THE
PRINCESS OF
TRELIAN

THE TRELIAN TRILOGY

The Dragon of Trelian
The Princess of Trelian
The Mage of Trelian

THE
PRINCESS OF
TRELIAN

MICHELLE KNUDSEN

CANDLEWICK PRESS

Copyright © 2012 by Michelle Knudsen

First paperback edition in this format 2017

Library of Congress Catalog Card Number 2011047174
ISBN 978-0-7636-5062-9 (hardcover)
ISBN 978-0-7636-6935-5 (paperback)
ISBN 978-0-7636-9455-5 (reformatted paperback)

17 18 19 20 21 22 BVG 10 9 8 7 6 5 4 3 2 1

Printed in Berryville, VA, U.S.A.

This book was typeset in Adobe Jenson Pro.

Candlewick Press
99 Dover Street
Somerville, Massachusetts 02144

visit us at www.candlewick.com

 *For Bridey,*
who knows about family,
and friendship

CHAPTER ONE

MEG CLOSED HER EYES, TRYING VERY hard to remember that she loved her little sister and that she did not truly want to throttle her. No matter how irritating she might be.

"But *why?*" Maurel asked again.

"Because it doesn't work that way," Meg said. Again.

"But I want to talk to him!"

"So go ahead. He's right there."

Maurel sighed with theatrical exaggeration. "Not *that* way. In my head. Like you do."

Meg let out a sigh of her own. She opened her eyes and propped herself up on her elbows. Her sister was standing above her, glaring down, her hands curled into little fists and planted fiercely on her hips. Maurel was lucky she was so cute when she was mad, or it would have been a lot harder for Meg to control her temper. Especially now, when her temper seemed so much shorter than usual. It was just because she hadn't been sleeping well — she was sure that was it . . . but it still worried her. She had come out here to spend a little time alone with Jakl, to recharge her emotions a bit. And to sneak in a nap if she could. The nightmares only seemed to trouble her sleep at night. So far.

Her dragon was sprawled around her on the grass, already feigning sleep. He often did that when Maurel was around, Meg had noticed. Maybe he was on to something.

"Maurel," Meg said wearily, "I have explained this to you. Several times. For one thing, we don't 'talk' to each other in our heads. It's more like we can feel things about each other. And for another, the link is only between Jakl and me. I couldn't share it with you even if I wanted to."

"But —"

"Maurel!" And for a second, the whole world disappeared in a bright-red burst of rage.

No, Meg thought, *no, no, no!* She had no reason to be so angry, but she was filled with it, burning with it, suddenly having to fight against the urge to throw herself at Maurel and *make* her be quiet. To grab the infuriating girl and — *No!* she thought at herself with everything she had. *Stop it!* Just barely, Meg managed to speak her next words in a kind of whispery growl instead of a scream.

"Maurel. If you ask me why one more time, you will be very sorry." *We both will.*

2

Maurel hesitated, and then, to Meg's immense relief, seemed to decide that her big sister might not be teasing. She sat down in a huff at Meg's feet. "It's not fair," she muttered, pulling at the grass.

No, Meg thought, breathing slowly and deliberately, waiting for that latest frightening flash of anger to finish draining away. Jakl's head had come up in alarm in response to it, but she could already feel him starting to relax again. Her current situation was many things, but fair wasn't one of them. She looked down to see she had dug a pattern of tiny crescent moons into her palms with her fingernails.

She loved her dragon. Sometimes she loved him so much that it scared her. And she loved having him as part of her life. Especially now that he no longer had to be a secret part. But there was no denying that Jakl had made everything very . . . complicated. Better, in some ways. Lots of ways. He made her stronger; he made her feel powerful and alive and not alone. Never alone. And she got to *fly*. She couldn't help grinning at that as the final vestiges of anger dropped away as though they had never existed. She felt Jakl shift interestedly in her head, and she grinned even more. The flying part was *phenomenal*.

But the link made a lot of things harder, too.

Meg gave herself a little mental shake. *That doesn't*

3

bear thinking about, and you know it. She couldn't change it now, even if she wanted to.

"Maybe I'll find my *own* dragon," Maurel said. "Then we'll have our own link and I won't let you talk to him, either."

"Okay," said Meg amiably. That was certainly too unlikely to worry about.

"Or maybe I'll have a link with Lyrimon," Maurel went on. "He likes me. He hardly ever hides from me anymore."

"Other animals can't —" Meg stopped herself. Let Maurel pretend if she wanted to. Especially if it would help keep her from pestering Meg about Jakl all the time. Although why she'd even want to pretend to have a connection with the mage's grumpy gyrcat was beyond Meg entirely. But Maurel had always had her own ideas about what was fun.

Meg poked Maurel with her foot. "Well, just be careful. He's not like a regular cat, you know. And he can hurt you if you annoy him too much. He's always scratching Calen."

"That's because he doesn't like Calen. But he likes me. He hasn't scratched me at all in over a week!" Maurel smiled so proudly at this that Meg had to laugh.

 4

Maurel laughed, too, always ready to put an argument behind her. "What's Jakl feeling now?"

"He's feeling sleepy. Leave him alone."

That wasn't strictly true, of course. Jakl's tail twitched at the mention of his name, but he went on pretending to sleep. He couldn't seem to decide how he felt about Maurel. He picked up on Meg's affection, but also on her not-infrequent irritation. And Maurel seemed to confuse him sometimes. Perhaps because she was the only person other than Meg who showed absolutely no fear of him. Meg thought people around the castle were learning to tolerate the dragon's enormous presence — some more easily than others — but even those who had begun to adjust were still clearly uneasy about having him around. Even Calen, who had spent more time with Meg and Jakl than anyone, maintained a respectful sort of nervousness. Then again, Calen was nervous about a lot of things. She was going to have to work on that with him.

Thinking of Calen reminded her how much she missed him. She wished he and Serek would get back from the Magistratum already. Calen had promised to send a letter by bird when they started the journey home, but she hadn't heard from him yet. She knew there was a lot they had to do there, but how long could it really take to tell the other mages about what had happened with Sen Eva and give Calen a new tattoo to mark his progress? She bet they were having all kinds of unnecessary meetings and performing time-consuming ceremonies instead of just getting down to business. Adults were always doing things like that. It drove her crazy.

"How about now? What's he feeling now?"

Speaking of things that drove her crazy . . . Meg gave up. She sent a private apology to Jakl and said, "He's feeling a deep, unshakable desire to take you for a ride. Want to go flying?"

Maurel was on her feet instantly. "Yes! Yes, yes, yes!" she shouted. "Let's go, let's go!"

Jakl opened his eyes and shot Meg a betrayed glance as he shifted upright, but he couldn't fool her. He was always excited to fly, even if Maurel was coming, too.

Maurel had already climbed up and was straddling the base of Jakl's supple neck. Meg followed and sat close behind her, wrapping one arm tightly around her sister's waist and gripping one of Jakl's smaller crests with her free hand. When they went up alone, she rarely held on at all anymore, but she didn't want to give Maurel any ideas.

"Ready?"

"Yes!"

"Let's go, then," Meg said. She didn't actually need to speak out loud for Jakl's benefit; he could feel her readiness and knew when she was ready to go. And she *was* ready — she could hardly stand to wait another second. It was always like this. Once the prospect of flight entered her mind, being on the ground began to feel intolerable. Every part of her longed to be aloft, away, free, *flying*, right now, right now, right now, right *now*.

She took a deep, shuddering breath as her dragon unfurled his long, lovely wings. She could almost feel them as though they were her own, strong and beautiful and ready to stretch and soar. With a powerful backward sweeping of his wings, he leaped up, dipping back down for half a second before he caught the wind, and then they were off, launching forward and up into the sky.

Oh, it was so hard not to let go, to slide into that place in her mind where she could lose herself in the feeling of flight and the link. Meg tightened her arm around Maurel, forcing herself to focus. Jakl wouldn't let Maurel fall — he'd be able to feel if she were slipping — but this was her little sister. Even at her most irritating, Meg still loved Maurel beyond words. She couldn't take even the slightest chance.

Jakl banked to curve around the castle, and Maurel

squealed with delight, staring down and around at everything they passed. Meg felt herself grinning again. The good thing about flying with Maurel was that she had absolutely no fear. Calen was always terrified of falling off, but as far as Meg could tell, that possibility never even occurred to her sister. So at least Meg didn't need to rein Jakl in too much. He could soar and spin and loop, and Maurel would love every second of it.

Meg closed her eyes and let herself go just enough to feel Jakl's pure joy in the act of flying, the rush of the wind and the feel of the air beneath his wings and the speed and the power and the colors of the world swirling above and below and around them. This was their element, where they belonged. Together. Always. She felt her heart would burst with the absolute perfectness of it.

After a while — seconds, hours, she could never hold on to her sense of time while flying — Jakl nudged her back to herself and began to slow, spiraling back down toward the ground. Meg opened her eyes again and watched the world come up to meet them. The world with all its complications and problems and troubles.

And speaking of trouble, their mother was standing in the courtyard, looking none too pleased.

"Uh-oh," Maurel said as Jakl landed lightly on the grass.

Meg felt Jakl consider taking off again, but she pushed that suggestion away. One did not simply fly away from Queen Merilyn.

"Meglynne!" her mother shouted, striding up to meet them. "What did I tell you?"

"It's my fault, Mother," Maurel said, slipping down from Jakl's back. "I made her take me. Don't be mad. It was fun!"

"Oh, it was fun?" the queen took hold of Maurel by shoulders and looked as though she would never let her go. "Fun to scare your mother out of her wits, watching you hang above the earth that way, waiting to see you fall to your death. . . ."

"Meg and Jakl wouldn't let me fall. You shouldn't be so worried." Maurel's expression brightened suddenly. "Maybe you should try it! Then you'll see how fun it is, and you won't get so mad every time I go up."

Meg bit her lip to keep from smiling at the way the color drained from her mother's face at Maurel's suggestion.

"She's right, Mother," Meg said. At her mother's startled glance, she added, "No, not about you coming up for a ride, but that we wouldn't let her fall. Really. It's perfectly safe."

"Meg, I . . ." The queen took a breath and hugged

9

Maurel against her. Maurel squirmed around to face Meg but couldn't quite extricate herself from their mother's firm embrace. "I know it seems that way to you, but to the rest of us, it's — it's not — we're trying to adjust, but I can't have you whisking your sister up into the air like that, putting her in danger."

"But she's not —"

"Please, Meg." Her mother shook her head wearily. "Just respect my wishes on this. Do not take Maurel flying again without permission."

Maurel stared up at the queen indignantly. "But Mother! That's —"

"That's enough, Maurel. Come inside now."

Maurel rolled her eyes at Meg and then let herself be dragged off toward the castle. Meg watched them go. Her mother just needed more time. It was a big adjustment, having a dragon around. Of course she was still a little nervous.

Jakl was the first dragon anyone in the kingdom had seen in at least thirty years. Maybe longer. Meg's father claimed to have seen one flying overhead one night when he was a little boy, but that was a long time ago. And when pressed, he admitted it was at least slightly possible that it had only been a large bat and a dark sky and a boy's imagination. Before Jakl came, people had assumed that the remaining dragons of the world were keeping to themselves in the mountains, or that maybe they had flown away across the sea or gone to any number of other places.

And they were glad of it, too. When there had been dragons, much effort had been directed at keeping them away. But there had never seemed to be very many of them. Even history books from before Meg's great-grandfather's time referred to them as creatures rarely encountered, even if it was not unheard of to see one flying around in the distance. Even longer ago, in the times Calen had told her about, when people actually sometimes sought out dragons for linking, instead of stumbling into linking accidentally, as she had — even then, it wasn't like there were dragons everywhere you looked. And for most of Meg's life, she, like everyone else she knew, had only vaguely suspected that dragons were still out there, somewhere, but nothing you might expect to actually *see*.

Until the one day when she did. And everything, everything changed.

"It will be okay," Meg whispered. She lay her upper body down against Jakl's scaly neck, warm from the sun, feeling his comforting presence beneath and within her. She closed her eyes, soaking him in. He was a part of her now. Her mother would come to accept that in time. Everyone would. Meg just had to be patient.

The tower bell sounded, reminding Meg that it was time to go in for afternoon lessons. Her lessons had practically doubled once Maerlie had married Prince Ryant of Kragnir, thus putting Meg next in line for the throne. Meg wouldn't officially become the princess-heir until the ceremony at Autumn Turning, but her parents had already begun increasing her tutoring sessions and responsibilities in preparation.

The king and queen had always kept their daughters informed of the general news and goings-on in the kingdom, but now Meg was allowed to actively participate in many of the tasks she'd only heard about before. She assisted her father while he reviewed treaties and legal documents, helped her mother manage the daily planning and correspondence, and sat in with both parents when they received petitioners once a week in the throne room. That was her favorite part of all. People came in with their problems and disputes, and her parents made decisions to set things right. Not that the other things weren't important, too, but documents and letters were only one step in a lengthy process. You had to wait so *long* to see any actual results. But when people were standing right before you, and you could make a decision right away, make a difference in their lives right then and there . . . that was wonderful.

King Tormon and Queen Merilyn were known for being fair and just, and you could see in the people's eyes how much they trusted and respected their king and queen. Meg wanted people to look at her like that someday. Her eldest sister, Morgan, was already making a name for herself in her adopted kingdom, and Meg knew that Maerlie would win over the people of Kragnir in no time. As princess-heir, Meg would get to stay here, in Trelian, her future husband (whoever he might be) joining her instead of the other way around. And while being a trusted and respected queen of an allied country would be nice, being one here in the kingdom she knew and loved would be the best of all. Sometimes she visited the royal library and peeked at the books that chronicled the lives of previous rulers and pretended her own story was in there, too. She would be Queen Meglynne, part of Trelian's own glorious story, essential, inextricable. She would do things that mattered, and be remembered for them.

She would be important, and her parents would be proud of her.

Meg left Jakl lounging in the field. The castle carpenters had made him a nice big enclosure down in the part of the outer ward past the stables (well past, so he wouldn't terrify the horses), but while he seemed to like it well enough, he usually preferred the field just beyond the gardens. Meg thought the enclosure was at least partially for show, in any case — something to make it seem as if her dragon were contained and housebroken. She smiled, thinking how he did seem to appreciate the enclosure whenever it rained. Perhaps he was just a little domesticated, at that.

She yawned, regretting her missed nap, and found herself walking more quickly. She was glad of her increased lessons for another reason as well: the busier she was, the less time she had to think about . . . other things. Less time to sit and worry and wish Calen were back, so she could talk to him and he could reassure her that everything would be all right.

She promised herself she would check in with the Master of Birds as soon as her lessons were done. Maybe there would be a letter from Calen, saying he was on his way home.

CHAPTER
TWO

CALEN GOT HIS FIRST LOOK AT the needle and fought the urge to close his eyes.

This was important — his first real mage's tattoo, his first mark beyond that of the initiate. The first one that he'd truly earned for himself. He wanted to remember every part of it. Even the slightly terrifying parts.

Master Su'lira was holding up a long, slender tool with a needle at the tip, examining the tiny blade in the light. The needle looked very, very sharp. Soon, Master Su'lira was going to stick Calen with that needle and use it to paint a delicate design under the surface of his skin.

It's all right, Calen told himself firmly, refusing to look away. *You've been through much worse than this.*

It was true. He had been lost in an unknown land, desperate to get home. He had been viciously attacked by villains and monsters. He had been forced to climb to heights no sensible person should ever, ever have to experience. Some of those heights had been reached while flying through the air on the back of a dragon, ridiculous distances above the ground. He had almost *died*. More than once. Being stuck with a needle should be easy compared to all that.

Master Su'lira turned back to his workbench, making adjustments. Calen let out a shallow breath. Not quite time. Not yet.

The marking room was small and private. Serek had explained that the process could sometimes take a long while, depending on the level of achievement of the person being marked. The official ceremony was always held separately, so all the other mages wouldn't have to sit there watching and waiting for what could be hours. Calen had felt himself go a little pale at the mention of *hours*, but Serek had dryly assured him that his mark would not take quite that long. Later, the official marking ceremony would formally acknowledge Calen's progress along the mage's path.

The room's walls were covered with panels of drawings and designs, which Calen guessed were examples of different kinds of marks. Serek had never explained the meanings behind his own markings: an intricate landscape of lines, swirls, and symbols twining across both sides of his face. It wasn't forbidden to explain the meanings; Calen suspected Serek just felt it was too personal to discuss. Or maybe he thought it would sound like bragging. Serek had more markings than most of the other mages they had met since they'd arrived, and each of those markings represented some new level of skill or achievement. Calen hadn't realized before that Serek might be a mage of some distinction. It had never even occurred to him. Serek was just . . . Serek. It was strange to see him here, in this new context, among others of his calling. Calen's last visit had been so long ago, and he had been so little, that he barely remembered anything beyond vague, half-formed images and feelings.

Master Su'lira turned sideways again, holding up the needle once more, and Calen wondered if another reason for the private room was so that no one else would be there to observe if any mages or apprentices started screaming, or crying, or fainted from the pain.

"Nervous?" Mage Serek asked from across the room. He was leaning against the wall, watching the preparations with his usual detachment. Serek had, of course, been through this procedure countless times. And no doubt without any cowardly whining or squirming. He had probably sat there reading a book and barely even noticed when the needle pierced through his skin.

Me, on the other hand . . . Calen thought, sighing.

"A little," he admitted. Serek could clearly already tell, anyway.

17

Serek nodded. "It will hurt a great deal, but the pain is part of the process. A reminder that we do not take on these responsibilities lightly."

Good old Serek. Always comforting.

"I know," Calen said. "I'm ready."

Master Su'lira turned toward him, smiling.

Calen mustered a shaky smile back.

"You must hold very still, Apprentice Calen," Master Su'lira said as he sat on the stool beside him. Calen nodded. The man smiled again. "No more nodding," he said.

Oh. Right. "Sorry."

"And no more speaking unless I ask you a question directly. If you need to say something, if you need to sneeze or cough, if you need me to stop for any reason, tap your hand here on the table to get my attention. All right?"

"Yes."

"All right. I am going to prick you just once to start, to show you how it will feel."

Calen held himself rigid as the needle came closer to his face. He shifted his eyes to look straight ahead. He could still see the needle in his peripheral vision, but at least now it didn't look like it was coming directly at him. Although, of course, it was.

"All right," the Marker said again, softly, and Calen felt a pressure against his skin. And then a bright blooming of pain. He inhaled sharply through his nose but managed not to gasp. Then Master Su'lira drew the needle back, and the pain faded quickly. Calen swallowed. He could do this. It hurt, but it wasn't unbearable.

"Are you ready for me to continue?" Master Su'lira asked, holding the tool a few inches away. "You may answer."

"Yes."

"All right." The Marker brought the needle closer again, and Calen felt the pressure and then the pain. This time, though, the needle prick didn't come and go quickly; he could feel the needle going in and out slightly, moving in tiny increments. The pain didn't stop or fade but stayed present, scratching, piercing, almost burning. *Ow*, he thought. *Ow, ow, ow!* But he didn't move. He tried to keep his breathing slow and even, through his nose, since his mouth was closed and he was afraid to open it now.

It wasn't really so bad. It still hurt, quite a bit, but he thought being scratched by Lyrimon hurt more. And it seemed to help if he tried to focus his mind on other things.

He was glad Serek hadn't wanted to bring Lyrimon

along on their journey, although he was a little worried about poor Maurel, who had volunteered to look after the gyrcat while they were gone. She seemed to be a pretty tough little girl, though. And Meg would no doubt step in if there were any problems.

He had been surprised to realize how much he missed Meg once he and Serek and their small armed escort had left the castle. He knew he would see her again in a few weeks, but almost as soon as they were beyond sight of the front gate, he had started to feel a little bit, well, sad. He supposed he had gotten used to seeing her every day.

He hoped they would be able to head back home soon. They had only arrived yesterday, and today was the marking and ceremony, and then tomorrow was the meeting with the council of mages who were in charge of things, and then maybe the next day they could start back. Surely it couldn't take too long for the mages to decide what to do about Sen Eva. Serek had sent letters with the whole story ahead of time, so the council already knew what had happened.

Master Su'lira's hand shifted slightly to a new area, and the pain flared up more intensely again. Calen clenched his teeth to stop himself from crying out.

He didn't want to ask the man to stop. He wanted to be able to sit there and take it, to be strong and get through it without needing a break. He tried again to think about other things. About Meg. About magic. About whether there would be a banquet as part of his marking ceremony. He liked banquets. At the banquet following Meg's sister's wedding, there had been every kind of food Calen could imagine. There had been a whole table just for dessert. Calen had had two servings of a baked apple concoction that was pretty much the best thing he had ever tasted in his whole life. Sweet and sticky and hot with some kind of syrup all over it and a delicate pastry crust that flaked off as soon as you touched it with your fork.

Ow, ow, ow, ow, ow!

Baked apples. Right. He would just keep thinking about baked apples. Hot, delicious, syrupy baked apples. Nothing painful about those.

Suddenly he became aware that the needle wasn't touching him anymore.

"Yes, all right," Master Su'lira said, sitting back. "We're all finished here."

Calen took a deep breath. Finished! That hadn't been too terrible, really. The pain was fading rapidly, and it was already hard to remember just how much it had hurt. But he was glad it was over. He started to reach up to touch his face. The Marker slapped his hand away.

"Do not touch!" he said. "You must wait until it's been healed." He looked over at Serek.

Serek straightened up and walked closer, eyeing Calen's face appraisingly. Then he raised one hand palm out, and Calen saw a faint haze of golden energy gathering around Serek's fingers. Gold laced with tiny threads of green and purple. At Serek's subtle gesture, the energy flowed swiftly toward Calen's face. His skin felt tingly for a moment, and then — nothing. No more stinging, no soreness. He looked up at Serek.

"The marking process itself cannot involve magic," Serek said, "but healing is allowed after it's over. There's no need for you to walk around with a bandage on your face." He twisted his lips into an almost-smile. "Besides, it takes away from the ceremony if your face is swollen and bleeding the whole time."

"Oh," Calen said. *Ugh.* "Um, thanks."

"The marks are also spelled so that they'll grow with you, at least until you reach your full height."

"Oh," Calen said again. "The green and purple."

Serek looked as though he wanted to say something, but he glanced at the Marker and just nodded slightly.

Calen still kept forgetting that no one else could see the colors he saw when someone was casting. That was another part of what they were supposed to talk about at the meeting tomorrow.

Master Su'lira brought over a hand mirror with a carved wooden handle. Calen took it and slowly held it up in front of his face.

His initiate mark had been a small symbol, a crescent moon with a double-headed arrow running through it horizontally and another line crossing it vertically, centered directly under his left eye. He was so used to seeing that in the mirror that he hardly noticed it anymore. But now — the vertical line had been extended at the bottom into a spiral that curled out and then in and terminated with a tiny star at the center. Along the line that led down into the spiral, on the opposite edge, were three small sideways points, almost triangles. They looked sort of like a sideways crown. Or dragon crests.

He looked back up to see Serek and Master Su'lira both standing before him, arms crossed. Serek's expression was neutral, as usual. The Marker was smiling and nodding to himself.

"It looks very nice, yes? A fine first true mark for you, Apprentice Calen."

"But what does it mean?" Calen asked.

"I cannot tell you that," Master Su'lira said. "I do not know the meanings. I only see what to draw."

Calen looked at Serek in total confusion.

"Master Su'lira sees the appropriate mark for each mage who comes to him," he said. "It's a kind of vision. Markers are gifted in this way and trained to read the symbols and signs they see in people. The mark itself comes from you; the Marker simply transcribes it. Only certain symbols, like the one indicating master status, are ever repeated."

"Oh," Calen said yet again, looking back into the mirror. "That's — huh." He traced the lines with his eye, trying to see what meaning might be there. He had thought there would be, well, a key or something. A set of standard symbols that stood for different things. It was sort of astounding to think that every single mage's marks were unique. He would have to pay more attention to the faces of the mages they met here.

"Do we go to the ceremony now?"

Serek shook his head. "No, not for a few hours yet. This is traditionally a time for quiet reflection. You can go back to your room for now if you like."

Calen nodded. He felt oddly exhausted, maybe from the pain, or from the healing, or just from the whole experience — the anticipation, the importance, everything. Quiet reflection seemed like a good idea. Especially if he could reflect while lying down on his bed.

He stood up and handed the mirror back to Master Su'lira. "Thank you," he said. "It's — I like it very much."

The Marker smiled and bowed slightly. "You are most welcome, Apprentice Calen. I look forward to seeing you again in the future."

Serek opened the door and then stopped in the doorway. Three mages stood just outside.

"Ah, Mage Serek!" one of them said. "We have been, ah, waiting for you. And for young Calen, of course." All three mages' eyes flicked to Calen before returning to Serek. Calen tried to remember if he'd seen them before. The mage who had spoken was the most heavily marked, his face half-covered with lines and symbols with sharp angles.

Serek didn't look happy. "My apprentice has just received his mark. As I'm sure you realize, this is not an appropriate time for conversation. If you will excuse us, I am going to take him back to his room now." With that, Serek pushed past the three men and walked quickly up the corridor. Calen hurried to follow.

"Ah. Yes. Of course," the mage said again, also

following. "It's just that we wished to speak with you before the meeting tomorrow, if possible. There are, ah, things to discuss. . . ."

He trailed off. Serek had stopped and turned around to glare at him. Calen knew the effect of that glare rather well. Trailing off from whatever you had been saying was one of the more common responses.

"Mage Brevera," Serek said with great emphasis. "Now is not the appropriate time. Do I need to make that more clear to you somehow?"

"But — ah — if we could just arrange a time that would be more . . . ?"

Serek rolled his eyes. "Very well. Meet me in the third-floor vestibule —" He broke off, frown deepening. The mages were shaking their heads and looking uncomfortable.

"Perhaps somewhere more private?" one of the other mages suggested. He was the least marked of the three, although he still had several marks beyond his master tattoo.

"Fine," Serek snapped. "Come up to my room in half an hour. Will that suffice?"

"But, the boy —" the third mage began. The marks on his face were softer, less angled. They seemed to weave in and out of one another, so that Calen couldn't make out very many distinct symbols at all.

The first mage cut him off. "Yes," he said. "Yes, that would be very agreeable."

Serek turned without another word and strode off toward the stairwell. Calen followed quickly behind. What had *that* been about? He wondered what they wanted to talk about that had to be discussed in private. There had been something a little disturbing about the way they'd looked at him. He glanced back over his shoulder. The mages were standing in a tight clump, whispering aggressively at one another.

He turned back to ask Serek about it, but one look at his master's face convinced him that now was not the time to ask questions. Well, that was all right. He was more than ready for that quiet reflection. There would be time enough to find out about those mages later. Right now, he kind of just wanted a nap. And to spend some time alone in front of the mirror, looking at his new mark.

CHAPTER THREE

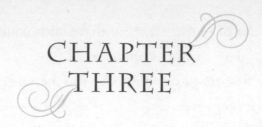

MEG WAS DREAMING. SHE KNEW SHE was, knew she was back in one of the same nightmares she'd been having for weeks now — but knowing didn't help her escape it.

In this one, she was lost in the woods, as she had been with Calen once, only this time she was alone. Jakl swirled in her head, a tangle of confused emotions, but he was nowhere nearby. There was something she had to do, something very important, but she didn't know what it was, or how to do it, or where to go. Every step seemed to take her farther in the wrong direction, even if she tried turning around to go back the way she'd come.

Something crunched behind her in the shadows. Someone was there. Jakl suddenly loomed inside her, filling her with rage and fear and panic. *No,* she thought. *No, no, I have to calm down, I have to think. This isn't the way.* But she could not control it; the waves of emotion rolled over her, through her, and she was lost, inside and out, and the danger was getting closer and closer and closer and there was nothing she could do.

She woke in a cold sweat, as she had so many nights before.

For a moment, Meg lay there, staring up into the dark, trying to make her heart slow down. Then she got out of bed, pulled on a pair of breeches and an overshirt over her nightgown, and stepped quietly out into the hall. Jakl was awake, concerned; she had to get better at shielding him while she was sleeping. He didn't need to suffer from her nightmares, too. But at the same time, she was a little glad. She liked feeling him there, ready to try to comfort her. She made her way down to the courtyard.

He was waiting for her when she stepped outside, green scales glinting in the moonlight. He lowered his long neck as she approached and turned to nudge at her with his big, worried head.

"It's okay," she murmured, wrapping her arms around as much of his neck as she could. She lay her face against him and closed her eyes. "We're okay." Why did she feel she had to keep reminding herself of that?

Because it's not really true — that's why.

She hated that little voice, the one that seemed to always speak her fears to her and make them feel more real. She tried to ignore it. They were okay. They *were*.

Silently, she climbed up and felt her spirits lift and

29

then let go as she and her dragon rose into the night sky. *We'll just fly for a bit*, she thought. Just fly, and not think about anything else.

Jakl had no objections. He soared up, over the castle, away into the darkness. They didn't come back until the first hint of dawn began to lighten the horizon.

In the morning, Meg slunk into her family's private dining room long after everyone else had started eating. A serving girl quickly brought her a bowl of porridge and a mug of tea as she sat down.

"We missed you at the briefing this morning," her father said, not looking up.

"Briefing?" Meg said, still not feeling quite awake. She wrapped her hands around her mug.

"With the Captain of the House Guard."

Meg winced. She'd completely forgotten. "I'm sorry. I . . . overslept."

"I noticed." Now he looked at her, not happily. "It's not the first time, Meg."

"I know. I'm really sorry. It won't happen again."

"You said that last time," Queen Merilyn said.

"I *said* I was sorry," Meg said. She felt her temper stirring and tried to tamp it down. "I didn't oversleep on purpose. I don't know why Pela didn't wake me."

"You never used to sleep so late," Maurel put in brightly. "Maybe you're sick or something."

"I'm not —"

"*Do* you feel all right, Meg?" asked her mother.

"Yes, I'm fine!" Meg snapped. Her mother's eyes widened. Meg took a breath, trying to regain control of her voice. "I'm sorry. Please, just — I just haven't been sleeping well. I'll ask Pela to be more aggressive when she wakes me from now on." Pela did seem to give up rather easily.

Her mother looked at her in that searching way Meg was beginning to hate, but she only said, "All right, Meg." The king didn't say anything. Maurel was already bored with the conversation, and had turned her attention to making designs in the surface of her porridge with her spoon. Nan Vera wasn't sitting with them; Meg must have missed her entirely. No doubt she was off giving baby Mattie her breakfast, which tended to be a messy affair that Nan Vera preferred to handle in private. Too many ruined tablecloths and dresses stained from flying food.

It seemed so empty at the table with only the four of them. Morgan had gone home to Prolua soon after the wedding, and Maerlie had left for Kragnir with her new husband shortly thereafter. Maybe Meg's tardiness wouldn't have been quite so noticeable if they hadn't become such a tiny group of late. Although she supposed she still would have missed the briefing.

She really would have to talk to Pela about waking her even when she didn't seem to want to get up. Meg had managed to avoid having a lady-in-waiting for years, but now that she was preparing to officially take on the responsibilities of the princess-heir, her parents had decided it wasn't proper for her not to have one. There had always been maids and servants, of course, but a lady-in-waiting felt . . . different. More burdensome. Pela was supposed to be Meg's companion as well as her attendant, and that meant Meg was supposed to spend time with her, doing . . . she wasn't even sure. Talking, walking in the gardens, sitting around doing ladylike things, she imagined. She suspected it was her parents' way of trying to get her to act more princess-like. Although they had also made the point that it was an honor for a girl to be appointed a lady-in-waiting, and it wasn't really fair of Meg to deny Pela that opportunity.

Guilt was a powerful motivating force, Meg had discovered. Especially once she'd been introduced to Pela, who was very sweet and nice and seemed so genuinely to want to fulfill her newly assigned role.

"Perhaps," her father said suddenly, breaking into

her thoughts, "you would feel more rested if you actually *slept* at night, instead of going for rides on your dragon."

Of course. Her dragon. She should have known it would come back to this.

"I couldn't sleep," Meg told him. "I just wanted some air."

"Meg." He looked steadily at her, an echo of her mother's worry on his face. "I know you need to spend time with Jakl. I understand that, truly. Serek has explained about the link, and I know we cannot expect you to act as though it does not exist. But you cannot . . ." He paused, searching for words. "People are beginning to . . . talk."

"Talk?"

"About the appropriateness of a princess having a dragon for a pet." He put up a hand to forestall her heated objection. "I know, that's not what he is. But from the outside, all people see is that the soon-to-be princess-heir has apparently adopted a dangerous beast to be her constant companion. It makes them . . . uneasy." His voice softened. "Surely you can understand."

She understood. It was everyone else who didn't understand. She understood that her parents claimed to have accepted what had happened to her, but they hadn't, not really. How could they? Their daughter was

33

linked to a *dragon*. Connected, body and mind, forever. She was still struggling to come to terms with it herself. She was the same, but also not the same. And now her mother was worried about her, and her father didn't know what to make of her, and Maurel — well, okay, Maurel seemed to not care at all about the dragon, except to think it was exciting. But everyone else was treating her differently now, holding her at arm's length, looking at her as though they expected her to sprout wings of her own any moment now and fly away.

She could feel the hot anger beginning to rise again inside her.

"I don't see how going for rides at night is any worse than going for rides during the day," Meg said, still trying to keep her voice calm.

Her parents exchanged a look. Then her mother said, "We'd like you to spend less time riding during the day, too."

Meg was on her feet before she realized it, looking down at her parents incredulously. "I thought you said you understood!" she said. "I *have* to spend time with him. Serek told you —"

"Why does spending time with him have to include riding?" her mother asked. "You can just visit him in that nice enclosure we had constructed. Or, if necessary, in the field beyond the garden . . ."

Meg stared at them. The edges of her vision seemed tinged with red. "If *necessary*? No. You don't understand at all. We have to fly together. It's — I can't explain it. But it's important. And I'm not going to start trying to hide him from everyone. I won't!"

"Meg —" the king began.

"I know you both wish we didn't have a dragon to worry about. But we do. And I'm very sorry if Jakl makes the people of Trelian uncomfortable, but they're just going to have to get used to it, aren't they?"

The king and queen exchanged another look, and then her father looked back at her with a strange expression. "Actually, Meg," he said, "not necessarily."

The room suddenly seemed very quiet.

Meg continued to stand there, looking back and forth between them. "What," she asked finally, "does that mean?"

The queen leaned over toward Maurel, who was staring down at her porridge and seemed to be trying very hard to pretend no one was arguing. "Maurel, please go and tell Nan Vera that you're finished with your breakfast now."

"Yes, Mother," Maurel said quietly. She fled without looking back.

The king waited until Maurel had gone. Then he said, "Meg. Please sit down."

"No."

He sighed but didn't insist. "While it's . . . traditional for the eldest child remaining in the kingdom to inherit the throne, it is not by any means required. If it seems that the people will not accept you as princess-heir, we might have to consider passing the title to Maurel instead."

Meg blinked, trying to take this in. "But — the ceremony, at Autumn Turning —"

"Can be adjusted, or delayed," her father said. He reached across the table toward her hand. "Meg, we don't *want* to do this."

She snatched her hand away. "But you're going to threaten me with it all the same," she said.

"We have to do what is best for this kingdom," her father said, his voice sharper now. "Which is what you should be thinking about as well."

"So you've decided that what's best for the kingdom is for me to hide what I am," she said bitterly. Her mother looked away. Her father just kept looking at her.

"Haven't you ever considered that there might be

advantages to having our own dragon, loyal to the kingdom?" she asked.

"But he's not loyal to the kingdom, Meg," her father said. "He's loyal to you. Don't you see? We need the people to accept you before we can ask them to think about the advantages of having a dragon. You must understand how frightening Jakl seems to those who don't know him, who don't know that he's connected to you so closely. People are wondering where he came from and why you are seen spending so much time with him. Once they are firmly in support of you, such things will become much easier."

"Accept me," Meg repeated in a flat voice. "They don't *accept* me? Because of Jakl?"

"Meg —" her mother began.

Meg shook her head in disbelief, no longer even trying to hold back her anger and indignation. "Jakl *saved* them! We would be at war right now if it weren't for him! Or worse!" She was shouting now, but she didn't care. "And Maerlie would be *dead*! Have you forgotten that?"

"Meg!" her father barked at her. "Control yourself!"

"No," she said, backing away. Everything in her vision was turning red now. She had to get out of there. "I can't talk to you right now. I have to — I can't —"

She turned and ran from the room, ignoring her

parents' voices calling after her. Jakl was responding to her anger, and she was glad. She ran toward the court-yard, toward the garden. She was *not* going to stop spending time with him. She was not going to hide who she was. Her parents would learn to accept it. Everyone would learn to accept it. She wouldn't give them a choice.

She was out and up and on Jakl's back and away in seconds. For spite, she flew him low over the city, letting everyone get a nice, long look at their terrifying dragon princess. Then she let go, freeing her mind of her parents' concerns, the ungrateful people of Trelian, all of it. She let Jakl fly where he would, and felt nothing but the wind and the sky and her dragon and the link shining strong and invisible and eternal between them.

Later, much later, she was sorry.

She was sitting on the fence outside Jakl's paddock, watching him roll around in the grass. As usual after one of her flares of temper, she couldn't quite understand why she'd gotten so angry. Of course she didn't like hear-ing that the people of Trelian were uncertain about her, but she did understand. Her parents were right — she had to win the people over, let them see that she could be the princess-heir they wanted her to be.

She cringed, thinking of her recent flight over the city.

Her anger was gone now, replaced with a kind of empty sadness. She didn't know what to do. She couldn't stop flying with Jakl altogether. But maybe she could make sure they flew out over the forest, where they wouldn't be seen. And she could try harder to be seen without him, to be seen doing . . . normal things. Appropriate princess-heir things.

Things that wouldn't make anyone uneasy.

This was probably another reason her parents had insisted on the lady-in-waiting, Meg realized. So that people could see her walking around in the company of another girl, doing girl things. . . . She had to admit it made a certain sense.

Resolved, Meg hopped off the fence and set off to find Pela. They could have their talk about the importance of timely princess waking while walking in the garden, and Meg would act like a regular human girl who was not at all connected to a terrifying, fire-breathing creature.

She felt Jakl stirring proudly as she thought that last part, and despite everything else, she could not help but smile.

Pela was sewing in the royal common room when Meg found her. She leaped to her feet when she saw Meg, her needlework tumbling from her lap.

"Oh, Princess! Did you want me? Normally you like to spend your mornings alone, and so I didn't think—"

"It's all right, Pela," Meg said, trying to ignore the girl's jumpiness. Pela reminded Meg of a nervous little bird. "You're right: lately I have been spending my mornings by myself. But I thought perhaps we could begin taking some morning walks together. It would be nice to stroll in the gardens after breakfast, at least on pleasant days."

"Oh, yes, Princess! That would be lovely. Shall we go now? I suppose it's not really morning anymore, but it's still early enough, don't you think? Just let me put my sewing away." Pela scooped up the fabric and thread from the floor and took off toward her quarters, which were, unfortunately, right across from Meg's own. Then she stopped abruptly and turned back. "Is that all right? I don't mean to make you wait; I could leave it here. . . ." She looked doubtfully at the chair where she'd been seated.

"No, it's fine, Pela. Please. I need to stop by my room as well." A few final moments to herself suddenly seemed like a very good idea. "I'll meet you by the garden entrance, all right?"

"Yes, Princess. Of course." Pela hesitated for a second, then seemed to understand that Meg wasn't going to race down the hall with her. "I'll — I'll see you very shortly!" She turned and resumed her run.

Meg took a deep breath and walked slowly after Pela. She understood that the lady-in-waiting was supposed to be nearby in case her mistress needed her, but placing the girl right across the hall seemed a little much. Meg had never needed any of her other attendants in the middle of the night, at least not since she was Maurel's age; what made her parents think she was going to need Pela? It was probably another instance of appearances, she supposed, to make Meg seem like a normal princess. Morgan and Maerlie had both had ladies-in-waiting in rooms next to theirs, after all. But that was different. *They* were different.

But that was the whole point, wasn't it? Meg was supposed to be more like them.

She reached her door and went quickly inside, not wanting to be standing in the hall when Pela came back out. Then she sat on the edge of her bed and closed her eyes. Her earlier rage was only a memory now, but she still felt tense, and she could safely assume Pela would do something to try her patience. She needed to try and stay calm.

Meg had known for a while now that the link tended to intensify her emotions, as Jakl felt what she was feeling and then added his own mirroring feelings to hers. Or the other way around. It could be a nice thing, when she was happy, or when he was, or when they were flying together and both of them got swept away in the joy of it. But when one of them was angry, it was . . . less nice. And lately it seemed to be getting worse.

No, she corrected herself. *Be honest.* It *was* getting worse. Her temper was out of control, sometimes setting her off with barely any provocation at all. Sometimes, she became so full of rage, so quickly, so *unreasonably,* that she was afraid she might do something terrible. More terrible than just snapping at Maurel or screaming at her parents.

She sighed, realizing that she still had to go and apologize to them at some point.

Eyes still closed, Meg forced herself to breathe slowly and deeply, the way Calen had taught her. Meg and Jakl were both still learning how to deal with the link, but the relaxation techniques seemed to help calm them. A little, anyway. When she actually remembered to use them.

Once she felt relatively centered again, Meg made her way down to the garden entrance. Pela was already there, seated on a stone bench near the doorway. She looked a little flushed; Meg suspected the girl had run full speed the entire way, just to make sure Meg would not have to wait for her.

Pela, of course, jumped up as soon as Meg appeared. "I'm ready, Princess! Shall we set out? Do you have a favorite path?"

"Pela," Meg said. "Please. Can you just, um . . . ?"

Pela's face fell at once. "Have I done something wrong, Princess?"

"No," Meg said hastily. "No, of course not. Let's just sit down a moment." She sat on the bench and waited for Pela to sit beside her. Pela sat but still looked mortified.

"Oh, you're dismissing me, aren't you?" she asked miserably. "I knew I would do something wrong. I knew it. I'm sorry, Your Highness. Whatever I did, I'm very sorry. I would never have —"

"Pela!"

Pela stopped, eyes wide. "Yes, Princess?"

Meg took another deep breath. "Pela, I want you to sit there quietly for a second and just listen. All right?"

Pela nodded.

"Good. Now pay attention. I am not dismissing you. You have not done anything wrong. We're going to start spending more time together, so we can get to know each other a bit." Meg tried to make her voice as kind and gentle as possible. "I can see already that I'm going to like you very much."

Pela's face lit up instantly. She began to open her mouth, but Meg quickly reached up and put her hand over it.

"Shh. I'm not finished." She eyed Pela seriously and did not take her hand away from the girl's mouth. Meg was afraid that if Pela said one more thing, she'd strangle her. That would not be a good beginning to their new relationship. "I like you, Pela, but I need you to do something for me. I want you to stop trying so hard to please me. You will please me most by just being yourself. Just—just try to relax a little, all right? Can you do that for me?"

Pela nodded vigorously. Meg cautiously took her hand away. The younger girl bit her lip and seemed to be ordering her thoughts. Inside her head, instead of through her mouth, for a change. That was a good sign.

"I'll try to do that, Princess," she said at last. "I do want you to like me. Very much."

"I do like you, Pela. And I'm sure I will like you even more the more I get to know you." She smiled. "Shall we go for our walk now?"

"Yes, Princess."

Meg stood up, and Pela did likewise. "Do *you* have a

favorite path, Pela? If you do, I would very much like to see it."

Pela smiled shyly. "I do, Princess. It's the one that goes past the cherry trees near the far wall. Do you know that one?"

"I haven't been that way in a while, actually. I would be very grateful if you would show me."

Pela positively beamed as they set out. She really was a sweet and friendly girl. Maybe she'd require less effort over time. Meg could hope so, anyway. She gave her lady-in-waiting one more considering glance. "Pela — do you think you could call me Meg?"

"Oh, no, Princess," Pela said at once. "I couldn't!"

Meg sighed. She hadn't thought so, but it was worth a try. With Calen she never had to think about behaving like a proper princess. She was always just Meg to him. But she knew she couldn't be that way with everyone. Just as she couldn't fully be her dragon-linked self with everyone, either. That was even clearer after what her parents had told her this morning.

They walked on, Pela chattering happily, and Meg did not fail to note the way the gardeners and the guards looked up to watch them as they passed. She was glad they were paying attention.

CHAPTER FOUR

CALEN PUT ON THE SPECIAL ROBES Serek had laid out for him and examined himself in the mirror. He still couldn't stop staring at his new mark. His hand stole up to trace its delicate shape along his cheek. It made his whole face look different. And now, with the fancy clothes, he barely recognized himself at all.

I look like a real mage, he thought with some astonishment. A young mage, and still an apprentice, but all the same — a mage. When people looked at him now, they wouldn't see an initiate. They'd see a mage with a true mark, and they'd know he was capable of real magic.

He knew he still had a lot to learn. *Tons* to learn. Even just learning how much more there was to learn would take nearly forever, he guessed. But somehow that didn't bother him the way it used to. Knowledge and power had once seemed like impossible goals, a distant destination he would always be approaching but would never quite reach. Now that he was actually on the path, *really* on the path, he could see things more clearly. It was true that he'd never know everything; he'd never get to the end of the journey, not really. But with every step, he'd know more than he had before. Even now, he could look back and see how far he had come. Suddenly, having all that learning ahead of him seemed exciting rather than exhausting. He wanted to learn everything he could.

There was a knock at the door. Before he could answer, the door opened and Serek strode into the room.

"Sure, come on in," Calen muttered.

"Ready?" Serek asked. "It's time to go down." He stopped then and took a long look at Calen. "The robes suit you," he said after a moment. "The mark does, too."

"Really?" Calen asked. "I mean, I like it. A lot. But it's so strange to see it there. I look so . . . different." He glanced once more at the mirror, fighting the urge to touch his face for the thousandth time.

"The first true mark is the strangest," Serek said. "Each one brings its own . . . feelings, I suppose. But the first one has the biggest impact. It was like that for me, anyway. I believe it is the same way for most mages."

Calen struggled not to stare at his master. Serek never spoke about feelings. Calen hadn't thought Serek even *had* feelings.

They left Calen's room and started down toward the ceremony chamber. Serek had told Calen what to expect. No banquet, unfortunately. Apparently it wasn't the kind of ceremony that came with special food. It was just the talking kind. Calen would stand up in front of all the assembled mages, and the council masters, the ones the other mages had elected to be in charge for the current cycle, would say some things to him, and he was supposed to answer yes to all their questions. Serek said it wouldn't take very long. It was just a formality, so he could be presented before the assembly with his first true mark, and then later on they would all just have dinner together in the dining hall as usual. Calen was slightly nervous about having to stand up in front of everyone, but it wasn't like he'd have to do anything difficult. He was pretty certain he could handle saying yes a bunch of times, even in front of an audience.

"Hey," said Calen, suddenly remembering. "What did those other mages want to talk to you about so badly?"

"Hmm?" Serek slowed his pace slightly, letting Calen come up next to him. Then the words seemed to register, and his face darkened. "Oh. Just some Magistratum non-sense. One of the reasons I've never wanted to be on the council is all the ridiculous posturing and politics."

"I don't think I understand," Calen said.

"Sometimes not all of the mages will see eye to eye on

something," Serek explained. "That's to be expected — we are a large enough organization, and part of our function is to discuss and debate matters of interest and come to some kind of consensus. But sometimes, certain of our number decide to run around outside of the council chamber, spreading rumors, stirring up trouble, and trying to get other mages to vote in a particular way. It's not the way the council was meant to work, and I have no patience for it."

Well, that was no surprise. Serek didn't have patience for anything. "So they were trying to convince you to vote their way? About what?"

Serek looked down at Calen silently for a moment. "Nothing you need to worry about," he said finally.

"But —"

"Calen."

"Okay, okay. Never mind," Calen said, holding up his hands in surrender. "It's none of my concern, and you'll tell me if and when there's a good reason for me to know, right?"

Serek half smiled at him. "Exactly."

They walked down two flights of stairs and turned toward the room where the ceremony would be taking place. A few other mages were entering the double doors ahead of them. Now Calen was starting to feel a little more nervous. *This is nothing,* he told himself firmly. *At least no one's going to stick you with a needle!*

They reached the doors, and Serek pushed them open. The room inside was large and shaped like a half-moon, with rows of seats arranged in a partial circle around a raised platform in the center. Right now about three-fourths of the seats were filled, and Calen glanced around at all the unfamiliar faces as he followed Serek down the center aisle. Most were full mages, although there were younger, less marked faces here and there: apprentices and initiates visiting with their masters. There had to be at least two hundred people. Maybe more like three hundred.

And this wasn't even all of them. Serek had explained that some mages stayed at the Magistratum for long stretches of time, either between assignments to particular households or because they had chosen to stay and work on shared projects or help with the central administration. Others visited for short periods to get their new markings, to do research, to register apprentices, or to bring an issue before the council.

There were probably another hundred or so mages scattered across the continent, assigned to kings, minor lords, town officials, and even sometimes private estates.

They acted as counselors, healers, and teachers and assisted their patrons with magic in whatever ways were needed, as long as they didn't violate the laws of the Magistratum. Others traveled around looking for new apprentices or responding to new requests for mage assignments. The Magistratum carefully monitored everything, though. No mages were ever permitted to run off to wherever they pleased. Too much had gone wrong before mages were organized and regulated by the council.

The chamber slowly quieted as Serek and Calen made their way down the aisle. By the time they reached the front, the room was silent. Serek led Calen around to the side and up a narrow set of steps. The two council masters sat waiting in large, ornate chairs in the middle of the stage. Serek bowed to each of them and said in a clear voice, "Council Master Renaldiere, Council Master Galida, I present my apprentice, Calen of Trelian."

Calen smiled. He liked that "of Trelian" bit. He'd never heard anyone call him that before.

Then Serek turned, walked back down the aisle, and took a seat that had been left open for him in the front row. Calen was left facing the council masters alone. The one on the left — Council Master Renaldiere — was a very old man, his hair white and kind of fluffy at the very the top of his head. On another man, that hair might have been funny, but the mage was so solid and imposing a figure that it was hard to imagine being amused by anything in his presence. Council Master Galida was a middle-aged woman, dark haired and attractive, with large green eyes and dark skin. Both of their faces were heavily marked, the lines and symbols on Galida's face lighter in color to stand out against her complexion. The two mages regarded Calen solemnly for a moment, and he fought the urge to fidget. Then Council Master Galida instructed him to turn around and face the assembly.

Calen's knees threatened to buckle, and he had to concentrate everything he had on his legs to keep them straight. He was looking out at a sea of faces, all staring right at him. Somehow it seemed like even more people from this vantage point than it had while he'd been walking down the aisle.

"Calen of Trelian," came Council Master Renaldiere's voice from behind him, "apprentice to Mage Serek and bearer of your first true mark. Do you claim full responsibility for your actions and their consequences, accepting the prices paid for all choices along the path that brought you to this place?"

"Yes," Calen said as loudly and firmly as he could. He

52

was relieved to hear that his voice sounded steady, not at all shaky, as he had feared it would be.

"Do you acknowledge the greater responsibility that accompanies all progress from this point forward along the mage's path?" Council Master Galida asked next. "Do you accept the prices and choices that are yet to come?"

"Yes. And yes."

"Do you willingly recommit yourself to the service of your master, your kingdom, and the mages' order above all?"

"Yes."

"Thank you, Apprentice Calen. May the blessings of the Bright Lady light your path and the wisdom of the Harvester guide your steps upon it."

The entire assembly murmured, "Blessings and wisdom" in response, and then it was over. Serek caught Calen's eye and nodded. Calen turned and bowed to the head mages and then started for the stairs leading back down from the stage. That hadn't been so bad, really. He didn't know why getting up in front of people had to make him so nervous. Sure, everyone had been looking at him, but it wasn't like they were going to *do* anything to him.

Calen raised his foot to descend onto the top step when suddenly an enormous *BOOM* crashed through the assembly chamber. He stumbled and just barely managed to fall backward onto the stage instead of head-first down the stairs. Somehow the sound had turned into strange, swirling smoke. No — not smoke. It was magic energy he was seeing, enough to fill the air around him and out into where the audience was, too. The energy was made up of lots of different colors, too many for Calen to sort out and identify.

As his ears began to recover from that first assault of sound, he could hear people shouting. Serek was suddenly at his side, asking something. Calen couldn't make it out, but he began shouting, "I'm all right, I'm all right!" in case that's what Serek wanted to know. He let Serek help him up from the stage floor and lead him down the stairs and into a corner. All around them, mages were on their feet, pushing, running, calling out to one another.

"Stay here!" Serek shouted into Calen's face, leaning in close enough that Calen could understand him.

"But—"

"Just do as I say for once!" Serek snarled, pushing Calen painfully against the wall. Then he turned and took off into the chaos that filled the room. Calen lost sight of him immediately. And then caught sight of something else. Shapes were starting to form all around the chamber. Shapes that seemed to have roughly formed arms and legs. And were they holding some kind of knives? Or maybe they were claws. And … Calen squinted, trying to make sense of the swirls of color and madness around him. And … and teeth? Were those teeth?

What *were* these things?

The shouts around him became confused and frightened as the shapes began attacking. People were screaming and running, climbing over the seats; some were rushing the stage. Calen saw mages fall under the blows of the magic-formed shapes, saw their arms raised in ineffective attempts to ward off the violent swipes of the intruders' limbs, saw their flesh part in red ribbons sliced by claws or knives or teeth or *something*, but he didn't see anyone fighting back. Why weren't they fighting back?

Because they can't see anything, he realized. The shapes were made of magic — swirling energy-creatures of black and red and violet with threads of green and other colors running like veins through the hazy forms of their bodies.

Calen looked desperately around for Serek; he had to tell him what was happening. A few mages seemed to have managed to cast protection spells, but most appeared too busy trying to escape the invisible assault to cast anything. Should he try to help? Somehow he knew Serek had meant for him to stay put and not do anything, but surely he wasn't supposed to just stand by when he was the only one who could see what was going on.

He shook himself free of his tangled thoughts. *Stop dithering and do something,* he told himself. The entire chamber was filled with writhing, fighting creatures; it was pure luck that none of them had found his little corner so far. He couldn't count on that luck lasting for long.

With a practiced ease, he cleared his head, preparing to focus on casting . . . something. Serek, curse him, still hadn't taught Calen anything useful about magical weapons. But Calen could figure something out. He knew he could. Something damaging but focused — he didn't want to hurt one of the mages by mistake.

Red energy was the most destructive; he'd seen Sen Eva use it as a weapon, and he'd seen Serek use it to try to wipe out an infection in a wounded soldier. There was a spell Calen had used to kill root-beetles on some plants in the Mage's Garden once. Maybe if he started with that but tried to make it bigger, more powerful . . .

He concentrated, drawing the red magic into something he could see between his palms. Then he thought about trying to shape it, like a beam, something he could send at the creature nearest him. When it felt like the right shape, the right intensity, he *pushed* it from him with all the force he could muster.

It shot from his hands just as he'd envisioned and struck the creature in the back of the head. The creature shuddered and turned around. When it saw Calen with his arms still held out before him, it let out an ominous-sounding growl, its blurry, magic-formed face seeming to snarl. It did not, Calen noted with a sick, sinking feeling, appear to be damaged in any way. Just enraged. Then it launched itself at him.

Calen tried to back away, but he was still in the corner. He did the only other thing he could think of: he flung up a shield like the one he'd used to fend off Sen Eva that time on the tower. The creature threw itself against the magic barrier, and now Calen could see quite clearly: yes, those were indeed teeth. Teeth and claws. Big ones. Only inches away from his face, held off by his hastily constructed shield.

He looked wildly around, trying to see if anyone might be near enough to help him. He saw Serek and Council Master Renaldiere pushing their way through a group of mages to reach the front edge of the stage. The council master shouted something, and Serek nodded. Then they both raised their hands and began to channel a mix of green, gold, and white energy. At another shout from Renaldiere, both men released the magic, sending a burst of mixed colors up and out into the chamber. Calen was still trying to figure out what the spell was supposed to do when the energy formed a thin, sheetlike form and then descended to land lightly atop everyone and everything in the room. A subtly glowing sheen of magic seemed to coat everyone, mages and creatures alike. And suddenly the creatures became solid, their blurred limbs and features shifting into horrible, fully physical reality.

Calen nearly screamed. They were far worse this way. The creature attacking him now had dark, bristly fur, huge, claw-tipped arms, and a terrifying, wolflike snout dripping with saliva as it tried again and again to bite him through the shield. Why, *why* would Serek and the others do this? They had just made the things more real, more terrible.

He got it about a second later: the spell made the creatures visible. To everyone. Now that the mages could see what they were fighting, they were far better able to defend themselves. The tide turned fairly quickly after that. All around the room, mages began casting defensive spells and magical attacks, and in short order the creatures began falling and fading, killed or destroyed or undone. Someone — a mage Calen didn't know — finally noticed Calen's difficulty and sent something red and powerful at the attacking beast. It slid to the ground, clearly dead, but Calen still waited a few more seconds to release his shield.

Mages who had been knocked down began to get back up, some with the help of other mages' hands or healing spells. A few did not get up at all. Calen couldn't tell if they were unconscious or . . . worse. He saw one young apprentice, a boy of maybe six years old, crying unashamedly. Other mages were turning toward the stage in search of the council masters.

"What were those things?" someone shouted toward Renaldiere and Galida — probably not for the first time, but the noise level had finally gone down enough that individual voices could be heard. A chorus of angry shouts followed, seconding the question: "How could we have been attacked here —?"

"How did they break through our defenses?"

"And who could have —?"

"And *why* —?"

Council Master Galida turned from the older woman she was speaking with and held up her hand against the rising tide of voices. "Peace," she called out to the assembly. Calen was chilled to hear that strong voice shaking a little. "We must act quickly to see if there is anything we can learn."

Calen saw other mages nodding at this, and then Galida and Renaldiere began calling up white energy, their hands held wide before them to focus the power. Other mages joined in, and before long nearly every mage in the room — every full mage who was able and wasn't busy with healing or helping someone else — was standing still, facing the stage, and creating his or her own sphere of white, glowing energy. Calen itched to cast with them, but he knew better than to try. He didn't know exactly what they were doing, and joining in blind could disrupt the spell. Or worse, change the effect to something other than what was intended. He knew first-hand that when different spells clashed, the effects could be dangerous and unpredictable.

White magic usually meant communication, or exploration. Or *information*. Would what they were casting now help them discover where the creature spell had come from?

Renaldiere said something Calen didn't understand, and all the mages raised their arms as one. At a final word from the council master, the white energy suddenly burst forth from every pair of outspread hands, shooting out and into and through the walls and ceiling. Almost at once, small bursts of energy began coming back through the walls. The council masters both cocked their heads as though listening. After a few minutes, the frequency of the return bursts dropped off, and then they stopped altogether. Galida shook her head in frustration. Renaldiere gestured at the assembly, and everyone released the spell.

"Thank you," Galida said to the group. Her face was drawn, but her voice was steadier now. "You may go; we will reconvene this evening to discuss what has happened." She picked out two mages near the stage. "Nyar, Espion, please see to the wounded. Draft whomever you need to assist you. Council members, please stay behind."

People began to disperse, some limping on the arms of friends, some helping Nyar and Espion see to those who hadn't risen on their own. Another group of mages began to dispose of the dead creatures that hadn't already been magically unmade. Everyone looked very worried. Serek spoke for a few minutes more with some of the other mages on the stage, then came back down to where Calen was waiting. He gave Calen a grim look.

"I see that you are practically bursting with questions," he said. "Wait until we get back to my rooms, and I will do my best to answer them. Do not ask me anything until we get there. Understood?"

"Yes," Calen said. He *was* practically bursting with questions, but he thought he could hold them inside for a few more minutes. He followed Serek back out through the double doors and up the stairs. Along the way, they passed small groups of mages clustered together, speaking in hushed voices. Several of them glanced up as they walked by, and it seemed to Calen that they kept their eyes on him a little longer than he was quite comfortable with. He was glad when they reached Serek's rooms, which were just down the hall from Calen's.

They entered, and Calen sat on a simple wooden chair next to a sturdy table in the main room. Serek's quarters were bigger than his own, with a separate bedroom and more places to sit. Serek sat down across from him. Calen waited, trying not to bounce in his seat. Finally Serek rolled his eyes and said, "Very well. Go ahead."

"What *happened?*" Calen asked at once. "Where did those things come from? There were so many colors, and I didn't — I didn't even know someone could do that, make *things*, creatures, whatever they were, just out of magic —"

"I don't know what happened, exactly," Serek said. "No one does at the moment. Other than whoever is responsible for it, of course. As for where they came from, well, that is something we are very interested in finding out." He looked at Calen appraisingly. "What did you see? You said there were a lot of colors?"

"Yes. More than I could really sort out. It's strange — I've never seen any other kind of magic that was so tangled up that way. It was like it was trying on purpose to be confusing."

"Maybe it was," Serek said thoughtfully. "Perhaps it was designed to keep us guessing, to make it harder for us to defend ourselves. It should not have taken us so long to figure out that there were invisible creatures, not just random forces. . . . Well, you may be right about the confusion aspect. We'll have to bring that up tonight."

"We? I'm going to the meeting?"

"You'll need to tell them what you saw, Calen. You're the only one who was able to see the spell, after all. When Renaldiere and I made the things visible, we altered the original spell. Helpful for fighting back, but not so helpful for discovering what the spell was in the first place, or where it came from. You might be able to give some valuable insight."

"Oh. Right. Of course." Calen tried to sound more confident than he felt. He wasn't sure there was anything he could tell them that would be useful. But he was glad he was going to the meeting. There was no telling if Serek would be as willing to answer his questions later on. He didn't always have much patience for Calen's wanting to know everything all the time. And he thought Calen was better off not knowing some things, although Calen failed to see how that could ever make any sense. How could it hurt him to know as much as possible? Weren't teachers supposed to *want* you to want to learn?

There was one thing Calen wanted to know most of all. "Whoever cast that spell, it had to be a mage, didn't it? But not — I mean, no one here would have . . ." Calen hesitated, then made himself ask what he really wanted to know: "Do you think it could have been Sen Eva? Or . . . or Mage Krelig?"

Mage Krelig was that scary portal mage who had been helping — or commanding, or using, or all three — Sen Eva. Serek and the other mages had figured out who the man must be from Calen and Meg's reports of what they'd heard him saying to Sen Eva and from the things he had apparently taught her how to do. He was the only mage of that kind of power whom anyone could remember having been magically exiled.

But there had been no sign of Sen Eva in months, and as far as they knew, Mage Krelig was still stuck in whatever faraway world he'd been exiled to, because his evil plan had fallen apart when Calen and Meg had helped to stop Sen Eva on the rooftop. Sen Eva had gotten away, but she'd failed to kill Meg's sister and start the war with Kragnir. And the prophecy Mage Krelig had talked about had something to do with a war. So without the war, he couldn't come back. So they were safe now. Or they were supposed to be.

"That's what we were trying to figure out with the mass casting," Serek said. "We were looking for any sign of an intruder, or anyone suspicious in any way. But we found nothing." He curled his hand into a fist, more frustrated than Calen had ever seen him. "I don't understand it. To enter the Magistratum undetected and cast something like that and then just vanish — it should not be possible."

This was very bad, Calen realized. It was one thing for him to be confused; he was still just an apprentice. But Serek was a lot older and knew so much. It was frightening to see him so completely at a loss. And surely the council masters were supposed to be really knowledgeable and powerful, and if *they* were confused, too . . . Well, maybe they just needed some time to think. Maybe at the meeting later, with everyone having calmed down a bit, they would be able to figure it out.

Calen tried to think of how best to phrase his next question. Serek looked at him for a moment, then said, "Spit it out, Apprentice."

"*Now* will you teach me some kind of attack spell?" Calen asked. "The creature I tried to kill almost killed me instead!"

Serek became very still. His gaze turned icy. "You tried to kill one?"

"I couldn't just stand there doing nothing!"

"That was absolutely what you should have done!" Serek stood up and began to pace angrily. "I believe I have told you countless times not to attempt spells that I haven't actually taught you, regardless of what you think you might be capable of!"

"But —"

"I assume whatever it was you tried to do failed?"

Calen dropped his eyes. "Yes," he said bitterly. "But I still —"

"Still haven't learned your lesson?"

"If you would just *teach* me how to attack with magic, I wouldn't have to try to make things up on my own! I don't understand —"

"Exactly," Serek broke in. "You don't understand. Which is why you should not be playing around with magic against my wishes."

"Playing—!"

"Enough," Serek said. "Go back to your room, Calen. I'll come get you when it's time for the meeting."

With extreme effort, Calen bit back everything else he wanted to say, restricting himself to a silent but furious glare as he stomped out. There was no arguing with Serek when he got this way. Calen had thought it would be different now that he had earned his first true mark. He thought Serek would finally teach him how to *do* things, real things, to use his magic like a real mage. It wasn't fair. Did Serek want him to always be helpless in the face of danger? Cowering in a corner instead of being able to protect himself and fight back?

He tried to tell himself that he didn't need to worry, that the full mages were going to know what to do, that he was just an apprentice and it wasn't his job to figure everything out. But he couldn't stop his brain from continuing to turn things over, wondering what was going on and why he couldn't shake the feeling that what had happened today was only the beginning.

CHAPTER FIVE

THERE WAS A KNOCK AT THE door. Meg looked up, startled. She was in the middle of changing into clothes a little more appropriate for dragon riding than what she'd had on, and she certainly wasn't expecting any company.

"Yes?" she called through the door.

"Princess? It's me, Pela. I'm so sorry to disturb you, but they said —"

Meg opened the door a crack, holding the dress she'd just taken off against her shift. "What is it, Pela?" They had just finished today's morning walk a little while ago. Meg had been surprised to discover how quickly she'd begun to enjoy them. Pela was already noticeably less jumpy, even after just a couple of days. And when she wasn't trying so hard to be the perfect lady-in-waiting, she was actually kind of fun to talk with — clever and observant and full of interesting stories about her family and the town where she grew up.

Still, Meg had been looking forward to some time alone with Jakl. He demanded even more of her attention than usual of late, growing anxious if she spent too much time away.

"It's —" Pela suddenly noticed Meg's state of undress. "Oh! Oh, Princess, let me help you with that. You shouldn't be standing half-dressed in doorways. And you know this is one of the things I can help you with, I've told you...." She slipped inside, forcing Meg to step back and make room for her or be run over. Meg obediently turned around in response to Pela's firm hands on her shoulders and gave herself over to the girl's enthusiastic ministrations.

"The guards asked me to find you," Pela said, taking hold of the soft fabric of Meg's shift in order to help Meg tug it off over her head. "It's — it's that boy. Wilem."

Meg spun around to face her, ripping the material from Pela's hands in the process.

"What happened? Did something happen? Did he escape? I *told* them to take every precaution." She was instantly furious, absolutely incensed, that the guards could be so careless! When she got her hands on them —

"No!" Pela said, clearly alarmed by Meg's reaction. "No, nothing like that, Princess. Please—don't be angry." She reached out and actually petted Meg's arm in long, slow strokes, trying to soothe her. "He only wants to speak with you."

"He — what? Wants . . ." The anger dissipated as soon as Meg understood that Wilem hadn't escaped, but with such suddenness that it actually made her dizzy. That reaction had been extreme, even for her. And now she felt so *strange* . . . shaky . . .

Meg stepped back and sat on the edge of her bed. Pela hovered anxiously in front of her.

"He . . . insisted, apparently," Pela said, watching Meg's face carefully. "He said it was extremely important, and he would speak to no one but you."

"He insisted, did he?" Meg muttered. Wilem was not in a position to insist on anything. He had been his mother's willing accomplice, pretending to care for Meg in order to gather information, planning to kill Maerlie in revenge for what he thought Meg's father and the king of Kragnir had done to his father and brother. True, Sen Eva had lied to him, told him he was avenging their deaths and carrying out his father's wishes. He had made no attempt to evade punishment once he found out the truth about his mother's evil plans. Meg knew he deserved some credit for that. But she thought she had given him more than enough already. He was still *alive*, wasn't he? He had no right to insist on anything.

Pela was still hovering. "Shall I tell them you won't see him, Princess?"

She wanted to say she would not see him. She wanted that very much. But Wilem was her responsibility now. She had to go see what this was about.

If it turned out he was wasting her time, she would make him very sorry.

"No. It's all right, Pela. I will speak with him. Tell the guards to have him meet me in the garden."

Pela darted out to relay the message and then returned to help Meg back into her dress; she certainly wasn't going to meet Wilem dressed like an errand girl in her patched-up pants and tunic. In fact . . .

"Pela, fetch me the dark blue silk, the one Maerlie sent."

Pela curtsied, seeming pleased. "Yes, Princess!"

When they left for the garden, Meg let Pela walk ahead so she could compose herself. It had been weeks since she'd last spoken to Wilem. Thinking about him still brought back too many terrible feelings. The shock at his betrayal and the fury at what he had done, and at the far worse things he had been planning to do. Shame and embarrassment at having believed that he truly cared for her. Shame, too, at having been so devastated by the loss of her false suitor, even in the midst of the danger facing her family and the kingdom. And most of all at not having realized, for believing in the lie, for believing it so completely that she let him *kiss* her . . .

That kiss, that night, had been magical. Even now, appallingly mixed in with the hate and anger was the remembered thrill of that sweet moment when he leaned toward her and she realized what was about to happen and the way her mind had seemed to go away for a time and her heart had felt so large and full and tender inside her. Her first kiss, her first romance — it should have been something to treasure forever. Instead it was a poisoned thing, a memory that made her feel small and stupid and cold.

Although perhaps cold was not quite accurate. Angry fire was growing inside her again. *Jakl,* she thought urgently at her dragon, *stop that.* With effort, she slid the barrier into place as Calen had taught her, muting Jakl's presence in her mind to a vague sensation that she was aware of but didn't feel quite so connected to. She could just barely sense him pouting on the other side. He hated when she cut him off that way. She didn't like it, either, but she couldn't face Wilem with Jakl reflecting and amplifying everything she was feeling.

She tried not to think about the fact that it seemed to be getting harder and harder to put up the barrier each time she tried it.

When she reached the doors that led to the garden, Meg took a few extra deep breaths. *You're not angry,* she told herself. *You're not upset. You don't even care. You don't feel anything about Wilem at all.* Then she stepped out into the sunny afternoon.

He was there, waiting for her, seated on a low stone bench, a guard on either side and another standing stiffly at attention, facing the steps she was now descending. She barely saw the guards, though. All she could see was Wilem, his dark eyes looking up at her with a strange blend of fear and hope, his face, though somewhat more haggard than it had once been, as heart-stoppingly beautiful as ever. For the hundredth time, she thought of how unfair it was that someone so treacherous could project such an attractive image to the world.

He stood as she approached. She stopped several feet away.

"Princess," Wilem and the attention-standing guard said at the same time. The guard shot Wilem an irritated glance, then turned back to face Meg. "Your Highness," he said this time, and seemed petulantly satisfied when Wilem remained silent. Pela stood awkwardly nearby, clearly uncertain whether to stay or go.

"Leave us," Meg said to the guards, "but stay in sight,

please." She turned toward Pela. "You may go, as well, Pela. Thank you."

The guards strode off obediently, and Pela looked both relieved and reluctant as she made her way back inside. Meg was left facing her enemy alone. He was taller than she was; she didn't like having to look up at him. She also didn't like being this close . . . facing each other, so like they had in that other time, before everything fell apart in such a horrible, painful mess.

"Sit down, Wilem," she said.

He sat at once, silently, watching her face. Waiting for her permission to speak, she realized. She crossed her arms, looking down at him. Looking down at him was much better.

"What is it that you want to say to me?" she asked coldly. She hoped it was coldly, anyway. She was definitely trying for coldly.

"I have been having dreams," he said without preamble. "Bad dreams. Very vivid and . . . disturbing." He paused, then added, "I believe they have something to do with my mother."

For a moment Meg could not think of one suitable thing to say in response to this. Her brain seemed unable to translate all of those words into meaning. Dreams. Like she'd been having? And something to do with Sen

Eva? That was the hard part to get her mind around. Of course they all knew Sen Eva would be back at some point. But not *now*, not yet. *Gods*, Meg thought. *Please not yet.*

"What—?" She licked her lips and started again. "What makes you think your mother is involved?"

"I can feel her there, while I'm dreaming," he said. "Her . . . presence. I can sense her as if she were sitting just out of sight in another room. And the dreams themselves . . ." He stared at the ground beside her feet. He looked so unhappy. She fought back a wave of sympathy. *Remember who he is!*

"What are the dreams about?" she asked.

He shook his head—in refusal or denial or frustration, she wasn't sure. "I can't remember most of them clearly once I wake up. They were infrequent at first, just once or twice a week, and I thought they were just regular nightmares. But lately they have been coming every night. Almost as soon as I close my eyes. In them, everything is dark and confused, and . . . sometimes I see myself doing things. Bad things that I don't want to do." He looked up at her again, and his eyes seemed full of pain, but she knew she could not trust those eyes. Not really.

"What kind of things?"

He hesitated again and then seemed to make some kind of decision. In a flat voice, keeping his eyes steadily on hers, he replied, "Sometimes I hurt you. Sometimes I hurt your family. Sometimes I kill the mage or his apprentice. Always, I end up fleeing the castle, running off into the night. And I can feel my mother there, in my head, telling me to do these things. Forcing me to do them. Showing me how and when and taking me through the steps to achieve each end . . ." Some of the flatness dropped from his voice. "I don't do them willingly. I don't — I don't want to hurt you. I swear it. And I don't want to escape. I want to pay for what I've done. I don't *want* to go back. But she wants me to. To do whatever I have to do to get free and go to her." He paused once more, and Meg had trouble making herself believe his anguish was false. "My mother is sending these dreams. I am sure of it."

"Sending them. You mean magically."

"Yes."

Meg automatically made the protective sign of the goddess. Gods, she wished Calen were here. And Serek. And the whole gods-cursed Magistratum with their stupid council and their meetings and rules and libraries and whatever else they could use to tell her what she was supposed to do with this disturbing information. Should she even believe it? She thought she had to. If he was lying to her about this, she could not see how that would serve a purpose, other than simply to upset her. And if he was telling the truth, she could not afford to ignore his warning.

"Do you think you are a danger to my family, Wilem?" she asked calmly. Far, far more calmly than she felt.

"I don't know." He closed his eyes, and she saw again how rough and drawn his face was now. Like someone who had not slept well in a long time. "I think — I think I might be."

"Because you think the dreams might succeed in making you do something against us?"

"Yes."

"Are they getting stronger?"

"Yes," he said, opening his eyes again. "The early ones were shorter, less . . . forceful. As though the early dreams were first attempts, practice, and now that she has figured out how to send them more effectively . . ."

Meg fought back a shudder. "You think she might be getting skilled enough to turn her suggestions into compulsions."

He nodded.

"Do you think she might be able to send the dreams to other people as well?" Her dreams weren't like that, really. Not like he had described. But maybe Sen Eva had other goals for Meg.

"I don't know," he said, glancing at her curiously. "Have you —?"

Meg cursed inwardly, a sudden fierce river of doubt rising within her. Doubt and an urgent sense of alarm. *Stupid, stupid girl!* She should not be giving him any information. What if all of this was some sort of ruse to get her to admit she was having nightmares herself? What if Sen Eva was using him to find out whether her attacks on Meg's sleep were working? This could all be part of some larger scheme — even his presence here, his apparent rejection of his mother and her plans — everything could be a lie. Everything. *Anything.* She had to be more careful. Why was it so hard to remember not to trust him? He'd fooled her with lies before. Would she never, *never* learn?

Meg stepped back and turned to signal the guards, who were watching attentively. As they began jogging toward her, she looked back at Wilem.

"I will increase your guard. If anything . . . changes, if the dreams get stronger, if you find yourself acting on anything . . ."

"I will tell you at once, Princess. Thank you." He seemed genuinely relieved. Grateful.

Meg turned away. She didn't want to look at him anymore. The guards arrived, and she gave them instructions to increase the security detail assigned to Wilem both day and night. Especially night. They acknowledged this without question, and Meg left them to it. She would have to go find her parents and let them know what Wilem had told her. Once Calen and Serek returned, they could ask Serek to investigate; surely there was some way he would be able to tell if magic were being used against Wilem in that way. Or against Meg.

She thought she would leave out the part about her own dreams when she spoke with her parents, however. Just for now, just until she could find out more about what they meant, or didn't mean. Her parents were concerned enough about her right now. There was enough they were still trying to get used to. This new issue, the dreams — the dreams could wait.

She felt Jakl tugging at her and suffered a twinge of guilt. He would have to wait, too. *I'm sorry,* she thought at him. *Just a little longer. I have to take care of this. I'll be there as soon as I can.* He didn't like that. She could feel him pulling her, wanting her to come *now,* but she had no choice. With an effort, she made the barrier a little stronger, pushing him more firmly away. Once again, it seemed a lot harder than it should have been.

Calen, she thought desperately, quickening her steps as she approached the castle doors. *Please come back soon.*

CHAPTER SIX

THE COUNCIL HAD DECIDED TO COMBINE the meeting with the evening meal. Calen found himself juggling a pair of plates piled high with dinner while trying to find Serek and the seat he hoped his master had remembered to save for him. Long, cloth-draped counters covered with food lined one side of the meeting chamber, and pitchers of water and wine had been set out among the tables where people were sitting. This was a different room from the one in which the ceremony had been held. While that space had been designed so that one person or a small group could present information to an audience, this one was set up as a series of large concentric circles — the intention being, Calen supposed, that everyone would mostly be able to see one another, and they could have a discussion as a group.

The mages were all talking among themselves, still clearly agitated about the afternoon's events. Calen thought he'd heard his own name mentioned more than once. It made sense, he supposed — the attack had happened during his marking ceremony. But it still made him uncomfortable. And it still seemed that certain mages' eyes kept lingering on him as he passed by.

He spotted Serek at last, seated in the second circle from the center. Calen made his way down the narrow aisle, edged behind the chairs of several other mages — none of whom seemed the least bit inclined to slide their chairs in to make his progress any easier — and finally reached the spot where Serek sat talking with the mage next to him. The seat on the other side of Serek was empty, Calen saw with relief. His arms were getting tired from holding up the heavy plates. He set Serek's plate down before him and then his own beside it. Then he slipped into the seat and tried to listen to Serek's conversation without seeming to.

"If you'd have asked me yesterday, I would have sworn there was no way anyone could penetrate the Magistratum's defenses like that," Serek's companion was saying. He seemed to be a fair bit older than Serek, but his face was not as heavily marked. His beard was entirely gray, and what little hair there was on top of his head was white. "Can't imagine how they managed it," the man went on, shaking his head. "I keep turning it over in my mind, listening to the theories being thrown around—all nonsense. No one really has any idea at all."

"Something will come out in the meeting," Serek said. "No one can cast something that large without leaving some trace behind. Not in the middle of a room full of mages."

"Which begs the question, of course: why there and then? You don't suppose—?" His eyes flicked up, and he suddenly noticed Calen sitting there. "Oh, ah . . . your apprentice has joined us, I see."

Serek turned to take in Calen and the plates of food. "Ah, thank you, Calen. Mage Anders of Everton, may I present Apprentice Calen of Trelian. Calen, Mage Anders is an old friend of mine."

"Old, indeed," Anders said, giving Calen a little nod of greeting. He seemed friendly enough, but he gave Calen one of those overly long looks that had been making him antsy all afternoon. "Congratulations on your marking, young Calen. A mage's first true mark is not an experience he ever forgets. Of course, yours may be more memorable than most, I suspect. Quite a show we had this afternoon, wasn't it?"

"Yes, sir," Calen replied respectfully. He was still stuck on the idea that Serek had called this man his friend. He hadn't thought Serek had any friends.

Anders opened his mouth to say something else, but just then the sound of a bell rang out. The council masters were sitting in the center circle, a quarter of the way around the room from where Calen and Serek were. Mage Renaldiere was holding a silver bell aloft in one hand. The other council members were seated along the same row to either side of Galida and Renaldiere. Conversations around the room quickly died down, and all the mages turned their attention to the center.

"I don't have to emphasize how serious the events of this afternoon were," Mage Galida began. "The members of the council have spent some time reinforcing our defenses and constructing several new layers of wards and alarms, but since we thought we were already adequately protected before . . . well, obviously we want to figure out what exactly happened, and how, and who was responsible. As we were unable earlier to determine anything about the source of the spell, we are here to see what further information we might be able to pull together and to determine appropriate action." She turned to look at Serek. "Mage Serek? I believe you have something to report."

Suddenly all the eyes in the room were on them. Calen swallowed nervously. He'd known he would have to tell about the colors; he just hadn't thought it would be the very first item on the agenda. He wasn't ready to have everyone looking at him again already.

Serek nodded. "Thank you, Council Master." He looked around and addressed his words to the surrounding tables: "As many of you have heard by now, my apprentice has a unique gift. He is able to see colors when magic is cast nearby, and is beginning to be able to identify types of magic by the colors associated with the casting. I know we meant to have a separate discussion about his ability, but in light of today's events, I thought it might be helpful to hear his interpretation of what happened in the assembly hall."

He looked expectantly at Calen. A murmuring had broken out among the mages, which only made it harder for Calen to will himself to speak. Did they have to stare and mutter like that? He was intensely aware of Serek's gaze, which seemed to be growing ever so slightly impatient.

Stop being such a baby, he told himself, and strangely it sounded like Meg's voice in his head. She would have no problem speaking in front of a crowd, of course. But more important, she would do whatever needed to be done without whining about it. He had a responsibility to help here if he could. He opened his mouth. "Well —"

"With all due respect," another mage broke in, "we

as yet have no documented proof of the apprentice's alleged ability to see these colors. How do we know that what he saw was anything other than his own imagination?"

"It was *not*—" Calen began, but Serek laid a warning hand on his arm.

"Why don't we hear what he has to say before arguing about its validity?" Galida said dryly. After a moment, the mage who had spoken nodded in acquiescence. All eyes turned back to Calen. He found it was easier to speak now that he was angry.

"I do see colors when people cast," he said, directing his words toward the council masters. They, at least, seemed to want to hear what he had to say. "When I cast, or when other mages cast around me. It is stronger with spells I know well, but over the past few months, I've been able to see more, even if the spells are unfamiliar. I didn't realize for a long time that I was the only one. I thought everyone could see the colors."

"And what did you see today, Calen?" Renaldiere asked.

"Everything," Calen said. "I mean, it seemed to be all different kinds of magic together. More colors than I've ever seen at one time before. And I could see the creatures that were attacking. I mean, before you and Mage

Serek cast that spell to make them visible. They were completely made up of magic energy, a lot of black and red and purple, but also some green, and some other colors — so many that it was hard to sort anything out, especially because I don't know anything about that kind of spell — making things, creatures, out of magic that way."

There was a great deal of muttering at this. Calen looked at Serek nervously.

"It could be that the unusual variety of colors Calen saw reflects the fact that the spell was designed to be hard to decipher," Serek said.

An older female mage from across the room raised her voice to be heard over the continued muttering from the other mages. She bore many marks, and her white hair was pulled back from her face with a bright, rose-colored scarf. Calen recognized her as the one Council Master Galida had been speaking with on the stage just before the mass casting. "I did sense a great, tangly confusion of magic this afternoon, friends. And" — she raised her eyebrows and glanced around significantly —"you all know I normally don't need to stretch to tease out what's being cast around me."

There were nods and murmurs of agreement at this. Anders leaned over and whispered to Calen, "Lisbette is highly skilled at sensing magic. She can usually identify a spell even from the energy that lingers afterward; it's quite extraordinary."

Mage Lisbette went on, "That spell didn't feel like anything I have ever sensed before. I am willing to believe that what the young apprentice says is true. Which says to me we are dealing with some kind of magic unfamiliar to the lot of us. Which is, to say the least, a matter of more than passing concern."

More muttering, more nods, some head shakes, lots of worried faces.

A man sitting a few rows back spoke next. "We have not yet discussed the possibility that the attack is connected to the recent events relating to the woman Sen Eva and her efforts to aid in the return of Mage Krelig."

Calen sucked in his breath. He had hoped he was just being paranoid about that.

The other mages had erupted into side conversations again at the man's words, and Council Master Renaldiere had to ring his bell for quiet. Then he nodded and said, "We might as well begin tonight. That topic is, of course, the main reason we called this general assembly. There does not seem to be any doubt that Sen Eva's benefactor is Mage Krelig; we are agreed on that. Mage Serek's report suggested that Krelig's attempt to return was thwarted by the events at Trelian, but as long as Sen Eva is still at large, we must assume that she may still be working toward that goal."

"But how *can* he return?" one of the apprentices Calen had noticed earlier asked. "Isn't that supposed to be impossible? Wasn't he exiled to keep him away forever?"

"They should have killed him when they had the chance," an older apprentice said. There were many mutters of support for that sentiment among the other apprentices, but also a lot of head shaking from the full mages.

"Mage Krelig was too powerful to either compel or kill," Galida said. "He had abilities beyond most of his peers, and no hesitation about using his powers to achieve whatever he wanted. Ironically, the early founders of the Magistratum were at a distinct disadvantage, as they were bound to follow the laws they wanted to impose on all mages, whereas Mage Krelig was free to cast whatever he wished. We think the only reason the mages of his time were able to manage exile was that he had been caught unaware, not expecting that particular form of attack. That might have been his weakness — he himself would not have thought of exile, since he usually just killed anyone who got in his way."

"As for whether he can truly return, we fear that is a real possibility," Renaldiere said grimly. "Mage Krelig had — has — the Sight, and we believe he has had a vision showing him how to get back."

"Part of what he requires is apparently a war," Serek said. "That's what Sen Eva was trying to achieve. She was trying to renew the war between Trelian and Kragnir in order to set certain elements in place for Krelig's return."

Calen shocked himself by speaking. "He said — when Meg — when Princess Meglynne — and I saw him, in the portal that Sen Eva opened, he said something about Queen Lysetta, the queen of Kragnir who died when she was visiting Trelian. He started the war, back then, with Kragnir, but I guess there was something else he needed, too."

"A partner," Anders said. "He needed someone on this side to help bring him through. He must not have been able to find one before."

"Or he found one and it didn't work," another mage said.

"How is he even still *alive?*" another of the apprentices asked. "Wasn't he exiled hundreds of years ago?"

"Again, we aren't certain," Galida said, "but we believe that time works differently wherever he was sent, and so less time has passed for him than it has for us."

"The important thing to make clear," Renaldiere said, "is that a war between kingdoms is not the danger we are afraid of. That would only be a means to an end for Mage Krelig, and the end would be . . . well, it would be catastrophic. We haven't faced an enemy like this in a long time. The Magistratum has done such a good job of keeping mages in order and controlling potential threats before they cause too much damage that we are rather unprepared for a mage of Krelig's caliber. He is very powerful, and very driven."

"And probably very angry," Anders said quietly from the other side of Serek.

"Not to mention *crazy*," Calen muttered, mostly to himself. Krelig had certainly seemed crazy when he'd been talking to Sen Eva through the portal that time.

"And he is also . . ." Renaldiere seemed to be searching for the right words. "He was more than just a mage who resisted the formation of the Magistratum. He does not want to return simply to try to disband us. He would bring about a return to the chaos and terror of the old times — mages unmarked and unsworn, acting without rules or restraint, using their powers to force others to bend to their will, and every one of them subject to the whims and goals of a madman of enormous power. A horrible fate not just for our order, but for the rest of the world as well. Including those kingdoms and villages many of us are sworn to protect."

Several moments of silence followed Renaldiere's remark. Calen hadn't really thought it through before; maybe a lot of the others hadn't, either.

"Could he really do that, though?" Calen asked into the silence. "I mean, believe me, I know he's evil and powerful and everything, but he's still just one man. Even with Sen Eva's help, could he really overpower the entire Magistratum?"

"Oh, yes," Renaldiere said. "I have no doubt of it."

The bare certainty in his voice was terrifying.

Council Master Galida was nodding grimly beside him. "From the beginning," she said, "Mage Krelig was known for being ruthless in his search for greater power. There are lengthy accounts in our histories of his violent acts, testaments showing him to be unalteringly cruel and without conscience or loyalties. He would kill every last one of us, destroy the Magistratum entirely, and kill anyone opposing him and anyone he even suspected of being a potential obstacle to his plans."

"Even acting alone," Renaldiere went on, "he has knowledge and power we could not hope to match."

"And you don't think he'll be acting alone," Mage

Anders said. It was not quite a question. "And you don't just mean this Sen Eva."

Renaldiere looked steadily out at the assembled mages. "I would not presume to accuse any of our number of being sympathetic to his goals . . . but it cannot be denied that there will always be those drawn to power, and Mage Krelig was known to be very persuasive in his way. His abilities allow him to offer significant rewards to his followers. We must face the probability that he will be able to recruit some other mages to his cause."

Angry mutters followed this, but Calen felt more frightened than angry. Mage Krelig was good at making promises. That's how he'd gotten Sen Eva to help him, after all. It didn't seem hard to imagine that he'd find things he could promise other mages that might win them over to his side.

"He also retains the portal knowledge that we have lost," Galida said, "which gives him additional powers of frightening consequence. The slaarh reported in Trelian, for example, were brought through a portal from somewhere. We must assume that Mage Krelig instructed Sen Eva on how to accomplish that. Although Mage Devorlin's journal does contain a lot of information from his own private, ah, experiments. We will be studying his notes very closely."

There was some general confusion at this, and Calen realized that not everyone knew about the journal. Serek seemed to realize the same thing. "We found a journal in Sen Eva's possession," he explained. "It was written by Mage Devorlin of Kragnir, who we believe to be the partner Mage Krelig had tried to cultivate in Lysetta's day. Sen Eva discovered the journal while serving as an advisor to King Ryllin and began experimenting on her own, unmarked and untrained. There was an accident of some kind in which her older son was killed and her husband lost. It seems she had been opening portals in an attempt to find her husband, when she found Mage Krelig instead."

"But why send such an attack?" one of the other council mages asked. "If it was Mage Krelig behind what happened this afternoon, what did he hope to gain? Damaging and startling as it was, it did not seem of sufficient strength or viciousness to cause serious harm to the Magistratum. Was it some kind of warning? And if so, to what end? One would not think Krelig would want to do anything to alert us to his continued attempts to return to this world."

"Seems likely the spell was intended to do more

harm than it did," said Mage Lisbette. "If he is coaching this Sen Eva from afar, she could simply have failed to perform the spell correctly."

"I believe," said another mage, "that there was a different reason." Calen recognized him as one of the mages who had been waiting for him and Serek after he'd gotten his tattoo that morning. "It was surely no accident that the spell was cast when and where it was. We cannot ignore the possibility that Mage Serek's apprentice is somehow involved with those who sent the creatures."

Calen's mouth fell open. *What?*

Serek got slowly to his feet, his eyes practically shooting sparks. "Mage Brevera," he growled, "you go too far —"

But Brevera rushed on, nearly shouting in his attempt to talk over Serek: "There are those of us here who have believed for some time that there is a danger associated with the boy. We have attempted to discuss this matter with Mage Serek, but he has been unwilling to consider our findings!"

Serek's expression grew even darker, but he did not raise his voice. "I have been unwilling to consider your findings in secret meetings behind closed doors, Mage Brevera. I have been quite clear on how I feel about that.

95

If you have accusations to make, make them here in full council, or keep your opinions to yourself."

"They are not opinions!" Mage Brevera answered hotly. "They are findings that my colleagues and I have verified through multiple divinations —"

"Privately cast divinations, of which your word is not sufficient evidence."

Mage Brevera stood up. "How *dare* —"

"Enough!" Council Master Galida shouted. "Mages, must we remind you of the council rules for debate?"

"No," Serek said at once. "My apologies, Council Master Galida." He sat back down.

Mage Brevera sat as well, muttering something that might have been an apology. Calen finally remembered to close his mouth, but he still felt as if the ground had fallen away somewhere far beneath him. He swallowed and then asked in a small voice, "What danger?"

Galida looked at him. "Did you say something, Apprentice Calen?"

Calen nodded and tried again, willing his voice to cooperate. "I asked what danger, Council Master. If there is some kind of danger associated with me, I would like to know more about it."

"Indeed," she said. "So would I. Mage Brevera, if you would be so kind?"

Mage Brevera smiled smugly. "Gladly, Council Master. As you know, Mages Thomil, Mettleson, and I routinely cast divinatory spells concerning the Magistratum, its members, and related events. We report our findings when they are significant so that appropriate action may be taken if necessary." Galida nodded, and Mage Brevera continued.

"For nearly a year, we have encountered disturbing trends in our findings. Until recently the warnings were vague and unfocused, and we were aware only of a general sense of danger approaching. I have reported this in the past, but since we had nothing specific or helpful to go on, there seemed to be nothing the council could do but wait for further signs. Those signs recently began appearing. We know that a newly marked apprentice will be directly connected to vast and destructive danger to the Magistratum. We —"

"Calen is hardly the only recently marked apprentice," Council Master Renaldiere broke in.

"With respect, Council Master," Mage Brevera said with a tiny nod of his head, "there is more. We know the danger involves a boy who is the first apprentice of his master and one who traveled here from the north. There are many little such facts we can relate. But most significantly, we know the apprentice in question has unusual abilities that others do not share. Can you doubt that our findings must point to this boy?"

There was more muttering from the assembly, and Calen saw far too many mages glancing in his direction. Serek sat stone-faced, listening. Calen wished his master would say something in his defense. Obviously there was some mistake. He certainly wasn't involved in any kind of danger affecting the Magistratum!

Mage Brevera looked at Serek with a sour expression. "We attempted to discuss the matter with Mage Serek in order to gain his permission for some, ah, testing of his apprentice so that we might further determine the nature of the danger he presented. Mage Serek refused to cooperate."

"Why did you not report first to the council?" Galida asked.

"Perhaps we should have, Council Master Galida," Brevera said, making what Calen thought was a very poor attempt to sound apologetic, "but we wanted to have more information before presenting our findings. Divination is such a difficult and inexact art, and we wanted to be sure before bringing any suggestions before the council. And until this afternoon, we were still uncertain. But now . . ." He hesitated, then went on in a rush. "We submit that, for the protection of the Magistratum,

Apprentice Calen be immediately subject to investigation to determine the further nature of the danger he represents."

Serek was suddenly back on his feet, and he and Brevera began shouting at each other across the chamber. Other mages joined in as well. Council Master Renaldiere was ringing his tiny bell like a madman, but no one was paying any attention. Mage Anders caught Calen's eye from the other side of Serek and gave him what seemed a sympathetic expression. That did nothing to assuage Calen's fears. What exactly did "subject to investigation" mean, anyway? It certainly didn't sound good. This was crazy! He hadn't done anything!

The sound of the silver bell suddenly became deafening, and Calen could see that the council master had cast an enhancement spell to amplify the ringing. Serek sat heavily back in his seat, and the shouting died down around them. He turned to look at Calen, and his face was angry and worried. Calen didn't mind the anger — he'd seen Serek angry more often than not, and at least this time he seemed to be angry on Calen's behalf, not at Calen himself — but the worry was ... well, worrisome. Serek did not generally appear worried. Calen was beginning to feel very scared.

"Thank you," Renaldiere said when everyone had

finally quieted down. He leaned over to speak with Council Master Galida for a moment, then addressed the room once more. "It does seem that we should be open to exploring every avenue that might help us figure out what happened here today. And the findings of Mage Brevera's group are not to be discounted out of hand. We believe there can be no harm and much possible good in allowing him to proceed with his investigation."

"I submit that the matter be put to a vote," Serek said quickly.

Council Master Galida looked at Serek with what seemed like regret. "I do not believe a vote is required, Mage Serek," she said. "No action is being taken other than an attempt to gather further information about Apprentice Calen's ability and his possible significance in relation to the mysterious casting we all experienced today. He is not being formally accused of anything or being placed under any kind of official reprimand or notice. We would ask that he comply willingly with this request. Overriding his refusal would call for a vote, but I cannot see any reason he should refuse, unless he has something to hide."

Serek seemed to be searching for some other objection he could make, but finally he only nodded. He turned to Calen. "They only want to learn more about your ability and to have you participate in some more divination spells," he said quietly. "We already knew your ability would be a topic of consideration during this visit. And perhaps the divination will be helpful. I don't like the way this decision was reached, but truly there's nothing to worry about. Just be polite and cooperate, and tell them the truth about whatever they ask you. We have nothing to hide from the council."

Calen wished Serek could have managed to erase the worry from his expression while telling him there was nothing to worry about. But his words made sense, and Calen knew there was no real reason to be afraid. *This is the Magistratum*, he reminded himself. *I'm one of their number. No one here is my enemy.* He wished he felt more certain, though, that everyone here was his friend.

"I believe we should adjourn for now," Council Master Renaldiere said. "Mage Secretary Ettien will form the committee to investigate the nature of the spell cast this afternoon, and Mage Brevera will lead the investigation of Apprentice Calen's abilities and possible connection to the attack. As originally planned, tomorrow morning's meeting will focus on what we can do to prepare for the possible return of Mage Krelig. We will have the records of Mage Krelig's crimes and subsequent exile available for examination at that time, and anyone with any information passed down via apprenticeship or personal connections should be prepared to share that information with the group tomorrow."

He rang his bell a final time, and the mages began to rise and collect their belongings and talk among themselves. Servants quietly stepped in to begin clearing away the food and table settings.

Calen and Serek stood up, and Serek led Calen through the crowd to where the head mages sat waiting. Mage Brevera and his colleagues were standing before the table as well.

"Come with us, please, Apprentice Calen," the man beside Mage Brevera said. Serek looked resigned, and Calen realized that Serek had known they would want Calen to go by himself. He threw his master a frantic look, but Serek only nodded at him firmly.

"Go on, Calen," he said. "I will see you as soon as they have completed their work." Serek stared fixedly at Mage Brevera when he said this last, and the other mage seemed as if he were going to say something in response but then thought better of it. Instead, the mage turned and led the way out through a narrow door behind the last row of tables. Calen followed, looking back once just before he left the room. Serek stood there, still looking in Calen's direction, but whatever he was seeing was something else, his gaze directed inward. Calen turned back around to pass through the doorway. He felt a sudden chill as the door clicked shut behind him.

CHAPTER SEVEN

Q UEEN MERILYN AND KING TORMON LOOKED
at each other grimly. Meg watched them and
waited, unhappy to have had to bring them such troubling news. Jakl was still pushing at the barrier she'd put
up, like a cat scratching at a closed door, clamoring for
her attention. *Hold on*, she thought at him. She didn't
like how insistent he felt, agitated and impatient. *I'll be
there as soon as I can.*

"I think you handled this well, Meg," her father said,
turning back to her. "Whether or not Wilem is telling
the truth, the extra guard makes sense. And once Mage
Serek returns, we can ask him to investigate the matter
further."

"Do you know when they'll be back?" Meg asked.
"Have you gotten any word?"

"No, Meg. I'm sorry. I am certain they will return as
soon as they can, but you know there were many important things for the Magistratum to discuss." He smiled at
her gently. "I know you miss your friend, too."

She smiled back, although she didn't much feel like it. She did miss Calen, more than her father could guess. But it wasn't like she didn't understand. Of course Serek had important responsibilities. Calen, too. He couldn't stick around here just to keep her company all the time. And really, she was glad he was getting some of the recognition he deserved. She hoped all the other mages were impressed with his special ability. She hoped he told them about the spells he'd refined, too, the techniques he'd worked out while they were trying so hard to get home, and then to get the evidence they needed against Sen Eva. Meg might not know much about magic, but even she could see that Calen was very talented. She saw the way Serek looked at him now, too, as if he couldn't believe he hadn't seen Calen's specialness sooner.

"I think it would be a good idea if you checked in with Wilem regularly," her father went on. "I would prefer that he not need to send for you through the guards. And this way he will know we are keeping a close eye on him. And you'll know right away if something changes."

Meg tried to swallow her misgivings. If there was one thing she did not want, it was to see Wilem every single day.

"Of course, Father," Meg said. "I will let you know the minute there is anything to report."

"Excellent. Thank you, Meg."

Her mother smiled at her, and being able to please her parents in this way was almost worth the unpleasant prospect of regular interaction with Wilem. They would see that she was perfectly capable of being the heir they wanted. She would show them, and the people of Trelian, and everything would be fine.

She stood up to take her leave, but as she opened her mouth to say good-bye, there was a sudden strange shifting in her head, followed by a wave of blinding pain. And then Jakl, flooding in, drowning her.

"Meg!" Her mother's voice, no longer sounding very pleased. Both of her parents were on their feet. Meg realized she was back in her chair and had grabbed her head with her hands. Had she screamed? She didn't think so. She was, however, moaning in pain. She clamped her mouth shut and tried to focus. This was certainly not helping anything. *Stop it, Jakl!* she thought at him, hoping her obvious dismay would make him back off. He was having none of it, though. With horror she realized she could feel him getting closer. Tired of waiting for her to come to him, he was coming to her instead.

Oh, no. No, no, no. This was not good. Not good at all. And it still hurt. Gods, what was he *doing* to her?

Meg's mother was reaching forward across the desk

106

as her father came around, knelt before her, and placed his hands over hers, on the sides of her head. "Are you all right? What is it, Meg? Talk to me!"

"I'm okay," she managed. With effort, she forced her face to relax, made herself ignore the pulsing pain. "I'm sorry. I don't know what happened. Sudden, uh, headache."

"Is it —?" The king looked at the queen, and Meg knew what they were thinking. They were right, of course, but that didn't make it any better.

"No, it's not the link," she lied. "It doesn't work that way. And besides, Jakl would never hurt me. It's just a headache. Maybe from not sleeping so well last night."

They clearly did not believe this. She didn't blame them. But she wasn't about to give them the truth. "Meg —" her mother began.

"I'm fine, really." She gently removed her father's hands and stood up. "I just need some air. I'm sure I'll feel better in a moment. Please."

She fled, trying not to look as panicked as she felt, leaving her father still kneeling beside her vacant chair.

Stop! she thought furiously at the dragon as she raced toward the garden. *Stop it right now, you gods-cursed thing! I'm coming — just wait!* It felt like he was ready to come right into the castle to find her.

And it still *hurt*. Why was he hurting her?

She kept running, one hand holding her head, the other hitching up her dress, ignoring the startled stares of those she passed in the halls. Finally she reached the garden doors and burst through them, eyes raised to the sky. Jakl was there, as she knew he would be, circling, screaming. People were running, terrified.

Wonderful.

He screamed again when he saw her. He was so *angry* — she'd never seen him like this. He dove toward her, and for just a second she was certain he was about to kill her. She stood her ground, too angry herself to be afraid and still unwilling to believe he would truly hurt her. Even though he *was* hurting her, still, now, every second. He crashed to the ground beside her, and she scrambled up on his back, wanting nothing but to get him away from here so they could have this out more privately. Whatever this was. This horrible flood of anger, flowing between them, feeding on itself with sickening intensity.

As soon as they were up again and moving away from the castle, she screamed back at him. "What is wrong with you?" She pounded her fists against his neck, knowing he could barely feel her blows but needing to strike out at him just the same. "Are you crazy? Are you trying to make everything even worse? Stop it! Stop it, stop it, stop it, stop it, stop it!"

She was crying now, she realized. From the pain and from the *wrongness* of it, that they were screaming at each other this way, that he could make her angry enough to hit him, that he could hurt her the way he was. She didn't understand.

Slowly, Jakl seemed to come back to himself. She felt him take in her fear and pain along with the anger, and he seemed to grow a bit confused as he grew calmer. He circled again, angling toward a clearing, and set himself down as gently as he was able to. She was off his back at once, striding around to face him. He arched his neck back slightly to look at her. He was breathing heavily, exhausted from his furious flight and from the effort of holding back his fire. She realized suddenly that if he'd had a little less control, he might have set the whole garden ablaze. Or worse.

Oh, Jakl.

They stared at each other, abashed. She felt the anger drain from her and noticed suddenly that her head didn't hurt anymore. Jakl lay his head flat in the grass and looked up at her in obvious apology. Meg sat beside him. "What *happened?*" she asked, stroking his neck. "What *was* that?"

109

He couldn't answer, of course. She doubted he would have been able to explain, anyway. He seemed as confused as she was. Nothing like that had ever happened before. She was pretty sure it was not supposed to. Calen had never mentioned anything in his various warnings, and he usually tried to cover every conceivable thing that could ever possibly go wrong.

One more thing she'd need to ask him about when he got back.

Until then . . . She looked at Jakl and sighed. "I'm sorry," she told him. "I didn't mean to stay away so long. There was an emergency. I knew you were waiting, and I was trying to come to you as soon as I could. But you can't . . . I need you to try very hard not to get so impatient. You scared me. You scared a lot of other people, too."

The waves of apology and shame coming at her through the link were getting overwhelming. "It's all right," she said gently. "Nothing really terrible happened. This time. But we need to make sure that never happens again. We both need to try very hard, all right?"

They sat that way for a while, Meg leaning her check against his neck, and then she climbed back up to let Jakl fly off the rest of their bad feelings. The rush of wind and speed, too fast for thought or fear, soothed them both, and finally she had him take them back toward the castle. The sun was getting low in the sky.

As he circled toward their usual landing spot, Meg noticed a lone horse racing toward the main gate. The rider was dressed in a courier's uniform. As she watched, the courier pulled up at the gate, dismounted, and ran forward, not even pausing long enough for the waiting gate attendants to take the horse's reins from him. The guards let him through without delay.

Meg felt a little knot of worry forming in her stomach. It must be bad news. The courier would hardly punish himself and his horse with such haste otherwise. Jakl tensed beneath her, sensitive to her sudden concern. "Don't worry," she whispered to him. "I'm sure it will be okay, whatever it is. It's not anything you need to worry about." She felt him relax again; perhaps he was just especially eager to please her after the craziness of that afternoon.

She slid from his back and hurried into the castle through the garden doors. Her parents usually received couriers in the small office adjoining the throne room. She headed there, a hundred different fears looming up inside her all at once. *Maybe something happened to Calen,* her mind whispered relentlessly. *Or to Serek, or to everyone at the Magistratum. Maybe there is trouble in Kragnir, maybe Maerlie is ill, maybe Morgan is ill, maybe more of those horrible monsters of Sen Eva's have been spotted and they are heading this way. Maybe it is Sen Eva herself, returned at last, back to finish what she started.*

She flew around the last corner and down the hall. She did not think her parents would mind her coming to hear what the courier had to say. This would be one of her princess-heir duties soon enough: receiving couriers and dealing with the news they brought.

She could hear voices as she approached. The courier was already reporting. It was a young woman, she realized, not a man; most couriers were male, but there were a few female riders as well. Meg hadn't been able to tell from her distant vantage point. She was about to enter, ready to apologize for interrupting but also to ask permission to stay and listen. Then she heard the word *dragon.*

Meg froze just outside the doorway.

"You're certain?" the king was saying. "Absolutely certain?"

"The findings were pretty clear, Sire," the courier replied. "Fires with no apparent cause, patches of scorched earth, and reports of a large creature seen flying overhead at night. There have been deaths, too. Not to mention severe damage to property and farmland. Something large and dangerous has certainly been making these attacks."

"And Lourin is convinced that Meg's — our — dragon is to blame?" The queen's voice, almost too soft for Meg to hear.

The courier sounded apologetic. "No other dragons have been seen or heard of in so many years, Your Majesty. When the signs first began appearing, King Gerald was not sure what to make of them, but when he heard about Trelian's dragon, he came to the logical conclusion."

Logical! There was no way Jakl could be responsible for the damage they were talking about. And certainly not for people's deaths! She had a sudden, reluctant flashback to his behavior earlier today, his nearly uncontrollable anger . . . but she pushed it aside. She would know. If Jakl were flying off in the middle of the night and terrorizing nearby kingdoms, she would know. She would.

Unless . . . unless her nightmares were shielding her somehow. Distracting her from what Jakl was doing when she was not with him . . .

Unless she was having the nightmares *because* of what he was doing when she was not with him . . .

No. She would not believe it. It wasn't possible. She would know.

Meg hesitated, unsure of what to do. She wanted to burst in and refute these ridiculous accusations. But she held back, waiting to hear what else the courier had to say, to hear what her parents said in response. Did they really believe it was Jakl?

"What action is Gerald taking?" the king asked.

"For now, he simply sends a warning—"

"A warning!" the queen exclaimed, but then bit back whatever else she might have wanted to say.

The courier went on, sounding reluctant. "He sends a warning for Trelian to call off its dragon and explain these attacks against the kingdom of Lourin. No immediate consequences are mentioned, but he asserts that if the matter is not resolved within four days, he will be forced to take action to protect his people." The courier paused, then continued, "I respectfully recommend sending a reply at once, Your Majesties. King Gerald seemed . . . agitated. I believe he has already sent word to Baustern and Farrell-Grast, to seek their advice and possible support in any action he may take against Trelian. I would be happy to return at once bearing whatever—"

"Thank you, Tessel," the king broke in. "We must

discuss this, and you will need food and rest before you will be able to carry any messages anywhere. Please report in to your dispatcher and then get yourself something to eat. We will summon you when we have need of you again."

"Yes, Your Majesty," Tessel said. And then before Meg could think of what to do, the young woman emerged through the doorway and saw her.

"Princess!" she exclaimed, her eyes going wide.

"Meg?" came her father's voice from within the office. In a moment he appeared behind the courier, and then her mother appeared behind him.

"I . . . heard some of what you were discussing," Meg admitted. No sense trying to deny it. She was itching to defend her dragon, in any case. "Jakl is not responsible for these attacks," she added firmly.

"Meg, come inside and sit down. Tessel, please go on."

Tessel dipped her head gratefully and hurried off. Meg went in and threw herself into one of the supplicant's chairs. Her parents reseated themselves in their own chairs behind a large desk carved with intricate designs. The king leaned forward and looked at his daughter intently. The queen looked at her too, but her face was still and unreadable.

"Are you . . . feeling better?" the queen asked after a moment.

"Yes," Meg said.

"How much did you hear?" the king asked.

"Enough," Meg said. "I heard that King Gerald is accusing Jakl of attacking his kingdom, which is absolutely ludicrous. Jakl would never do such a thing. And if he did, I would know. It's not possible."

"How sure are you about this?" her father asked gravely. "Think, Meg. Don't just answer in anger. This is very serious. We cannot afford to make the wrong decision here."

Meg took a deep breath and tried to force herself to think objectively. Was she sure? Really, *really* sure? She thought she was. And yet . . . the nightmares, and the way Jakl had acted earlier, the anger, the searing pain in her head . . . Could he be doing things without her knowledge? But even if he could, why would he attack another kingdom? It made no sense.

"I will admit that I still do not know everything about the link," she said at last. "But it seems impossible to me that Jakl could travel so far away from me and do these terrible things he is being accused of without my knowing. And he would have no reason to do so. He has no enemies other than the ones we share with him. He certainly has no understanding of political arrangements or ranks or even kingdom boundaries, as far as I know. His world is much . . . simpler than that. I cannot imagine he would have some reason, some driving cause to attack anyone unless they were actively threatening him. Or me. And to sneak away somehow, to fly all the way there and back and make these attacks in the middle of the night — honestly, that would take planning, and strategy, and thinking about actions and consequences. Jakl is intelligent, but not in the same way we are.

"He interprets things through my feelings, the ones that he shares with me through the link, and so maybe if I had had some reason to hate Lourin and to wish them ill . . . but even then, I cannot see him taking such independent action. It's just not the way his mind works."

The king nodded, taking this in. "Your argument makes sense, Meg. And yet there is still the evidence to consider. I doubt very much that King Gerald will just take our word for it that we have not been sending our dragon to attack his kingdom. Even if he understood the nature of your connection to Jakl, which of course he does not, how could we expect him to believe the opposite of what the evidence seems to suggest without presenting some proof of our own?"

"Then we will just have to find that proof," Meg said. "Something is making these attacks; it's not Jakl, so it must be something else. Maybe we can find out what. If we are convinced of Jakl's innocence, then there must be a way—"

"Meg," the queen said quietly, "how can you be this certain? He is, as you have said yourself, a wild animal. You cannot control him directly—his behavior this afternoon proved that, I think."

Meg winced; of course they would have heard about Jakl's frightening display when she left them earlier.

"It seems at least *possible*," the queen went on, "that he can take actions on his own without your consent or knowledge."

"Mother, it doesn't work that way!"

"I believe that you think that. I want to believe it as well. But I do not see how we can swear it is true to King Gerald until we prove it to ourselves first."

Meg took a deep breath. She tried to put herself in her parents' place. They were just trying to protect the kingdom. That was their primary responsibility. Hers, too, of course.

But . . . they were wrong. Jakl was not doing this. Something else was going on in Lourin.

"How can we do that?" Meg asked at last. She tried to sound completely reasonable, even though she felt nothing of the sort. "What would make you feel thoroughly convinced?"

Her parents looked at each other, considering.

"We could confine the dragon —" the queen began.

"No!" Meg cried before she could stop herself. That would not work. Not the way Jakl had been acting lately. He would not take well to being confined under the best of circumstances, and now, with him being so . . . so unpredictable . . . she was afraid of how he might react. What he might do. She knew he wasn't responsible for what was happening in Lourin, but her mother was right that she could not truly control him. What if they tried to confine him and he fought them? Hurt someone? *Killed* someone? By accident. She knew it could only possibly happen by accident . . . but it could happen. She could not let him be put in that position.

"Please," Meg said. "He would — he would hate that. There must be another way."

"I believe," her father said after a moment, "we had better think a bit more on this before deciding on a course of action. We must somehow convince King Gerald that his country is not under attack by Trelian, but perhaps we can come up with a different solution. We have a little time. It is too late to send a courier back with our reply tonight, in any case."

That seemed to settle the matter for now. Meg's parents left to get ready for dinner and gently suggested that Meg do the same. Meg nodded but remained in her chair for a few minutes after they left.

She could not let them lock Jakl up, not even temporarily, not even for the very best of reasons. She could tell they were holding on to that idea, that they would want to try it if another plan did not present itself. And she wouldn't be able to talk them out of it. Not without revealing why she was so worried, and if she told them the truth, they'd probably be even more eager to chain the dragon to the ground. They couldn't really understand. It wasn't their fault, but that didn't change anything.

She had to think of something else.

CHAPTER EIGHT

"BLUE," CALEN SAID IMPATIENTLY.

"And now?"

"Red."

"And now?"

"We've been through all of these spells already. More than once. Why are you still —?"

"You were instructed to cooperate," Mage Brevera said. "Now answer the question."

Calen sighed. "Orange swirled with white."

They had been doing this for hours. Calen shifted on the hard wooden chair, feeling uncomfortably crowded in the cramped little room, filled as it was with the three mages and himself. Mage Brevera's two companions, Mage Thomil and Mage Mettleson, took turns casting various spells in front of him while Mage Brevera ordered Calen to identify the colors involved. They were repeating spells now; Calen didn't know if they'd run out of easy spells to cast or if they were just trying to trick him. He still didn't understand what they were trying to accomplish. And they still wouldn't explain how he represented a danger to the Magistratum.

"Now," Mage Brevera said, "tell me what *kind* of spell I'm casting." He raised his hands and concentrated on a spot between them. A tendril of golden energy formed and began spiraling outward, circling the mage.

"A healing spell of some kind," Calen said. A flicker of fiery orange joined the gold. *That* was different. And interesting. Calen leaned forward, trying to piece it together. "Oh, that's . . . wow. Healing and . . . protection? Like to help make someone better while stopping them from getting sick with something else . . . or . . . hurt. Oh! Like in battle, maybe? To protect a soldier from further harm while you're fixing his broken leg or whatever?" That was clever! Calen could easily see the uses for a spell like that one.

The mage released the spell, and the colors dissipated into the air around him. Calen looked up at him excitedly. "Can you make it bigger to include more people? Or modify it, maybe to conceal the soldier as well as protect him? Maybe with some black . . ." He trailed off as Mage Brevera's already impressive frown grew even deeper.

"We are asking the questions, Apprentice," the mage told him. Then he began to cast another spell.

Calen identified three more spells, then decided

that whether Mage Brevera liked it or not, he had had enough. "Stop," he said. "Please. It's got to be really late by now, and I'm very tired. If you're going to keep making me do this, at least let me go get some rest. I'll come back again first thing in the morning."

"*We* will decide when it's time to stop," Mage Brevera said.

"Well, you can keep going as long as you like," Calen said, standing up, "but I'm finished." He was too tired and annoyed to be afraid of the consequences of talking back to the mage. He'd been told to cooperate. He *had* cooperated. But now he was done. It was getting hard to keep his eyes open, let alone concentrate on what Brevera was casting.

"Sit down!" the mage barked. He pushed Calen back down into the chair.

Calen sat there for a moment, astonished. "Hey!" he said. He wanted to stand back up but didn't know what he would do if Brevera pushed him again. Push him back? Surely he wasn't supposed to get in pushing matches with full mages, but Brevera had been the one to start it. . . . Even now the mage loomed before him, clearly not about to back down.

"Brev," Mage Thomil said, leaning forward to place a hesitant hand on Brevera's arm, "it is getting rather late.

123

And we're all getting a bit tired. Perhaps starting again in the morning is not a bad idea."

For a moment no one said anything. Calen glanced at Mettleson, who stood silently, looking rather blank. Deliberately so, Calen suspected. Brevera was clearly the boss, and this was the first time either of the other mages had contradicted him in even the slightest way. Mettleson was apparently perfectly willing to let Thomil be the one to risk Brevera's temper, even though Mettleson himself had to be just as tired. Calen's opinion of the man dropped even further.

"Very well," Brevera said at last. "Take him to his room."

"I can take myself to my room," Calen said, but Brevera shook his head.

"You will be staying under our observation until the testing is complete," he said.

Calen blinked. "You're not letting me go back to my room?"

"Please," Mage Thomil said. "Just come with me. The room we have ready is quite suitable for your needs. You will return to your master just as soon as we finish with the tests."

"And when will that be?" Calen asked.

Thomil glanced at Brevera, who just stood there

looking grouchy and unpleasant. Mettleson still looked blank. "Please," Thomil said again to Calen, gesturing toward the door.

Calen went. He was certainly eager to get out of this room, even if he wasn't going to get to go back to his own room yet. He supposed he could spend one night where they wanted him to. Surely they would finish up tomorrow.

Thomil led Calen down the corridor to a door at the far end, right next to where the passage terminated in a narrow window. There was a small, pointless-seeming table with nothing on it set before the window ledge. It was too dark to see the view, whatever it was. Calen sighed and let Thomil usher him into the room. The mage lit the room's two candles with a flick of his hand. The room was small and spare, but the bed was made and there was a pitcher of water and a bowl on the nightstand. Not exactly all the comforts of home, and nothing like the far nicer chamber he'd been given next door to Serek's rooms, but it would be fine for just one night.

"I'll come for you in the morning," Thomil said.

"All right. Thank you, Mage Thomil."

The man nodded and stepped out into the hall. Calen sat down on the bed as the door closed. A second later, he was startled to hear the sound of a key turning in the lock. He sprang up and tried the door, just to be sure. They had locked him in. Suddenly the room felt more like a prison cell than just a place to sleep.

Calm down, he told himself. *You can't really blame them for not trusting you to stay here after you made it clear you didn't want to.* Except, he'd agreed to stay, hadn't he? Who were they to think he'd lie and break his word?

It was insulting, really. But more than that, he just didn't like being locked in. What if there was some emergency? He supposed he could try to contact Serek if necessary. But . . . not yet. Not about this. Serek would just think he was being unreasonable. He could almost imagine his master's irritated voice: *What does it matter if they locked you in, if you were planning to stay in the room anyway?*

Calen noticed a pile in the corner and took one of the candles over to investigate. Someone had brought his things from his rooms. Well, at least he could change his clothes and wash up. That had actually been pretty considerate of them. Maybe he really was being unreasonable about all of this. Sure, Brevera was obnoxious and surly, but he was just doing his job, after all. And Thomil seemed all right.

Calen got himself ready for bed and lay down on the

narrow mattress. Somehow, even though he was very tired, it took him a long time to fall asleep.

In the morning, Calen was up and dressed and waiting impatiently by the time Thomil came and unlocked the door. When the mage led him back to the testing room, Calen stopped in the hallway, dismayed.

"Aren't we going down to breakfast first?"

Thomil looked uncomfortable. "We'll have something brought up."

They did, but not until after Calen had suffered hungrily through another hour of spell identification under Mage Brevera's unfriendly direction. When a servant finally knocked on the door and was admitted bearing a tray, there wasn't very much on it. The mages had already eaten, Calen realized with irritation. Probably while he had been sitting there waiting for them to come release him.

He took his time, ignoring the exasperated sighs of Brevera and the worried glances of Thomil. Mettleson still didn't seem to have an opinion about anything. He just waited silently, sitting on the edge of a table and staring into space.

Once Calen had finished his meal, they resumed the endless testing. They continued until lunch, which was also brought up to the room — this time by two serving maids, bearing much more fully laden trays. After lunch they switched over to divination spells. Calen was relieved at first, since at least this was different and divination was especially fascinating to him. But they wouldn't explain anything they were doing, and he was unfamiliar with the patterns. Sometimes the mages had him hold the cards or dice or bones or whatever they were using before they began; other times they just looked at him while doing the spells themselves. After one whispered conversation, during which the mages huddled in a corner, Thomil approached Calen, bearing a small knife.

"What is that for?" Calen asked suspiciously.

"We need a drop of your blood," Thomil said.

"Uh . . . no. Sorry, but I don't think so." Were they *crazy?*

Thomil looked over his shoulder at Brevera, who stood with his arms crossed firmly over his chest. Then he turned back to Calen. "Please," he said. "It won't hurt. It's for the next spell."

"Not unless you explain to me what you're doing this time," Calen said. "You're the ones who keep saying I represent some sort of danger to the Magistratum. If that's true, I deserve to know what it is."

"That is what we are attempting to divine," said a new voice. It took Calen a second to realize it was Mettleson. "We do not yet know exactly how you will harm the Magistratum —"

Calen pounded his foot against the floor, barely missing Thomil's toes. "I'm not going to harm anything!"

"And the more talking we do about it," Mettleson continued, ignoring Calen's outburst, "the less effective the divination spell is likely to be. I believe you know enough about divination to understand that, Apprentice."

"Don't waste time cajoling him," Brevera growled. "Just take his blood and be done with it."

Calen gaped at Brevera. Thomil closed his eyes for a moment. "Please, Brev," he said wearily. He opened his eyes again and looked at Calen. "It is not a harmful spell," he went on in a softer voice. "And really, it won't hurt. If you refuse, Mage Brevera will only send for the council masters to give you a direct order to comply. Assuming he doesn't just take it himself by force. I would like to get these tests over with as much as you would, and your cooperation is the quickest way to make that happen. Please, Calen. Hold out your hand."

Calen closed his mouth and tried to think. He didn't like the calm way Thomil had informed him that Brevera might just take his blood without his permission. That was not okay. Absolutely not okay. Things were definitely getting out of hand now, he decided. He glanced at the door. He had no doubt that if he tried to run, one of the three mages would be able to stop him before he reached it. And he knew that they could restrain him magically if they chose to. They could do . . . almost anything they wanted to, he realized. His recent lunch felt like a hard little lump in his stomach.

Slowly, he held out his hand.

Thomil nicked him swiftly with the knife, a narrow swipe that nonetheless resulted in an impressive welling up of Calen's blood. He then healed the tiny cut immediately, before it had a chance to do more than sting. At least he'd been telling the truth about its not really hurting.

The mage carried the bloodied knife back over to where Brevera and Mettleson waited near the larger table in the room. Mettleson seemed to be leading the divination procedures, even though Brevera was clearly still in charge of the whole operation. As Calen watched silently, Mettleson picked up a small pouch made of some kind of shiny black cloth and held it open. At Mettleson's command, Thomil tipped the knife over the pouch and let the blood slowly drip down into it. Calen felt a little sick. Mettleson pulled the pouch's drawstring closed again and shook the contents vigorously, then spilled them out across the table. The three men leaned forward, muttering and pointing to different stones and patterns in their arrangement. Calen looked away, not wanting to know if he could see his blood marring the surfaces of any of the stones.

When the mages told him he'd be staying in the locked room again that night, Calen was too shaken to object. He followed Thomil obediently down the hall and sat down on the bed. He watched the door swing closed and heard the key turn in the lock on the other side.

They threatened me, he thought after Thomil's footfalls had faded away. But as soon as he thought it, he wasn't sure. Had they, really? Did Thomil's assertion that Brevera would have taken his blood whether or not Calen assented count as a threat? Or had Thomil just been trying to be convincing, in order to avoid trouble? They hadn't really hurt him. Just . . . scared him.

Calen thought again about contacting Serek. But Serek had told him to cooperate. And Calen wanted his master to see that he could do what was required. How would he ever prove that he was capable of so much more than Serek allowed him if he called for help as soon as things got difficult?

Calen made himself get up and get ready for bed.

What was he really afraid of, anyway? Brevera and the others weren't *evil*. He could think of a lot of unpleasant things to call them, but they were still all on the same side. They weren't going to do anything terrible to him. Okay, the blood thing had been ... startling, but if they needed it for the spell, then he shouldn't be a baby about it. It was in his best interest to help move things along, really. Sooner or later they would realize they'd made a mistake about him. They had to, because it *was* a mistake.

Surely they'd finish up tomorrow, anyway. How much more could they really need from him?

But they didn't finish up the next day. They kept testing long into the evening, and when Calen finally asked them when they would be finished, no one responded — not even Thomil, although he did at least have the grace to look somewhat guilty as he ignored Calen's question. They took his blood again that day, too. Twice. Calen didn't object either time, although he wanted to. He kept telling himself it would be over soon, and as Thomil had said, the best way to hurry it along was to cooperate.

But that night, when Thomil led him once more back to the locked room at the end of the corridor, Calen stopped outside the door.

"Please," he said. "Can I at least talk to Mage Serek? I don't think he realized how long you would want to keep me here."

Thomil would not quite look at him. "I'm sorry, Calen. I don't think Brevera will allow that. Please just continue to cooperate. Don't — don't argue with him or give him any reason to be more suspicious."

"But —" Calen reached out and took hold of Thomil's arm. "I don't *understand*. Why is he suspicious at all? What are you trying to figure out with all the testing? I swear, I did not have anything to do with that attack. What is it that you think I've done?"

Thomil sighed. "It's not what you've done. It's what you will do."

"I'm not going to —"

"Yes. You will." The mage finally met his eye. "Mettleson is extremely gifted in divination. All three of us have talent in that area, but Mettleson is the most skilled Diviner to come through the Magistratum in many years. There is no doubt about this, Calen. You represent a danger to us. A serious danger, involving — in some way — Mage Krelig. We just can't figure out exactly what you'll do."

This was crazy. Crazy! And wrong. Calen narrowed his eyes. "I know a little about divination," he said.

"You can't know anything with that much certainty. It doesn't work that way. Events are always in motion, and things can change. Whatever you see, or think you see — nothing about the future is set in stone."

"That is true about most kinds of divination, yes," Thomil agreed. "But Mettleson has a touch of the Sight. When he's sure about something, he's sure. He knows that you will act against the Magistratum. If we could just figure out how, maybe we could —" He stopped and looked up the corridor, suddenly seeming to remember where they were. "Please, Calen. Just . . . just continue to cooperate. Personally, I believe that you don't intend any harm. But that doesn't matter. You will cause harm all the same. Brevera is a difficult man, but he's dedicated to protecting the Magistratum. He will do anything to ensure its safety."

Thomil looked at Calen silently for a moment. Calen didn't like the expression on his face.

"Be careful," Thomil said finally. "Don't . . . provoke him."

He gestured, and Calen went into the room without another word. Thomil locked the door behind him.

It was definitely time to contact Serek.

He had done it twice before, months back, without really knowing what he was doing. The first time he had reached out to Serek in desperation, when he had realized Sen Eva was trying to kill him and Meg, after they'd overheard her plans. The second time Sen Eva had also been trying to kill them, and he'd had to borrow some of Meg's strength in order to cast the spell, feeling his way through the whole process as he went along. Since then, Serek had taught him how to do it properly, letting him practice during lessons but warning him (*several* times) not to otherwise use the spell except in emergencies. Serek claimed it could only be used to contact other mages, but Calen had learned long ago that not everything Serek said was impossible really was, so he had wasted no time in trying it out on Meg. They hadn't been able to work it out, though. He was sure there was a way to do it, but he was going to have to keep experimenting, trying to find the key.

For now, though, he only had to contact Serek, and that he knew how to do. He took a deep breath and cleared his mind, pushing all the worry and irritation and exhaustion away to a place where it couldn't distract him. He began to gather the magical energy he needed, opening himself up to it, feeling the potential power of it growing inside him. Carefully, he created a picture of Serek in his mind, preparing to open a channel of communication between them. And then, once he was ready, he sent out the beam of white energy he'd constructed, just the right amount to get Serek's attention without scaring the pants off him, which is what had happened that first time, when Calen had sent everything he'd had at his master in his panic and lack of knowledge. Amusement tugged at the edges of Calen's consciousness as he remembered this, but he pushed it away, forcing himself to focus. The energy streamed out, seeking Serek, and — smashed into some kind of barrier.

Calen jerked backward, startled out of his careful concentration. *What*—? He must have let himself get distracted after all. He composed himself and tried again. But again he felt the spell come up against a wall of some kind, stopping its progress.

They're blocking me, he realized, fear and anger growing in equal measure inside him. *Brevera and the others are blocking me from communicating with Serek.*

He tried again, even though he suspected it was hopeless, pushing as hard as he could against the barrier. Nothing. It felt very solid and secure, and he didn't see a way to get around or through it.

He thought for a moment, then sent a flicker of magic at the candles, blowing them out. That worked, and lighting them again worked, too. It seemed he could cast at will within his room, as long as he didn't try to send anything outside of it. That was somewhat comforting, although not immediately helpful. Unless . . . He looked at the door.

He thought of Thomil's final words in the corridor, and how anxious and unhappy the man had seemed. Thomil did not think Brevera was going to release Calen anytime soon. They were keeping him here against his will, as a prisoner. Blocking his ability to communicate with his master.

And Thomil was clearly worried about what Brevera would do if Calen opposed him.

This had gone far enough. It wasn't right, what they were doing, keeping him isolated this way. He needed to tell Serek what was happening.

Calen stood up and faced the door, ready to cast whatever it took to break through it. He'd start small, though. If he could open the lock quietly and slip out, that would be a lot better than blasting the door down and causing a racket that everyone in the building could hear.

Besides, he'd never blasted a door down before, and he wasn't quite sure how to do it.

He didn't know how to open locks, either, but he knew how to get information about an object. Serek had been teaching him about that — using magic to study things and figure out how they worked. Carefully, he reached out a tiny tendril of energy and guided it toward the keyhole.

As soon as his spell touched the lock, a burst of magic came flying back at him and threw him against the floor, knocking the wind out of him. He lay there for a moment, catching his breath. Ow. That had hurt. *Okay,* he thought shakily. *Clearly, they have anticipated this idea as well.* He didn't quite have the nerve to try again.

Feeling somewhat cowardly, Calen told himself he would find his chance tomorrow. Somehow. He changed his clothes and went to bed.

In the morning, Thomil gave Calen a long look, but didn't say anything to indicate he knew about the spells Calen had tried the night before. Calen bet he knew, though. He bet they all knew, and now they'd be on their guard against any further attempts to get away. He tried not to let himself get discouraged. He had to get an opportunity sometime. He just had to stay alert and make sure he was ready. Maybe when the serving maids came up with breakfast, or lunch . . .

Gloomily, he followed Thomil back to the testing

room and sat down in his uncomfortable little chair. Brevera stood before him but did not start casting anything. He stared at Calen as though trying to see inside his head.

"Who taught you to identify spells?" he asked finally. "Was it Serek? Or someone else?"

"No one taught me," Calen said. "I told you —"

"Stop lying!" Brevera shouted, his face going red with anger.

Calen stared at him, appalled. "I'm not —"

Brevera spoke over him, his voice dropping in volume but still tense with fury. "You seek to hide the truth from us, but we can see some things without any doubt. The signs clearly show that you will be near the center of the events to come. This . . . ability, this color-sight you have, must be the key. It gives you an advantage that could make you very dangerous. Do you think we cannot see it? Do you think we will just allow you to use this power freely?"

Calen swallowed. "I don't know what you're talking about. I can't help that I can see things you can't."

The mage's eyes narrowed. "Show me how to do it, then. Prove to me that you aren't hoarding this ability for your own secret reasons."

Calen blinked in surprise. "I — I can't! I didn't learn how to do it, I just do it. I don't know how to teach you."

Brevera lunged forward and grabbed Calen's shoulders. "Enough! No one can do what you are doing. Someone must have taught you. Someone, perhaps, who knows things the rest of us do not." He stared into Calen's eyes again, looking for something he was not, apparently, finding. Then he shook Calen, hard. "How long have you been in contact with Mage Krelig?"

"*What?* Are you *crazy?* I'm not in contact with him!" Calen looked wildly around, hoping Thomil would step forward to calm down Brevera, but Thomil was standing back with Mettleson. He did not meet Calen's eyes.

"You are a liar and a danger to the Magistratum," Brevera said. "What were you hoping to gain with that stunt during your ceremony? Were you trying to assassinate the council masters? Or perhaps you were trying to kill me, to stop me from revealing your secrets?"

"Please," Calen said, trying to speak slowly and carefully. "I swear to you, I didn't do anything. You're making a mistake."

"I don't believe you," Brevera said.

Now Thomil spoke. "Brev. I think we should wait."

"No," Brevera said, not taking his eyes from Calen.

"It's too dangerous. He has already tried to escape once. Everything we saw is going to come to pass if we don't stop him."

"S-stop me from what?" Calen asked. "I told you, I'm not doing anything!"

"There are other ways," Thomil said. "We should go to the council —"

"No!" Brevera turned and faced his colleague. "They will hesitate; they will debate; they will let Serek come up with some defense. Don't you see? We must take responsibility. We are the only ones who realize the true danger."

This was getting very scary.

There was a sudden knock at the door. The mages spun to face the source of the sound. Calen saw that Brevera had half started a spell but then released it. "Breakfast," Brevera said, shaking his head. "I'll get rid of them." He started for the door, then stopped. "Watch him."

Calen had been getting ready to run, but now Thomil and Mettleson came to stand between him and the door. He knew he would never get past them. But maybe he could still call for help —

The door opened, and Calen took a breath to start shouting, but suddenly Brevera was flying backward into the room. A blaze of purple and orange energy surrounded him. Thomil and Mettleson began to turn but froze before they could move more than a few inches. Bewildered, Calen looked up to see Serek standing in the doorway. Mage Anders peered in from behind him.

"Good morning," Serek said to Mage Brevera, who was still on the floor — pinned there magically by Serek, Calen could see. The other two were being held still by Anders, who nodded cheerfully to Calen when he noticed him staring. Brevera looked like he was trying to say something in response, but Serek's spell prevented him.

"I've come to retrieve my apprentice," Serek went on conversationally. "I think you have had him long enough." He looked at Calen. "Are you all right?"

Calen nodded, still too stunned to speak. He got up and walked toward the door. He rather felt like he was dreaming. Serek and Anders both shifted out of the way to let him pass. Once he was through, he turned around to see what else was going to happen.

Serek and Anders seemed to be wrapping the other mages in bands of magical energy, literally tying them in place and stopping them from moving or speaking or, Calen assumed, casting. Serek went on talking as though nothing unusual was going on.

"I appreciate your efforts on behalf of the Magistratum," he said to Brevera, who looked nearly insane with rage. "But I'm afraid I have run out of patience, and it's time my apprentice and I were leaving. I'm not sure what you told Galida and Renaldiere to make them support your actions, but I've decided not to comply with their recommendation of cooperation. Good-bye, Brevera." He nodded at the other mages in turn. "Thomil, Mettleson."

Then Serek stepped back and closed the door firmly. Anders cast another spell at the door itself — a multicolored affair that Calen was too shaken to try to figure out right at the moment. Serek took Calen's arm and walked him swiftly down the corridor.

"Where —?" Calen began.

"Not now," Serek said, his conversational tone abruptly gone. "We've got to hurry. Anders has bought us a little time, but it still might not be enough. We're, ah, leaving against the recommendation of the council. Which is not a matter to be taken lightly, but I'm afraid it was the best choice under the circumstances. I'll explain later. For now, just try to keep up."

Calen nodded and tried to obey. He looked back to see Anders hurrying along behind them.

CHAPTER NINE

MEG FOUND TESSEL IN THE KITCHEN, sitting at one of the long tables with a bowl of stew. The courier looked tired. Meg hesitated in the doorway but then pressed forward. She needed to ask about Lourin. There had to be something more, something to help prove that Jakl wasn't involved.

"Tessel?"

The young woman looked up, surprised. "Yes, Princess?"

"Can I ask you some more about your message? About what you saw in Lourin?"

"Of course," Tessel said. She set down her spoon. "What do you want to know?"

Meg sat down across from her. Tessel was a few years older than she was, maybe about Maerlie's age. Her long, brown hair was tied back in a hasty-looking knot, still messy and windblown from her recent journey.

"I wanted to know . . ." What did she want to know? Meg sighed, feeling defeated before she had even begun.

"I know my dragon has not been attacking Lourin," she said. "I know this, but I can also see why King Gerald would think otherwise. I need to find a way to prove Jakl is innocent."

Tessel touched the stem of her spoon but didn't pick it up again. "I'm not sure how I can help, Princess."

"I'm not sure, either," Meg said. "I'm sure you told my parents everything you know already. I don't know what else to ask you. But there must be something. Did you see the scorched ground and fire damage yourself?"

"Yes."

"And . . . the people who were killed. Is it certain they died from burning?"

"Yes, Princess. I saw them — the bodies — with my own eyes. They were burned, all right. Witnesses said they saw a flash in the darkness, a stream of fire coming from a source they could not see. Everyone agreed it was no natural flame, no cooking fire or house fire gone out of control or anything of the sort."

"Wait — a source they couldn't see? So no one is claiming to have actually seen the dragon?"

"No, they do claim to have seen him," Tessel said. "Or to have seen *a* dragon, at any rate. Just not specifically when they saw the fire. But several people said they saw a dragon fly across the sky."

Could there be another dragon out there? It wasn't impossible. Jakl had come from *somewhere*, after all. Maybe he had brothers and sisters. Or parents. Or cousins or something. But even if that were the case, how could she prove it?

"Did any of them get a close look at it? Did they mention how big it was, or what color?"

Tessel shook her head. "No, Princess. I think they saw it only at a distance. Except perhaps, um . . . those who were killed."

Meg pushed away another thought of Jakl's struggle to contain his fire that afternoon. She didn't know what she was trying to accomplish here. She should let Tessel have her meal and rest. She stood up.

"Thank you, Tessel. I'm sorry to have disturbed you."

Tessel shrugged apologetically. "I'm sorry I couldn't be more help."

Meg turned and left the kitchen, not sure exactly where she wanted to go. Jakl floated at the edge of her consciousness, gently pulling at her, but she didn't think she should go to him. He had to get used to spending some time apart from her. Otherwise he would only get more impatient whenever she couldn't be there when he wanted her.

She didn't think it was good for her, either, to go to

him whenever she wanted to. It was so easy to get lost in their time together, and she was afraid that it would get harder and harder to come back. Especially when she had such difficult and complicated situations to come back to. She didn't want to have to worry about Lourin and King Gerald. She didn't want to have to check in with Wilem every day. She didn't want to worry about Sen Eva and that portal mage person and every other terrible danger that hovered constantly on the horizon.

Meg heard the whiny edge to her thoughts and felt instantly disgusted with herself. *Too bad,* she thought firmly. *If you're going to be the princess-heir, it's your job to worry about these things. Stop being such a baby.* She felt like rapping her knuckles with a stick the way Nan Vera used to whenever any of her charges sufficiently annoyed her. Meg had always deeply resented the knuckle rapping, but she was beginning to understand the impulse. Gods, she was irritating when she whined. Even just inside her own head. And it certainly wasn't very princess-like.

All right then, she said to herself. *What can you do? Other than whining and worrying, that is. What can you do?*

There was nothing she could do about Wilem at the moment; she'd already talked to him today. She didn't have to make herself deal with him again until tomorrow. And they didn't know yet what Sen Eva might be up to, and so taking action wasn't really possible. That left the situation in Lourin. What could she do about that?

You can find a way to prove Jakl is innocent.

Well, yes, sure, all right. But how? Tessel had already told everything she knew. The only way Meg could find out anything more would be to go to Lourin herself.

She stopped in the hallway, not seeing the walls around her or the servants crossing the corridor where it met the main hall up ahead or anything else.

But . . . she couldn't, could she? Wouldn't someone try to stop her?

Not if she didn't tell them she was going.

Meg grinned in a way that felt decidedly wicked. And wonderful. She knew how *that* worked, after all. It wasn't like she didn't have lots of experience sneaking off on her own. Maybe it was different now that she was going to be the princess-heir . . . but if she didn't make it plain to everyone that Jakl was innocent, she wouldn't ever get to be the heir. Lourin would want revenge upon the creature they thought was responsible for those attacks. If her parents didn't turn Jakl over to them, there could be a war. Meg couldn't let Jakl be punished, of course. But she couldn't let there be a war over him, either. Jakl would have to be sent away, for his own safety, for the safety of the kingdom. And if that happened, Meg would go with him. She wouldn't have any choice. They'd be exiles, cut off from her family and her home. Forever.

So she would just have to stop it from coming to that.

She turned around and started back down the hall, still not really seeing anything around her, trusting everyone to get out of her way as she walked faster and faster and then gave in and started running. She reached the kitchen just as Tessel was leaving, no doubt about to get some well-deserved rest. Well, she could wait a few more minutes. Meg grabbed the startled young woman's arm.

"Princess? What is it?"

"Walk with me," Meg said, whirling around toward the kitchen entrance and pulling the confused courier along with her. "I'm sorry, I know you're tired, but I need to ask you a few more things."

"What — what things?"

"In private," Meg said firmly. She didn't say another word until they were through the doors and a good distance away from the castle. She forced herself to slow down. To anyone watching, it would seem they were simply having a stroll in the gardens. It was a nice enough evening for walking; it shouldn't seem too odd.

"I need to know . . ." Meg began finally. And stopped.

She tried to think of how to ask what she needed to without giving herself away. Then she decided it didn't matter. She would just order Tessel to keep quiet. "All right. Listen. I'm going to Lourin myself to see what I can find out. I need you to go over your information for me once more, everything they showed you, and tell me where exactly to look for the scorch marks and — and the other things they are considering to be evidence. If you can, maybe you could sketch me a little map of the city and show me where to go."

Tessel was staring at her in horror. "Princess, you can't go to Lourin!"

"Of course I can," Meg said calmly. "I just need you to tell me what I need to know, first."

Tessel was still staring. "You *can't* — I mean, I can't . . ." She took a breath and started again. "If something happens to you, because of information I gave you . . . Lourin is not a good place for the heir of Trelian right now. People there are very angry. If they caught you, it would — it would be very bad."

"They won't catch me. I'll have Jakl with me."

"What? No! Princess!" Tessel struggled visibly to control her words and tone. "You can't bring your dragon there! That would be —" She floundered for a moment, then seemed to find some inner resolve. "It would be madness. You would only be proving to them what they already think is true!"

"I won't let Jakl be seen. I'll have him wait for me somewhere out of sight."

Tessel crossed her arms. "Then how will he protect you?"

That was a good point. But Meg waved it away. "Don't worry about that. I'll figure something out. All I need from you is information."

Tessel shook her head. "I am sorry, Your Highness, but I can't let you do this. You can go ahead and report me to the king and queen, if you like, for my disobedience. But somehow I don't think they would see fit to punish me for not helping you run off and get yourself killed."

Meg felt an all-too-familiar spark of anger beginning to form inside her.

"Tessel, listen to me. This is something I have to do. I cannot explain all of the reasons to you. But either I go with your information to guide me or I go without that information. Given those two choices, do you think you can bring yourself to do as I ask?"

"Princess, *please*. Be reasonable. You can't —"

"Either help me or send me off without any help at all. It's your choice."

Tessel hesitated, frowning deeply. "There is — there is a third choice, Your Highness." She took a slow breath, as if to put off her next words for a few more precious seconds. "I could go with you."

Now it was Meg's turn to be shocked. "What?"

"At least that way I wouldn't be sending you into danger alone. Maybe I could help you to not get killed if you are discovered." Tessel tilted her head back over her shoulder toward the sheath slung across her back. It was empty now, while she was in the castle, of course, but all couriers carried either swords or bows while out on assignments, and all were given basic combat training. They were supposed to be protected by law and custom, but there were plenty of criminals who didn't care about law and custom. And a lone rider might seem an easy target for robbery, or worse.

"Tessel, I appreciate your offer," Meg said. "But that is out of the question."

Tessel drew herself up and looked at Meg straight on. "I'm coming with you, Princess. I don't want to, believe me. But you're not leaving me any other choice. If I let you go alone, and something happens . . . Well, at least if I'm there, if something happens, I won't have to face the king and queen alone after you die."

Meg started to object again, but Tessel cut her off.

"If you refuse, I will start screaming for the guards right now. I bet they'll be able to stop you before you reach your dragon."

The spark of anger was growing into a twisty, burning flame. Meg could feel its tendrils working their way up and into her veins, heating her blood. Who was this girl to think she could try to tell her what to do? Yes, she was older, but she was a *courier*, sworn to serve, not someone who should dare to make demands of the princess-heir. Tessel knew it, too; a glimmer of fear was plain despite her resolve.

That fear seemed to grow as Meg watched, and she realized that her own face must also be betraying what she was feeling. She closed her eyes and forced herself to breathe, in and out, slowly, in the way Calen had taught her. She wouldn't be this angry if it were Calen telling her not to go. A *little* angry, maybe, but Calen had earned the right to at least *try* to boss her around. He was her best friend, and he'd saved her life enough times to be able to tell her anything he chose. This girl, this courier, was no one to her; she had no right to try to, to try to —

To try to stop you from getting yourself killed?

Meg pushed that thought away. She had to go to Lourin. It would be far worse to do nothing and let Jakl become the center of a war between the kingdoms! She knew this was the right course of action. It had to be.

Maybe taking Tessel with her was actually a good idea. She could show Meg exactly where the attacks had occurred, show her this supposed evidence . . . and keeping the courier close would mean she couldn't betray Meg to her parents.

"All right," Meg said finally, opening her eyes. "You can come with me. Do you know where my dragon's paddock is?" She waited for Tessel's nod. "Meet me there at twelfth bell. Don't be late, or I'm going without you. And Tessel —" She held the courier's eyes for a long moment. "Don't say anything about this to anyone. Swear to me that you won't."

"I won't," Tessel said. "I swear it." She narrowed her eyes. "Unless you go without me, in which case I'll go right to the king and queen."

"Just be there," Meg said. Then she turned and started back toward the castle to get ready for dinner and to pretend she had no other plans for the night.

CHAPTER TEN

IT HAD TAKEN TWO TRIES TO slip out without alerting Pela. The first time Meg opened her door, Pela immediately peeked out of her own to see what her princess might need, and Meg had to let the girl fetch her a snack from the kitchen before she could try again. At least Pela hadn't asked any difficult questions about Meg's unprincess-like attire. Dresses were uncomfortable to ride in and tended to get dirty and torn. Meg kept a supply of breeches and boots and old shirts and jackets to wear for dragon riding, none of which would ever meet Pela's standards of what her princess should be seen wearing. Meg had tried to keep most of her body hidden behind her door until Pela went back into her own room. Not for the first time, she wished she had that magic spell of Calen's that made him invisible. The whole way through the castle, from her rooms to the garden entrance, she kept expecting Pela to pop up behind her, demanding to be helpful. She'd never had trouble slipping out past Pela before; Meg wondered if her parents had asked the girl to keep a closer eye on her. Probably.

It was a relief to finally get outside. Meg made her way slowly down past the stables, keeping to the shadows as much as possible. When she reached the end of the little path that led to Jakl's paddock, Tessel was already waiting. The paddock included a huge, barn-like building, and it opened onto a private field where Jakl could roll around in the tall grass without spooking or crushing any horses or people or decorative three-hundred-year-old heirloom trees. Tessel was standing a few feet back from the fence, watching Jakl warily. Jakl was pretending to be asleep.

As Meg approached, the dragon suddenly leaped to his feet, startling Tessel into stumbling back several more feet. She looked immensely relieved when she noticed Meg. Tessel walked over to meet her, glancing back over her shoulder once or twice at Jakl, who was pacing her along the fence.

The courier must have managed to catch a quick nap; she looked alert and freshly washed, if not especially happy. She'd changed into fresh clothing as well — dark pants and a matching top and jacket — although she still wore her courier sash diagonally across her chest. "I guess we're, uh . . . flying?" she asked.

Meg nodded. She had considered, briefly, the idea that she and Tessel should sneak out and meet Jakl somewhere else, but decided it would be too difficult trying to get them both past the gate guards. She also didn't entirely trust Tessel not to get them caught and detained by the guards on purpose. Meg would get in trouble when word got back to her parents that she went out flying at night again, but she didn't see any other choice. And if she came back with a solution to the trouble with Lourin, surely her parents couldn't be *too* angry with her.

Meg climbed the fence, and Tessel followed. Jakl sat on his hind legs like a cat, staring down at Tessel as though she were something he might like to eat. Meg tried to suppress a smile.

"Is he —? Can I —?" Tessel had stopped again and was staring up at him. With visible effort, she turned away and looked at Meg. "What should I do?"

"He won't bite," Meg said. *You hear me?* she thought at him. *Don't bite.* "You can walk up and touch him, if you like."

Tessel did so, walking slowly forward and then reaching out to place a hand on Jakl's foreleg. "He's so warm!" she said with some surprise.

"You'll be glad of that when we're up in the sky," Meg said. "It gets cold up there."

Tessel stepped back from the dragon again and turned to face Meg. "Princess, may I ask what your plan is, exactly?"

"I want to see this evidence that seems to indicate the attacks were made by a dragon. The area where the fires were, anything else that you can show me. I hope to find some clue as to what really attacked Lourin. If King Gerald is convinced the culprit is a dragon, he might not be looking very hard for evidence that suggests anything else."

Tessel looked a little skeptical, but she only nodded. "I can show you what they showed me," she said. "What will we do if someone sees us?"

"I don't think I'll be recognized, dressed like this. The city of Lourin is large enough that strangers shouldn't automatically be regarded as suspicious. You should probably take that off, though," she added, nodding to Tessel's courier sash.

"Oh . . . yes, of course." Tessel slipped the sash over her head and tucked it into a pocket.

"I'm hoping it will be late enough that we won't run into anyone on the streets," Meg continued. "And if we do . . . we can pretend we're lost or something. We shouldn't need to stay too long. I just need to find something to help me figure this out. There *must* be something

158

there." She realized she was clenching her fist, and made her fingers relax. "I know it wasn't Jakl, so there must be a sign of something else."

Tessel looked as though she might want to argue further, but Meg brushed past her and climbed up onto her dragon, settling at the base of his long neck. She reached back to help Tessel up after her. The courier hesitated only a moment before taking Meg's hand and scrambling up.

"Is there anything I need to know about dragon riding?" Tessel asked once she was seated behind Meg.

"Just hold on to me," Meg said. "Don't be shy about holding on tight. I won't break."

"All right," Tessel said. She obediently tightened her arms around Meg's waist.

Jakl launched upward into the night. Tessel gasped and gripped Meg even tighter. Meg barely felt it; she was half gone already, swept up in the excitement of flying.

Before long, though, she forced herself to draw back and focus on her surroundings. She felt Jakl let her go reluctantly; he liked it best when she was right there with him, when they were flying together with one consciousness, but he understood that passengers required a little more attention on her part. Plus she had to keep an eye on their progress. She'd studied the maps in the library carefully after dinner, fixing the relative locations of Trelian and Lourin firmly in her mind. She thought Jakl was picking up enough of that information through the link to keep them on course, but she felt better watching for landmarks herself, just in case.

Lourin was Trelian's closest neighbor to the west. A war with Lourin alone would be bad enough, but part of the problem was that a war with Lourin would almost certainly not *be* a war with Lourin alone. Lourin was closely allied to two other nearby kingdoms, Baustern and Farrell-Grast, and would no doubt call on both of them for aid. Trelian could find itself facing all three kingdoms combined.

But that's not going to happen, Meg reminded herself. *I'm not going to let that happen. That's what this little journey is all about.*

They continued on, Tessel a silent presence behind her. Meg knew Lourin was usually a comfortable two- to three-day ride for a mounted party, and that couriers, riding fast and changing horses frequently, could make the journey in a day if need be. But Jakl sliced through the sky far faster than even the speediest horse could gallop. It was only a little more than an hour before Meg could see the three-forked river that marked Lourin's eastern border.

At Meg's gentle nudge, Jakl began spiraling down, looking for a place to land. Tessel had said the fires had occurred in farming areas on the eastern outskirts of the city. Meg didn't want to risk flying Jakl any closer, not when the people there were sure to be actively watching the skies. She wondered again what they'd really seen, what creature really had been making the attacks. If it had been another dragon, maybe Jakl could talk to it somehow, make it stop whatever it was doing.

If it had been something else . . . The only other alternative she could think of was one of those monsters — the slaarh — that Sen Eva had been able to command. And that would be very, very bad. For all kinds of reasons. It was possible, she supposed, that from a distance, someone might mistake one of those giant flying monstrosities for a dragon. But as far as she knew, the slaarh couldn't breathe fire.

Of course, at one point, she hadn't known there were slaarh that could fly, either. Who knew how many variations of those horrible things there might be?

Meg suppressed a shudder. She just had to find something here, some clue, some piece of information that would lead to the truth. However frightening it might be. Knowing had to be better than not knowing, even if the truth turned out to be terrible indeed. She

161

held that conviction firmly in her mind, trying to take some courage from it.

Jakl landed in a small clearing near the river. Meg told him to stay put and set off with Tessel through the dark woods. She glanced back only once; Jakl was crouched low to the ground, peering after her. He didn't like staying behind. Meg tried to send reassuring feelings toward him through the link. But she also realized she was a little glad that Tessel had insisted on coming along. The woods were thick and strange, and thinking about the slaarh and Sen Eva had made her jumpy.

When they reached the edge of town, Tessel led the way along the edges of several fields before she finally stopped and pointed. Before them lay a long stretch of scorched earth, the few remaining bits of trees and brush blackened into spindly dead sticks. Beyond them, Meg could see the ruins of a house that clearly had been burned to the ground.

Tessel leaned close. "There are two other houses like this farther in, plus a few other burned trees and patches of farmland. And you can see the way the ground and plants appear trampled, as if something very big was walking here. That's part of the evidence they are talking about, too."

Meg could see what Tessel meant. None of that

162

really proved that it was a dragon, but she had to admit it was ... suggestive. Especially when no other explanation came immediately to mind.

"It just doesn't make any sense," Meg whispered. "Why would any creature, dragon or not, attack houses and farms like this? Were any animals carried off? Was it searching for food?" Maybe whatever it was had been hungry, and when farmers appeared to defend their live-stock, it had attacked them then?

Tessel considered. "I don't think so," she said. "I don't remember anyone talking about missing animals. Which is probably another reason they think it was a deliberate attack upon the kingdom."

None of this was helping. "Let's go see the other houses," Meg said.

Tessel opened her mouth to reply, but before she could speak, her eyes widened and one hand reached up and over her shoulder to draw her sword. Meg spun around and stared in dismay. Five men, armed with spears, swords, and farm implements, stood facing them. Several other people, men and women both, were com-ing out from around the ruins of the house and gather-ing behind them. Meg turned back, about to urge Tessel to run with her, but she could already see more figures moving to block their escape.

"Well, now," one of the men before them said calmly. "And here I thought old Arnie was crazy for expecting whoever'd done this would come back to try again so soon. Seems I owe you an apology, Arnie."

"Accepted and forgiven," a second man replied. He was stooped and graying, the old metal hoe he grasped appearing to function more as a cane than as a potential weapon. "Crim'nals always return to the scene of the crime. Learned that lesson more than once in my day."

Meg struggled to find her voice. "We — we're not criminals," she said. "We're not here to cause any trouble."

"Then why are you here, young miss?" the first man asked. "We don't see too many strangers creeping 'round here after last bells, and those we do see rarely turn out to have honest intentions."

From behind her, Meg heard Tessel whisper urgently, "Don't tell them who you are."

Meg hesitated. She'd thought that telling them who she was, that she'd come to investigate the cause of the damage, might be the best course. Surely they'd see that she wasn't capable of doing any harm here herself, that they hadn't brought any means of doing mischief. . . . But perhaps Tessel was right. How would it look, the princess-heir of Trelian sneaking around here in the dark, unattended except for one young courier?

They might think to wonder how she'd gotten here, alone, with no carriage and no horses.

They might think to ask about her dragon.

"We're — we're lost," Meg said. "We got separated from our families in the woods, and we were trying to find someplace to stay for the night."

"That so?" the man said. "Well, if that's true, you'll have nothing to worry about. You just come along nice and quiet up to the castle. King's advisor told us to alert her if we came across any strangers, and reasons or not, you two are strangers here, and you can make your stories to Miss Delana."

He turned to a gangly teenage boy beside him and sent him to run ahead to let the castle guards know they were coming.

"You know, Neale," Arnie said, looking at Meg with narrow eyes. "Seems to me this girl's about the age and type of that one we were supposed to especially watch out for." He nodded toward her. "Got that yellow hair and well-spoken manner o' voice, and the old clothes that don't seem quite right for her. Just like Delana told us."

Meg felt a sinking sort of dread alongside her growing fear.

The first man — Neale — clapped Arnie on the back. "Seems I owe you thanks as well as an apology, then.

Even shared among the lot of us, that reward would be a mighty welcome thing." His voice was almost jovial, but when he turned back toward Meg and Tessel, his eyes were hard and cold.

"So —" One of the women had come up from behind them to address Arnie and Neale. She looked back and forth between the men and Meg. "This is really her, then? That dragon-girl? The one who . . . ?" Her voice faltered, and she swallowed before continuing. "The one who killed my Franklin?"

Oh, no.

"Stop," Meg said. "Please listen." She felt Jakl stirring, becoming aware of her rising fear. *No,* she thought fiercely. *Do not come for me. Do not, do you hear me? Just wait. Wait.*

Some of the people were muttering angrily now. The woman who'd just spoken had been joined by a younger woman, who put her arms around the older one and glared at Meg with such clear and intense hatred that Meg took an involuntary step backward. She felt Tessel move closer behind her and half turned to see the people from the other side beginning to step toward them. Tessel was facing them with her sword ready, her back against Meg's.

Frantically, Meg tried to think. She could let Jakl

come, let him swoop down and try to rescue them, but she wasn't sure he could just pluck them safely out of the crowd. If the townspeople didn't scatter at the dragon's approach, some of them might get hurt as he tried to get to Meg and Tessel. And that would certainly not help to prove that Jakl wasn't a danger to Lourin.

Tessel seemed ready to fight, but that didn't seem like a good plan, either. She could get herself killed. And again, they didn't want to hurt any of these people. She needed to convince them *not* to hate Trelian, not give them more reasons to do so.

"Please," Meg said. "Don't — don't hurt us." If they tried to harm her, Jakl would be on them in seconds, and nothing she said or did or thought at him would convince him not to kill them all in order to save her. "I swear it's not as you believe. Take us to King Gerald. Let me talk to him and explain why I'm here. I promise you, I do not intend you any harm."

Neale spoke again, still looking at her coldly. "Your promises don't count for much here, dragon-girl. But we'll take you to Miss Delana, because that's what we've been instructed to do. You Trelian folk may be savages and murderers, but here in Lourin we follow a more decent path."

He gestured, and several of the largest men came forward. Tessel tensed behind her.

"Put down your sword, Tessel," Meg said softly.

"What? Princess, no . . ."

"I don't want anyone to get hurt. We'll go speak to this Delana, and perhaps she can convince the king to see me. I don't see that we really have any other choice."

Slowly, Tessel lowered her sword.

Neale waved the other men on impatiently. Meg hoped she wasn't making a terrible mistake. *Jakl, no matter what you sense happening here*, she thought at him urgently, *do not come for me. Not unless I call you. No matter what.* She had to trust that she could handle this herself. After a moment, she felt his reluctant acquiescence.

Tessel allowed her sword to be taken from her, and both girls quickly found themselves held firmly by the surrounding men. They paused only long enough to tie Meg's and Tessel's wrists uncomfortably behind their backs, then began marching them forward.

By the time they reached the castle gates, a small group of guards was waiting for them. They parted to allow a tall, well-dressed woman to come through. This had to be Delana, the advisor.

"We kept a watch, just like you asked," Neale said, ducking his head respectfully toward her. "This one fits that description you gave us. We think she might be Trelian's dragon princess."

Delana drew closer. Her face was not one Meg recognized, of course, but there was something hauntingly familiar about her expression.

"You have done very well," she said, looking out at Meg and Tessel's captors with approval. There was something familiar about her voice, too. "Be assured that King Gerald will show Trelian and all the world how we respond to spies and villains sent into our midst!"

There were shouts of angry assent from the people around them.

Meg's heart sank further. She tried to hold on to the hope that the king himself would not be so determined to see them as the enemy.

Delana stepped aside to clear a path, and the men holding them began moving again, pulling Meg and Tessel roughly through the gates. Meg looked up to find the advisor's gaze locked on her. The woman smiled viciously when she caught Meg's eye.

It was the smile that did it. Meg gasped, her legs suddenly weak underneath her. *No, it can't be, it can't be her —*

Delana's smile grew as she watched Meg's reaction. Then she fell out of view as the men continued to drag

Meg and Tessel toward the castle. Meg twisted violently against the hands that held her, struggling to turn and see the woman again, to convince herself that it wasn't true, it couldn't be — she didn't have the right face — but somehow, impossibly, it *was* her, all the same.

Sen Eva had come back.

The men holding her tightened their grip. "Hey, now! None of that," one of them said angrily, shaking her.

"Princess! Princess, what is it?" Tessel's voice seemed far away, even though Meg knew the courier was right beside her. Nothing seemed quite real. Even the ground beneath her feet seemed shifty and less than solid. Meg didn't answer, couldn't answer, she just kept trying to break free. She had to stop Sen Eva, had to warn her parents — oh, gods, they weren't ready. Sen Eva was going to catch them all unprepared and none of them would be safe —

She made one last desperate effort and ripped free of one of her captors, but the other held her fast. There was a sudden sharp pain at the back of her head, and then the world went black.

CHAPTER ELEVEN

"PRINCESS? PRINCESS MEGLYNNE, can you hear me?"

Meg opened her eyes. It took a few blinks to make them focus. And then all she seemed able to see was dirt and darkness.

"Princess?"

Meg groaned and tried to sit up. This was more difficult than it should have been, since her hands were still tied tightly behind her. Her arms and shoulders ached terribly. And her head. *Ugh.*

Jakl was hovering anxiously at the edge of her awareness. He was worried but trying to obey her wishes of keeping away. *Good,* she thought. *I'm all right. Just— just wait.*

"Tessel?"

"Yes. Are you hurt?"

"I don't know. I mean, everything hurts, but I think I'm okay." She finally managed to twist herself upright. She could just make out Tessel sitting a few feet away, her back against a plain, rough wall. A faint bit of light was coming in from a small window, high above. She thought it was daylight, not moonlight, but it was hard to tell. The place they were in was still very dark. "How long was I unconscious? And where are we?"

"Several hours? I'm not certain, but I think the sun's up. As for where, I believe this is the Royal Prison of Lourin."

"What?" Meg stared around, trying to see more of their surroundings. "They shouldn't have . . . Did they tell the king who we are? He should not have —"

"I'm not sure what they told him," said Tessel. "They knocked me out, too."

Even if King Gerald's attendants had not wanted to wake him in the middle of the night, etiquette should have required them to put Meg and Tessel in a guest room, under guard, until the king was ready to see them.

Then Meg remembered that Sen Eva had somehow changed her face and made herself King Gerald's advisor, and she was suddenly grateful that they were only in the king's prison and not dead.

Sen Eva. Meg remembered the way the woman had smiled at her, and her stomach clenched into a tiny ball of fear. She still couldn't believe it — their enemy, here in Lourin, and somehow not looking anything like her true self. But Meg was absolutely sure it was her. And Sen Eva *knew* Meg knew, and didn't seem to care at all.

They were in more danger than Tessel realized.

Meg closed her eyes and reached out through the link. *Jakl,* she thought as clearly and forcefully as she could, *find Calen. Go now. Find him and find a way to let him know where I am.* She pictured Calen in her mind as clearly as she could, tried to feel how much she needed him, tried to feel it enough that Jakl would know what she wanted. She knew he understood her when she spoke to him directly, but from this distance, she wasn't sure how much she was really getting across. *Feel this,* she thought desperately. *Please, Jakl. Get Calen. Go get him right now.*

She couldn't tell whether he understood. She knew he felt that she was afraid, and she thought he understood that she wanted him to go, to fly away from her, and she tried to take heart in the knowledge that he'd understood her last night when she told him to stay away. In a moment she could tell that he'd begun flying, back in the direction of home. But did he know what she wanted? Was he going to find Calen or just going away?

But wait — *home* was wrong. Calen wasn't there. She tried to bring to mind maps she'd seen showing the location of the Magistratum, far to the south. Very far.

Calen must either still be there or just be starting his way back. She pictured the Magistratum itself, images pieced together from books and Calen's descriptions: a huge, square fortress with no towns around it for miles.

That's where he is, she thought at Jakl. *Hurry. Please.*

She couldn't tell if he had understood or not. He was far enough away already that she could no longer sense which way he was going.

"Princess?" Meg opened her eyes again. Tessel was looking at her with concern. "Are you all right?"

"Yes. No. I was just — just trying to think." She bit her lip, trying to make herself focus. "We have to get out of here," she said.

"How?" asked Tessel. Meg's eyes were adjusting quickly to the dark; she could see the other girl much more clearly now. She almost wished she couldn't — Tessel looked utterly defeated. "This is just what I was afraid of. I should never have let you come here, Princess. I should have betrayed you to the Trelian guards for your own safety."

"No," said Meg. "It's good that you didn't."

Tessel gave an odd, half-choked laugh. "How can you say that? Look what's happened!"

"No, trust me." She tried to meet Tessel's eyes in the darkness, but the other girl's face was turned slightly away. "Tessel, listen to me. That woman, the one who calls herself Delana? She's . . . an enemy of the kingdom. A terrible enemy. It is a very good thing that we know she is here."

"An enemy? But . . . how can that be? She's King Gerald's advisor."

"I don't know. She's — she's in disguise somehow. And she must have something to do with what's happening here — the attacks and the anger toward Trelian. I have to get back and warn my family. She's very dangerous."

Tessel shook her head. "I don't think you understand how much trouble we're in right now, Your Highness. I don't think King Gerald is just going to let us go."

"I'll figure out something," Meg said. "I have to."

Tessel looked at Meg for a moment without speaking. Then she asked, "What do you think your parents will do when they discover you're gone?"

Meg had been trying not to think about that. In her original plan, she would have been back before they had a chance to notice her absence. "They'll be angry, of course. But once they learn what I've discovered —"

The older girl was shaking her head again, in denial or — disgust?

"What?" Meg asked her.

Tessel hesitated; from what Meg could see of her

expression, she hadn't meant to display such an obvious negative reaction. "It's not my place to say," Tessel said at last.

"You can say whatever it is you're thinking," Meg said. "Really. I want to know."

"I think — I think you might need to consider your actions more carefully sometimes. I don't mean any offense, Princess. But to have come here, to have risked yourself and risked making Lourin even more angry . . ."

"I'm trying to find a way to convince Lourin *not* to be angry!" Meg said. "It seemed the only way —"

"But it probably wasn't the only way," Tessel said. "I understand that you wanted to act, that you wanted to do something to help. But there's a reason you didn't tell your parents what you were doing. There's a reason you didn't want to alert the guards. And you should think about that. If coming here was the right decision, why hide it?"

"Because —" *Because you don't understand about my dragon. Because my parents don't really understand, either, even though they know about the link. Because I was afraid of what would happen if I let my parents try to chain Jakl up somehow, and I can't bear just sitting and doing nothing when anyone I love is in danger, and if he goes crazy again while chained to the ground, lots of people I love could*

be hurt. Or worse. But she couldn't say any of that. "Just because they're my parents doesn't mean they always know best," she said instead. "Sometimes they make the wrong decisions, too."

"Of course," Tessel agreed. "But so does everyone. Even you."

Meg bit back an angry retort. It was hard to argue that this had been the right decision when they were sitting in a prison cell and had no idea what was going to happen to them.

But if she hadn't come, they would not have found out about Sen Eva. Didn't that have to count for something?

"I can see that you love your dragon," Tessel went on gently, "but I'm not so sure that the princess-heir can afford to put love before duty."

"I didn't! I'm here *because* of my duty!" But even as she said it, she wondered if it were really true. She had a duty to her kingdom, but was that really what had led her to sneak off to Lourin in the middle of the night? And what about her duty to her parents, to obey their wishes? And her duty to the people of Trelian, including this unfortunate young woman she'd led into terrible danger? Hadn't she a responsibility to protect Tessel as much as she did the people of Trelian in general? And had coming here really been the best way of protecting anyone other than her dragon?

But she had a responsibility to him, too, didn't she? How could she choose between them?

Meg looked at Tessel with a new level of respect. "Do they teach this stuff in courier training?" she asked.

Tessel gave her a small smile. "Not exactly. But they do teach us about duty. To our commanders, to each other, to our kingdom. Being a courier is a little like being a soldier in some ways. You have to know where your first responsibility lies at all times. They teach us to keep that straight in our hearts and minds, so that we know what to do if something happens out on assignment somewhere."

"That sounds nice," Meg said wistfully. "To always know what to do."

"Well," Tessel said judiciously, "some situations are certainly clearer than others. But it helps to know in your heart what your first priority is. Deciding that makes other decisions easier."

Meg fell silent. What was her first priority? A year ago, she would have said her family, without question. But the princess-heir had to put her kingdom first. Her parents, as much as they loved their daughters, had a responsibility to the people of Trelian. Which is why

Meg and her sisters' marriages would be arranged for political gain, why they were taught what they needed to know to lead a kingdom, why they could not simply follow whatever was in their hearts. But now, since the link, Jakl was a part of her. More than that, he was dependent on her. Her, and no one else. How could she not protect him?

She realized she could barely sense him now. It felt strange to have him so far away. They hadn't been separated by this much distance since the time she and Calen had been sent so abruptly and violently away from Trelian by Calen's accidental alteration of Sen Eva's spell, meant to kill them. The link had still been so new then that it had taken her a while to realize what she was — or wasn't — feeling. But now she was very aware of Jakl's absence. The link was still there, of course, and she wasn't nearly as far away from him as she'd been that other time, but he was so faint, she couldn't sense anything other than that he was alive — somewhere. She had no idea where he was or how he was feeling or whether he'd found Calen or anything else. She felt disturbingly incomplete.

Would Sen Eva try to kill her again? Now that she was caught, without Calen or Jakl to help her? Would Sen Eva try to use her captivity against her parents?

There were no limits to what she could imagine Sen Eva doing, really. She fought back another wave of fear. Being terrified was not going to help.

Instead, she tried to make herself focus. *Duty and responsibility.* If she had to, she knew she could sacrifice herself for her kingdom. But did she have the right to sacrifice Jakl as well? He hadn't asked for this any more than she had. Even if he'd linked to her on purpose, he had no idea what it meant to be a princess or a queen. He would die for her — she knew that. But would he die for Trelian? Did she even have the right to ask?

She just had to hope that no one would have to sacrifice anything right now. King Gerald would send for them eventually, and she would try to convince him that Trelian was not his enemy. Maybe he would be able to protect them from Sen Eva, once Meg alerted him to his advisor's true identity.

And if King Gerald could not be reasoned with, surely Calen would come and get them out of this mess. Somehow.

If Jakl could find him.

And if they could get back here before it was too late.

CHAPTER
TWELVE

SEREK LED THE WAY DOWN CORRIDOR after corridor, always keeping to out-of-the-way passages and stairwells that no one seemed to use very much.

"But I don't understand," Calen said, nearly breathless with trying to keep up. "Shouldn't we be telling the council what Mage Brevera was doing? Why are we running away?"

"It's not that simple," Serek said back. "And what part of 'not now' did you fail to comprehend? Stop asking questions and just keep moving."

Calen stopped asking questions out loud, but he couldn't stop them from running through his head. None of this made any sense to him. The Magistratum was supposed to be a safe place, the place they had come to in order to get their questions answered and to figure out how to find Sen Eva and stop her once and for all. All of the mages were supposed to be on the same side, weren't they? The good side. Not the side that locked up apprentices and forced their masters to burst in and rescue them and then run quickly and quietly away.

But if Brevera and the others really thought he was working with Mage Krelig . . . did that make them bad or just wrong?

Serek finally stopped near a plain-looking door at the bottom of one of the stairwells. Calen halted beside him. Anders arrived a few steps behind.

"Are you sure you want to do this?" Serek asked the older mage. "It's not too late to change your mind and stay."

"I've already done more than enough to get myself in fairly serious trouble," Anders said jovially. "I might as well continue." He looked at Calen. "You know, I was just thinking only a month or so ago that my life could use a little more excitement. And now here it is. Hurrah!" He raised his hands briefly over his head and did a quick little two-step dance. Calen stared at him in consternation.

Anders turned back to Serek. "The horses should be right outside. Shall we?"

Serek pushed the door open to reveal a narrow alley. They hurried along to where it opened onto a small rectangular area with several large crates piled to one side. A young boy was standing there, holding the reins of three horses in his fist. Each of the horses had several bundles tied to its saddle. Seeing the bundles made Calen remember his own bundle of belongings, no doubt still piled up in the room the mages had been keeping him in. He supposed there wasn't anything irreplaceable in there, although it would have been nice to have a change of clothes.

"Excellent work, my young friend!" Anders said to the boy. He reached into his pocket and took out a small sack. "Coins for you and some treats for the animals, eh? And an extra bit to pay the stable master if he gives you any trouble."

Anders handed the sack to the boy and took the reins from him. The boy flashed him a quick grin, then scampered off around the corner. Anders handed the reins of the largest horse to Serek and one of the others to Calen. "Jorry's a fine lad. Always good for a bit of under-the-table business when I need something taken care of. He's got a collection of mangy animals he's rescued and needs the extra coin to buy them food and such. A veritable animal orphanage! If you're ever in the market for a puppy, let me know."

Calen had a brief, enchanting vision of bringing home a large dog to take on Serek's irritable gyrcat. He looked over at Serek.

183

"No," Serek said, not looking at him. He was tightening the girth on the saddle and checking the straps. "Check your horse, and let's get moving."

Calen was no expert rider, but he'd been on horseback often enough to know what to do. "Nice girl," he said softly, patting her neck as he checked the saddle.

"That there's Killer," Anders said.

Calen jumped back in horror, and Anders laughed. "Oh, just kidding. Does she look like a killer to you? Her name's Posy. She's a sweetie. Serek, *yours* is called Killer. Mine's Franny. They are all good friends, except for Killer, who likes to bite everyone. Just keep him in front, Serek, eh? He's not one for following."

Serek acknowledged this with a lazy wave of his hand and neatly hoisted himself up onto Killer's back.

Calen led Posy over to one of the crates and used it as a mounting block. That was less embarrassing than having her wander off while he was midhoist would have been. Anders did the same, which helped Calen feel a little better.

Once he was up, Anders turned Franny back to face the building. Frowning slightly in concentration, he lifted one hand and created a swirl of orange, white, black, and blue energy. As Calen watched, the swirl expanded and then spiraled out around Anders, Calen,

184

and Serek before flowing back along the alley toward the door, circling there, then shooting into the door itself and disappearing.

Calen had never seen magic behave in quite that way before. It was almost as though Anders had given the spell instructions somehow, telling it where to go and what to do.

"That was . . . how did you . . . ?"

Anders grinned at Calen over his shoulder. "You don't get to be as old as I am without learning a trick or two, my nice young friend."

"But —"

"Now, now. Time to go!" He waggled his eyebrows at Calen and then turned his horse away from the alley. Serek was already riding Killer off along the rough dirt road. At minimal urging, Posy and Franny fell into companionable step behind him.

Calen wondered if Serek's admonishment against questions included all questions, or just those addressed to him. Anders didn't seem inclined to explain about the spell he'd just cast, but Calen had more pressing questions, anyway. After a moment, Calen leaned toward the older mage, whose horse had come up nearly even with Posy.

"So, shouldn't we be, um, running?"

185

"Yes," Anders said. "Most definitely. But there's a rocky part up here when we enter the woods. I imagine once we get past that, we'll be speeding along with all possible haste."

"Will the Magistratum be sending mages after us?"

"Hmm? Oh, yes. I imagine so." Anders smiled at Calen, then looked ahead and began humming a little tune to himself.

Calen stared at him again. Anders was clearly not a normal person. "But . . . aren't you worried? Shouldn't we all be worried? What will they do if they catch us? Why are we running away in the first place? Where are we going? Why are you coming with us? What are we going to do?"

Anders looked at him silently for a moment. Then he turned toward Serek's back and called out, "Boy, you weren't kidding about the questions, were you! Does he ever stop?"

"Only when he's unconscious," Serek called back dryly.

"But—"

"Try not to worry so much, Calen," Anders said. He reached over and patted Calen's leg reassuringly. "I know there's a lot you don't understand. Let's just get some distance between us and our soon-to-be pursuers, and

 186

at some point we'll stop, and then I'm sure Serek and I can answer at least some of your many, many questions. For now I'll just say that it's quite possible some big, terrible things are happening, or are about to happen very soon, and different mages have different ideas about how to deal with them, and Serek and I have different ideas from Mage Brevera and his friends. Now, pay attention — you're about to be smacked in the head with a large branch."

Calen turned just in time to see the branch in question coming directly at his face. He ducked and then was distracted from further attempts at conversation by the fact that Posy seemed to like walking as close to every tree as possible. The horses fell back into single file as the path narrowed out, and for a while the only sounds were the horses' hooves against the rocky ground and Calen's occasional curse as he failed to avoid getting smacked or scratched by passing foliage.

When the ground smoothed out again, Serek glanced back to make sure they were all past the rocks and then kicked his horse into a canter. Posy lurched to follow, and Calen grabbed at her mane to avoid being thrown backward. Anders let out a whoop from behind him and then sped past on the right, laughing like a maniac and urging Franny to even greater speed. Killer cast an eye at the approaching Franny and went even faster, making Anders laugh again as he followed closely behind. Thus inspired, Posy's canter quickly became a gallop as well. Calen tried to be glad that at least horses only flew along the ground, not at ridiculous distances above it like dragons. Sure, he could still die a painful death if he fell off, but at least there wouldn't be that horrible waiting part as he plummeted through the clouds and sky and all that.

"Good girl, Posy," he told her nervously. "Just don't sprout wings, okay?" He felt somewhat more secure as he got used to the rhythm of her feet, but kept the fingers of one hand tangled in her mane, just in case.

An interminable time later, Calen finally became aware that the other horses were coming to a stop up ahead. "Whoa, girl," Calen said, but Posy had apparently already assessed the situation and was slowing of her own accord.

"We're only taking a short break," Serek called over to him. "Just enough time to rest the horses a little and eat something."

Anders was casting another of those swirly energy spells, this time sending tendrils of magic in several different directions, including back along the way they'd come. At some point Calen was definitely going to make the old man explain how he did that.

But right now he had a different question, one that had occurred to him as he had tried in vain to ignore the pulsing ache in his legs and rear end as the horses had alternately walked and trotted and cantered and galloped, depending on the terrain and whether Serek thought they needed a rest. Even when they'd been walking, they'd been spread out enough that talking hadn't really been possible. So Calen had merely started cataloging questions in his head to ask later.

He got down from Posy's back, tied her reins to a nearby tree, and walked over to where Serek and Anders had already dismounted. Anders was rummaging through one of the packs and setting out food items beside it.

"Serek? Why are we doing this?"

Serek rolled his eyes. "I believe you have been told several times now that I will explain —"

"Yes, yes, I know." Calen ignored his master's glare at the interruption. "But I don't mean why are we running. I mean, why are we *running*? I mean, on the ground, on horses? Why don't we use that purple transportation spell? Something like that one that sent Meg and me to, uh, wherever that place was we ended up?"

189

Anders glanced up at him. "I believe you just answered your own question, young Calen."

Calen tried to recall exactly what he'd just said. "What? You mean because I didn't know where we were sent? I thought that was just because it was an accident. I didn't even know what I was doing when that happened." He looked accusingly at Serek. "I know you know how to transport things. You showed me! In your study that time!"

"Exactly. I know how to transport *things*. Objects, in my direct line of sight, to another location also within my direct line of sight." Serek accepted a little plate of food from Anders, who appeared to be in the process of setting out an entire picnic complete with wine and cookies. "How many times have you seen me transport myself somewhere? How often did you notice other mages popping in and out of sight during your stay at the Magistratum? Why do you think we spent two and a half weeks riding and camping to get to the Magistratum if we could have just appeared there?"

"Well . . . okay." Calen accepted his own little plate of food and sat down on the ground, facing the others. "I guess I kind of thought it was something you saved for emergencies. But if you can look at a thing and move it to the other side of the room, why not a person?

And why do you need to see where you're sending something?"

Anders chuckled to himself. Serek took a bite of meat wrapped in a kind of soft, flat bread. "Because — Lord and Lady, Anders, this is delicious!"

"Wait until you try the cookies," Anders said.

Serek took another bite and chewed slowly before speaking again. "Because, Calen, transporting living things is not the same as transporting objects. And transporting things to a place you can see is different from trying to transport things to an unknown location."

"But why does the fact that it's different mean you can't do it? I mean, it's not impossible! It happened to me and Meg, didn't it?"

Serek and Anders exchanged a look.

"Well," Serek said after a minute, "you and Meg were actually very lucky."

"What do you mean?"

"He means," said Anders, "that many people who experiment with that particular kind of casting are never seen or heard of again." He paused, then added, "Well, not alive, anyway."

Calen had a hard time swallowing his latest bite. "What?"

"Attempting to transport human beings magically is

actually strictly forbidden," Serek said. "Even short distances, even from one side of the room to another. That kind of transporting is certainly possible, if rarely of any practical purpose. And that's because it's relatively easy to transport something you can see to another location you can see. Just like you saw me do with Rorgson's skull in my study."

"But then why —?"

"It's forbidden because mages couldn't always agree on what acceptable short distances were, and whether or not it was okay to transport someone to a place you knew well even if you couldn't see it. Sometimes that worked out all right, and sometimes . . ."

"Sometimes people ended up reappearing in very awkward ways. Like under a cart, or half-embedded in a rock wall," Anders put in helpfully. He held out another little tray. "Cookie?"

Calen stared at him. "Half . . . embedded?"

Serek shot Anders an exasperated look. "That was one extreme case. Or . . . maybe two. But the point is that trying to transport a person to a place you can't see is tricky at best and lethal at worst. And mages who tried sending people to places they didn't know well . . . well, many of those people disappeared forever. And so just to avoid any potential confusion on the rules, the Magistratum voted to prohibit any transporting of people. At all. There are very occasional exceptions, where mages have done so in emergencies and then petitioned for permission after the fact, but even then, it did not always work out for the best. I'm sure Anders can give you lots of unpleasant examples later on if you'd like to hear them."

"You bet," Anders said, nodding enthusiastically.

"But in any case, that is why we are riding horses instead of simply magically appearing in the royal gardens. And as for the other part, about line of sight — even with objects, it's very difficult trying to send something to a place you can't see. Difficult and dangerous, since there's always the chance someone might be, say, standing in the place you decide to transport your object to."

Anders leaned forward and mouthed the word *half-embedded*, his eyebrows raised emphatically.

"Oh. I . . . okay." Calen swallowed again, the lump of food in his throat still not seeming to want to go down. "Got it."

Serek looked slightly uncomfortable. "I probably should have mentioned all of this sooner, hmm? It

193

rather slipped my mind in all the excitement when it first happened, and then . . . well. You haven't been, ah, experimenting, have you?"

"No." Calen felt a little faint at the idea. Thank the gods he hadn't thought to try!

"Good. Don't start."

Calen nodded, looking down at his plate and trying to muster up some appetite for his remaining lunch.

"So," Serek went on, after accepting a cookie from Anders. "We have a few more minutes before we need to start moving again. Perhaps we can answer some of your other questions."

"Maybe just one at a time, though," Anders put in.

Right. Calen tried to refocus. His mind kept calling up disturbing images of people half-embedded in walls. He wasn't even sure what to ask. "What — what's *happening*?" he asked finally. "What were Mage Brevera and those others trying to do? And why?"

"Or three at a time," Anders said agreeably.

Serek finished his cookie and brushed some crumbs off onto the grass. "You know from the meeting that Mage Brevera thinks that you present a danger to the Magistratum. He also thinks you helped to cause that attack at your marking ceremony, but that, of course, is ludicrous. In any case, he and the others have been trying to determine exactly what kind of danger you pose and how it might be averted before it's too late. He had also suggested taking some rather drastic measures to attempt to nullify this alleged danger even if they couldn't figure out exactly what it was."

Calen didn't like the sound of the word *nullify* in this context. He was afraid to ask exactly what that meant.

"Others, including me," Serek went on, "believe that you are involved in the danger in some way but not as the cause. It's a matter of interpretation."

"I'm still on the fence," Anders said.

Calen frowned at him.

"Well, it's the truth," Anders said, seemingly unruffled. "But even if you are the cause of the danger, I don't agree with the idea that you should be locked up or —"

Serek cleared his throat.

"Or, uh, anything like that," Anders finished. "If we went around taking drastic action on every single evil omen some fool mage thought he saw foretold in a deck of cards, we'd never get anything else done."

"I think you came just in time," Calen said. "Mage Brevera was getting angry. He said — he asked me how long I'd been in contact with Mage Krelig. He thinks I'm working with him somehow! He seemed about to . . . about to do something. Thomil was trying to get him to wait."

"Ah," said Anders. "That explains it."

"Explains what?" Calen asked.

Serek answered. "When I realized Brevera and the others were blocking us from communicating — I had tried to reach you with a summoning spell, to make sure you were all right — well, that was sufficiently ominous that I decided to go to the council masters and demand that you be released. But Anders thought . . . um . . ."

"Oh, just tell him," Anders said.

Serek raised his eyebrows at Anders, and the older mage nodded in confirmation. Serek shrugged and said, "Anders, ah . . . sees things. Every once in a while."

"Sees things? Like things that aren't there?" Calen asked. This would not actually surprise him.

"Sort of," Anders said. "But not the way you mean. I see things that are going to happen. Sometimes."

"Like prophecies? You have the Sight? Like Mage Krelig does?"

"To a degree. I don't get them too often, although lately they've been coming a bit more frequently than I'm used to. And they're usually more about current events, or the very near future, than about far-reaching, prophecy-type things. I've always thought of them as

 196

glimmers. Little glimpses of the future. Or of possible futures, I should say. Often there's some choice to be made, and I can see glimmers of both possible outcomes of a given decision."

"And you had one about me?"

"I had one that suggested we should go and retrieve you at once, without trying to get the council's approval."

"Did you — did you see what Mage Brevera was planning to do to me?"

"I saw enough that I knew we should get you out of there before he got to do it. Luckily, Serek knows about the glimmers and trusts them, as I do."

"But the other mages don't know, do they?" Calen asked, looking back and forth between Serek and Anders. "That's why you had to give Serek permission to tell me. It's a secret."

"It's . . . just something it seemed better not to advertise. For many reasons. So I will thank you to keep this information to yourself," Anders said. "Assuming, of course, that we live long enough for it to matter. Depending on who catches up with us first, we may find ourselves the victims of some mysterious accident before we can be brought back to the Magistratum for questioning."

"Yes," Serek said, rising. "We should get moving."

"But — but why couldn't we just go to the council and tell them what happened?" Calen hurried after Serek toward the horses. "Why did we have to run away?"

"Because," Serek said, "we have no proof other than Anders's vision, which is a secret, and your own testimony, which Mage Brevera and the others would no doubt deny. And Anders's vision also suggested that we might be best served by leaving the Magistratum for the time being. Your part in all of this is very controversial, Calen, and if we stayed, even the council might have seen fit to keep you confined until they felt they knew more about what was happening. There were . . . several meetings while you were being investigated, and there were many conflicting opinions on what was to be done about you. I thought it was best to look into matters on our own. It's my hope that we'll come up with something concrete we can bring back to the council and convince them of some other course of action."

"How will we do that?"

Serek and Anders stopped walking and exchanged another look. "I . . . do not think that is something we should discuss with you," Serek said.

"But . . . you said you don't believe what Brevera does, about me being a danger —"

"No," Serek said. "I said I don't believe you're the cause of the danger, but I cannot doubt that you are going to be involved. Some of the fortellings were very specific, Calen. Which makes me think it is best *not* to involve you in our efforts to sort this out. I am also suspending your lessons for the time being."

Calen stared at him. "Suspending . . . but *why*? That makes no sense at all! Shouldn't you finally be teaching me to defend myself if I'm going to be involved in some kind of danger? This doesn't seem like the time to *stop* teaching me!"

Calen expected Serek to be angry at the outburst, but his master only shook his head. "I am sorry, Calen. We can't know how you are going to be involved. If you are somehow . . . compromised, your knowledge could be used against us."

"Compromised?"

"He means—" Anders began.

"I know what he means," Calen said. "I just can't believe he would think that I would ever, ever help Mage Krelig."

"Not willingly, perhaps," Anders said. "But Mage Krelig is more powerful than you can imagine, Calen. He might be able to . . ." He trailed off, a strange expression on his face. He was looking past Calen, up at the sky.

Serek and Calen both turned to look.

An enormous shape was flying straight at them. It was dark, and fast moving, and very large.

Serek dropped his empty plate, red energy building at once between his palms. This seemed to jolt Anders back to himself as well, and he started casting something of his own, red and orange together.

"Wait," Calen said suddenly.

"Move aside, Calen," Anders said. "Go farther back into the trees, but don't run."

"Wait," Calen said again. "I think —"

He saw Anders preparing to strike and reached out abruptly, pushing the mage off balance. He saw the spell dissipate with relief.

"Hey!" Anders said, whirling to face him and showing the first hint of real anger Calen had seen. "Don't ever —"

"It's all right, Anders," Serek said, releasing his own half-formed spell.

"It is not all right!" Anders objected. "It is most certainly —"

"You were about to cast at an ally," Serek said.

"I — what?"

Calen didn't stay to hear the rest of Serek's explanation. He ran forward, waving his arms. "Jakl!" he cried. "Jakl, here! What is it? What's wrong?" Because something must be wrong. Something must be very, very wrong.

What was Jakl doing all the way out here — without Meg?

CHAPTER THIRTEEN

CALEN STOOD THERE WAVING HIS ARMS like an idiot, wondering why Jakl hadn't landed already. Then he realized he was probably standing in the only possible spot where Jakl could touch down, and he moved back hastily. Jakl landed at once, narrowly missing the trees on one side and actually breaking a few branches on the other.

Calen ran forward again immediately. "What is it? What's wrong? Where's Meg?"

Jakl just looked at him.

"I'm guessing the dragon hasn't learned to speak since we saw him last," Serek said, coming up beside Calen. Anders was a step or two behind, looking a bit unnerved.

Calen shot his master an irritated glance. "This is not the time to be sarcastic!" he said. "Something must be really wrong." He turned back to the dragon, searching for signs of . . . he didn't know exactly. A recent fight? A clue? A note from Meg strapped to his back?

Jakl flattened himself farther down on the ground. That message seemed pretty clear. Calen started to climb up.

Two pairs of arms pulled him right back down.

Calen rounded on the mages angrily. Serek put up his hands in a placating gesture. "Calen, just wait for a second. Let's think about this."

"There's nothing to think about! Meg must be in trouble. I have to go help her. Right now." He swallowed and looked at Anders apologetically. "I'm sorry about pushing you. I shouldn't have done that."

"No," Anders said. "You should not have. It's incredibly dangerous to interfere with another mage's spell in progress. But I understand why you did."

"I really didn't even have to," Calen admitted. "I forgot. Dragons are pretty much immune to magic. You couldn't really have hurt him."

Anders looked somewhat skeptical at this but said nothing. Calen decided that Serek could be the one to explain. He needed to get going.

"Calen," Serek said again.

"What?" Calen said impatiently. At Serek's darkening expression, he made himself take a breath and added, "I'm sorry. I didn't mean to be rude. But Meg . . ."

Serek nodded. "Yes, I know. But we need to be smart

about this. At the very least, Anders and I should go with you."

"I beg your pardon?" Anders said, turning to look at Serek.

"We need to get ahead of the Magistratum. The dragon can move a lot more quickly than horses can."

"Yes, certainly, but where exactly would he be taking us? Is it possible to, ah, steer this creature?"

Jakl turned his head toward the older mage.

"No offense intended, Mr. Dragon," Anders added politely.

"His name is Jakl," Calen said. "And he'll be taking us to wherever Meg is. After that . . ."

"Can he carry all of us?" Serek asked.

"I don't know," Calen admitted. He turned to look at the dragon. Jakl was pretty big. It seemed like he could fit four people on his back. The three of them, plus Meg when they found her.

Jakl threw himself back against the ground, with what seemed obvious impatience. "I think that's a yes," Calen said.

"All right," Serek said. "Jakl, please give us just a moment to collect our things."

"Can he understand you?" Anders asked as the two men hurried back toward the picnic and their packs.

204

Calen couldn't hear Serek's response and didn't really care. He itched to get moving, to find Meg. He leaned forward and stroked Jakl's long neck. "You're itching to get out of here, too, aren't you?"

Jakl cocked an eye at Calen but otherwise didn't move.

"Don't worry," Calen said. "We'll help you. Everything will be all right." He said that last part several times, for both of them. His mind was spinning with all the possible things that could have happened. All the recent talk about big, terrible events and dire predictions and his personal involvement in whatever danger was approaching was not helping. If anything happened to Meg . . . but no, she had to be all right, at least for now. Maybe in trouble, but not . . . not really hurt or anything. Certainly not . . . certainly still alive. Otherwise Jakl wouldn't be here, seemingly okay. He held on to that thought and tried to feel better.

Anders's voice rang out suddenly from where they'd left the horses. "Good-bye, Franny! Good-bye, Posy! Good-bye, Killer! Be nice!" Calen turned to see Anders looking after the horses as they trotted back along the road, back toward the Magistratum.

"That should confuse our pursuers, at least for a little while," Anders said to Calen as he walked back over to where the dragon waited. Serek was still putting a few last items into his pack.

"How did you get them to head back home?" Calen asked.

"Oh, horses always want to head back home. I just helped by creating a little illusory carrot to start them on the way."

"Illusory carrot?"

"Just what it sounds like. A fake little image of a carrot, dangling just out of reach. It will fade fairly quickly, but by then they'll be well enough on their way that they'll be dreaming of their stalls and fresh hay and whatever else horses like about being home. And I imagine they'll run into whoever's been sent after us before they get all the way back, anyway."

"How do you do that? With your magic? Your spells before were like that, too, weren't they? The ones you sent at the door and back down the road behind us. Like you tell them where to go and what to do."

Anders considered him with interest. "You really can see what mages are doing when they cast, can't you? That's very impressive, Calen. My goodness. Well, in a sense you're right — that's exactly what I'm doing. It's a bit like casting a series of spells that I want to happen in sequence, and then sending them off in a little bundle.

I can show you more about it once we're done running through the woods and flying through the air and all of that." He turned his gaze to Jakl. "So what's it like, riding a dragon?"

"Terrifying," Calen said at once. Jakl looked up, his expression almost showing signs of indignation. "Well, it's true," Calen said defensively. "We go very high in the air and very fast, and I always want to throw up a little bit." And this would be the first time he'd ever ridden Jakl without Meg there with him, he realized. Not wanting to look like a coward in front of her was usually what made him hold himself together. He hoped he'd manage not to scream or faint this time, without her.

And then Serek was there, and it was time to go. And as eager and desperate as he was to get moving, he'd now had too much time to anticipate the ride, and climbing up onto Jakl's back was a hundred times harder than it had been just a few minutes earlier. *Meg needs you*, he told himself firmly. *So stop whining and just hold on.*

Serek sat behind him, and Anders behind Serek. It felt a little odd to have Serek's arms around him — Serek wasn't exactly the hugging sort, after all — but Calen knew he'd be grateful to have someone holding on to him once they were up in the air.

Jakl waited a moment, apparently making sure they

were all settled, and then he launched himself into the sky.

Calen closed his eyes and concentrated on not falling. He could hear Anders whooping with excitement behind him. If the mage thought fast-moving horses were fun, he must be loving the dragon. Calen hoped the old man was holding on, at least. Serek didn't say anything, but Calen thought he felt just the slightest tightening of the arms around his waist.

After a while Calen was able to make himself open his eyes. Not that it mattered, really. Mostly all he could see were clouds, with occasional glimpses of trees and landscapes below. He wondered where they were going. Maybe they should have discussed some kind of plan, he realized belatedly. He'd have to trust that whatever they needed to do to help Meg would be obvious once they arrived. He hoped the ride would be quick. He hoped they all made it there in one piece.

He hoped Meg would still be okay when they got there.

CHAPTER
FOURTEEN

THE SUN—IT WAS DEFINITELY THE sun—had moved some hours across the sky when the sound of a distant heavy door opening and closing made Meg and Tessel both turn to face the bars of their cell. In a few moments, heavy footfalls approached, and then a pair of Lourin guards appeared. "We're taking you to see the king," one of them said. "You're not going to give us any trouble, are you?"

"No," Meg said. "Not at all."

The guard who'd spoken nodded once. "Good." He gestured, and the other guard inserted a key into the lock and swung the door open.

Meg and Tessel began to try to struggle to their feet, which was awkward with their hands tied behind them. The first guard hesitated, frowning, then spoke to his partner. "Untie their hands, Borle. They're not going anywhere."

"Thank you," Meg said. At least the guards weren't being unnecessarily cruel. That seemed promising.

Although it still made her uneasy that they had thrown the princess of a neighboring kingdom into the king's prison in the first place.

Borle untied them and then stood back, letting them exit the cell under their own power. At first Meg's arms hurt even more after being freed, and she heard Tessel gasp with pain beside her, but after a few moments the pain began to dull into prickly pins and needles. The first guard led them back up the corridor between the cells, with Borle following behind them. All the other cells they passed were empty.

The guards took them up several flights of narrow stairs, and then down a long hallway, until they reached King Gerald's throne room. The first guard stepped forward and bowed, announcing, "The prisoners, Your Majesty."

"Thank you, Stefan," the king replied. He was sitting on the single throne at the center of a raised platform in the front of the room. There was no queen of Lourin; King Gerald was older than Meg's father was, but for some reason he had never married. There were rumors that he would be wed to one of the daughters of Baustern when she came of age; Meg felt sorry for her, if that were true. It couldn't be any girl's wish to marry a man old enough to be her father — maybe even her grandfather, by that time. A princess must marry for the good of the kingdom, but still . . . some matches must be harder to accept gracefully than others.

Stefan and Borle retreated to the back of the chamber and took positions on either side of the doorway.

"So," King Gerald said, beckoning them closer. "You're the one responsible for our recent troubles."

"No," said Meg emphatically. Politely, but emphatically. "I assure you, King Gerald, I am not. I came here, in fact, to try to discover the truth of what's been happening, so I could clear my dragon of blame. And there's —"

"If that's true," a familiar voice said from behind Meg, "Why come in secret in the middle of the night?"

Meg turned to see the woman she knew was Sen Eva striding into the room. She still looked like a stranger, but Meg had no doubt. She wanted to scream, to weep, to run away, to fly at the woman and try to scratch her eyes out. But she made herself stand still, hiding her fear and anger. Tessel tensed visibly beside her but kept silent. They watched Sen Eva walk up and stand beside the throne, as if she belonged there. Could King Gerald know who she really was?

"I'm sorry," Meg said. "I don't believe we have been officially introduced. Who are you?"

Sen Eva's eyes twinkled at Meg, but she said nothing.

211

King Gerald said, "Delana is one of my trusted advisors. She has been with me for many years, and I rely greatly on her guidance." There was an odd cadence to his speech when he said these words. He was lying, of course, but Meg had a terrible feeling that he thought he was telling the truth.

"Delana asks a good question," the king went on. "Why would your parents not send you to speak with me directly?"

"They did not send me at all. I came on my own, to see if I could prove that my dragon is not responsible for the attacks you have suffered. To be honest, I did not think you would simply take my word for it. I had hoped to find some evidence to clear his name."

"I'm afraid I find that very hard to believe," King Gerald said gravely. "The evidence seems very clear to us. And when Trelian's response to our warning is to send someone here in secret . . . well, you can see how that does not help to convince us that you have nothing to hide."

"It wasn't Trelian's response. It was just my own —"

"It doesn't really matter," the king said. "My people are frightened and angry, and I have a duty to protect and reassure them. And truly, if you did come without your parents' consent, that hardly makes you less of a danger. We assume your dragon carried you here, rogue princess; summon him now, so we can destroy him and put all of these fears to rest."

"What?" Meg said. "No! I swear to you, he is not responsible! Don't you want to find out the real truth?" Calm, calm, she had to say calm. "Killing my dragon will not protect your people if there is some other creature behind the attacks."

The king did not even seem to hear her. "We have called representatives and witnesses from all the districts to a public execution," he said. "We will go there now, and you will call your dragon."

"King Gerald, please," Meg tried again. "Think about this. Even if I could somehow summon him here, what would stop him from attacking you, if that's what you think he is capable of? It doesn't make any sense."

"We will be ready for him this time," he said. "You will call him, and you will keep him from acting against us. We know that he protects you. If we have a knife to your throat, he will not attack."

Meg felt her mouth go dry. *If we have a knife to your throat* — how could he so casually discuss such a violent threat against the princess of another kingdom? Was King Gerald really not worried about the risk of starting a war with Trelian?

Her breath caught in her throat. Starting a war . . .

Meg's eyes darted back to Sen Eva almost against her will. That's what this was all about. Sen Eva was still trying to start a war. Trying to set the conditions for the portal mage to return. She must have been planting the evidence against Jakl from the beginning. That, and then influencing the king somehow to make him believe that Trelian was attacking.

"Please. You . . . I don't believe you are thinking clearly," Meg said. Her voice sounded a little desperate to her own ears. It wasn't that she was worried they'd really be able to hurt Jakl. Even if she could make him appear right now, he wouldn't allow them to get close enough to hurt him. She was far more worried about him hurting them. If they threatened her physically, she didn't think she'd be able to control his reaction. He would attack. And it would be her fault, and people would die, and there would be war. Sen Eva would get what she wanted, and Meg would have helped. And from everything Calen had told her, Sen Eva's succeeding in bringing the portal mage back would be a very, very bad thing.

She could not let that happen. "King Gerald, if you'd just let me help you discover who is really responsible —"

"We know who is responsible," said Sen Eva. "Really,

child, why continue to deny it? Call your dragon, and let us put this matter to an end."

"No," Meg said. She kept her eyes on the king. "Please, you're not listening. I can't —"

"You must," the king said. "It is the only way." He reached up and patted Sen Eva's hand, which was now resting on his shoulder. "Delana assures me it is so."

"Your Majesty," Meg said, "this woman is not who she claims to be. I don't know what she has told you, but she —"

"Now you're just being foolish," the king said. "I know exactly who she is. Delana is one of my trusted advisors. She has been with me for many years, and I rely greatly on her guidance."

Meg felt a chill as he repeated the words he'd said earlier. Sen Eva's smile widened confidently. "Call your dragon," she said. "Now."

"I'm sorry, King Gerald," Meg said. "I can't do it. It's not possible. If we could just figure out some other way . . ."

The king nodded as though he had expected this. "Delana said you would not be reasonable." He nodded to Stefan and Borle. "We will be forced to take drastic measures in order to secure your cooperation."

The guards came forward. Borle took hold of Tessel

and bound her hands behind her again. Tessel looked at Meg, her eyes wide.

"No, you don't understand," Meg said. "I can't summon him. He's — he's waiting for me where we left him. I can take you to him, but I have no way to bring him here."

"Now, Princess," said Sen Eva. "I know that's not the truth."

"Let's go," King Gerald said, rising.

"Please, Your Majesty —"

"Bring them," he said over his shoulder. He walked out ahead of them, Sen Eva at his side.

"I'm sorry," Stefan murmured, binding Meg's arms as well. Then the guards walked them out after the king and Sen Eva.

They were led down another long hallway and down stairs and out to a kind of public amphitheater. It was packed with people, except for a large cleared space in the front, which was blocked by barriers and armed guards. An excited muttering began when they saw the king, but it turned angry when Meg and Tessel were brought into view. *They hate me,* Meg realized. *They think I control Jakl, and they think he killed their people and burned their farms.*

She felt herself hating them back in response and had to force herself to remember it wasn't their fault.

216

Sen Eva was manipulating all of them somehow. *She* was responsible. *She* was the enemy.

The king led the way up onto a raised platform at the front of the amphitheater. Meg was horrified to see a tall, black-hooded figure waiting for them beside an empty chair and a small table. The insignia on his chest marked him as the castle torturer. Trelian didn't have one of those, but she knew other kingdoms sometimes did. Lourin was apparently one of them.

Judging by the look on her face, Tessel recognized the significance of the black figure as well. She shot another terrified look at Meg.

Meg had to do something. She couldn't let them do what they were apparently planning to do. But she couldn't summon Jakl even if she wanted to; he wasn't here. And even if she could do it and somehow keep him from burning them all into cinders, she couldn't let them kill him. Not even just because she loved him. In this case at least, love and duty served the same end. If they killed him, she would almost certainly die, too. And when her parents learned that she had died here in Lourin, Sen Eva would still get her war.

But she didn't know what to do instead. How long had it been since Jakl had left? Could she hold out until he brought Calen? Would Calen even be able to help them? Or would she just be bringing him into danger like she did Tessel? Maybe sending for him had been a mistake. *Another* mistake. What if Jakl returned without him? What if the dragon came just as Sen Eva wanted, and Jakl reacted to Meg's being in danger in the way that she feared he would?

This was bad. This was very bad. And it was all her fault. Tessel was right; she hadn't been acting like the princess-heir. And now all of them were going to pay the price.

King Gerald and Sen Eva sat in large, cushioned chairs at one edge of the platform. Borle brought Tessel forward and pushed her into the other chair, the one right in front of the torturer. His face grim, the guard secured her arms and legs to the chair and then backed away.

The torturer produced a black roll of fabric. He placed it on the table. Then he slowly unrolled it to reveal an assortment of shiny metal tools.

"Please," Meg said. "Wait."

The king ignored her. "People of Lourin," he called to the audience, "you have asked me to take action in response to the attacks we have suffered at the hands of our neighbor kingdom. You see before you the princess-heir of Trelian, the one who controls the dragon. She is going to call him here for us, and we will execute him. Thus will you be assured of your safety from this day forward!"

The crowd gave a great cheer.

"This is a lie!" Meg shouted. "You are all being deceived!"

People shouted back at her, calling out insults and angry threats, and some began to throw things — bits of trash and rotten food and more than a few rocks. One of the rocks struck her on the cheek just below her eye. Meg turned to try to shield her face and saw King Gerald raise a hand, palm out, toward the crowd. They quieted and waited for him to speak.

"Sometimes a king must do difficult things in order to protect his people. As you see, the Trelian princess refuses to cooperate. This forces us to compel her by other means. The other girl is the princess's companion. Perhaps her suffering will affect the princess-heir in a way our own suffering does not." He seemed to falter suddenly, and Sen Eva placed her hand on his arm. Then he spoke again in a stronger voice. "Delana assures me that it is so."

Meg lurched toward Tessel, not even sure what she meant to try to do, but Stefan's strong hands grabbed her and held her back. She could tell that Tessel was trying to be brave, but when the torturer held up the first of his instruments, her nerve broke. Tears began to leak from her eyes.

Maybe they're just trying to scare me, Meg thought desperately. *They wouldn't really . . . She's a courier. They're not supposed to —*

And then the torturer leaned forward and made a swift, short cut along Tessel's inner arm. She screamed.

"Stop!" Meg shouted. "She's — she's a courier! You can't . . . check inside her pocket, her sash —"

The shouts of the spectators drowned her out. The torturer leaned forward again.

"Please!" Meg screamed again. This was horrible, and all her fault; she had to make it stop. "Please! I'll — I'll call the dragon. Please, just stop."

The noise of the crowd intensified, and the torturer raised his head to look at the king.

Sen Eva whispered something to him, and King Gerald nodded. "Continue," he said to the torturer. "The princess has already proven herself to be deceitful. You must continue your work until we actually see the dragon before us. It is the only way to be sure."

Tessel struggled in her chair, but the restraints held her fast. Meg struggled, too, trying to break free of Stefan's grip, trying to get to Tessel, to save her from having to pay for Meg's stupid, impulsive decision. But she couldn't get free any more than Tessel could.

Below the stage, the crowd continued to cheer and urge the torturer on. "What's wrong with you?" Meg screamed at them. Did they really think torturing an innocent girl was somehow going to solve their problems?

She turned to look at the king and saw Sen Eva grinning at her. Meg's hatred burned within her like true fire. *One day, I will kill you,* she promised silently. *One day you are going to pay for everything.* Her hatred felt too big to contain; it burned stronger and brighter until she couldn't understand how Stefan was still holding her, how he didn't pull away from the force of the heat.

Jakl, she realized suddenly. He was getting closer. She was feeling him again, and he was feeling her, adding to her rage and hate. She welcomed it, drawing his anger into her, trying to feel it in every corner of her being. *Hurry,* she thought at him. *Oh, hurry. I need you.* She was no longer worried about what he might do to the people of Lourin. She looked at them, watching, cheering, calling for Tessel's blood. They sickened her. She wanted Jakl to burn them all.

No, she thought. *No, no.* She was losing herself again. She had to stay present. She still had to stop this war

221

from starting. She couldn't let Jakl hurt anyone. She had to remember.

She felt him push himself harder, struggling to reach her. She could hear his roar, feel the rushing of the wind as he flew. She tried to stay focused, tried to remember. It was hard, with the fire burning so hot within her.

She was dimly aware that somewhere, in the background, Tessel was screaming again.

CHAPTER
FIFTEEN

IT WAS HARD TO TELL HOW much time had passed when Jakl suddenly seemed to press forward with new effort. The clouds sped by even faster than before, and Calen made himself stare very intently at Jakl's neck so he could try to stop noticing the clouds. He didn't really need to *see* how fast they were going.

There was a shift in the dragon's body below them, and suddenly they were dropping through the sky. Calen squeaked involuntarily before he realized it was a controlled, if still alarmingly swift, descent, not the dragon plunging downward to all of their deaths.

They seemed to be approaching a small city. It was no place he'd been before; he could see an unfamiliar castle in the distance. Not one of Trelian's provinces, then. Someplace else. He had no sense of which direction they'd traveled, no idea where they were in relation to the Magistratum or anyplace else. Maybe Serek or Anders would know. Or Meg could tell them later. After they reached the ground safely and rescued her from whatever danger she was in and all made it safely back home again.

As Jakl dropped lower still, the castle grew closer. Calen could see more details below — houses and fields, trees and roads. And up ahead, in an area adjoining the castle proper, a large group of people stood facing a raised platform with a large cleared area before it. There were several figures on the platform, a few seated, the rest standing.

A few heads turned in their direction, and then suddenly everyone was shouting and people were racing every which way. As they drew nearer, Calen saw with relief that one of the figures on the platform was Meg. She was struggling to break free from a guard, but she seemed all right. Awake and alive, anyway, and not visibly damaged, except for what looked like a cut under one eye. But she was screaming — screaming at the guard, at the people near her, screaming at Jakl. . . . What was she saying?

Jakl screamed back, then lurched crazily to the side, and Calen threw himself against the dragon's neck, trying to grab on to whatever he could hold. He heard Serek swearing behind him. A volley of crossbow bolts flew through the space they'd occupied a moment earlier.

Calen was beginning to make out some of Meg's

words. He heard her scream, "Jakl, no fire! No fire, do you hear me?" and then Jakl lurched again, this time rising up as he did so. Maybe to get out of range of the bolts, Calen thought. Why didn't Meg want him to use his fire? That would make whoever was shooting at them stop and run away, wouldn't it?

Jakl changed direction again, looping around in a stomach-twisting arc and circling low around the outside of the amphitheater. Calen had a moment to realize they were upside down, and then Jakl shuddered violently, and they all fell off.

Calen had only just inhaled to scream when the ground came up to meet him. The air rushed right back out of his lungs, and he rolled over onto his back and watched Jakl circle back up into the sky. *What—?*

"I gather the dragon wanted us to dismount," Anders said from the ground beside him. "That was certainly, ah, efficient."

Serek was already on his feet, racing toward the platform. Where Meg was. Calen scrambled up and hurried after him.

People were shouting and running all around them. Calen could see groups of archers and crossbowmen still trying to take aim at the dragon. Other guards around the cleared area were holding swords and axes.

225

He had no idea how they expected to reach Jakl with those.

Calen reached Serek's side just as they arrived at the platform. Meg stood at the edge, free of the guard who had been holding her, although it looked like her hands were still bound. Her hair and eyes were wild, her expression a strange mix of relief and fear and pain.

"Sen Eva!" she shouted down to them. "It's Sen Eva, she's here!"

Calen's blood turned to ice at the sound of that name. He spun around, staring, but he didn't see her anywhere. Serek had climbed up onto the platform and was trying to untie Meg's hands, telling her to calm down, but Meg was shaking her head urgently.

"Serek, the woman in the green dress, behind you, it's her — I swear it!"

Calen turned to look. A woman in a deep-green dress was speaking in harsh tones to a group of huddling townspeople. That wasn't Sen Eva. It didn't even look anything like her. Had Meg gone crazy?

He took a few steps closer, trying to hear what the woman was saying above all the other shouting and Jakl's cries from where he was still circling in the sky.

"You see the way she called the dragon down to attack

226

you," the woman was shouting to the people around her. "You saw it with your own eyes!"

She did *sound* a little like Sen Eva. That was unnerving. But she *wasn't*; she was clearly not the same woman. He looked closer. There was something odd about the woman's hands. They seemed blurry. Blurred with — he squinted. Then gasped.

Magic energy. That's what he was seeing. His mind flashed back to the first time he'd met Sen Eva, when he'd realized what she was. An unmarked mage, an aberration. And now here she was again. Oh gods, it *was* her. Somehow. But her face! How could she . . . ?

"Serek!" Calen said, stepping quickly back to the platform. "She's casting. She is. Something subtle, but it's there."

Serek stared for a moment and then leaped down from the stage and ran toward her. The woman was facing away from him, but as the people around her noticed his approach, she turned to see what they were looking at. Her eyes widened. "You!" she said.

Serek grabbed her arm and then jerked as if burned. *He can feel her ability,* Calen realized. The test of touch Serek had never gotten a chance to apply the last time around.

Serek released her while at the same time flinging a shield around himself to protect against whatever she might cast. Calen vaulted up onto the platform beside Meg and flung up a shield of his own.

But Sen Eva didn't cast anything at them. Instead she backed into the crowd, shouting, "You see! Now they have sent their mage against us as well!" The light touch of energy was still flowing from her hands, blue and white and purple, flowing from her and trickling through the crowd around her, flowing through the people and continuing onward. They did not seem aware; they reacted only to her voice, nodding and taking up echoes of her words to pass along to the people behind them.

"Trelian's mage!"

"Trelian moves against us!"

What?

Calen turned toward Meg in confusion. She shook her head at him. "Later. I'll explain everything. Right now we just need to get back." He finished releasing her hands, and she started to thank him, then stopped as her eyes moved to look at something behind him. "Who's that?"

Calen spun back around — all this turning and looking was starting to make him dizzy — to see what new threat was coming at them. But it was only Anders, standing at the edge of the square and appearing very confused as he looked back and forth between Serek and Calen and everyone else.

"It's okay. He's a friend of Serek's," Calen told Meg.

She stared at him, then shook her head again as if filing this startling bit of news away for later. He suspected they would have a lot to fill each other in on once they were back home.

Meg stopped rubbing her wrists suddenly and reached toward his face. "Your mark," she said. "Oh, Calen. It's beautiful."

Then a commotion from behind them made them both turn. Serek was surrounded by the townspeople, who were pushing and shoving him, preventing him from going after Sen Eva. Anders was running to Serek's aid but seemed uncertain what to do. Calen understood — they couldn't cast anything harmful and risk hurting the other people, but they couldn't do nothing and let Sen Eva get away. . . .

"Don't hurt them!" Meg cried desperately. "They already think we're attacking them! If anyone else is hurt . . ."

Anders hesitated a moment more and then sent a burst of grayish energy at the crowd. Some sort of confusion or fog spell, from what Calen could see. The people stopped fighting, rubbing at their eyes or staring around as if unable to see clearly. Anders reached in and grabbed Serek's arm, then pulled him away from the crowd.

"Meg," Calen said, "can Jakl carry all of us? You and me and Serek and Anders and, uh, who's that?" There was a girl slumped — unconscious? — in a chair at the edge of the platform. She was bleeding from several cuts along her arms and two across her cheek.

"Tessel," Meg said in a strange, flat voice. "She's a Trelian courier. They were . . . torturing her."

"What? *Why?* No, never mind. Tell me later. Just help me get her out of there." Calen ran toward the girl and began inspecting the clasps that held her to the chair. "I think I can . . ." He looked up to see that Meg hadn't moved from where she was standing.

"Meg?"

"It's my *fault*," Meg said.

"What are you talking about?"

"She shouldn't have been hurt. She shouldn't have been here at all." She looked at him, and her eyes were brimming with tears.

Calen straightened and walked back over to Meg. "What's wrong?" he asked, searching her face. "What happened? How did you even get here?"

"I was trying to — I had to —" She stopped and shook her head in frustration. "I thought I was doing the right thing. But I can't tell what that means anymore."

"Meg." Calen grabbed her shoulders. "You're not making any sense." He looked her in the eye, still searching. "What's going on? What *happened?*"

She looked back at him, struggle visible on her face. "I'm so angry, Calen. The people were cheering. She was bleeding and screaming, and they were shouting for more. I *hate* them. I wanted to . . . I had to make sure Jakl didn't hurt them, but I wanted him to. I wanted him to set them all on fire and burn them to ashes where they stood." Her voice was rising, her eyes losing focus in a very alarming manner. "I still want to. Burn them, and burn King Gerald, too, and *everyone*, everyone who . . ." She blinked, and her eyes seemed to clear, but she still seemed off, confused. Jakl screamed again above them, and she took a deep breath. "I can't . . ."

"Yes, you can," Calen said, far more calmly than he felt. "Come on, Meg. I know you've been through something bad here, but it's okay now. Everything's okay. If it's Jakl confusing how you feel, you know how to block that."

She shook her head. "Doesn't work anymore. Something's wrong. And it's not just him. *I'm* angry. So much. I *hate* —"

Calen shook her by the shoulders. Not too hard — he didn't want to hurt her — but he needed her to snap out of this. He didn't like it, whatever it was. "Stop it, Meg! You need to focus. You're just . . . confused right now."

Her eyes widened suddenly. "Confused . . . Calen, we have to tell Serek. Sen Eva was influencing King Gerald somehow, confusing him, making him believe she'd been his advisor for years."

Serek and Anders were still looking for Sen Eva among the townspeople. "Serek!" Calen shouted.

The two mages ran over, and Meg repeated what she'd said. Then she looked around. "I don't know where the king went — the guards must have taken him back inside."

Serek started at once for a stone archway at the far end of the platform. He called back over his shoulder. "Calen, you come with me. Anders, stay with the princess and do not leave her side!"

"And help that girl," Calen told Anders. "She's a Trelian courier. They — they tortured her."

Anders turned toward the girl in the chair, and Meg gave Calen a grateful look before following the older mage. She seemed to be mostly back to herself again. For now, anyway.

Calen ran after Serek, into the castle. "How do we

find him?" Calen asked. But almost immediately a guard stepped into their path, his sword held at the ready.

"Stop there, Mages," he said.

"Are you loyal to your king?" Serek asked.

The man's face hardened. "Of course."

"Then you'll want to take me to him."

The guard stood his ground. "I can't do that."

"Has he been acting strangely lately?" Serek pressed. "Not quite himself? Giving orders that don't seem to fit normal protocol?"

Now doubt showed in the guard's face. But he shook his head. "That's none of your —"

"He has been under the influence of a very dangerous woman," Serek broke in. "She's a mage in secret, and she's used her magic to convince the king and everyone around him that she's been his advisor for years. Deep down, I think you know better. She's probably made you uneasy from the start, yes?"

Another guard stepped out of an adjoining corridor. Calen thought it might be the same one who'd been holding Meg on the platform. "It's all right, Marcus," he said to the first guard. Then he turned to Serek and Calen. "Come with me."

He led them to a small but well-appointed room behind several locked doors. An anxious-looking man

233

who had to be King Gerald sat on stuffed chair. Another guard, looking equally anxious, hovered nearby. He put a hand on his sword as Serek and Calen walked in. "Stefan?" he asked, looking to the guard who had led them inside.

"It's all right," Stefan said again.

"Did you find Delana?" the king asked plaintively. "Where is she?"

Stefan knelt before the king's chair. "These men can help, Sire," he said gently. Then he rose and gave Serek a hard look. "I trust that you do mean to help," he said. "If you try anything else, you won't leave this room alive."

Serek nodded impatiently and stepped toward the king. He placed one hand on the side of the king's head and began to send out tendrils of white energy laced with blue, letting them flow from his hand and into the older man before him. After a moment, Serek drew in a sharp breath and then looked up at Calen.

"Do you see anything? Besides what I'm doing? Anything in or around King Gerald?"

"No," Calen said. He squinted, trying to make sure. But he didn't see anything unusual other than Serek's own magic. "Is there something I should see?"

"I would have thought so, but maybe — maybe your sight only applies during the actual casting. This is something else. Something Sen Eva must have laid the groundwork for over time, then strengthened with new magic as needed."

"What is it?" Stefan asked.

"A kind of persuasion spell. Something to make King Gerald trust his new advisor and make him believe she'd been here far longer than she had." He looked at the guards. "She must have touched you with this as well," he said. "Unless you can remember when she arrived — fairly recently?"

Stefan seemed to be struggling with something. "I — I would have sworn she had been here for years. But when I try to think of specific incidents or times . . ." He shook his head. "I don't know. She has felt . . . wrong to me, somehow, but I thought I just didn't like her. King Gerald has held questionable company before, from time to time." He took a breath. "Can you remove whatever spell we are under?"

"Yes," Serek said. Again he touched the king, who had sat still and silent like a small, worried child during this conversation. A slow seeping of bright orange — neutralizing energy — left Serek's hands. After a moment, the king started as though waking from an unintentional doze in his chair. He stared at Serek and Calen and then looked around at his guards.

"What . . . what is happening here?" he asked.

Serek raised and spread his arms, one hand in the direction of each guard, and sent a quick burst of the same quality of orange energy at each of them simultaneously. They both looked startled, and then dismayed.

"Sire," Stefan said, "we have been the victims of magical treachery."

The king looked suspiciously at Serek and Calen, and Stefan hastened to add, "Not by these mages, Majesty. A — a common enemy. The woman who called herself Delana."

"Delana!" the king said indignantly. "Delana has been my . . ." he trailed off uncertainly. "No, that's not right." He looked again at Serek, and then at Stefan.

Serek stood. "I'll leave you to explain. I must get the princess-heir back to Trelian."

Now the king seemed to come fully back to himself. "The dragon-girl! No, I cannot allow —"

With the barest flick of his fingers, Serek cast again at the king and his guards — a version of the immobilization spell he'd used on Mage Brevera and the others. Calen stared; was Serek allowed to do that to a king?

"I apologize, King Gerald, to you and to your men," Serek said. "But I have a duty to take the princess home, and you have been fed a great deal of misinformation that is still clouding your judgment. You will find your-self able to move again shortly; I trust you will think carefully and sort out the truth before taking any further action against Trelian."

He turned to leave, and Calen hurried after him, glancing back only once to see the king staring furi-ously after them. They ran back outside to find Meg and Anders waiting, Tessel supported between them. Anders was holding some sort of blocking spell around them — intended, Calen could tell by the colors, to both protect them and make them less noticeable to anyone who might forget the dragon long enough to remember that the princess was still there.

"Can the dragon carry all of us, Your Highness?" Serek asked.

"I — I don't know," she said. "He only needs to get us a safe distance away from here, if he can't make it all the way. Although . . . I don't know how we'll get to him while they're still shooting at him. He's already . . . it's very difficult to keep him from fighting back. He's so angry. . . ."

Calen was struck by the tension in Meg's face. She shouldn't be struggling with Jakl that way. He frowned. Now wasn't the time, but he was clearly going to have to find out what was going on. If she was having trouble

237

with the link . . . He hated that he hadn't been here to help her.

"Can we stop the arrows somehow?" Calen asked Serek. "Give him a chance to come down and get us?"

The two mages looked at each other. Then Anders had Meg help him lower Tessel gently to the ground. He turned toward the confusion of people and guards and began sending clouds of blue energy spiraling out from his upraised hands.

"Sleep spell," Serek said, adding his own casting to Anders's. "Do you think you can join in, Calen? I know we haven't practiced combined casting, but given that you can see what we're doing . . . I think you'll be able to match our progress. Just try to stay even with our levels. Don't push; only follow. Do you understand?"

Calen nodded. He cleared his mind and then let his own casting begin, matching his own spell to what he could see of Serek's and Anders's. There was something he wasn't quite getting, he could tell. . . . Serek and Anders had truly combined their casting somehow, and his own magic was only supplementing theirs, not really joining . . . but he thought it was enough. It felt . . . strange, almost as if the combined spell were pulling at his magic somehow, helping it flow from him more easily.

Around them, the people who were just beginning

238

to come out of their disorientation from Anders's last spell suddenly fell to the ground. People dropped in a widening circle as the spell grew outward. Calen trusted Meg wouldn't count this as hurting them; the worst anyone would experience might be a bruise, or maybe a headache.

Anders sent additional tendrils of the spell outward, toward those outside the amphitheater. Calen followed him, and he could feel when his magic encountered the bowmen and dropped them as well. In moments, everything was quiet.

Jakl swooped down in a heartbeat, somehow managing not to squash any of the sleeping people as he did so. Serek released the spell and gently told Calen to do the same. "Anders will finish it," he added.

Calen turned to Meg and helped her with Tessel. Between the two of them, they managed to help the barely responsive girl up and onto the dragon's back.

Anders had finished off the spell but was watching the sleeping townspeople, probably checking for any signs of movement. Serek was stepping carefully among the slumped forms, looking at faces and clothing. Looking for Sen Eva, Calen realized. Well, of course. They couldn't just leave her there, could they?

But after working his way through the entire crowd,

Serek looked over at them and shook his head. Then he walked back toward them and climbed up behind Calen. Anders followed behind Serek.

"Where did she go?" Calen asked Serek over his shoulder.

"I don't know. She had ample time to flee while we were with King Gerald. But we can't risk staying here longer. We've got to get back and tell the king and queen what's happened." He sighed. "All of it. I'm afraid the situation is even more complicated and urgent than we'd feared."

"Those really terrible things are already starting to happen, aren't they?" Calen asked.

Serek didn't answer. But he didn't really need to, Calen supposed. It had kind of been a rhetorical question. The reappearance of Sen Eva alone was enough to qualify as terrible, and with this talk of war and Meg being held prisoner and the Magistratum chasing after them . . . Calen was afraid they were already well beyond terrible and onto . . . whatever was worse.

He was still trying to think of the right word for "more than terrible" as Jakl launched back into the sky and headed for home.

CHAPTER
SIXTEEN

H ER PARENTS WERE SO FURIOUS THEY couldn't even look at her. Meg understood why they were angry. She didn't blame them. Her father was pacing as he spoke, looking at Serek, Anders, and Calen in turn. Her mother followed the king with her eyes, her expression grim.

Jakl had been able to make it all the way back after all, though he'd needed what strength Meg could share with him toward the end. Which had meant that when they'd arrived, both she and Tessel had had to be half carried up into the castle. Tessel had been taken straight to the infirmary. Mage Anders had healed the worst of her cuts and bruises back in Lourin, but she had still kept slipping in and out of consciousness. He'd said she probably just needed some time to recover from the shock and pain of what had happened.

Meg hoped she'd be all right. If Tessel was all right, maybe there was a chance that Meg could forgive herself for what had happened.

She kept thinking back to what Tessel had said in the prison cell about duty and responsibility. It seemed obvious now that she had put her dragon first, ahead of everything and everyone else, no matter how she'd tried to justify it. Going to Lourin had seemed like a way to clear Jakl's name . . . but Tessel was right that it probably hadn't really been the *only* way. And had she bothered to try and think of alternatives? No. Not really.

Meg knew she could be impulsive. She knew she had to try to control her actions better. But she was also afraid that what was happening lately with Jakl was adding to the problem. She had thought at first that the nightmares were only affecting him while they were going on, but maybe they were staying with him in some way. Or maybe Jakl's rages were causing the nightmares, and Sen Eva had nothing to do with it. Either way, she had to figure it out. Soon. When the crowd had been screaming for Tessel's blood and she'd felt Jakl approaching, it had been very, very hard to hold on to herself and what she had to do. She'd kept slipping, losing herself in Jakl's anger and her own, unable to separate the two. If Calen hadn't been there to help her come back to herself . . .

But he had been. She just had to remember that as long as she had Calen, she would be all right. He would remind her who she was if she forgot again. And he was back home now, and he would stay with her and keep her . . . keep her herself. It would be all right. It had to be.

"We must send word to King Gerald at once," her father was saying. "Before anything else, we must convince him that we are not at war." He strode over to the door of the meeting room, opened it, and told the guard there to send for a steward and writing materials. Then he turned back to Serek. "You're certain you removed the — the magic that Sen Eva was using to control him?"

"Influence, not control. But yes. And I would hope they would be on guard against her, now, so that she wouldn't be able to get close enough to enspell him again. But he may still consider us to be the enemy, Sire. Even if Sen Eva does not return to him, his people will remember seeing the dragon attack, and he will remember that I left him immobile in his castle as we made our escape."

"You had no choice," King Tormon said. "And you were only trying to help clean up Meg's mess. If Gerald declares war against us, you will not be the cause."

Even now, Meg noted sadly, he didn't look at her. Not even to accuse her.

"We must try to explain in our message just how insidious Sen Eva can be," Serek said. "Convincing King

Gerald will serve no purpose if she is still secretly in the kingdom, stirring his people into rebellion."

"For all we know, she will convince the people to overthrow the king if he fails to act as she desires," Anders added.

"For all we know, he may still decide we are to blame for everything that has been happening," said the king.

"For all we know, our letter will never even reach him," said the queen.

There was a moment of unhappy silence following this comment.

The steward arrived, and the king had them all wait while he penned a hasty letter, then had the queen sign it alongside his own name. He had the steward make two copies and signed both of them as well, then sealed them all with his ring and the wax the steward had brought and sent the steward to run the letters up to the Master of Birds. The birds flew fast; the message would arrive in Lourin in a few hours.

"A courier would be better," the king said, "but the birds will be quicker, and given what happened to that poor girl . . . well, the birds will be safer, too. Although we should still send a courier to follow up. With soldiers, for protection. Bah! I never thought such a thing would be necessary, but it is clear we cannot be certain how far these people will go. Not with Sen Eva's influence to be considered." He ran a hand through his graying hair. "Damn. I thought we'd have more time than this."

"We all did, Sire," Serek said. "Or we hoped so, at any rate. I need to send word to the Magistratum at once and tell them what is happening. That events are already in motion."

"What?" Calen asked. "Aren't we hiding from them? Weren't we just running away from them this morning?"

"They would certainly have come here looking for us regardless," Serek said. "This was never a hiding place, only somewhere to come to regroup. And in any event, Sen Eva's appearance changes everything. Until now all of our arguments have been speculation: what it will mean if she reappears, what we should do to prepare, what steps we should take now, and so on. But I can verify her presence in Lourin, and now it will be clear that she is actively trying once again to advance her goals."

"What are her goals?" the queen asked. "Revenge? Or does she really believe in that prophecy about the war and that other mage's return? Surely that's not . . . that can't actually happen, can it?"

"We are very afraid that it can, Your Majesty," said Serek. "There are other mages who disagree —"

"Idiots," muttered Anders.

"But the signs seem very clear to the rest of us that if certain elements are all in place, Krelig will indeed be able to cross back over to our world."

"Why is the war so important?" Calen asked. "What does that have to do with his coming back?"

"We don't really know," Anders said. "We think he had a vision that told him he could not — or perhaps *should* not — return unless there was a war going on. It could be as simple as needing the rest of us to be distracted enough that we won't be able to organize ourselves to stop him. Or there could be something more to it. . . . Again, we just can't know for sure. Our divinations give us only hints. Mage Krelig's vision may have told him more." He shrugged. "Or not. If he's like, ah . . . others . . . who have the Sight, he has probably learned to trust his visions even if he doesn't understand them."

"We do know that he must have someone's assistance on this side, however," Serek said. "The portal spell needs to be cast from both this world and the other. If we can only find Sen Eva again and get her into custody . . ."

"I can't believe we let her get away!" Meg said. Then she realized how that might sound. "I don't mean that you did anything wrong, Mage Serek. I just mean . . . she was right there. I should have done something earlier. Somehow. When I first realized who she was."

"You have done quite enough," said the queen, finally looking at Meg. Her eyes were cold and angry.

"Mother, I —"

"Enough," said the king wearily. "Meg, I know how you feel about the accusations against Jakl, but you must understand how wrong it was for you to go off on your own that way. We are lucky to have you back in one piece."

"And it appears you have only made things worse in the meantime," her mother added.

"Sen Eva made things worse!" Meg cried, jumping to her feet. "I'm not the one —"

"Enough, I said!" The king's shout cut through the room. Meg stared. He hardly ever raised his voice that way. "Meg," he went on, after a moment, "perhaps you should go and get some rest now."

Meg wanted to object, but she didn't have the heart to keep trying to defend actions she now regretted. And she didn't want to provoke her father to yell at her like that again.

"I'll walk with you," Calen said. He looked quickly toward his master. "If that's all right with you, Mage Serek."

"Yes, go on," Serek said, waving a hand toward the door. "The rest of us have much to discuss. I'll find you when I need you."

Grateful, Meg held the door for Calen, and they both stepped out into the hall.

"So," Calen said, once the door had closed behind them, "what's going on with the link?"

"Let's go down to the garden," she said. "Oh, Calen, there's so much I need to tell you."

They started down the stairs. When they reached the first landing, Pela suddenly popped up before them.

"Princess!" she said. "They told me you were back! Are you hurt? What happened? Why did you run off that way with that courier girl? They said she was in the infirmary. They said — oh!" She stopped abruptly and looked at Calen. "The mage's apprentice. Hello." Pela's eyes darted quickly around — probably, Meg realized, looking for a chaperone. Meg tried not to smile.

"Hello, Pela. Yes, I'm fine. This is Calen. Calen, have you never met Pela, my lady-in-waiting?"

"Uh, hello," said Calen.

"Can I do something for you, Princess?" Pela went on. "Help you change into a dress, perhaps?" She looked meaningfully at Meg's clothing. Meg glanced down and was astonished to realize just how dirty and disheveled she was.

"Oh," she said. She hadn't even considered stopping to change before going to tell her parents what had happened, and then they had all started talking, and fighting. . . . "Um, maybe that would be a good idea."

"Meg—"

She held up a hand. "I'm not stalling, Calen—I promise. But I shouldn't really be seen sitting around in the garden in tatters like this. Meet me in an hour?"

"All right," Calen said. He hesitated, then added, grinning, "You do look pretty awful."

Meg swatted at him as he ducked away, and then she let Pela lead her off toward her rooms. Pela babbled on about all the things the servants had been saying and asked endless questions about Tessel and Calen and Anders and Serek without waiting for any of the answers. It was just as well; Meg didn't feel much like explaining the little she could explain or coming up with suitable excuses for not explaining the rest.

She had to admit that it was lovely to let Pela take care of her. Without once waiting for direction, Pela called up some hot water for a bath, helped Meg out of her dirty clothes and into the tub, and helped her to wash and dry and change into fresh clothing. Meg felt rather more like herself again once she was clean.

She sat at her dressing table to let Pela put up her hair. It made her think of the way Maerlie used to arrange her hair for her sometimes. She wished her sister were here now. Maer had always been so good at making her feel better. Although she would certainly not have supported Meg's secret journey into Lourin. She'd probably be just as angry with Meg right now as their parents were.

"I wish you had told me," Pela said suddenly, breaking into Meg's thoughts.

"What?" Meg looked at the younger girl in the mirror, but Pela's eyes were still on Meg's hair.

"About going to Lourin. I could have helped you."

"Pela —" Meg broke off, unsure what she meant to say. *I couldn't trust you not to tell my parents? I didn't want to risk getting you in trouble? I couldn't possibly explain why I needed to go there without telling you things I need to keep secret?* Those were all true, but she didn't feel like she could say any of those things straight out. "I know you want to be helpful," she said instead, "but there are some things I just need to do on my own."

"But you didn't do it on your own; you took that courier girl with you." Pela frowned and twisted up another section of hair. "But I didn't mean you should have taken me with you. I just meant you should have told me. I can't help you if you won't let me."

Meg was still trying to think of how to respond when Pela stepped back and smiled at her in the mirror. "All done, Princess," she said brightly. "Now you look just like you should. Do you like what I did with your hair?"

"Yes, Pela. Thank you." Pela was right; she did look much more princess-like now.

"I'll take care of those dirty clothes," Pela said. "Unless you'd like me to walk you down to the garden?"

"No, that's all right." Meg stood and started for the door, then turned back. "Thank you, Pela. Truly. You really are a great help to me."

"Of course, Princess," she said. She gave Meg a little curtsy and ushered her out the door.

Calen was waiting for Meg on one of the stone benches. She almost stopped for a second just to stand there and appreciate how wonderful it was to see him, here, finally, back where he belonged. She was sure he was glad to be back, too. He'd only had a chance to tell her tiny snippets of what had happened at the Magistratum, but it certainly did not sound good, for the most part. Except for his new mark. He seemed very proud of it, holding his head up with a little more confidence than he had before. She was glad to see it.

251

She sat down beside him and smiled unashamedly. "It's so good to have you back home, Calen," she said.

"It's good to be back," he said. "I, uh . . . you know . . ."

"Missed me?"

"Yeah." He looked up to catch her grinning at him. "Just a little," he added hastily. "Not a whole lot, or anything."

"Oh, of course."

They sat there for a moment, Meg still smiling, Calen picking at a loose thread on his sleeve.

"So," he said, finally. "Tell me."

Her smile fled, and she looked at him seriously. "I don't know what's happening to me, Calen. To us." She told him about Jakl's sudden rages, the way it was getting harder and harder to maintain the barrier when she needed to protect herself from the dragon's emotional influence. "And it's not just Jakl," she added. "It's me, too. Sometimes I get angry all on my own, and he's the one who's influenced by me. It's like . . . like there's always this terrible rage, waiting inside me, and sometimes it just washes over me. But either way, wherever it starts, we both end up feeling it by the end. And then it just gets worse, and feeds on itself through the link. . . ." She trailed off, knowing Calen understood.

"That's definitely not good," he said, frowning. "I

need to figure out why that's happening. We can't have Jakl going all crazy one day, and you not being able to stop him." He hesitated, then added, "Or have you going all crazy instead."

"Right," she said. "There's also . . . I've been having these nightmares. I thought maybe they had something to do with it. Jakl is definitely experiencing them with me in some way. Emotionally, at least, if not the specific images. They're different from regular bad dreams. And . . . Wilem has apparently been having them, too."

Calen looked up at her sharply. "Wilem?"

"Yes. Not the same kind, though. His sound . . . well, I meant to tell you and Serek about them right away when you got back, but with everything else that happened I didn't get the chance. Wilem thinks Sen Eva is sending his nightmares. You know, magically, somehow. He says the dreams are about him hurting people and running off to join her. About doing things he doesn't want to do. He's worried that he might be a danger to my family."

"Of course he's a danger," Calen said. "Have you forgotten who you're talking about?"

"No! No, of course not. Although I don't think . . . he did tell me about the dreams voluntarily. Made the guards come find me so he could tell me directly, in fact."

"You don't think he could have had some hidden motive?"

"Well, it did occur to me," she admitted. "Maybe he was trying to find out if I was having dreams, too. I almost . . . I didn't quite tell him. But he may have guessed."

"Hmm." Calen fell silent, thinking. "I don't like the sound of any of this. We need to tell Serek, definitely. As soon as possible."

"Could we — could we not tell my parents? About my dreams? I told them about Wilem's, but I just . . . didn't want to tell them about mine."

"What? Why not? Meg, it could be important!"

"I know," she said. "I know! It's just . . . they don't know how to deal with the link, or the dragon, and they already look at me so differently. And they're talking about the people not supporting me as the princess-heir because of Jakl, and I'm still trying to figure out how to make them have more confidence in me. . . . I don't want to give them one more reason to think there's something wrong with me." She was horrified to realize she was close to tears. She hadn't meant to talk about this.

"Meg, of course there's nothing wrong with you. I'm sure they don't think that!"

She shook her head. "You haven't seen the way they

look at me sometimes. Like I'm a stranger. Like they don't know me at all." Now she did start crying. She wiped angrily at her face, not looking up.

Calen reached over and took her hand. She squeezed it gratefully but still couldn't bring herself to meet his eyes.

"It's going to be all right," he said. "I promise. I'll figure out why all this is happening. And in the meantime, your parents . . . they're just trying to adjust, Meg. You are different. You know that. But not in a bad way." He laughed a little. "Hey, if I could get used to the new you, they will, too. You'll see. They just didn't have the same, um, close-up level of introduction that I did."

She smiled a little at that, but it still hurt to think of how they looked at her. Especially today, when she got back. She'd thought they would be glad to see her. Angry, of course, but mostly happy that she had made it back all right and with such important information. At least now they knew about Sen Eva! But they'd been too incensed to acknowledge any amount of value in what she'd done. Meg knew she'd been wrong to go, but . . . she had still hoped her parents would appreciate the positive side, small as it was. And that their relief that she was all right would be . . . well, that it would be the most important thing to them. And it wasn't. Clearly, it wasn't at all.

She couldn't help wondering if they secretly wished she just . . . weren't here. If they wished she and Jakl could go off somewhere and not keep scaring all the loyal subjects and striking fear into neighboring kingdoms and generally complicating the lives of everyone around them.

And really, no matter what Calen said . . . there *was* something wrong with her. The way she was feeling lately, the anger, the slipping away from herself . . . The link kept changing her, making her feel so out of control, so different, changing her thoughts and feelings and influencing the way she acted, letting her put other people in danger. . . . There was something very wrong with her, indeed.

But she didn't want to try to convince Calen of that. Not when he was the only one who believed in her.

The doors to the garden entrance opened, and a pair of kitchen boys came walking toward them. One was carrying a basket, the other a stoppered bottle and two cups.

"Princess?" the first one said, dipping his knees respectfully. "Miss Pela said you and Apprentice Calen missed dinner. She had us bring you out something to eat." He frowned thoughtfully at the bench, then made little waving motions until Meg and Calen realized what he wanted and moved to make more space between them. The two boys quickly unpacked the contents of the basket on a little linen square and set out the bottle and cups, then bowed and retreated into the castle.

"Wow," Calen said around a mouthful of food. "I think I like this lady-in-waiting of yours."

Meg smiled. "Me, too."

She hadn't realized how hungry she was until the food was in front of her. Calen seemed to feel the same. Conversation lapsed as they both concentrated on filling their empty stomachs.

"So," Meg said after a while, trying to pull herself out of her dark mood. Although Pela's thoughtful little picnic had already done much to help with that. "Tell me about the Magistratum! Did it hurt, when you got your mark? What was it like? Did you have to let people watch?"

He told her the whole process, and she oohed and gasped in the right places, and she could tell he liked describing how much it had hurt and how he'd managed to endure it without doing anything embarrassing. The story got less fun when he told her about the attack at the marking ceremony, though. And less fun still when he told her about those other mages, the ones who took him away and locked him up and forced him to give them drops of his blood.

"Oh, Calen," she said after he described trying to contact Serek and realizing he couldn't do it. "That must have been awful. I'm so sorry you had to go through that."

"Me, too," he said. "And I still don't understand what they think I'm going to do. I wish they could at least be clear about what they think makes me a danger to the Magistratum. Then maybe I could do something about it."

"Hey," she said firmly. "You told me that Serek said you might just be involved in the danger, not the cause of it. Maybe you'll be the one to stop the danger, whatever it is, and that's how you'll be involved! Don't go taking everything those other mages said to heart. If Serek thinks they're wrong, then so do I."

"Anders is still on the fence," Calen said, somewhat bitterly. "And even Serek . . . he's not really sure that the other mages are wrong. He just didn't want them to lock me up or — or do anything unpleasant to me while they were trying to figure it all out. But he also won't tell me what he and Anders are doing to figure it out. Or even what they really know so far."

He looked up at her, and his eyes were more angry than she'd ever seen them.

"Serek's even suspending my lessons! And so now this big danger is coming that I'm going to be right in the middle of somehow, and I'm going to end up completely unprepared and unable to avoid it or fight back or defend myself because they won't *teach* me anything." He kicked at the ground with his foot. "I hate this. Everyone is afraid I'm going to do something terrible. And there's nothing I can say or do to convince them it's not true."

"Who is Anders, anyway?" Meg asked. "How long have he and Serek known each other? And from where?"

"I don't know. You know how Serek is about sharing personal information. And I didn't have that many opportunities to talk to Anders alone. He's kind of . . . odd. But he knows how to cast in ways that I've never seen before. I think he's very smart, even though he acts a little . . ."

"Eccentric?" Meg suggested.

"Yeah. Maybe now that we're not running for our lives, I can find out more about him and ask how he knows Serek. I got the feeling it was from a long time ago, somehow."

"Just one more mystery we'll need to figure out," Meg said. "Although perhaps that one's not quite at the top of the list."

"Yeah," Calen said again. "I guess it's somewhere down below figuring out what Sen Eva is up to."

"And what those mages think you're going to do."

"And what's going on with Jakl, and your link."

"And who attacked the Magistratum during your marking ceremony. And why."

"And what's causing those nightmares, for you and Wilem."

They looked at each other grimly.

"I thought the Magistratum was going to take care of everything," Meg said. "Weren't they supposed to take care of everything? Weren't you and Serek supposed to show up and tell them what happened, and then they'd just, you know, fix everything?"

Calen sighed. "That's what I thought, too. But they can't even agree on what the problems are, let alone what to do about them."

"It's all going to be okay somehow, though, isn't it?" Meg asked. "Eventually?"

"Yes," Calen said. He said it with such conviction that she couldn't help but believe him.

"I'm really glad you're back," she said quietly.

"Me, too, Meg. Really glad."

Then they sat there in the moonlight, being glad together, and didn't say anything else for a long time.

CHAPTER SEVENTEEN

MEG NODDED AT THE GUARDS OUTSIDE Wilem's door. One of them turned and knocked loudly, calling, "The princess is here to see you!" Then they all waited for him to come and let them in.

Calen didn't know why everyone was being so polite. Wilem was a criminal. They shouldn't have to knock or ask permission to enter. He was a little worried that everyone was forgetting who Wilem was. What he'd done, or almost done. He would have thought Meg, at least, would never forget . . . but now he wasn't so sure. She had seemed almost concerned about him, when she'd told Calen about the dreams.

The door opened. Wilem immediately stepped back, and one of the guards escorted him to a chair. Meg and Calen followed him inside. Once they were seated as well, Meg told the guards to close the door and wait outside.

"Are you sure, Your Highness?" one guard asked. He looked less than happy about the idea.

"Yes, we'll be fine. I'll call you if we need you."

The guards retreated, closing the door.

"Good morning, Princess," Wilem said respectfully. "Hello, Calen."

"Good morning," Meg said back.

Calen didn't say anything. He studied Wilem across the small, low table that separated him from where Meg and Calen were seated. Wilem looked a bit different from how Calen remembered. Thinner, and he seemed tired. *Well, we're all tired,* Calen thought, although actually that wasn't quite true; he'd slept better last night than he had in what felt like weeks. He was glad he'd had the chance to rest and wash and change before coming here. Not that he cared what Wilem thought about him, of course. But it would have bothered him to be sitting here all rumpled and dirty while Wilem looked like he was ready to go off to some fancy dinner. He seemed rather better dressed than a prisoner ought to be, in Calen's opinion.

"How have the dreams been?" Meg asked. Meg had told Calen that her own sleep had been free of nightmares last night, but she'd had such nights on occasion before; she didn't seem to believe that meant they were going to stop for good.

"Worse," Wilem said. "Last night — last night I woke up with my hand on the door."

Meg looked worried at that. "What were you dreaming about?"

"I can't remember," Wilem said. At Calen's contemptuous snort, he continued, "I swear. I wish I could. I know — I know it was not anything good." He glanced at Calen. "I see that you have returned. I assume Mage Serek is back as well? Will the two of you be able to stop this somehow?"

"Maybe," Calen said. "You're certain they're not just regular nightmares?"

Wilem shook his head. "They feel different. As if someone else is there, in the dream. Directing me, somehow. Princess Meglynne has certainly told you that I believe it to be my mother, trying to influence my actions."

"Was last night the first time you woke up in the process of doing something?" Calen asked.

"Yes. Last night's dream was stronger than any other so far. Everything felt more urgent, somehow."

Calen shared a glance with Meg. That made sense. Sen Eva could be trying to advance her plans, whatever they were, more quickly now that she knew they knew she was up to something. Assuming the dreams really were her doing. And assuming Wilem wasn't just lying.

Meg had told Calen more about the dreams she'd

been having, too. Hers didn't seem to involve anyone trying to get her to do things, though. They were just dark and confusing and full of intense emotions. She often felt like there was something she was supposed to do, but unlike in Wilem's dreams, that was never clear. There was a sense of everything being wrong, especially in relation to Jakl. That worried Calen most of all. He did not like what Meg had been telling him about the link, or about Jakl's strange behavior.

So if someone was sending the dreams to both of them, it seemed clear that there were different purposes to them.

"We're going to talk to Serek next," Meg said. "We'll let you know what he wants to do."

"You know where to find me," Wilem said, half smiling. Meg seemed about to smile back, then stopped herself. Calen didn't see what there was to smile about. He stood up, and Meg followed his lead.

As they went back down the hallway, Meg asked, "Do you think he's lying?"

Calen shrugged. "I think he's a liar. I can't tell if he's lying about this in particular, though. It is hard to guess what reason he might have to do so."

"I think he really is sorry about everything that happened," Meg said.

"I don't care if he's sorry," Calen said. "I still don't trust him. Anyone who would do the things he was going to do, for any reason . . ."

"I know. I just keep thinking about how his own mother was lying to him, practically his whole life, poisoning his mind . . . it's hard to see his behavior as entirely his own fault."

"Maybe not entirely, Meg, but he still knew the difference between right and wrong. He was going to kill Maerlie. You can't just forgive something like that."

"No, of course not! I didn't mean that. I just meant . . . I don't know." She shook her head. "If someone you trusted completely convinced you that in order to right some terrible wrong, you had to kill someone . . ."

"Meg, listen to yourself. Would you let yourself be talked into killing someone? Even by someone you trusted completely?"

"I'd kill Sen Eva," she said darkly. "Wouldn't you?"

"Well, that's — that's different," Calen said, a little shaken. "She tried to kill you. Us. And your sister, and who knows who else. She was behind everything."

"Well, what if I had just told you everything that she'd done? What if you weren't there, and only had my word to go on? You trust me, don't you? Wouldn't you believe me if I told you she was dangerous and had to be stopped?"

"Yes," Calen said. "I would believe you. And I would

try to help you however I could. But I don't think I would let myself be talked into trying to kill someone. Not even her. Not even — not even for you. Even after everything, if she was standing right in front of me, right now, and I had the chance . . . I don't know. I don't know if I could do it."

Meg was silent, apparently thinking this over.

"And don't forget," Calen went on, "Sen Eva had convinced Wilem that your father was responsible for killing his brother and father. But he wasn't even planning to take his revenge on your father directly. He was going to kill Maerlie, who even Sen Eva admitted had nothing to do with their deaths."

"I know. I haven't forgotten that."

"Why are you trying so hard to understand what he did?"

"I'm just trying to figure out if we can trust him. If maybe he really could be on our side, now. He gave himself up, Calen."

"Unless that was all part of the plan."

"I know. I thought of that, too. But you were there. Did it seem like part of the plan to you? When she left and he stayed?"

It had definitely not seemed like part of the plan. But how could they know for sure? Some people were really good at being deceptive. "I don't know, Meg. It just seems safer not to trust him. Why give him a chance to trick us all a second time?"

She was quiet again for a moment. "Yes," she said then. "I guess you're right."

Serek listened with his usual lack of expression as they explained to him about Wilem's and Meg's dreams. Anders was there, too, and he asked lots of questions to clarify things they said.

"Fascinating," Anders said when they were through. Meg and Calen both stared at him. "Well," he went on, "terrible, too, of course, but you can't deny that it's fascinating. Manipulation through dreams! This Sen Eva must be powerful, indeed. Such a shame she's, ah, evil and all that."

"Yes, we're all very disappointed about that part," Calen said dryly.

Meg laughed. "Sorry," she whispered when Calen raised his eyebrows at her in inquiry. "You sounded a lot like Serek just then."

Before Calen could object — he did not sound like Serek! — Serek himself stood up. "We'll have to be there tonight when Wilem falls asleep," he said as he walked over to the bookshelf behind his desk. "I'll need to do some research, but I think we should be able to figure out whether someone is sending him the dreams or not."

"Will we be able to tell for sure if it's Sen Eva?" Calen asked.

"Possibly. Although if anyone is sending them, she seems a fairly safe bet. The more important question is whether we can block them somehow."

"Can we?"

Serek eyed Calen over his shoulder. "That's what the research is for, Apprentice. Grab a chair and get comfortable."

"But I thought you were suspending my lessons," Calen said, then cursed himself for being an idiot.

Serek turned around to face him. "I am. This isn't a lesson; it's research. Are you saying you don't want to help?"

"No, sir."

"Then get to work."

Calen did as he was told. Meg stood up. "Thank you, Mage Serek, Mage Anders. I'm going to go let my parents know what we've discussed."

She frowned a little, and Calen suspected she was wondering whether her parents would even want to talk to her right now. They had been really, really angry.

Calen thought he understood why; it must be hard having a daughter like Meg, who didn't always do as she was told. Of course, he didn't always do as he was told, either, but that was different. And Meg always — well, usually — had a good reason for doing the things she did. But having an impulsive daughter who was also a princess, who also happened to be linked to a dragon . . . well, no wonder the king and queen were having trouble adjusting. He hoped they would get more used to everything soon, though. Meg seemed really upset about the way they were acting toward her.

"Oh, but wait, Meg," Calen said, suddenly remembering. "What about *your* dreams?"

Serek looked up from the book he was holding. "I think we should deal with Wilem's dreams first. They seem the most immediately dangerous. If we're successful with Wilem tonight, we can try blocking Meg's tomorrow. Is that acceptable, Princess?"

"Yes, I think so." She looked at Calen uneasily, though. Again Calen thought he knew what she was thinking. If Meg's dreams were causing Jakl's crazy behavior, they might be even more dangerous than Wilem's. They hadn't explained that part to Serek and Anders yet. Meg had wanted to wait, and Calen . . . Calen had agreed

269

because it was what she wanted. Well, he would help her with that part on his own. He knew more about dragons and linking than Serek and Anders did, anyway. And one more day probably wouldn't make much difference.

That night, they went back up to Wilem's chambers. It was crowded in the small bedroom; Anders sat on one side of the bed, Serek and Calen on the other. Meg had insisted on being present as well, even though she wouldn't be doing anything other than watching. Serek had made her promise to be absolutely silent and still the entire time. She stood off to one side, leaning against the wall. Wilem sat down on the bed, still fully dressed, looking faintly embarrassed.

"I must admit," he said, looking around at them, "I can't see how I'm going to be able to fall asleep with all of you here."

"We can help you with that," Anders said. "Just lie back and relax."

Wilem obediently lay back, and Anders closed his eyes. They'd talked about this earlier, back in Serek's study. They didn't think anyone sending the dreams would be able to tell whether Wilem's sleep was natural or magically induced, but just in case, Anders was using the magic only to make him fall asleep, not to keep him asleep. As Calen watched, Anders touched Wilem's forehead with a whisper-thin tendril of blue energy. Wilem's breathing changed at once, becoming slow and even. Anders released the magic and opened his eyes. They would wait long enough to feel certain Wilem was safely deep in slumber and then start the rest of the spell.

There had been some discussion between Serek and Anders regarding whether Calen should be allowed to be present for this whole procedure. Ultimately, Serek had decided that if Sen Eva was able to use dream magic in this way, it might be a good idea for Calen to know how to block it. After all, what if Sen Eva's influence was what would lead to Calen's acting against the Magistratum as everyone feared he would? Anders had argued against trying to circumvent predictions in that way, but in the end he'd agreed that in this case, the benefits outweighed the risks. Calen tried to be grateful, but he was still angry that there had been any question about it at all.

But Calen was there *only* to observe, Serek had informed him. Several times. It was a delicate enough spell even for experienced mages like Serek and Anders, and they were not going to start teaching Calen how to fully participate in a joint casting, anyway. They'd had to work out exactly how to focus the spell based on similar

271

techniques that other mages had written up. There wasn't a lot of information about trying to control other people through their dreams, since no properly marked mage would likely attempt such a thing. Not following the rules kept giving Sen Eva all kinds of unfair advantages, in Calen's opinion.

There had been information about a kind of voluntary dream sharing, which was what they would be using to gain access to Wilem's dreams. Calen wondered if he'd inadvertently used some variant of this same spell when he'd worked with Meg to summon Jakl, back when they'd been lost in the forest. Serek still wasn't sure how he'd managed that at all, since Meg wasn't a mage herself, and she shouldn't have been able to participate in any kind of casting. One more mystery for the list, Calen supposed. The list was getting very long.

"I think he's ready," Anders said quietly. Serek nodded. They began casting in unison, white and black energy — communication and concealment, as far as Calen had been able to reason out so far. There was also a touch of blue energy, which had something to do with sleeping and soothing. The two men's spells were perfect mirror images. The colors gathered, swirling together to create a kind of soft-edged beam. Then, slowly, the beam extended to form a delicate link among Anders,

Serek, and Wilem, joining them within the circuit of the spell.

"Now, Calen," Serek said quietly, "see if you can join in without adding anything. And be careful."

Very carefully, Calen tried to open himself to the spell, drawing off a tendril of the magic energy flowing between Wilem and Serek. He let it flow through him, not touching it, not adding anything, just letting it pass through his consciousness and back out toward Serek and continuing along its way. Serek hoped this would let Calen share in what they were seeing without his being actively involved in the casting. Once Calen felt secure in his position within the circle, he whispered to Serek, "Okay."

"All right," Serek answered. "Stay back, no matter what happens. Here we go."

The beam of energy began to widen, growing fainter and more diffuse as it slowly spread to surround them. Wilem's image grew hazy to Calen's eyes, and then the bed and Serek and Anders and the rest of the room were gone, and there was nothing but blue-gray haze all around him.

And then suddenly he could see Wilem again. Wilem seemingly both lying down, asleep, and sitting up in his bed, wide-eyed with alarm.

"No," Wilem said, his voice hoarse. "Please stop this." Calen didn't think he was talking to anyone actually there in the room.

Something that was not quite a voice, not quite a thought, passed through the shared space between them. It carried images with it — images of Wilem sneaking through the dark shadows of the castle hallways, images of his room guards slumped down on the floor, images of hands pushing doors open and hands holding knives and hands reaching toward a sleeping figure on a bed. The sleeping figure shimmered into different shapes: it was Meg; it was Maurel; it was Queen Merilyn, King Tormon; it was Serek; it was Calen himself.

Calen tried to hold himself still, not reacting, not doing anything, just watching, but he could feel his slow, careful breathing threatening to quicken beyond his control. Those images definitely seemed to be coming from somewhere else; Wilem was not creating them on his own. Wilem was still struggling, the images beginning to swirl increasingly swiftly around him, becoming a tangible force that seemed to lift him from the bed, pushing him up and toward the door. The cycle always seemed to end with images of Wilem leaving the castle, escaping into the night, running toward . . . something.

Someone. A familiar presence, waiting to welcome him. Wilem seemed terrified, seemed to be resisting, but Calen still wasn't sure about that part. He knew Wilem was a good actor. His apparent terror could all still be part of the plan.

Something shifted in the magic energy flowing through him, and Calen tried to focus on what was happening there. He heard Serek's voice, from a strange distance, cry out, "Now!" And then it was like a portcullis slamming down, surrounding Wilem and pushing Calen back out into the room. Calen caught a glimpse of a solid wall of orange and black as he fell backward and landed painfully on the floor, his chair overturned beside him.

Serek's face came into view above him, and he felt hands helping him back up. Meg was there, righting his chair and looking very shaken. "Are you okay?" she asked.

"Yeah. Yeah, I think so." He looked at Serek. "Was that supposed to happen?"

Serek actually looked slightly embarrassed. "Sorry," he said. "I'd forgotten that since you weren't involved in the casting, you wouldn't be prepared for the shield going into place. I had to, ah, sort of push you out of the way. Are you all right?"

"Yeah," Calen said again. "Just a little dizzy. That was — that was pretty interesting."

"What happened?" Meg asked. "I couldn't see anything except Wilem having convulsions on the bed, and then you slammed back out of your chair."

"We were sort of watching his dream," Calen said. "I think." He looked at Serek. "Is that what that was? And then you blocked it, at the end?"

Serek nodded. "Those dreams are definitely being sent. I couldn't tell for certain that it was Sen Eva, but she still seems the most likely guess."

Calen glanced up and saw Anders finishing up something with the last part of the spell. Tying it off somehow? He supposed that made sense; they needed something that would continue to block the dreams without their being there every night.

After a moment more, Anders released the ends of the spell and reached forward to touch Wilem on the shoulder. The older boy's eyes flew open, and he sat up.

"Did it work? Did you —?"

"Yes," Serek said. "You should be protected now from any further dreams of that sort. She should not be able to get past the shield."

"Could you see them? The things she was trying to get me to do?"

Serek nodded. "It definitely appeared to be compulsion magic, filtered through the dreams. Powerful, but you should be all right now."

"Thank you," Wilem said, sounding genuinely grateful.

Serek nodded again, and Anders stood up, wiping his hands together. "Fascinating!" he said. He looked at Serek. "We must write up a paper on this for the Magistratum. You know, for when we're allowed to go back someday. I've got to go record some notes before I forget."

He headed out, murmuring excitedly.

"Where did you say you met him again?" Calen asked Serek.

"I didn't," Serek said shortly. He turned back to Wilem. "Let us know, of course, if you do experience any other troubling events."

"Yes, Mage Serek. I will."

Serek turned and headed out after Anders.

"Well," Meg said, "I suppose we should let you get some real sleep now." She seemed suddenly uncomfortable in the now far-less-crowded room.

"Thank you, Princess," Wilem said.

Meg gave him a half smile and an awkwardly dismissive wave and then turned for the door, leaving Calen standing there by himself. He and Wilem regarded each other for a moment in silence.

"Yeah, well, good night, I guess," Calen said finally.

"Good night, Calen. And thank you, too."

Calen gave the older boy a Serek-like nod and then hurried to catch up with Meg.

CHAPTER EIGHTEEN

MEG FELT THE DREAM CLOSE IN around her. She fought it, tried to break free, but couldn't. She was lost in the forest again, and Calen was lost, too, and she had to find him, but she didn't know how. She tried reaching out to Jakl for help, but touching him through the link was like touching fire — she pulled back in pain and fear and confusion. *What's wrong? Jakl, what's wrong, what is it?*

She heard him roar in response from somewhere nearby, but she couldn't see him. He was so angry, *again*, and she still couldn't understand what was causing it. *Is it my fault?* she thought at him desperately. *I'm sorry, I'm sorry, Jakl, please, just come to me and we'll figure it out. We'll make it all right again, I promise, just please. . . .*

But it was no good — he was only growing angrier. She could feel his rage like terrible twining flames reaching for her, trying to surround her, consume her, burn her away until there was nothing left of her at all. She tried to run, but there was no running that would let her escape the link. Jakl reached for her endlessly, and she could feel herself starting to burn. It was agony, and not just physically. *Jakl, what is it? Please stop, stop hurting me, I don't understand, I don't understand, it hurts, you're hurting me, please. . . .*

He could hear her; she knew he could. He understood exactly what he was doing.

And he didn't care.

She woke up screaming.

Pela was there in an instant, sitting beside her on the bed, trying to soothe her. "It's all right, Princess, it's all right, just a dream. You're here and safe with me now, do you see?"

Meg didn't respond; she reached out for Jakl, terrified but needing to know how much of the dream had been real. Was he raging again, as he'd been that day he came for her in the garden? No . . . she didn't think so. He was angry, but she thought he'd been dreaming, too. He seemed more confused and afraid than anything else. She forced herself not to flinch from him as he reached back toward her. *It's all right,* she thought at him. *We're going to find a way to make this stop — I promise.*

He seemed to be struggling with something; she

waited to feel him accept her reassurance, to relax, to let go of his fear, but he didn't seem able to do so. Instead she felt the confusion growing again, and the anger along with it. Suddenly he wrenched himself away from her, screaming in rage and pain.

"No!" she cried aloud, feeling him slip back into that frightening place where she couldn't reach him.

She became aware of Pela's fingers digging into her arm. "Princess!" she was shouting. "Princess, what is it? What's happening?"

"Pela, I'm — I'm sorry, I didn't mean to frighten you. I have to go —"

"What is it? That sound, is it your dragon?"

Meg realized she wasn't just feeling Jakl's screams through the link; she could hear him with her ears as well. He was closer than she'd thought.

"Oh, no, no," Meg whispered, pushing herself from the bed and stuffing her feet into her boots. She burst through the door and down the hall.

Pela followed after her, still shouting. "Princess, come back! Where are you going?"

Meg couldn't stop to explain. She had to get to him before something happened. "Get Calen!" she shouted back over her shoulder. Pela dashed off at once, without another word.

Already Meg could hear other voices in the castle, people crying out in alarm and confusion.

Jakl, please, she thought, *stop this, I'm coming, please, listen to me. It was a dream, just a dream, you're fine, we're both fine. . . .*

She let the flow of thought continue, barely even aware of the words she was forming in her head, just trying to reassure him that everything was going to be all right. Unfortunately, she wasn't at all certain that it *was* going to be all right. This was more than just the nightmare. Something was happening to him. To both of them. She was losing him somehow, but she didn't know to what, or how, or why.

It seemed to take forever to reach the garden entrance. Meg ran out into the night and looked up. He was there, circling, screaming into the night sky. With horror, she realized the castle guard was already outside. They had crossbowmen with them. She knew they'd all been instructed never to harm the dragon, but they hadn't been told why. She didn't know how faithfully they'd keep to the order if Jakl looked as though he were going to attack.

She ran out to the field she and Jakl often used for takeoffs and landings and general lounging and screamed at him through the link to follow her. She couldn't tell if

282

he was even aware of her right now. He reminded her abruptly of a horse she'd seen once who had trampled a wasps' nest and been stung so many times that it drove him mad. The horse had broken a fence, wounded two guards, and killed a stableboy who tried to stop him before he was brought down with arrows. He had screamed until the last, kicking and writhing in his pain until he finally died. Meg swallowed and tried to push the image from her mind. That was not going to happen to her dragon.

She stood in the center of the field and stared up at the sky, watching him. She reached for him again through the link, trying to push past the swirl of confusing emotions that seemed to block her way. *Jakl, listen to me! Nothing is wrong! Come down here and let me try to help you!*

She felt a glimmer of response and pushed harder. He was in there, some part of him wanted to come to her, she could feel it. She had to help him find his way through the anger and fear. *I'm right here*, she thought. *I'm waiting for you, I'm not going anywhere. Come down. Please come down.*

A flicker of motion caught her eye, and she saw several guards approaching her, some fixed on her position, others looking warily upward. She pointed at them and

shouted, "No! You stay back! I have to take care of this."
The guard nearest to her hesitated, and he was close
enough that she could see him trying to decide whether
to listen to her. For a moment, she opened herself up to
Jakl's anger and willed some of it to flow through her,
adding to what she was already feeling on her own. She
lowered her voice slightly and spoke just to the closest
guard. "If you do anything to make him worse, I swear I
will make you very, very sorry."

Something in her expression must have convinced
him. With a wave of his hand, he started back and beck-
oned the other guards to follow.

Siphoning off that bit of Jakl's anger had seemed
to help. There was more of him trying to reach back
to her. She wondered suddenly why she had even
had to *try* to take on his anger; it should have come
through relentlessly, overwhelming her, whether she
wanted to feel it or not. What he was feeling now
was far too strong for her to try to block, even if she
had dared to consider it — and she couldn't have; she
needed the link wide open for her to be able to try
and help him right now. So she should have been feeling all of his anger, but she wasn't. Somehow he was
experiencing all of it, alone, as if the link had become
one-way, taking her dream-emotions and sending

them through to Jakl and not letting him release them back to her.

Could that be what was happening? Could Sen Eva — if the nightmares were truly her doing — be directly affecting the link, interfering with the way it worked? The thought made her sick inside. It was like having a traitor inside her own heart. Jakl needed that link to reach back to her. If he couldn't . . . gods, no wonder he was going crazy.

Meg closed her eyes and tried to draw off more of the dragon's anger. If she could take more of it, maybe he'd be able to calm down enough to come back to himself. Whatever was wrong with the link, it wasn't blocked entirely. She could pull some of Jakl's emotions back to her if she thought consciously about it. He hadn't been able to share with her on his own, but she could help him, now that she knew what was going on.

It's all right, she thought at him again. *I see what to do. I'm going to help you.* It was maddening, that someone should intrude upon their private connection in this way. Jakl was *hers,* they were each other's, and for someone else to touch that, to interfere in the way they were joined together, to hurt her and especially to hurt *him* . . . She thought she already hated Sen Eva as much as it was possible to hate another person, but the woman kept

285

finding new ways to be loathsome. When Meg found her again, she would not miss her opportunity a second time. She was going to make her pay, to hurt her for everything she had done, for everything she was trying to do. The woman was evil; she was barely even human. She deserved to suffer, to be in pain and torment and to die horribly, and if Meg had the chance, she would — she would —

The rage inside her became too much for rational thought, and she opened her mouth and screamed up at the stars, hating them for shining down as though nothing were wrong, as though nothing were happening. She hated them — she hated *everything*. She —

She heard something, but she couldn't seem to focus. It felt like someone was touching her, but she didn't . . . she couldn't . . . she felt —

"Meg!"

There it was again. Her name — someone was calling her. . . . In that moment of realization, she felt Jakl suddenly there again, back to himself and trying to reach her as well. She shook her head, trying to clear it. She felt . . . she was so angry, she didn't know what to do with it, how to stand here without bursting into flames of rage. Like the dream — oh, gods . . .

"Meg, can you hear me?"

She turned, and there was Calen, standing beside her, his hand on her arm. His face was bleeding.

"Calen?"

"Yes, I'm here." He seemed immensely relieved to have her attention. She noticed the guards standing back several yards behind him, all of them watching her.

"What happened to your face?" She reached out toward him and then froze, staring at her outstretched hand. Her fingernails were bloody.

"Did I . . . ? Oh, gods, oh, Calen, did I do that?" Her voice was a whisper. She couldn't seem to look away from her fingers.

"It's all right," he said. "Don't worry about that now."

The ground shook as Jakl landed as close as he dared. He was next to her instantly, his head pressing against her side. She reached down to touch him, reassured by his warm presence, both here and in her mind again, clearly, no longer muddled and distant.

"What happened, Meg?" Calen asked gently. "What happened?"

"I think . . ." Her voice hurt from screaming. She swallowed and tried again. "I think it's Sen Eva. Through my dreams. She did something to the link, Calen. Or was doing something. The link wasn't working. Jakl was trapped, alone with all that anger . . ." She could still feel the remnants of it inside her, embers waiting to be fanned back into flame. She tried to take deep breaths and calm herself down.

"It's all right," Calen said. "We'll figure out how to stop it. Serek is here, and Anders, and we can go with them right now and explain, okay?"

"No," she said. "No, I need to stay here for a little while."

Calen's eyes went to Jakl and then back to her face. "Of course," he said. "Whatever you need. That's fine."

Serek came up behind him then. Meg wasn't sure how much he had heard, if anything. She saw Pela standing nearby, as well, looking worried. And then her parents were there, too. Her mother knelt in front of her and looked searchingly at her face.

"Are you all right, Meg?"

"Yes, I think so," she said. The fear in her mother's eyes made her want to cry. "I'm sorry," she said miserably. "It wasn't our fault. She did this to us. Jakl couldn't help it."

Her father came forward and hugged her tightly, making a valiant effort to pretend he didn't notice the way Jakl refused to move and therefore made the mechanics of the hug a little awkward. "It's all right. We just want you to be safe, that's all. We'll . . . figure out the rest somehow, don't worry."

Meg closed her eyes for a moment, losing herself in the comfort of her father's strong arms. He hadn't hugged her like that in a long time. Not even when she'd come back from Lourin. Perhaps especially not then. Neither of her parents had seemed inclined to want to hug her then.

A shout from Nan Vera made them all turn, and then Maurel was there, darting past everyone to throw her arms around Meg, too. It ended up being a bit of a mess of arms and Meg and dragon, but Meg didn't mind one bit. This was good, having these important pieces of her family here around her. This helped her remember who she was, too.

Her father stepped back, picking up Maurel, and Meg repeated her wishes about staying outside for a bit longer. Serek murmured something to the king that she couldn't hear, and her father nodded reluctantly and let himself be led back inside. The queen squeezed Meg's hand once and then followed. Serek left, too, and Pela, and the guards, and everyone, except Calen.

"Can I stay out here with you?" he asked.

"Yes. Yes, please."

They sat down in the damp, dew-covered grass. Meg leaned back against Jakl, and the dragon curled around her so that the tip of his nose was resting beside her lap. Calen arranged himself to face her. She saw Jakl's tail twitch across to Calen and twine itself loosely around his body. *Yes,* she thought at him. *That's right. Calen's here with us, too. We're not alone.*

Jakl responded with a gentle reflection of her own feelings, and she finally felt the last of the anger and fear slip away into nothingness. They sat together that way for a long time. No one came out to bother them, and Calen never once seemed the slightest bit impatient to bring her inside.

They did go inside eventually. It was chilly out there in the field, and Meg was still only wearing her nightgown and boots. Jakl's warm body helped, but not quite enough. And they had to go in and figure out what could be done to stop the dreams. This could not happen again.

Jakl did not want her to go, but he seemed to understand the necessity. She hugged him tightly around the neck one more time, and then she and Calen walked slowly back toward the castle. A guard posted at the door let them know that Serek and the king were waiting for them in Serek's study.

When they got there, Anders opened the door and ushered them inside. Meg explained again what she thought had happened, repeating what she'd told Calen out in the field.

"He didn't . . . no one else was hurt, were they?" Meg asked when she was through. She thought she would know if Jakl had harmed anyone, but with all the confusion inside them both, she wasn't entirely sure.

"No one was hurt, Meg," her father said. "Just frightened."

"I'm sorry," Meg said. "I should have told you what was happening. I just — you were already so uneasy about the dragon, and I — well, I was just afraid to tell you. I know it was wrong. Cowardly. I know I haven't been behaving as I should be. I will do better, Father. I promise."

"Don't worry about any of that now, Meg," he said. "Let's just see what Mage Serek can do to help." Meg couldn't quite read her father's expression. She suspected he wasn't entirely sure how he was feeling right now, either. All of this was so confusing. For all of them.

She looked at Serek. "I should have let Calen tell you how bad it was getting, too. We shouldn't have waited this long."

"Yes, well," Serek said, "let's see what we can do, now that we know."

"How is any of this even possible?" Calen asked abruptly. "Dragons are resistant to magic. Sen Eva shouldn't be able to hurt Jakl."

"We've been discussing that," Serek said. "We think the problem is that she's attacking Meg and, through her, the link, and since Meg is not protected in the same way Jakl is, she is vulnerable. And then Jakl becomes vulnerable, through her."

"Oh," Calen said. "I . . . guess that makes sense."

"Will I have to go to sleep again, for you to stop her?" Meg asked. That seemed like a very bad idea, but if it was the only way . . .

Serek and Anders exchanged a look. "We've been talking about that, too," Serek said. "We do need you to be sleeping in order for the spell to work. But since we've done it once already, we think we can do it more quickly this time. You might only need to be asleep for a minute."

"The trickier question is whether your link to the dragon is going to affect the spell somehow," Anders said. "We don't want to accidentally cause some other kind of trouble while trying to protect you from Sen Eva."

"Wait," Calen said. "How do you . . . ?"

"Serek explained about the link to me," Anders said.

He turned to Meg. "I understand it is very privileged information, Princess. I will keep your secret."

"Unfortunately, Sen Eva seems to understand even more than we do about the link," Serek said. "We know she realized there was some kind of connection between you and the dragon during the fight on the tower, but it seems she has since figured out a great deal more. Which we have to assume means Mage Krelig also knows about the link, and perhaps is the source of Sen Eva's greater understanding."

"Oh," Meg said. "But . . . you're still going to try, aren't you? You have to try!"

"Yes," Serek said. "But Calen is going to be conducting the main part of the spell."

"What?" said Calen.

"You're the only one of us who has any experience with the link," Serek explained calmly. "You've used magic involving the link before."

"But I didn't know what I was doing! And I won't now, either! I could hurt them —"

"He just needs to argue and tell us how dangerous it's going to be first," Meg broke in. "I've seen it before. Don't worry — he'll come around."

"Meg!" Calen shouted, not sounding the least bit amused.

"You have to do this, Calen," she told him. "You know you can, and you know that it will be even more dangerous not to try, so stop stalling and let's just get it over with, all right?"

He stared at her, opened his mouth, then closed it again.

"Oh, fine," he said grumpily. He turned back to Serek. "What do I need to do?"

"It's going to be the same spell you watched us perform on Wilem," Serek said. "I'll talk you through it as we go. Anders and I will be with you, but you'll need to lead the way."

Calen nodded, and Meg could see him leaving his objections behind and focusing on the task ahead. She trusted him to do this for her. He just needed a push sometimes — that was all.

Meg lay down on the floor in the center of the room. It seemed silly to march up to her bedroom, especially if she wasn't going to be asleep for very long. Calen ran into his room for a moment and came back with a pillow, which he tucked gently under her head. She smiled up at him, and he gave her a quick smile in return. And then he was all business, as he and the two mages prepared to cast the spell.

"Ready?" Calen asked her when he and the mages had finished discussing the logistics among themselves.

"Yes."

"All right. Anders is going to put you to sleep. And then . . . I don't know how much you'll be aware of. Wilem didn't seem to know that we were there."

She nodded understanding, and then Anders touched her forehead, and then everyone was gone. Or maybe she was gone. At some point, she became aware that she was dreaming again. Fear seized her instantly, and she struggled not to panic. *It won't be like the last one,* she told herself. *Calen and the others are here with you, even if you can't see them. They won't let anything bad happen.*

Still, she felt the familiar confused sense of fear. She was in the forest again, and lost again, and she could feel Jakl growing confused and afraid along with her. *It's all right,* she thought at him. *Just hold on.* She didn't know whether to reach for him or not. She should have asked Calen. Before she could decide, she felt Jakl reaching for her instead. She could feel him wanting to be as connected as possible. He didn't feel angry, not yet. Just frightened.

And then she felt something else, a shadowy thing

coming at her out of the darkness. Jakl screamed in recognition, and she realized this must be Sen Eva's presence. She'd never seen it approaching before; it had always just been there, as soon as she was sleeping. Maybe Sen Eva had not expected her to go back to sleep again so soon. Meg tried to run from the shadow, but there was no place to run here. She felt Jakl latch on to her tightly, and she did the same to him. *I won't let go,* she promised. But even as she said that, she felt something changing, felt her sense of him growing fainter. *No, no!* she cried out, or tried to, but she couldn't seem to speak or move or do anything to stop what was happening. She felt anger blossoming inside her again, but she didn't know if it was the dream or just her own real anger at Sen Eva for what she was doing to them. She clutched desperately at Jakl through the link; she could feel that he was terrified, but he kept slipping further away, even as the terror seemed to start shifting into something else.

And then suddenly something else was there, something bright and not-shadow, and it pushed at the darkness, forcing it back. The shadow's hold on them loosened, and she felt Jakl's presence flow back through to her in a wave of emotion, confused and angry but not yet out of control. The brightness seemed to move around her, leaving a trail of comfort and protection until she was surrounded by what felt like a wall of safety. The link flowed freely through that wall, but somehow she knew that nothing else would be able to penetrate it.

And then she was awake, staring up at a trio of concerned faces.

"Did it work?" she asked. "Was that you, Calen? The brightness? It was, wasn't it?"

"Brightness?" he asked, moving back and helping her sit up. "What did you see?"

"I could see Sen Eva coming at us, or what I assume was her," Meg said. "A dark shadow. And then there was something else, this brightness, and it made a wall that kept her out and away from us." She could feel Jakl's relief underscoring her own. He felt protected now, too.

"Huh," Calen said. "Yeah, I guess that was me. Well, us. I didn't know you'd be able to see us at all."

"Fascinating!" Anders said, shaking his head in wonder. He was already headed toward Serek's desk — looking for something to take notes on, Meg supposed. Her father stepped over from where he'd been standing, back out of the way. He looked back and forth between her and Serek.

"Did it work, then?" he asked. "Will that stop — stop whatever was happening?"

"Yes, I think so," Serek said. "Although obviously you should let us know, Meg, if you feel anything out of the ordinary the next time you go to sleep."

"I will," she promised. She thought she might even be able to let herself try to sleep again tonight. Seeing that brightness, she felt safer than she'd expected to. She looked at Calen and was pleased to see that he looked rather proud of himself.

"Thank you," she told him seriously.

"You're welcome," he said, smiling.

"Yes, well done, Calen," Serek said. Meg caught Calen's eyes widening at the praise, although he tried to hide it. She knew Serek rarely said anything so directly positive to his apprentice.

"Well," the king said. "If we're finished here for now, I think we should go upstairs and let your mother and Maurel know everything is all right. I suspect they are both waiting up for us, worried."

"Oh, Pela, too, most likely," Meg said, feeling guilty. For once, she wasn't at all sorry that Pela's room was so close to her own. Pela had been frightened, but not at all hysterical or useless. She'd been swift in running to get Calen when Meg told her to, without hesitating or

298

asking pointless questions. She'd said she'd wanted to be helpful. Meg had to admit Pela was doing a good job of proving just how helpful she could be.

Calen stepped ahead to open the door for the king, and Meg followed her father into the hallway. She looked back and gave Calen one more grateful smile before they turned the corner and were out of sight.

CHAPTER NINETEEN

W ELL," ANDERS SAID ONCE MEG AND her father had left, "never a dull moment in Trelian, eh?"

"Why is Sen Eva doing all of this?" Calen asked. "I mean, I understand that she's trying to start that war for Mage Krelig. But why send nightmares to her own son? And why is she trying to — to do whatever she was trying to do to Meg's link with Jakl?"

Serek sat on the edge of his desk. "There's a lot we don't know yet," he said. "It's possible she's just trying to stir up as much confusion and trouble as she can. She may be trying to get revenge through Wilem, trying to compel him to attack those here in the castle whom she holds responsible for unraveling her scheme last time around. And Wilem himself seemed to think she was trying to get him to escape and join her. As for Meg . . . perhaps the more erratic the dragon's behavior, the more likely Lourin will believe he is responsible for the attacks against them. Or that might be about revenge also; she might be trying to punish Meg for her part in what happened. Or there could be some completely different reason we're not even considering."

"So then what do we do?" Calen hated how their enemies always seemed one step ahead. Why did the bad guys seem to have plans and courses of action all laid out, while the rest of them were just stumbling around, trying to keep up?

Serek and Anders exchanged another of those irritating glances. "Maybe you should try to go get some rest, Calen," Serek said.

"No," Calen said. "I don't want to go get some rest. I want to know what's going on. I want to help figure it out."

"Calen," Serek began in a slightly dangerous tone.

"You let me help with the dream magic, didn't you? And I did, I *helped*. You even said I knew more about the link than anyone, and I was the best one to do the spell. Why won't you let me keep helping? How can I prove —?" He heard his voice getting louder and tried to lower it again. Which was hard because they were making him so *mad*.

He looked back and forth between the two mages. "Isn't it supposed to mean something that I got my first true mark? You're acting like nothing has changed at all."

"I have already explained that we cannot risk—"

"I'm not going to betray anyone!" Calen shouted. "Why won't you believe me?"

"I do believe you," Serek said. "Which is why I don't know how to interpret the signs we have been seeing. Mage Brevera and his friends believed you were already in league with Mage Krelig in some way. I know that you are not. But I cannot guarantee that you will not be in the future. I don't believe for a second that you would willingly betray the Magistratum, but I have no proof to offer in defense of that certainty."

"But—"

"*But,*" Serek went on, "there is still a chance that something will happen to change things. Maybe you will end up involved with Mage Krelig in some other way, through some accident, some strange chance . . . in which case any knowledge you had about our plans to fight him could be dangerous."

Calen just stared at him.

"It's nothing personal," Anders said brightly. "Just taking precautions. You understand."

"No," Calen said. "I do not understand. I would never, *never*—"

"Think about it this way," Serek said. "Wilem

probably never thought he would be involved with a villain the way he was. But someone he trusted lied to him and coerced him into actions he didn't fully understand."

"I am *nothing* like Wilem!" He didn't like the way Serek's words echoed Meg's own thoughts about Wilem's behavior. "I don't care what his reasons were. He still knew he was going to kill an innocent person. Do you really think I am capable of something like that?"

"I think," Serek said, "that none of us truly know what we are capable of in any given situation until we are in it. Certainly I would not think, right now, that you would kill someone. But given the right motivation . . ." Serek sighed. "I'm not explaining this well, I'm afraid. No one is calling you a potential murderer, Calen. And I do not believe you have any ill intentions. But if there is *any* chance that you will be placed in a position where your knowledge of our plans could be used against us, then I must take suitable precautions."

Calen didn't know what to think, let alone what to say. He was still trying to come up with a response when there was a knock at the door.

"Now what?" Serek muttered as he went to answer it. A castle guard stood there, looking apologetic and nervous. He murmured something Calen didn't hear.

"What?" Serek exclaimed.

The guard started to speak again, probably to repeat himself, but Serek cut him off with an impatient wave of his hand. "Yes, all right, I understand. You can send them here, yes." He closed the door as the guard hurried away.

"Trouble?" Anders asked.

"Probably," Serek said. "Five mages, demanding to see me but insisting they are not here to arrest us."

Anders cocked his head, considering. "Five of them together probably could have forced their way past the guards if they'd wanted to," he said.

"That was my thought, too," Serek said.

"What do you think they want?" Calen asked. "Or are you afraid to tell me?"

Serek gave him an exasperated look. "Don't be difficult about this, Calen. Things are difficult enough already."

Which didn't actually answer the question, Calen couldn't help but notice.

A minute later they could hear voices in the hallway, and then the door swung open. "Your . . . uh . . . guests, Mage Serek," the guard announced. He gave a quick bow and hurried away.

Five mages walked in through the open door. Their faces were all moderately to heavily marked, and their expressions were serious. Calen didn't recognize any of them.

"So," Serek said. He nodded to two of the men. "Edgard, Porlin. I don't believe I know the rest of you. Welcome to Trelian. Are you really not here to arrest us, or was that just a lie to get past the guards without causing a scene?"

"It's the truth," the one Serek had called Edgard said. "Quite the opposite, in fact. We're here to join you."

For the first time in possibly ever, or at least as far as Calen could remember, Serek was momentarily speechless.

"I'm sorry," he said after a moment. "You've quite lost me. Join me in what, exactly?"

"Join your faction," one of the other mages answered. He offered his hand. "I'm Charlack, by the way."

At Serek's continued blank stare, the first mage spoke again. "I see that you are perhaps not aware of the events that have taken place at the Magistratum since your departure."

"You cannot possibly have come from the Magistratum since we left," Anders said suspiciously.

"No," the other mage Serek had recognized — Porlin — said. "We were not there. We received messages from colleagues regarding the situation, and made our decisions accordingly. We are the first to arrive only because we happened to be closest; more will follow, over time, as quickly as they can."

"More!" Serek looked utterly bewildered. "You must explain yourself. Right now."

Porlin nodded and began, "The mages have become . . . divided. There are some who now believe that you and Mage Anders and your apprentice are all in league with Mage Krelig and are plotting to aid in his return. There are others who believe that you were simply misguided in your attempt to release your apprentice from Mage Brevera's detainment, and who expect you to return once you receive assurance that Mage Brevera won't carry through his plans to, uh . . ." He hesitated, seeming to notice Calen for the first time. "To . . . neutralize him via possibly overaggressive means," he finished somewhat awkwardly.

"What does *that* mean?" Calen demanded.

"Quiet," Serek said. "And yourselves?"

"We believe you are best suited to lead the efforts to prevent Mage Krelig's return and to capture or kill him if he does manage to come back."

"What?" Serek asked. "That's — that's out of the question. I'm not leading anything. I'm certainly not participating in some kind of uprising against the council, if that's what this is. Where do they stand on all of this?"

"They are still trying to maintain some kind of order," Edgard said, "but more and more mages are declaring their intentions to join one or another faction despite that."

"We are also of the belief that your apprentice might be the key in bringing down Mage Krelig, rather than Krelig's ally against us," one of the other mages added.

Suddenly Calen liked these mages a lot more. Not everyone thought he was the enemy, at least.

Serek ran a hand through his hair. He seemed as out of sorts as Calen had ever seen him. "Are you really standing there calmly informing me that the Magistratum is dissolving as we speak?" Serek asked.

"Not necessarily," Edgard said, at the same time that Charlack said, "Yes."

Edgard looked at Charlack and sighed. "Not necessarily," he said again, a little louder. "At least some of us believe we can convince the council to support our side, in which case we could try to win back some of the other mages and reclaim a majority. After that, even those who don't agree might be more likely to return to the fold."

"All right. Just — just hold on," Serek managed. "We

need to sit down and discuss this and stop it before things get entirely out of hand."

"Sounds like it's a little late for that," Anders said.

Serek ignored him. "There's a meeting room on the second floor that can hold all of us," he said. He turned to Calen. "You stay here."

"What? No —"

"Calen!" He was practically growling. "Do not test me on this. Trust me that I'm trying to do everything that I can to protect Trelian and the Magistratum."

When Calen opened his mouth to object further, Serek cut him off. "Or don't trust me, curse you, but obey me anyway. Once we are past this crisis, we can go back to full training. For now I have to keep you ignorant of certain things. That's just how it must be."

With that, Serek turned and led the other mages out and down the hall. Anders paused before following them. "I know it's frustrating to be kept in the dark," he said. "But Serek really is doing what's best. Try to accept it, eh?"

He clapped Calen on the shoulder and went out after the others.

Calen stared after them. How did Serek expect him to just sit here after hearing that the Magistratum was coming apart and Calen himself was part of the reason for it? Maybe the *whole* reason. Could this be the danger everyone had been worried about? Only that would mean that the trouble was caused by the warning that there would be trouble. He supposed prophecies could work that way, but he still doubted this was really what everyone was so afraid of. Not that it wasn't terrible that the mages were taking sides against one another, but surely the real danger had to do with Mage Krelig. Everything kept coming back to that.

He started pacing, trying to think. And almost immediately tripped over something and went sprawling. A yowl followed by a painful swipe of claws revealed the something in question to be Serek's gods-cursed gyrcat.

"Argh!" Calen shouted, grabbing for the hateful creature. But Lyrimon had already faded back into near invisibility, blending in and becoming less there than whatever was around him. Which was why Calen never saw him until it was too late. Gods, but he hated that stupid cat!

At least now he knew enough about healing to be able to do something about the cuts. He caressed his aching calf with soft golden energy, adding a bit of blue to ease the sting. He glanced around, still trying to see where Lyrimon had gone. He thought longingly for a moment of casting something to make the cat visible against its will, like whatever Serek and Council Master Renaldiere had cast to reveal those magic-creatures, but it wasn't really the same situation. Lyrimon was a real animal, flesh and blood, that had the ability to blend and fade. There was probably still something Calen could figure out to counteract the cat's ability; he was sure that if he spent enough time thinking about it . . . but Serek probably wouldn't like it. And now didn't seem like the best time to make Serek angry. Angrier.

Calen's eye fell on Serek's desk. In the top drawer, he knew, was Serek's set of spirit cards.

Maybe if Serek wasn't going to tell him anything, he should try to find something out for himself.

The idea of doing something made him feel infinitely better. He hated just waiting here in ignorance. Surely it couldn't really hurt to see what he could find out. Serek had taught him more about divination since his first use of the cards, back when he'd first met Meg. And Serek was always saying that Calen had a real talent for divination. Of course, he was also always saying that divination was difficult and unreliable, along with a whole bunch of other warnings, but still, it wasn't like Calen had to *act* on whatever he saw. He just wanted to get a better sense of what was happening, what kind of danger he was supposedly so involved in. Maybe if he knew more about it, he could avoid doing whatever terrible thing everyone was so afraid he would do.

He glanced at the door. Serek and the others would be gone for a long time. He certainly had time to do at least one quick reading of the cards.

All right, then. Before he could change his mind, he got up and took the cards from the drawer. He sat in Serek's chair, shuffling the cards and focusing his mind on the question of the portal mage and what his own involvement with him might be. He decided to use one of the most basic patterns for the cards: a simple three-card spread representing past, present, and future.

When he felt he had shuffled them enough, he lay the top three cards down in front of him. He took a deep breath, trying to stay calm and relaxed. It was important to stay focused and not let anything he saw distract him from the reading.

The first card represented the past. It showed a baby in a cradle, and as Calen looked at it, the familiar feeling of *connection* came over him, the cards seeming like living beings, as if they were trying to touch him, to tell him important things. The message in this card was instantly clear: innocence. That must refer back to the time before any of this started, before Sen Eva and her evil plot and maybe even back before he'd met Meg.

The second card, the present, showed a small boat caught up on rocks in the middle of a river. The boat wanted to move, to get off the rocks and flow freely along in the water toward its destination, but it was stuck. Stuck like Calen was, unable to do anything because of the suspicion hanging over him.

The third card showed the future — or what the future could bring, if the present did not change. The image on this card was of a king, smiling from atop his golden throne. But it was upside down, which made the smile look like a frown. And it didn't represent a king, not literally. It meant a person who had reached some pinnacle of achievement, some place of fulfilled destiny or ambition. Or it should have, but because it was reversed, it signified the opposite: a person unfulfilled. Who never became what he should have been. Never did what he was meant to do. And along with that, there was an echo of a larger disappointment, a larger sense of things not being the way they were meant to be.

Calen placed the cards back into the deck and began shuffling again. That hadn't really told him anything he didn't already know, or at least suspect. He needed . . . he needed to know what he could do to *change* that future.

He glanced at the door again. That hadn't taken long at all; he had time for one more reading. He probably had time for several more, really, but he wanted to be safely engaged in other activities by the time Serek or Anders returned. He wanted to have a ready answer for what he'd been doing while they were gone, if they happened to ask.

So just one more. Something to tell him what he should do. How he could change that outcome.

There was another small spread he knew, one that used four cards. It was helpful when there were choices to be made because it showed two sets of actions with their likely consequences.

Calen shuffled a few more times, thinking about what he should do to help with the portal mage situation. Then he dealt four cards: action, consequence, action, consequence.

The first card showed a little boy being scolded by a father or teacher. Calen's calm almost slipped at this one; it was so eerily reflective of his relationship with Serek. The action suggested here was compliance, he thought. The boy submitting to the will of his elder.

The consequence card showed a spinning coin. He'd

seen this card before; it always meant that there was some reason a certain idea or action or result couldn't be seen clearly. That there were too many forces in play, too many factors that could affect the outcome. Calen sighed. That wasn't particularly helpful.

The third card showed a traveler setting out on a journey. This meaning seemed pretty clear as well—Calen striking out on his own, deciding to take action even if Serek didn't approve.

He turned to the fourth card and again almost lost his composure. He closed his eyes to refocus, then opened them again. It was the universe, a dark expanse of the heavens showing the sun and moons and stars. It seemed to suggest . . . everything.

Calen sat back in his chair, drained and excited and a little nervous. That was about as clear a message as you could ask for. The cards were definitely saying that if he did nothing, they didn't know what would happen, but if he set out to try and change things, he could achieve something really important.

Maybe this was how he could prove to everyone that he wasn't the danger they thought he was. Maybe the real danger was in sitting still and doing nothing. Maybe, if he . . . if he . . .

If he what? That was the part the cards couldn't tell

314

him exactly. He would have think about it carefully. Maybe he should wait to see an opportunity. Maybe he would know it when he saw it.

A yawn took him over for several seconds, and he realized it must be really, really late by now. He should try to catch some sleep. He gathered the cards back together, wrapped them carefully, and placed them back in the drawer exactly as he'd found them.

In the morning, he'd tell Meg what he'd seen. Maybe she'd have some ideas for what he could do. But even if he didn't know exactly what his plan was yet, he felt good just knowing he was going to make one.

CHAPTER TWENTY

MEG WOKE UP FEELING BETTER THAN she had in weeks. She could tell Jakl felt good, too; he practically gleamed at her through the link, energetic and happy. They hadn't slept all that long, really, just a few hours, but there had been no dreams, and no fear of dreams, and that had made an enormous difference.

Pela had waited up for her last night, and Meg had explained what she could about the nightmares. She told Pela that Sen Eva had been sending them to both her and Jakl, but she avoided actually explaining about the link. She thought Pela suspected at least some part of the truth about Meg's relationship with the dragon, but Pela didn't say anything other than that she was glad Meg would be able to sleep easier now.

Meg let Pela dress her without complaint and went down to breakfast. Nan Vera was there with baby Mattie; she said Meg's parents had gone off to an important meeting and Maurel was still asleep. That was fine with Meg. She didn't really want to talk about what had happened last night. Nan Vera didn't say anything about it, either. She just made polite small talk about the baby and the weather, and Meg was grateful.

She was still feeling good enough after breakfast that she thought she would check in on Wilem first thing, to get that unpleasant duty out of the way. If his sleep had been free of dreams as well, it need only be a short visit.

The guards admitted her and gave her the usual disapproving frowns when Meg told them to close the door, but she insisted. She didn't think Wilem would try anything with the guards right outside. And she didn't need the whole castle gossiping about the dreams, which is what would surely happen if she left the door open and the guards heard their conversation.

Wilem was sitting at the table, an open book and the remains of his breakfast before him.

"Good morning, Princess," he said, rising.

"Good morning." She approached the table but didn't sit. "I came to see how your sleep has been. No more dreams, I trust?"

"No," he said. "Whatever the mages did seems to have worked."

Meg nodded. "I'm glad to hear it." She turned to go.

"Princess Meglynne —" He reached out a hand to

317

stop her, but didn't quite touch her with it. "I had hoped to ask you: is there anything I can do? To help?"

"To help with what?" He already did daily work around the castle under the guards' supervision, helping with whatever odd jobs needed doing.

"With the efforts to stop my mother and what she's trying to accomplish."

That stopped her. "What —? How?"

"I don't know," he said. "I just —" He looked down for a long moment, then met her eyes again. "I know I can probably never make up for my part in what she was trying to do. But I would still like to try. If there's anything, any way I can help . . . You know she is capable of terrible things. But I know her better than anyone else. I might have some insight or information that could be useful."

"You didn't know her quite as well as you thought, though, did you?" Meg asked.

Wilem flushed. "No. I suppose not. But I do still know a great deal about her."

Meg studied his face, trying to see the truth there. "Why would you want to help us against your own mother?"

He kept his eyes on hers, steady and serious. "Because whatever else she is to me, she is also very dangerous. I think she truly believes that mage will somehow bring Father and Tymas back to her. She would do anything, sacrifice anyone, to make that happen. She made that clear when she lied to me. When I think about what she was doing, how she convinced me it was necessary to — to commit murder . . ." He shook his head. "I cannot pretend I owe her any loyalty after that. Or believe that there are any limits to what she might do. And I — I want you to know that I regret my own actions, so much. . . ."

He took another step toward her. He was too close now; she should tell him to step back, but she couldn't seem to look away from his face.

"Please," he said. And then he took her hand, and she was so startled she just stood there and looked down at it. It felt . . . nice. Not like the hand of a monster. But wasn't that what he was?

The door opened, and Calen's voice preceded him. "Meg, Nan Vera told me you were up here —"

He froze, shock plain upon his face. Meg pulled her hand out of Wilem's grasp. Calen looked at her, then at Wilem. Then back.

"What — what is this?"

"What is what?" Meg tried to keep her voice light. Her heart was thumping. Why was her heart thumping like that?

"What are you *doing?*" Calen sounded more incredulous with every word. "Meg—have you forgotten who he is? I never would have thought—I can't—" He took a few steps backward, shaking his head. Then he turned and strode out.

"Calen! Calen, wait!" She threw Wilem a furious final glance—he was just standing there, looking stricken—and then took off after Calen. Jakl was beginning to react to her emotions, and she tried to send him reassuring feelings. *Just stupid human stuff,* she thought at him. *Nothing to worry your dragon head about.*

She caught up with Calen down the hall.

"Calen, stop! It's not what you think!"

He stopped and turned to face her. "No? You weren't standing there holding hands?"

"No! He grabbed my hand right before you came in. We weren't 'holding hands.' It wasn't like that."

He started walking again. "Looked like that to me."

"Calen, please. He was asking me if he could help us in the fight against Sen Eva. I think he was just trying to show me he was sincere." She stepped alongside him, but he didn't turn to look at her.

"Like last time?"

"This is different!" *Was it?* Was she really just letting herself be lied to all over again?

320

"Why would he want to help us fight his own mother?"

"I asked him the same thing! He wants to try to make up for what he did. For what he'd been willing to do. She lied to him, Calen."

"He's probably lying to *you*," Calen said through gritted teeth. "Why can't you see that? Why do you keep letting him talk to you at all? I thought you hated him. Remember how much you hated him? What happened to that?"

Meg blinked. "I . . . I do hate him, Calen. Of course I do. But I really think he wants to try —"

He spun to face her again, cutting her off. "No, you don't," he said. "Lie to yourself if you want to, but don't lie to me. And stop trying to let him off the hook. Stop trying to forget what he did. Some things can never be forgiven, Meg. No matter what he thought his reasons were."

"Calen, he feels really terrible about everything."

He raised his eyebrows in mock surprise, but his eyes were cold and hard. "Oh, he feels terrible? Oh, in that case, sure, go ahead and hold hands with him all you want! You might as well let him kiss you again, too!"

Meg was shocked into speechlessness. Calen whirled back around and continued down the hall. In a moment, he had turned the corner and vanished from her sight.

Meg stood where she was, staring after him. Calen had never spoken to her like that before. Ever. She'd never seen him so angry.

She was angry, too . . . but it was so mixed up with other emotions that she couldn't sort any of them out. For once Jakl seemed to be the one keeping his distance through the link; he probably didn't know how to feel, either.

Stupid . . . boys! Meg thought to herself in frustration. Calen had no right to be mad at her. He's the one who had completely misinterpreted the situation. She had certainly not been "holding hands" with Wilem. *He* had taken *her* hand. That was entirely different. And why had he done that? Why had he thought he had a right to touch her?

Because you've been too nice to him, she answered herself.

Maybe. Probably. She didn't know. She did still hate him. She thought she did, anyway. Or at least, she knew she should. But was it wrong to want to believe that he wanted to try to make up for what he had done? Was Calen right that some things could never, ever be forgiven, no matter what the reasons were behind them?

Was it true that people deserved to pay for their mistakes forever?

The topic of forgiveness and who deserved it reminded her that she'd wanted to look in on Tessel again this morning. Her guilt weighed heavily on her as she made her way down to the infirmary. She'd stopped by a couple of times the day before, but the courier had been sleeping each time.

She was sleeping now, as well. The physicians said it happened this way sometimes, that a person would sleep a great deal following a traumatic event. They said Tessel would start to spend more time awake when she was ready.

Meg sat beside Tessel's bed and looked at the bandages. She wondered if Tessel would have scars from the cuts, if she'd have to remember what had happened to her every time her eye fell on one of them. If the memory of being tortured before a screaming, bloodthirsty crowd would ever become less painful, or if it would stay fresh and terrible in her mind forever.

It was a long while before Meg headed back to her rooms.

Pela was waiting outside her door when she arrived. "*There* you are! Your parents are looking for you. They're waiting for you in their study."

Meg obediently turned around and headed back downstairs. Maybe they wanted to tell her what their meeting was about this morning. She had been unofficially relieved of duties since her return from Lourin — her father had pointedly suggested that she rest and "reflect on her recent actions" for a while. Maybe her parents were ready to start letting her resume some of her princess-heir responsibilities. That would be welcome news. She was eager to start proving herself to them again. And having more work to do would leave less time for thinking about everything else.

She made herself smile at the guard in the hallway outside and then pushed open the door to the study. One look at her parents' faces told her this was not about anything good.

"What's wrong?" she asked from where she'd stopped, just inside the door.

"Sit down, Meg," said her father.

She sat. She tried not to imagine what new terrible thing could have happened now. The king was holding a piece of parchment in his hand.

"A courier from Lourin brought King Gerald's response this morning," her father began. "He seems to be somewhat recovered from Sen Eva's influence. But he still isn't certain he believes we are not behind the

324

attacks. He is willing to discuss matters, however, and will hold off on a formal declaration of war pending our negotiations."

She looked back and forth between her parents. "But — but that's good news, isn't it?"

"Yes. But there are certain . . . conditions." The king sighed, then looked at her squarely. "Meg, he is insisting that you and Jakl be confined to the castle grounds, at least until matters are sorted out. I realize you —"

Meg jumped back to her feet. "That's ridiculous!"

"Meg," her mother said, "given all that has happened, and especially given how things must seem from Lourin's perspective, it is not at all unreasonable for King Gerald to ask for this. And we will agree, and graciously, because our priority must be to prevent hostilities from escalating."

"I will not —"

"Sit down, Meg," her father said. When she hesitated, he added, "Right now."

Meg took a deep breath and made herself sit down again. *Stupid*, she scolded herself. She was supposed to be showing her parents how responsible she could be. How able she was to put Trelian's needs before her own. And her dragon's.

She tried to make her voice calm and reasonable.

325

"Father," she began, "I understand. I do. But can't we tell King Gerald that we promise not to approach his lands? Surely that's all he really cares about. . . ." Her father was shaking his head.

"King Gerald was very clear about what he wanted," her father said. "He does not want to take our word for it that the dragon will not approach his boundaries. He does not want to risk harm to his allies, either. He is sending an army to wait at our borders, Meg, and he will have soldiers stationed here, watching the sky and the roads. I believe he sent outriders along with the courier, in fact, so some of his men are already here. We cannot refuse him this, not if we want to avoid sparking hostilities. Jakl must not leave the castle grounds. Not to fly, not to hunt, not to go for a stroll along the Queen's Road. He will stay right here, and so will you."

An army. Oh, gods. Jakl had been slowly stirring again as she had responded to her father's announcement, and she could feel him fully focused on her now, aware of her agitation. She tried to soothe him through the link, but it was hard to do while she was so upset. And frightened.

"But it's not fair," she said. She heard the whine in her voice and hated herself for it. "Jakl didn't do anything! They're punishing him for something that's not his fault!"

"Fair has nothing to do with it," her mother said. "Of course it's not fair. Ruling a kingdom is not about what's fair and what's not. You must learn that, Meg. If you are to be the princess-heir, you must be able to put the good of the kingdom before everything else."

"I know that," Meg said, trying to stay calm, trying to ignore the "if" in her mother's last statement. "I just—" No. *No.* No arguments. She had to show them that she could do this. She took another deep breath. "All right. Of course, if that's what we need to do. I'll try to make Jakl understand."

Her father sat back in his chair. "Well . . . good. Thank you, Meg." The relieved glance that passed between her parents was irritating but, she supposed, not undeserved.

"With the Lady's blessing, we will have this sorted out soon," her mother added. "It's only temporary, Meg."

Meg nodded and rose to leave, trying to focus on feeling glad to have pleased her parents rather than on the heaviness in her heart. Jakl wouldn't really understand, and he would not be happy.

She went out through the gardens, past the neatly manicured shrubs and delicate trees and then to the outer ward and the path to Jakl's paddock. He was out in his field, waiting for her.

She could feel his inquiry, wondering what was wrong. Underneath she could feel his desire to take her flying. It made her want to weep.

"I'm sorry," she said. "We won't be able to go flying for a while." She pressed her face against his warm scales. "We have to stay here. Both of us. Because of . . . because of that nonsense happening in Lourin. It's not fair, but we have to. Do you understand?" She tried to send him images from her mind, visions of them here together, not being miserable.

"It won't be so bad, really," she said, trying to convince them both. "At least we'll be together. And it's only for a little while."

Please let it only be for a little while.

A flicker of his attention through the link made her turn to see what he was seeing. Maurel was standing a few yards behind her, rocking slightly on her feet in the tall grass.

"Hi, Meg," she said. "What are you doing?"

"Nothing," Meg said, sighing. "Nothing at all."

Maurel came the rest of the way over and reached out to pet Jakl's nose. He bent to make it easier for her to reach. "Are you going to go for a ride?" Maurel asked hopefully.

"No," Meg said. "We're not — we're not allowed."

Maurel stopped petting and looked up at her. "Did you get in trouble?"

"Not exactly." Meg didn't know how much to explain. "Do you know about what's going on with Lourin?"

"That they're mad at us? Yeah, I know that. But it's dumb. We didn't do anything to them, did we?"

"No, we didn't. But they think we did. And they think Jakl in particular did some very bad things. So until Mother and Father can work everything out with King Gerald, Jakl and I aren't allowed to go flying."

"Oh," Maurel said solemnly, taking this in. "I'm sorry. I know you like flying."

"Thanks, Maurel. I'm sorry, too."

Meg sat in the grass and leaned back against the dragon. After a moment, Maurel sat beside her.

"Is it hard, having a dragon?" she asked after a while.

Meg looked at her. "What do you mean?"

Maurel shrugged and plucked a piece of grass to play with. "I don't know. You don't always seem very happy, since Jakl came. You get angry a lot."

Meg thought about how to answer that one. "Well, it's complicated sometimes," she said finally. "But mostly I really like having a dragon. I know that I've been angry a lot lately, but some of that — some of that was . . ." Meg was again unsure how much to say. She didn't want to upset her sister unnecessarily. "Some of that was because I was having bad nightmares. They made me feel very angry even when I didn't have any reason to be. It wasn't real, but I didn't know that."

"Was Jakl having them, too? Is that why he was so angry last night?"

The queen had already put Maurel back to bed by the time Meg and her father had finally gotten back upstairs last night. She had thought her parents would have explained things to her this morning, but maybe they hadn't. Or maybe Maurel just needed to hear it again. From Meg. She probably suspected by now that grownups didn't always tell her the full truth about everything.

"Yes," Meg said seriously. "That's exactly what happened. But we fixed that. Calen and Mage Serek did some magic to protect us from the nightmares. So it won't happen again, okay?"

Maurel nodded. "Okay."

They sat quietly for a bit, Maurel twisting pieces of grass into a chain, Meg just sitting and thinking. After a while Meg asked, "Do you wish I didn't have Jakl?"

Maurel didn't answer right away. "No," she said finally. "I like him. And I know you like him. But . . ."

"But what?"

Maurel looked up from her grass twisting. "But

you're different now. Sometimes I wish you could have stayed the same."

Meg reached over and pulled Maurel close to her, wrapping an arm around her shoulders and squeezing. "Sometimes I wish that, too," she whispered.

They both got quiet again after that. Meg leaned back and closed her eyes. She wondered what Calen was doing, and if he was still mad at her. Then she decided she didn't want to think about that. She would just sit here in the sun with her dragon and her sister and not think about anything unpleasant for a little while.

"Meg?"

"Hmm?"

"If I found a dragon, would it make me different, too?"

"Probably," Meg said, her eyes still closed. The sun was warm and soothing on her face. "But I thought you wanted to have a link with Lyrimon."

"That's just pretend," Maurel said, a little reproachfully. "I want to have a link for real. Plus Lyrimon can't fly."

"That's true," Meg agreed. "Also, he is very grouchy."

"If I had my own dragon," Maurel went on, "he could be friends with Jakl, and we could all go flying together."

"That sounds nice," Meg said. "Jakl would probably like to have a friend."

"Maybe there's still other baby dragons in the woods somewhere. Jakl's probably not the *only* one."

"Maybe. But I wouldn't get your hopes up, sweetie. Dragons are very rare these days, remember?"

"But rare doesn't mean just *one*," Maurel said. "Jakl must have had a mommy and daddy, right? Maybe he had brothers and sisters, too."

Jakl was dozing, but Meg felt him stir sleepily at the idea of other dragons. Meg had never really wondered before if he might be lonely for others of his kind. It must be strange for him, to be all alone like he was. He had Meg, of course, but that wasn't the same.

She tried to picture it: Jakl with other dragons around him, flying, playing — would they curl up to sleep together like giant, scaly kittens? The thought made her smile. It also made her feel a little . . . jealous? Jakl sent something warm and reassuring and slightly amused at her through the link. Which made her smile again.

She still wondered, though. She had human companionship in addition to her connection with Jakl. Those relationships were very important to her. Did Jakl wish for the companionship of other dragons as well?

CHAPTER
TWENTY-ONE

MEG DIDN'T SEE CALEN FOR THE rest of the day. That wasn't really so unusual — it wasn't as if they spent every moment together, after all — but the argument they'd had made his absence feel conspicuous and significant.

Her thoughts of dragons in the paddock had dissolved into an unplanned but not entirely unwelcome nap. Maurel had wandered off by the time Meg had awakened, and Meg had gone back inside and tried to keep herself busy and distracted. But she still had spent most of the afternoon and evening wishing Calen would appear.

She refused to go seek him out herself, though. He was the one who had stormed off. It was up to him to come back to continue the conversation.

But he didn't, and she woke up the next morning feeling both grumpy and sad.

At breakfast, her parents mentioned that Serek had some vistors: other mages who had come to discuss important events at the Magistratum. Apparently they had arrived a couple of nights ago. Serek had come to see the king and queen yesterday evening to let them know and to alert them that more mages might be on the way. Maybe that's what Calen had been coming to tell her about the day before. Before he'd gotten so angry about that misunderstanding with Wilem.

Meg seized upon this new information as a good excuse — a good *reason* — to go talk to Calen. If he wanted to bring up their argument, that would be his choice. Her only intention was to find out about Serek's visitors. That was it.

She still didn't understand why Calen had gotten so angry in the first place. She knew he didn't trust Wilem, but she thought it was the hand holding — the hand *touching* — in particular that had set him off, not just the fact that she was considering Wilem's offer to help them fight his mother. And that didn't make any sense at all.

Calen was right about one thing, though. Meg was definitely finding it harder to hate Wilem.

She *wanted* to, but somehow she didn't feel the hate burning inside her as she once had. She knew he could be lying to her, knew he could still be pretending . . . but she couldn't believe that whole scene on the rooftop, when

Sen Eva's secrets had come spilling out and Wilem had been so shocked, so horrified. . . . Meg couldn't believe that had all truly been just an act.

But if she didn't hate him, that left . . . what? She couldn't *like* him. It wasn't as though they could be friends. So if they weren't enemies, and they couldn't be friends . . . she didn't know what they were. She didn't want them to be anything! But he was here, possibly for a long time to come. And she couldn't just ignore him entirely, as much as she might want to.

Wilem had truly seemed sincere about wanting to help. But she knew she couldn't really trust him.

She just wished he didn't sometimes make her feel as though she could.

As Meg approached the mages' chambers, she could hear voices coming from inside. Loud voices, and many of them.

She knocked, and after a moment, Calen opened the door.

They looked at each other, and Meg watched a series of emotions flash across Calen's face: surprise, relief, anger . . . shame? She wondered what her own face looked like. The silence began to feel uncomfortable.

"I came to find out about the mages," Meg said. "To

ask you about them. My parents told me this morning that they were here."

"Oh. Okay."

"Was that—was that what you came to tell me about yesterday?"

"Oh, uh . . ." He hesitated, then went on, "Yeah. That's all. It wasn't really that important. I knew you'd hear about them before long anyway."

They fell silent again. Meg hated how awkward this felt. She just wanted things to be back to normal.

"So . . . what's going on?" she asked when it seemed clear he wasn't going to say anything else without prompting. "Why are they here?"

She peered past Calen into the room beyond. There were at least five strangers that she could see, all mages with various degrees of marking across their faces. They appeared to be having a fairly heated discussion with Serek and Anders.

Calen glanced over his shoulder and then slipped out into the hallway, closing the door behind him. None of the men seemed to notice.

"They came two nights ago," he said, leading her a little way down the hall so that the voices fell to muffled background noise behind them. "They've been arguing ever since."

Meg couldn't help it. She said, "Lots of that going around lately."

Calen crossed his arms and leaned against the wall, looking at her. "Yeah," he said finally. "I guess so."

"Why—" Meg started after a moment, at the same time that Calen said, "I didn't—"

They both stopped. Waited.

"Go ahead," Meg said.

"I'm sorry I got so angry," Calen said. "I didn't mean to say those things to you. I just—I just want you to be careful. You're not—you're not always very careful, you know?"

Meg pursed her lips in annoyance, but he wasn't really wrong, was he? "I suppose that's fair," she said. "But it really wasn't what you thought, Calen. He took my hand, and for a second I was too startled to do anything, and that's when you came in and saw . . . what you thought you saw."

Calen looked like he was mulling over several responses. Finally he said, "But you can see, can't you, that he's trying to win back your trust? That he's trying to—to get close to you again? Surely he could have told you he wanted to help us against Sen Eva without having to touch you."

"Yes," she said. "You're right, of course." She almost

added that he was right about her not really hating Wilem anymore, too. But somehow that seemed like a bad idea, if she wanted them to get past this argument.

"I'll be careful, Calen," she said instead. "I promise." He nodded, but he didn't quite look at her. What did he want her to say? "I'm not — I'm not going to let him get close to me again."

He looked up at that, but his eyes met hers for only a moment before sliding away. "Okay," he said.

They stood there for a minute more, leaning against their opposite walls. The silence felt different this time, Meg thought. Less . . . hostile. But she still didn't like it.

"So," she said, trying to make her voice as normal as possible, "the mages?"

"Right," Calen said, nodding and looking at her again. He took a breath. "Things have, um, apparently gone a little crazy at the Magistratum since we left."

They went over to a little padded bench that sat tucked in a nook nearby. There was a tapestry across from it, showing some kind of battle scene. Meg looked at Calen instead.

He explained about the mages' unexpected arrival and their alarming news. "The group that's here now, they came here to join with Serek. They said others are on the way, too. They want him to organize a group of mages who are willing to go after Sen Eva and Mage Krelig right now."

"But that's wonderful!" Meg didn't understand what the problem was. "Calen, I'm sure if enough mages went after her together, they would have no trouble overcoming her no matter how powerful she's become. Gods, that's exactly what we need! I thought the Magistratum would have gone after her right away, back when Serek first explained what was happening. I never understood why they weren't doing anything."

"It's not that simple, Meg. If we do this, go after Sen Eva as a separate group, without the support of the council . . . it would be a very serious thing. The Magistratum was formed for a reason — to keep mages from running off and doing whatever they wanted all the time, from using their magic to achieve their own personal ends. If we break off from them . . . it could have very dangerous consequences. Maybe even worse than what's happening now with Sen Eva."

Meg was startled to realize that Calen actually looked a little frightened.

"It could be the end of the Magistratum, Meg. If mages start deciding to take matters into their own hands . . . we won't be the only group to do so. If we start this, other groups will form, too. Groups with different ideas of what to do. Groups that might decide that we need to be stopped before we do the wrong thing."

Meg stared at him. "Are you saying there could be a war among the mages?"

"Yes. Or at least, that seems to be what Serek is afraid of, and he knows a whole lot more about it than I do. If that happened . . . it would be terrible, Meg." He got up, too agitated to sit still. "Do you know about the time from before the Magistratum was formed? It was like that all the time. Mages fighting each other, and everyone was afraid of them. . . . Whole kingdoms were destroyed! It would be really, really bad for that to start happening again."

"What do you think Serek is going to do?" Meg asked.

"I don't know. I think he's going to try to wait, to petition the council to make a decision. If the council masters would just decide something, maybe all the infighting would just stop."

"If he does end up leading this group, what do you think they'll do?"

"I have no idea." He sounded suddenly bitter.

"What do you mean?"

He scowled and dropped back onto the bench, pushing his fist into the soft cushion beneath them. "It's because of those signs I told you about — the ones that say I'm going to be involved with Mage Krelig in some way. Serek has decided that the less I know about their plans to fight him, the better. He won't tell me anything now."

"But — but that's crazy! Do they really think you would help him? He's terrible! Worse than Sen Eva!"

"Exactly. But apparently I'm just too great a risk. So I'm supposed to sit around being useless." He looked at her, and for a moment, it seemed as though he were about to say something else, but he only shook his head.

The sound of running feet in the hallway made them both look up. It was Nan Vera, looking harried.

"What's wrong, Nan Vera?" Meg asked.

"It's Maurel, of course," the older woman replied wearily. "She was supposed to come meet me before lunchtime and never showed up. I've given up on *you* appearing regularly at meals," she said with a withering, squinty-eyed glance, "but Maurel has always been good about mealtimes, even when she's off causing gods-know-what mischief before and after."

"I'm sure she just lost track of the time," Meg said. Although . . . it was true that Maurel tended to time her misbehavior not to conflict with meals. "I can help you look for her, if you like."

"I'll help, too," Calen said. "Serek's not going to miss me while he's still arguing with the other mages."

"Thank you both," Nan Vera said. "I'm sure you're right, that she's only forgotten the time, but . . . well, with everything that's been happening lately, I'll just feel better when we know where she is."

"Of course," Meg said. She stood up, and Calen did, too. "Did you check outside yet? We can start there. She may have gone back to visit Jakl." But then Meg stopped, a terrible thought beginning to take shape.

Nan Vera was nodding. "Good. I'll keep looking inside. I've been alerting all the guards I pass as well. They know to bring her directly to me if they find her." She smiled a little grimly. "No matter what excuse she gives. You know how she is about talking her way out of getting in trouble."

"Nan Vera," Meg said. The older woman looked at her, and her smile faded at whatever she saw in Meg's face. Meg swallowed and said, "I think she may have gone into the forest."

Nan Vera stared at her. So did Calen. "Why would she do that?" he asked.

"She was talking . . . Yesterday, she was asking questions about Jakl, about whether there could be other dragons out there, waiting to be found. I thought — I thought she was just daydreaming — you know, pretending she was going to have a dragon, too, and that he and Jakl would be friends. . . ." She closed her eyes for a long moment. "I wasn't really paying close attention. I didn't . . . I should have remembered who I was dealing with. Oh, gods."

"I'll go tell your parents," Nan Vera whispered. She turned and hurried away.

"Meg," Calen said, "you don't know that's what happened. She could be anywhere. You know how Maurel likes to hide and play games."

"I know," Meg said. "But she never misses lunch, Calen. I know that sounds silly, but it's true. Not ever. What if she went out there looking for dragons and something happened to her? What if —?"

She thought of Lourin's soldiers, of wild animals, of wandering thieves and bandits.

She thought of Sen Eva. And she thought of the slaahr.

343

"Even if she did go outside the castle grounds," Calen said, speaking slowly and calmly, "she probably just got lost in the woods or something. The guards will bring her back. She'll hear them calling and come right back to us. You'll see."

But by evening, they still hadn't found her.

CHAPTER
TWENTY-TWO

THEY WERE ALL IN ONE OF the king and queen's
fancy meeting rooms: Calen, Meg, the king and
queen, Nan Vera, Serek, and Anders. Even Meg's littlest
sister Mattie was there, cradled carefully in the queen's
arms. Calen half wondered why Serek hadn't invited
those other mages to come, too, but he guessed this was
private Trelian business, not really anything to do with
the Magistratum. Maurel *could* still just be off exploring somewhere. She could be hiding to get attention, or
she could have lost track of the time, or maybe she really
did get lost somewhere off the castle grounds — which
of course couldn't be very fun for her, but surely they'd
be able to find her and bring her back safely if that were
the case.

Calen was more worried that something else had
happened. Something less easily made right again.

He looked at Meg and knew she was thinking the
same thing.

There was no real reason to think that Sen Eva had
anything to do with Maurel's disappearance. Except

that whenever something bad happened lately, Sen Eva seemed to be behind it somehow.

"The guards are walking a search pattern around the castle grounds and the surrounding forest," the king was saying, "but so far they haven't found anything, not even a sign that she's passed through a certain area. Nan Vera, I know you've checked all her usual hiding spots, and Meg and Calen have searched likely places as well. We've got the entire castle staff on alert, but somehow I doubt she's still inside the castle. I am open to suggestions for other ways to look for her."

Calen raised his hand tentatively. "Did anyone check — there's that secret passage where they found that other queen that time. . . ."

"Yes," King Tormon said. "We looked there, and I've got guards checking all the other secret passages we know about. It wouldn't surprise me if Maurel knows about a few that we don't, but I have to believe that she would not stay away this long by her own choice."

"Do we think it could be Sen Eva?" Meg asked. She looked back and forth between her father and Mage Serek. "Now that she can't get at us through the dreams, maybe she decided to try a different way?"

"I do think it's a possibility," Serek answered. "We know she is not a woman who gives up easily."

The queen looked horrified. "Surely she can't just enter the castle or the grounds without us knowing? I realize she is powerful, but have we no defenses at all against such a thing?"

"I wish I could reassure you, Your Majesty," Serek said apologetically, "but I'm afraid she is capable of much that is beyond our own abilities. Perhaps she lured Maurel off the grounds somehow. Or perhaps she found a way inside. Now that we know she can change her appearance, who is to say she did not merely walk right past the guards at the gate in the guise of someone they knew?"

"Or just influenced them to let her in, the way she influenced King Gerald," Calen added.

Everyone was starting to look a little sick as the implications began to sink in.

"I am ashamed to say we did not think to ward the entrances in some way," Serek said. "We have done so now, of course, and will know if any mages, marked or not, attempt to enter the castle grounds. But obviously we are a little, ah, late on that front. I am deeply sorry. I never suspected Sen Eva would attempt to physically return here."

"I still think Maurel went out on her own," Meg said. "I told you: I think she went out to find her own dragon. Once she was outside, Sen Eva wouldn't have had any trouble just — just grabbing her. . . ." She looked like she was going to cry.

"But why —?" The king was making an obvious effort to keep the conversation moving forward. "Why would she want to take Maurel? I don't see how this would serve her ends unless she planned to blame it on Lourin to interfere with the peace negotiations."

"You are sure that it is not Lourin?" Nan Vera asked. "There are those soldiers they sent; maybe they had a different mission from the one you were told about."

The king shook his head. "I have to believe that King Gerald is dealing with us in good faith. He would have no reason to abduct our daughter. He would know that such an act would only provoke hostilities, and I truly believe he does not want to be at war."

"But with Sen Eva whispering in his ear —" the queen began.

"We've discussed that, Merilyn, and he seems to be no longer under her influence."

"But we can't *know* —"

"There may be a way I can help," Serek broke in. "If you have something of Maurel's I can use, we can try a locator spell. They're not foolproof by any means, and the results can sometimes be too muddled to be of practical use, but I'd say we've reached the point where it's worth trying, at least."

"Yes," the queen said at once. "Please, anything you can try would be most welcome, Mage Serek."

The king nodded agreement, and Nan Vera ran out to fetch something from Maurel's rooms. "Something small!" Serek called after her.

Anders leaned over toward Serek. "Do you want me to assist on this?" he asked.

"Actually," Serek said, "I'm going to have Calen assist. He's got a talent for divination, and we might as well use every advantage we can."

Anders raised his eyebrows. He didn't look insulted or anything, just surprised. "I see," he said. "I'll look forward to seeing this, I think."

"But—" Calen began.

Serek spoke over him. "Run back to my study and grab the small pouch out of the top right drawer of my desk."

Calen darted out the door. If Serek didn't think this counted as continuing Calen's lessons, Calen was not going to argue. He supposed this was another case where the benefits outweighed the risks. And anyway, this probably counted as an emergency.

By the time Calen returned to the meeting room,

Nan Vera was back and Serek was seated at one side of a small table in the center of the room. A map of the kingdom was unrolled on the table's surface. He gestured for Calen to sit down across from him. Calen handed him the pouch, and Serek opened it and withdrew a piece of string and a small, dark stone shaped almost like a flat arrow.

Nan Vera handed Serek the object she'd brought back from Maurel's rooms: a small stuffed toy that looked like some kind of lizard with lots of teeth. Calen looked up at Nan Vera, who seemed a little embarrassed. "It's her favorite. She sleeps with it on her pillow every night."

"It's just fine," Serek assured her. He tied the string around it and then knotted the end of the string around the stone. Then he passed everything to Calen and told him to hold the string by the other end, so that the lizard and stone swung freely at the bottom.

"All right," Serek said in that calm, soft voice he used whenever he was talking Calen through an unfamiliar spell. "Clear your mind, and then I want you to picture Maurel as fully as possible. Give me your free hand first; this will work better if we're in physical contact. I'm going to do the casting, and I want you to simply allow the spell to work through you. Do nothing but focus on Maurel in your mind. Do you understand?"

Calen nodded and placed his free hand on the table, palm up. Serek grasped Calen's hand in his own, and then Calen saw the beginnings of the spell starting to form around them. He quickly closed his eyes and pictured Maurel, her bright smile, her always-slightly-messy brown hair, her lighthearted demeanor and near fearlessness in most situations. As he focused, he began to see things he hadn't even remembered: the dimple on her left cheek when she grinned, the way that one strand of hair tended to fall across her eyes no matter how many pins Nan Vera tried to secure it with.

He felt a sudden overwhelming desire to see her in context, and realized that must be Serek's part of the spell working on him. *Where are you?* he thought, seeking her out with his mind. He could feel the magic energy around him, flowing through Serek's hand into his own, seeming to touch the image in his mind and push through it to where the real girl was, somewhere, somewhere not very close but not really very far away, either. He felt the string begin to move purposefully beneath his fingers, swinging in a widening pattern. He resisted the urge to open his eyes and see what it was doing. His job was to focus on Maurel, to see her, to see where she was, to find her. . . . *where are you, where are you, Maurel, we're going to come for you, we're coming, tell us where you are. . . .*

He could see her! Not just the image he'd created in his mind, but Maurel herself. She'd been crying; she was afraid but not alone; someone was there, someone who frightened her, and he could see trees behind her, and there was a row of tall rocks pointing at the sky and the sound of water rushing, crashing — a waterfall? — and it was getting dark and —

The hand holding the string was suddenly pulled down forcefully, slamming painfully against the table, and he heard a collective gasp from the others in the room.

"Don't move, Calen," Serek said. "But you can open your eyes."

Calen did so. His hand was flat against the map, and Serek was taking careful note of where the stone had fallen underneath his hand.

"Is that where she is?" Calen asked. "It worked, didn't it?"

"Did it feel like it was working?" Serek asked.

"Oh, yes," Calen breathed. "I could see her."

"You could?" Meg asked at the same time that her mother rushed forward and asked, "Is she all right? Could you see if she was all right?"

"Yes," Calen said, still feeling a little dreamy from the

vision. "She was scared, but all right. I couldn't see who was with her, but she definitely wasn't alone. She'd— she'd been crying, I think. And— oh! There were these rocks, a row of tall, narrow rocks pointing up at the sky, and I could hear rushing water nearby. . . ."

"That's Bellman's Pass," King Tormon said. "It must be. That's more than a day's fast ride from here. How could she . . . ?"

"That points to Sen Eva's involvement more than anything else, I'm afraid," Serek said, sounding troubled. "All right, Calen, you can move your hand now. I've got the map marked, although it sounds like we know where to look in any case."

"We'll send a full company," the king said. "Soldiers, not House Guard. If Sen Eva's truly taken her—"

"Serek." Anders spoke suddenly from where he'd been leaning against the wall to one side of them. His voice sounded strange. He was standing bolt upright now, awkwardly, one hand pressed to the wall as if for support. He was staring at some fixed point in the air before him.

Serek turned to look at Anders and then froze in his seat. "Quiet," he said softly. "Nobody move— nobody speak."

"Choose carefully," Anders said in that same, strange

voice. "Mage Krelig stands on the brink of return. All depends on what is decided now. Soldiers will not be enough."

"Me," Meg said. "Of course, I'm going."

"You cannot," her father said. "Lourin."

"You're not serious," Meg turned on him. "You're going to let —"

"What part of 'Quiet. Nobody move — nobody speak' did you not understand?" Serek snapped at them in a low voice. "Be silent!" The king frowned at him, and Serek added hastily, "Uh, Your Majesty. Your Highness. Please."

Anders spoke again: "Choose carefully, or Maurel will not return."

The queen gave a choked sob at this, and Meg looked stricken.

Anders blinked suddenly and seemed to come back to himself again.

There was an uneasy silence.

"What just happened?" Meg asked.

"Anders has visions," Calen said.

"Visions? You mean he sees things that are going to happen?"

Calen suddenly remembered that it was a secret. "Oh. Oh, I'm sorry, Mage Anders. I forgot I wasn't supposed to . . ."

"It's all right, Calen," Anders said, lowering himself into a chair. "Everyone here just saw it happen anyway."

"But what did it mean?" Meg asked.

"I have to admit, that was not one of your more helpful sightings," Serek said. "Choose wisely? What would the wise choice be in this situation?"

"Not soldiers alone," Anders said. "Maybe not soldiers at all. Soldiers are not going to bring back the little princess. I think . . . I think I saw that boy. What's-his-name. The good-looking one with the nightmares. Willard."

"*Wilem?*" Calen asked.

"Ah," said the king. "Maybe she wants to trade hostages."

"Not just him, though," Anders said.

"Not him at all!" Calen said. Everyone turned to look at him. "Have you all forgotten who he is? We can't let him go!"

"We can if Sen Eva is willing to trade Maurel for him," said the queen.

"Merilyn," the king said. He sounded as though he were going to say more to her, but didn't. Instead he turned back to Serek. "But if that's the case, why didn't she let us know she'd taken Maurel? If she wanted to arrange for a trade, she should have contacted us."

"Maybe she knew we'd figure it out," Serek said.

"Or maybe she meant to let us worry in ignorance for as long as possible before she contacted us," said the queen.

"Who else did you see?" Meg pressed Anders. "Did you see me?"

"Sorry," Anders said. "I just know that boy has to be among those who go after the little princess. And it matters a great deal who else goes, but I can't say who the choices should be." He looked at Serek. "It was an odd vision. Usually they are clear, showing two outcomes of a choice. This was . . . muddy. As though too many elements are still undetermined."

"But wait!" Calen said. "That's just crazy! We can't send Wilem. That's probably the worst idea I have ever, ever heard! Uh, no offense, Mage Anders," he added.

"None taken!" Anders said cheerfully. "I agree — it sounds like a terrible idea. But it's the right one, all the same."

"What about those other mages, the ones who came to see you?" asked the king. "Could they help with this?"

"Calen," Serek said suddenly. "You need to leave."

"What? Why?"

"You know why."

356

King Tormon looked back and forth between them. "What's this about?"

Calen crossed his arms and waited for Serek to answer.

"There have been portents," Serek said, "that indicate the possibility that Calen could become involved with Mage Krelig somehow. It seems best to us to keep him, ah, ignorant of the details of our plans in that area. If we believe Sen Eva has taken Maurel, which is certainly how it seems, then the situation is too close to Mage Krelig for Calen to participate further."

Calen felt everyone's eyes on him. He felt like a criminal.

"It's nonsense," Meg said. "Anyone who knows Calen can see that."

"Thank you, Meg," he said.

Serek sighed. "I have complete faith in Calen's loyalty," he said. "But we cannot take risks —"

"Yeah, yeah," Calen said, getting up from his chair. "I'm going." He walked out without looking back.

This was so stupid. Serek knew he could help. He knew! Hadn't he *just* had Calen assist with the location spell? And he said he didn't doubt Calen's loyalty. But those were clearly just empty words, because if he really trusted Calen, he wouldn't have sent him away.

The castle halls were dark and empty. It was getting late, and Calen knew should probably just go to bed, but he was too worked up to think about sleep. He needed to do something — he couldn't bear just sitting around, not even knowing what was being decided.

He stopped suddenly, an idea taking root in his brain.

Maybe he didn't have to just sit around. Maybe this was the opportunity he'd been waiting for. While the rest of them sat around talking and wondering who to send after Maurel, he would just go. He would go on his own and rescue her himself. And then Serek would see that he was firmly on Trelian's side.

He started walking again, considering. He could see the location from the map in his mind. It was more than a day's fast ride, and he wasn't all that fast a rider. He needed some other way to get there. He wished Serek and Anders hadn't told him all that scary stuff about transporting. If he didn't know how dangerous it was, maybe he wouldn't be afraid to try it.

Of course, that might have left him half-embedded in something by accident.

If only there was a way to get around that problem. Why did it happen? It happened because people couldn't see what was already in the spot they were transporting to. But if you could see where you going, and if you could

358

be reasonably sure no one would walk into your path in the instant you traveled there . . .

He went back to his room and sat on his bed. Serek had said not to experiment. And he'd never really shown Calen how to transport something. Calen had seen him do it once, though, when he'd moved Rorgson's skull in his study. And Calen had done it himself that one time by accident, but he didn't want to repeat that experience. There was also that issue of transporting people being forbidden by the Magistratum. But . . . Serek had said something about emergencies, and getting permission after the fact. Surely this counted as an emergency. Maurel's life was in danger! And if he brought her back safely, would they really be able to punish him for it?

He considered the plant guide on his bedside table. He knew that transporting used purple energy, which was about motion and change. He concentrated on the book and began to surround it with waves of pure violet, thinking about moving it just a few inches over on the table. He tried actually pushing at it with the magic, but that wasn't right. He tried lifting, tried coaxing the magic to take the book apart and put it back together. (He was kind of relieved when that didn't work.) He tried various approaches, forcing himself to keep going and not get discouraged or upset. He was like steel. Like stone.

359

Focused on his task. It didn't matter how long it took, or what else was going on elsewhere in the castle. He would figure this out eventually. He knew he could.

And finally, he did. It was a matter of surrounding the book with energy, clearly envisioning it in the new location, and then a forceful kind of *willing* it to be *there* instead of where it currently existed. The book silently disappeared from one side of the table and instantly reappeared on the other.

Calen reached over and picked it up. It seemed all right. The pages were still in the right order, and the cover hadn't melted or turned inside out or anything else terrifying. It was the same book, just shifted in space. Perfectly fine.

He practiced for a while with the book, moving it to various locations around his room. He was tempted to try moving it somewhere else, like to Serek's desk drawer, but he refrained. He was only going to do this spell when he could see the target destination. No exceptions. He thought he'd be able to make it serve his purposes just fine.

It was a couple of hours later when he first attempted to move himself.

CHAPTER
TWENTY-THREE

M EG FLEW THROUGH THE HALLS, RIDING her fury like a maddened horse. At least she knew it was her own anger this time — not dream-tainted — and perfectly justified. She had left her parents and the mages arguing about what that "choosing wisely" nonsense meant, and she couldn't listen to one more second of it. She didn't care what it meant. They should let her go. She thought again, for the hundredth time in the last few minutes, about just leaving. About climbing up on her dragon and flying off to save her sister. But then Lourin would declare war, and there would be no question that it was entirely her fault. And her parents would never forgive her. Well, maybe they'd forgive her when she returned with Maurel. But maybe not even then.

She felt Jakl responding to her anger and cursed in frustration. She couldn't let him get upset. If he thought she was in trouble, he might try to come to her, and even just flying across the castle grounds could be enough to set off Lourin.

Easy, Jakl, she thought at him. *It's okay. I'm okay. It's just — just more stupid human stuff. I'm going to come see you very soon — I promise.*

She felt his concern ease off a bit, although not entirely, since of course he could still feel that she wasn't really okay. And then she felt him say — feel — think? — very clearly: *stupid human stuff.*

Meg stopped abruptly in the middle of the hall.

It hadn't been actual words. Not exactly. But it had been some kind of deliberately sent *feeling* of those words. As if Jakl had translated them into a kind of emotion and sent them back at her.

She turned at once and headed out to his paddock.

Jakl was lying in his field in the moonlight, mostly on his back, with his neck twisted around so that his head was right side up as he watched her approach.

"What in the light of the Lady was *that?*" she asked him. She climbed over the fence and grabbed his head and looked into his right eye. "You're — you're talking now?"

But he wasn't; she knew that. It was something else. Not talking. But still . . . communicating. More clearly than ever before.

She sat, and he rested his head against her.

"Wow. All right. That's — that's new, then. Can you say — think — whatever that is . . . Can you do it again?"

He just cocked his eye up at her. She wasn't even sure he exactly understood what she was asking. He always seemed to understand her in general, although she'd assumed he was mostly picking up the feelings behind her words, not really listening to the words themselves. So maybe he was just associating certain feelings with the words she spoke while feeling them . . . ? Trying to explain it to herself was starting to give her a headache.

"I guess it doesn't matter," she told him, stroking his neck. "You just startled me — that's all. I guess we're getting to know each other better and better all the time, hmm?"

He sent a general feeling of affirmation at that.

In the morning, when Meg went down to breakfast, she was determined to be calm and clearheaded. Her parents weren't there. Nan Vera was feeding Mattie and looking very sad.

Meg picked up her spoon. "They're going to get her back, Nan Vera." She made herself take a bite of porridge, as though that would prove that things were normal, that everything was going to be all right.

"Oh, of course. Of course they will. I know." Nan Vera wiped Mattie's chin with a corner of a napkin. "I just hate thinking about how scared she must be, stolen away by that horrible woman. . . ."

"I know," Meg said softly.

"But those mages will figure out something," Nan Vera said with determined confidence. "They know all kinds of things. We'll have our little troublemaker back before you know it."

Meg made herself finish eating, even though her appetite was nonexistent. Then she went off to find her parents. Mage Serek and Mage Anders were just walking out of the study when she arrived. They gave her distracted nods of greeting and hurried on their way. Meg went inside to join the king and queen.

"Good morning," she said, demonstrating her calm clearheadedness. She sat down in one of the empty chairs. "I apologize for my behavior last night. I should not have stormed out the way I did. I was . . . upset. Obviously. But I know that my behavior was inappropriate."

"It's all right, Meg," her father said. "Of course you're upset. We all are."

Her mother came over and sat beside her. "We know you're just worried about your sister."

Meg was almost disappointed to be let off the hook

so easily. Couldn't they see how sensible and reasonable she was being now? But she supposed it was better if they forgave her bad behavior in the first place. "Have you worked out a plan to go after Maurel?" she asked.

"Yes," her father said. "Serek is going to escort Wilem. We'll send a few soldiers with him, just in case they can be of any use. They're leaving as soon as possible."

"Good," Meg said. "I'm glad Serek is going. Are they bringing any of those other mages along with them?"

"No. Serek said this was Trelian business, not Magistratum business. I'm not sure I agree, since if Sen Eva is involved, then apparently this Mage Krelig is also involved somehow . . . but you know how Serek can be. I have to trust that if he thought those other mages were truly needed, he wouldn't leave them behind."

"It still doesn't make sense to me," the queen said. "If they all went, wouldn't they be able to overpower Sen Eva without any trouble?"

The king spread his hands. "You know we cannot force him. He is sworn to us, but to the mage's order above all. If he thinks bringing the other mages would violate some law of the Magistratum . . ."

The queen waved her hand as if to brush this argument aside. "I don't care about the law of the Magistratum. I care about getting our daughter back."

"I know," the king said. "I know, Merilyn."

"He's not even bringing Anders?" Meg asked.

"Anders said he definitely did not see himself going in his vision. He seems to feel very strongly that he should stay behind."

"I guess if we're going to trust his visions, we can't really argue with that," Meg said. "Have you told Wilem about any of this yet?"

"We were just about to," said her father. "If he refuses . . . well, him at least we can force to go along."

"I don't think you'll need to do that," Meg said. "He wants to prove that he's not on Sen Eva's side. This will give him a chance to do so." She took a breath, steeling herself, then added, "I can go talk to him if you like."

"Thank you, Meg," the king said. "That would be very helpful. Once you've explained the plan, have the guards bring him down to the courtyard as soon as he can be made ready."

"Be careful," her mother said.

Meg gave her mother what she hoped was a reassuring smile. Then she left and headed for Wilem's chambers. This was good. If she couldn't rescue Maurel as the dragon-girl, then she would help as much as she could as the princess-heir.

Wilem seemed surprised — but not displeased — to see her again so soon.

"I have some things to tell you," she said, not wasting any time. "Do you still want to help us stop your mother from carrying out her plans?"

"Yes," he said at once.

"Good," she said. "Because Serek is taking you to her today."

He stared at her. "What?"

She sat down in the chair across from him and explained about Maurel's disappearance and Anders's vision.

"But —" he looked at her helplessly. "I don't *want* to go back to her. If they're planning to trade me for your sister . . ." He broke off suddenly. "No. That's just as it should be. If I can help by buying back your sister's life with my own, I'll be glad to. And maybe I can do something to stop my mother's plans once I'm with her."

"Thank you, Wilem." She felt like she should say something else, but she couldn't think of anything. She wasn't sure if she should believe him, even now. He seemed sincere, but he had fooled her before, hadn't he? Could this *all* be part of a plan to reunite him with his mother? There was no way to know. And it didn't matter.

They had no choice; they had to do whatever it took to get Maurel back.

Meg stood up. "They want you down in the courtyard as soon as possible. I don't know what you need to bring with you — anything you'll need for camping out overnight, I suppose."

He got up, too, and stood facing her. "Thank you. For this chance. I want . . . I had hoped that in time you would be able to believe that I am no longer your enemy. I know I haven't done enough to prove that to you yet, but . . . I hope that day will come."

Meg didn't know what to say. She should tell him to forget it, that she would never trust him again. She should tell him that she didn't care what happened to him. She should say that he *was* her enemy, and he always would be, and there was nothing he could ever do to change that.

But she didn't say any of those things. Instead she found herself reaching forward to touch his hand for just a second. "May the Bright Lady shine down upon you," she whispered. Then she turned and walked quickly out of the room before he could say or do anything in response.

They left within the hour. Meg watched them ride off: Serek with Wilem's horse tethered to his own, the small company of soldiers spreading out to ride ahead and behind. Calen and Anders stood in the courtyard, waving good-bye. Well, Anders was waving; Calen was just standing there with his arms crossed. Still angry about being excluded, Meg guessed. And who could blame him? It was horrible that his own master suspected him of being a possible danger.

After a moment Calen turned and walked over to her. "How are you doing?" he asked.

"Better than last night," she said. "Still angry about not being able to help, but . . . I do understand, I guess. If we can get Maurel back without starting a war with Lourin, then that's obviously what we should do."

Calen's eyebrows went up. "You sound very resolved. And, uh . . . strangely reasonable."

She smacked him on the arm. "I can be reasonable," she said. "Sometimes, anyway. Once I have a chance to calm down."

"Hmm."

"How about you? The reason they're leaving you behind seems far less rational to me. Are you still really angry?"

"Yeah," Calen said. "But being angry won't solve anything, I guess. I'm sure Serek thinks he's doing the right thing."

She smiled. "You sound strangely reasonable, too."

He smiled back. It was almost a grin, actually. "I've had some time to think things out," he said. "I was really angry last night, but today . . . today I'm feeling a lot better."

"Good. Do you want to come with me to visit Jakl? I'm trying to spend as much time as possible with him to help make up for not being able to let him fly."

"Maybe later," he said. "I've got some things I need to take care of first."

"Oh. I guess you still have chores and things even if Serek suspended your lessons, huh?"

"Uh, yes. Exactly." He looked at her. "I'll see you later, Meg."

"Sure. Bye, Calen!"

But Calen didn't come all that morning or afternoon, and finally she went to look for him to see if he wanted to have dinner together. Things still didn't feel completely back to normal between them, but she thought they were getting better. He hadn't seemed mad at her today, anyway. And there were still so many things she wanted to talk to him about. She had planned to tell him about Jakl's new thought-feelings when he came to meet her, until she'd realized he wasn't coming. She thought he must have gotten caught up in something magic related;

he did tend to get lost in those giant books sometimes, especially now that he was allowed to go into the mage's library without asking permission. And she had no doubt he'd keep up his own reading even if Serek wasn't teaching him anything right now. He wasn't in the library, though. Or in his room, or Serek's study, or the Mage's Garden, or anywhere else she looked. She finally tracked down Anders, who was sitting in a meeting room with the visiting mages, discussing something that they quickly stopped discussing as soon as she came in.

"Nope, haven't seen him," Anders said when she asked. "Probably off sulking somewhere. That's what I would be doing!" He ushered her out, unconcerned.

Meg found herself out in the hall with the door closed firmly behind her. She didn't know why she was worried, exactly. It's not like she always knew where Calen was during the day. Except that he was usually either in the mages' quarters or doing tasks for Serek or spending time with her. And she wanted to talk to him. Maybe he was wandering around as well, and they just kept missing each other. She was sure he'd come find her eventually.

She took the opportunity to go visit Tessel again in the infirmary. This time, when she peeked in, she saw that Tessel was sitting up in bed, looking at a book. Meg

371

almost ducked back out before Tessel could see her but made herself walk in, instead. She owed Tessel a lot. Hiding from her was just cowardly.

"Good evening, Tessel," Meg said quietly. "Are you . . . ? How are you feeling?"

Tessel looked up and Meg almost flinched, anticipating anger, or fear, or maybe even hatred in the older girl's eyes. But she didn't see any of that.

"Princess," Tessel said. "They told me you'd been in to see me."

"Yes." Meg sat on the chair beside the bed. "I'm — I'm so sorry, Tessel. For what happened. You were right to try to talk me out of going, and I should never have let you come along."

"It's all right."

"No!" Meg said. "It's not all right! They tortured you! You could have been killed! And it's my fault; I made you put yourself in danger —"

Tessel shook her head. "But they didn't kill me. And I'll — I'll be fine. I'm not sleeping as much now, and my dispatcher said I might be able to return to my duties in a few more days, if the physicians clear me."

Meg blinked. "Return . . . But after what happened . . ."

"A courier position comes with certain risks," Tessel said. "Not, um, precisely the kind of risks I'd expected in this case, but I'm certainly not going to quit now. I still have my duty. I'm eager to get back to it."

"I feel like you're letting me off too easy," Meg said. "You should hate me for what happened."

"I . . . did, at first. But you thought you were doing the right thing, at least in the beginning. And everyone makes mistakes." She twisted her mouth up a little. "If you weren't sorry, if you hadn't seemed to think better of what you'd done — well, that might have made it harder for me. But in my heart, I can't blame you for doing what you thought was right."

Meg felt tears pricking her eyes for what seemed the hundredth time in the last few days. "Thank you, Tessel. I am sorry. Truly. And if there is ever anything I can do for you . . ."

"I will let you know," Tessel said. "I promise."

Meg rose and turned to leave, letting Tessel get back to her rest. She walked past rows of mostly empty beds but paused on the way out, near a door that went to a private room. She knew three soldiers still lay in that room, still suffering from the poison of the slaarh that Sen Eva had set against them. There had been six at first. Three had died. Serek was still working with the physicians, trying to keep the remaining three from dying before he could devise a cure. The men lay in a permanent sleep,

373

barely able to take in enough food and water to keep them alive. More death and suffering that Sen Eva would pay for one day.

Meg left the infirmary, wishing more than ever that she knew where Calen was. She knew he was probably just busy with something. Surely he would come and find her soon, and he'd be simultaneously apologetic and excited about whatever it was that had kept him away all day.

She went to have dinner with her parents and tried to ignore the gnawing fingers of concern in her belly that wouldn't quite go away.

CHAPTER TWENTY-FOUR

CALEN WAITED UNTIL SEREK AND THE others were well on their way. Then he took a deep breath, cleared his mind, and called up the energy for his invisibility spell. Serek hated when Calen called it that, since true invisibility was supposed to be impossible, but it accomplished the same purpose. Besides, he didn't care very much about what Serek thought right now.

He held the spell in place while walking up the Queen's Road to the spot he'd selected. Luckily, the wards that had been placed around the castle would alert Anders only if mages tried to enter the castle grounds, not leave them. One less thing to worry about. His route was slightly roundabout compared to the one Serek's group had taken, but Calen didn't want there to be the slightest chance of running into them along the way.

When he was far enough away that he couldn't be seen from the castle, he dropped the invisibility spell. He didn't want to try holding that while working the other magic at the same time. Maybe someday, but right now he thought he'd done all the experimenting he cared to do. He was already nervous enough. Part of him still couldn't quite believe he was doing this. But he told that part of him to be quiet. He knew he'd read the cards correctly, and they'd told him he needed to take action. And it wasn't like he didn't have a plan. He would get close enough to see where Sen Eva was holding Maurel, and then he would use his invisibility spell again, and just walk in and grab her. As long as he covered her mouth before she could scream and give him away, he thought he could get her inside his spell area without any trouble. And then they could just walk right out. He would come back along the route that Serek was taking — just walking, this time — so he could show him — them — that he'd already rescued Maurel himself, and they could all just turn around and go home.

But first — first he had to get there. He'd practiced plenty last night, but only very short distances across his room and back. This would be the same principle, though. And he'd only go as far as he could see.

Carefully, he called up the violet energy and wove it around himself. He fixed his eyes on a spot some fifty feet up the road. *Concentrate, stay focused. . . .* He took a breath, cleared his mind, and *willed* himself forward.

The world spun around him for a second, but when

he found his feet again, he saw that he was exactly where he'd intended to be. He gave a little whoop of triumph — it was working! He focused again, on another spot up the road, a little farther this time, as far as he could clearly see. Then he jumped again.

He had to stop and rest. He'd gotten maybe halfway there, in just a few hours, but it was a lot more draining than he'd anticipated. He had plenty of time, though; Serek and the others wouldn't get to Bellman's Pass until tomorrow morning.

He sat against a shady tree and pulled out the little package of dried fruit and meat that he'd tucked away before he left. He felt good. Really good. He knew he should feel a little guilty, and okay, he supposed he did. But that didn't matter very much. He knew he was doing the right thing. And it felt so, well, good to be using magic to accomplish something really significant. Not that the locator spell hadn't been important, or the dream protection they'd done for Wilem and Meg . . . but he'd only been assisting on those spells, really. What he was doing now was entirely his own. He'd thought it up himself, and it was working, and he was going to save Maurel and do something that would really show Serek how much he had underestimated his apprentice. He couldn't wait to see the surprise and grudging respect in his master's eyes.

He rested until he felt ready to go again. Then he gathered his magic, fixed on his location, and jumped.

He almost came upon the pass before he realized it.

It was dusk. He completed a jump to a spot along the road and suddenly heard voices. In an instant he'd called up his invisibility spell. Then he looked carefully around.

He couldn't see anything from where he was, but there was a bend in the road ahead, and the voices were coming from just beyond it. He crept forward. As soon as he rounded the bend, he saw the pointed rocks of Bellman's Pass before him. He could hear the rushing of water somewhere a little farther off.

For a moment he couldn't seem to catch his breath. He'd been so elated with the success of his spell that he hadn't let himself think about the fact that he'd be facing Sen Eva. *But you're not facing her, not really*, he reminded himself. *She won't even know you're there, until it's too late.*

He made himself continue stepping softly toward the rocks. He still had to be careful not to make any noise; the spell only masked sight, not sound. He wondered suddenly if he could come up with some variation that could hide any noise he made, too. Why hadn't he ever thought of that before? That would . . . he shook his head. *Focus!* He could think about applications of magic later. If there was a later. *Stop that.* This was no time to let nerves overtake him. He had a job to do here, and he was going to do it.

With a few more steps, he was able to see what he needed to. His confidence slipped another few notches.

Sen Eva was there, as expected. She was standing, facing partly away from him, and still looked like that stranger they'd seen in Lourin, but there was no question in his mind now that it was her. He could see Maurel, too; she was sitting on the ground, her hands bound behind her. She wasn't crying now, although she still looked miserable. Calen couldn't blame her. She was surrounded by more men than he could count, rough-looking men who must be working for Sen Eva. They didn't seem to be soldiers, exactly, but they were all dressed in black and had the look of people waiting around for someone to tell them what to do.

And beyond them, through the gaps in another row of those tall, pointed rocks, he could see black shapes moving. Enormous black shapes. He could see only glimpses of them, but he knew what they were. Slaarh. Those horrible oily-black monsters that Sen Eva had somehow called up from somewhere to do her bidding. Gods, but he hated those things.

Well, with any luck they would just stay there on the far side of the rocks, and he wouldn't have to worry about them. He had enough to worry about as it was. He would somehow have to maneuver through those ranks of men in order to get close to Maurel — and then get back through them again, somehow, without accidently touching any of them, since that would instantly give him away. He wasn't untouchable any more than he was unhearable, unfortunately.

Oh — *wait*. He didn't have to maneuver anywhere. He could jump there. It wasn't far. He could see it clearly. There was a space right beside Maurel that he could fix his eyes on.

Except if she moved, or if any of the nearby men chose that moment to take a step or two to the side, they'd be in his path. He could end up . . . he didn't even want to think about it. He certainly didn't want to risk *doing* it. He stood there, frozen with indecision.

"Welcome, Apprentice Calen," Sen Eva's voice called out suddenly. Her voice was still the same, not changed by whatever process had altered her appearance. "Why don't you come over here and join us?"

Calen's heart lurched. He was certain his spell was

380

still in place. How could she —? Maybe she'd heard a noise and was just guessing. Maybe she was just trying to trick him into revealing himself. He would not let that happen. He took a step backward.

"Please," she said, turning now to look at him. "I am afraid I must insist."

There was a rustling in the trees, and then more of those black-clad men poured out and blocked the road behind him. They didn't seem able to see him; their eyes searched the place where he was standing, passing over him with no recognition. But somehow Sen Eva knew exactly where he was. She was staring right at him.

Maurel had sat up straight, a terrible hopeful expression on her face as she looked wildly around for him. Calen said nothing; he still felt it must be a trick of some kind. How could Sen Eva see him when the men and Maurel clearly could not?

As though reading his mind, she said, "It would be humiliating indeed if I allowed you to fool me with the same spell twice. I can see you quite clearly, standing there on the road. And if I do this —" Calen felt a strange tug in the air around him, and suddenly the magic of his spell dissipated into nothingness —"my men will be able to see you quite clearly as well."

Two of the men on the road now approached. They

381

each grabbed one of his arms and began to propel him toward Sen Eva. Calen struggled, though he knew it was hopeless. Their grips were like iron.

They released him once he was standing before Sen Eva but stayed close, near enough to stop him if he tried to run or anything else. Not that he had any brilliant ideas for what to do, anyway. He was nearly paralyzed with fear. This was not the plan!

The woman looking back at him was a stranger, and yet she wasn't. The expression on her face was all too familiar.

"How did you do it?" he asked finally. "Change your face that way?"

She laughed contemptuously. "There are realms of magic that you and your masters cannot even imagine. I have access to power you will never know, Apprentice." She made the word sound like an insult.

"Calen?" Maurel's small voice was pleading. Sen Eva laughed again.

"Yes, dear. Young Calen is here to rescue you! Sadly, it does not seem to be going very well." She looked at Calen curiously. "And where is the princess, I wonder? I know she would not let you come alone."

Calen felt a rush of relief and struggled not to let it show in his expression. Sen Eva did not know everything.

For a moment, he'd thought she did. If she didn't know everything, there was still a chance they would get out of this. Somehow. There had to be.

"Now," Sen Eva went on, "part of me would like to just kill you right now, but I suspect you may still prove useful in some small way, and so I will refrain. For now. You may have a seat beside your little friend there. If you attempt the slightest bit of magic, I will know. And then I will kill her."

Maurel whimpered at this, and it nearly broke Calen's heart. He sat down beside her and put an arm around her shoulders. "Don't worry, Maurel," he said. "We'll get you home. I promise."

Sen Eva shook her head, smiling.

All this time the men around them had been watching impassively. The ones up on the road had turned back around to face away, perhaps keeping an eye out for Meg or whoever else Sen Eva suspected might be with him. Calen didn't know what to do. He didn't know if there was anything he *could* do. He was afraid Sen Eva wasn't bluffing about being able to tell if he tried doing any magic. He couldn't risk testing her on that, not with Maurel's life at stake. He didn't doubt that Sen Eva would kill her. She had been planning to kill Maerlie, after all, and had tried to kill him and Meg, too.

Near where Sen Eva was standing, there was a small cleared area between two of the tallest pointy rocks. It looked almost like a narrow doorway, and all the weeds and grass had been removed somehow from the space around it. He noticed Sen Eva watching him looking at it, and she looked expectant, as though she were waiting for him to comment. He didn't, just to spite her. Even though he really wanted to know what that was all about.

He supposed he could just wait until Serek and the others arrived. He hoped that their plan, whatever it was, would still work. It would not exactly be the triumphant encounter he'd been imagining, though. His cheeks burned at the thought of Serek's finding him here, needing to be rescued along with Maurel. *No.* He couldn't let that happen. He had to do something.

"All the pieces are not yet where they need to be. . . ." Sen Eva murmured to herself. She looked up at the sky, then back down at him. "Do you think she will come after you right away, or must I do something to draw her attention?"

He supposed she meant Meg. Calen didn't say anything. He just looked back at her with what he hoped came across as brave defiance.

She twisted up her mouth but only said, "Fine. Be stubborn if you wish. I could make you talk, but I believe I'll give it a little while longer to play out on its own. If you interfere too much, you risk changing the forces at work, and I certainly don't want that, not now."

Calen had no idea what she was talking about. He wondered if she'd gone entirely crazy since they had last seen her. She had seemed to be well on her way back then. No sane person would be doing the things she was doing — kidnapping, murder, following the evil orders of a creepy mage who spoke to her in portals from another place and promised her impossible things . . .

If only he could try something without her knowing. He couldn't just sit here! But what if whatever he tried didn't work, and she hurt Maurel? How could he ever face Meg after letting her sister get killed? No. No, he had to wait. For . . . something. He just wished he knew what.

Maurel was still leaning against him. "Don't worry," he told her again. "It's going to be all right."

"Liar," Sen Eva said sweetly. She looked at Maurel. "It's definitely not going to be all right, little girl. People are going to die. Probably your whole entire family. There's going to be war, and chaos, and if you do happen to survive, you'll probably wish you hadn't."

Maurel had started crying again. Now she turned her face against Calen's chest and sobbed. Calen glared at Sen Eva with helpless fury. "What do you want?" The words fell from his mouth before he could stop them. He hadn't meant to say anything, but he didn't understand the point of any of this. What was she waiting for? What was she expecting to happen?

"I want a great number of things," she said coldly, all mocking sweetness gone from her voice. "And I am going to have them this time." She paused, considering. "But it's still too soon."

"Did you — did you send those creatures, the ones that attacked the Magistratum?" Now that he was talking, he couldn't seem to stop.

"Hmm?" she said. "Ah, yes — did you enjoy my little gift? Did they do anything exciting before your friends were able to contain them? We weren't sure what would happen, exactly, only that they would stir up the hornets' nest, help to widen the divide in some way."

"But *how* — I mean, why?"

She smiled again, chillingly. "You do wish you knew how, don't you? Your masters don't teach you anything quite so useful as mine does."

She looked away, back toward the road. "I know your friends are watching somehow. If your failed attempt is not enough to make them take the next step, perhaps . . ." She looked at Maurel, then at one of the men standing guard. "Do something to make the little girl scream for her sister, Erick."

"No!" Calen shouted, and he lunged upward, trying to stand and push Maurel behind him at the same time. He didn't even know what he intended to do. He just knew he could not let Sen Eva hurt Meg's sister. He felt the magic energy gathering within him and wavered, wanting more than anything to strike out but terrified that Sen Eva would just kill him, and then kill Maurel, too. He stood frozen, *again*, unable to act, unable to do anything useful at all, shaking with confusion and fear and helpless rage.

Sen Eva barely even glanced at him. She lifted a hand almost dismissively in his direction. Calen's only comfort was that he could see that the magic was blue, not red, before it struck him and everything went black.

The first thing Calen saw when he opened his eyes again was Maurel's worried face. She was leaning over him and nudging his head with her knee.

"Calen!" she whispered. "Calen, please wake up!"

He groaned. "Maurel, what? Stop it. What do you —?"

And then he remembered, and struggled to come fully awake.

"Wake up, wake up, wake up!" Maurel said, emphasizing each "wake up" with another violent knee-nudge. *Ow.* She was definitely Meg's sister, all right.

"Okay, I'm awake — stop it," he said, pushing himself upright. It was morning. How was it morning already? Whatever Sen Eva had done to him had apparently kept him unconscious all night. His lips tasted like dirt. He shook his head and then looked around. "What's —?"

He suddenly remembered the last thing he'd heard Sen Eva say. "Maurel! Are you all right? Did she —?"

Maurel sniffed. "She told that man to hurt me," she said, indicating the guard who had been closest to them last night. He was farther off now; Calen supposed the men took turns at guard duty. "But I screamed before he did anything, and then he left me alone." She scrunched up her face. "Was that bad? She wanted me to scream. Should I have tried not to? I couldn't — I couldn't really help it. I was so scared, and I thought you were dead."

"No," he told her. "You were right to scream. We don't want them to hurt you, Maurel. You didn't do anything wrong." He hoped that was true. What did Sen Eva think making Maurel scream would accomplish? Did she think Meg was hiding just out of sight somewhere and would come running if she heard Maurel screaming?

"Ah, you have come back to us," Sen Eva said,

striding over to them. "Your princess is tardy. I would have thought she'd be here by now, but I think she must still be at the castle. That doesn't make sense to me, but I think I would be able to tell, if . . ." She paused and seemed to listen to something he couldn't hear. "I shouldn't . . . I don't want to interfere. . . ." She shook her head and looked at him again, considering. "Well. Perhaps a little nudge won't hurt."

She shouted an order, and several men ran off toward the second row of rocks. And then one of those terrible slaarh screams tore through the air around them. Maurel screamed again and leaned desperately into Calen. Even the men guarding them seemed uneasy. Calen put his arms around Maurel, shaking, as one of the monstrous creatures rose clumsily into the sky from behind the row of tall stones. One of the men was riding it, holding on to a chain looped around the creature's disgusting head and neck. The slaarh screamed again and took off in the direction from which Calen had come. In the direction of the castle.

Sen Eva stood there watching them, smiling. Behind her, more slaarh were lumbering up into the sky. These didn't have riders. Calen didn't know what any of it meant. What was she sending them to do?

A shout from some of the guards made Sen Eva

turn. And then she froze, staring, as Wilem walked into the pass.

Calen stared. What was Wilem doing here alone? Was this part of Serek's plan?

"Hello, Mother," Wilem said.

"Wilem," she said. Her coldness slipped, and a terrible hunger showed on her face. "Have you — have you come to your senses, then? Are you truly —?"

"No," he said, and her face closed up at once, slamming like a heavy door. "I am here to try to reason with you, if I can."

"I should have known you would never truly understand." Her voice had changed again. The hope and arrogance both were gone, and she sounded just like a regular person having a regular, if disappointing, conversation. She sat down on a flat rock and looked sadly at her son.

"I don't understand," Wilem agreed. "I wish you could let this go."

She laughed bitterly. "It's far too late for that, I'm afraid." She seemed about to say something else, then changed her mind. "I won't get drawn in to talking to you. I don't know what you hoped to accomplish by coming here, but it was foolish. And now you'll have to stay. Why don't you have a seat with your new friends? Please don't speak to me again. I can't allow you to distract me, and if you try, I'll be forced to take unpleasant measures."

Wilem's eyes widened when he saw Calen. Then he looked back at his mother, clearly confused. "But — we thought, I thought . . ." He stopped and tried again. "Are you not willing to make a trade for Princess Maurel?"

"A trade? Oh, I see." She shook her head slowly. Almost regretfully. "No, I'm afraid you have misinterpreted the situation, my dear. I did not truly expect that you would come to me, although I could not help but try. Can you blame me for not wanting to give up hope of having you by my side in the new order?"

"What new order? Mother, why are you doing this?"

"You know why," she said. "And now please stop talking to me, as I asked. Or I will have to silence you."

He stood looking at her a moment more, then came and sat beside Calen without another word.

Calen was trying to figure out how to ask where Serek was without actually giving anything away to Sen Eva, when there was a commotion up near the road.

The soldiers who had ridden off with Serek the day before suddenly rushed the pass and clashed with the outer perimeter of Sen Eva's men. Sen Eva glanced at the fighting for only a moment. Then she turned and scanned the surrounding area.

391

Bolts of red and orange energy suddenly came flying at her from behind the fighting men. Sen Eva threw up a protective shield just in time and sent her own red magic flying back toward the source.

Serek! It must be. Calen's embarrassment was nothing compared to his immense relief. Now things would be all right. Wilem must have been intended as a distraction, or maybe he really had meant to attempt negotiation before they resorted to fighting. It didn't matter now. Serek came slowly into view, still casting. Calen waited to watch Sen Eva fall before Serek's magical attack.

Except she didn't. They kept firing things at each other, but nothing seemed to land. They both had shields before them, and they were both apparently able to block whatever the other mage was sending. Sen Eva had obviously had a lot more practice than Calen when it came to fighting with magic — which really wasn't very surprising, he supposed, given that he knew pretty much nothing. Serek also appeared to know a lot more than he'd ever deigned to share with his apprentice. Which, again, wasn't really a surprise.

Finally Sen Eva pointed a hand in Maurel's direction. "Surrender or I'll kill her," she said. "Right now."

"No, you won't," Calen said, and flung up a shield of his own.

"Calen?" Serek asked, staring at him in obvious bewilderment. And in that moment of confusion, Sen Eva fired at Serek again.

Calen fired a second later, barely thinking, trying to send something to protect his master. Desperately, he willed his magic to reach Serek first, or at least to catch up with Sen Eva's and alter it somehow. Serek belatedly tried to refocus his own magical defenses. Calen couldn't see if he had managed to cast anything before there was an explosion of color where Serek had been standing a moment before.

Calen lurched to his feet, pulling Maurel with him. *I killed him,* he thought. *I distracted him and I killed him and now he's going to be dead and it's my fault, my fault, my fault. . . .*

But no! He wasn't dead. He was . . . what? Calen squinted, trying to understand the chaos of color that still swirled around his master. It looked as though Serek had managed to put up some kind of shield, but it had — it had fused, somehow, with the other magic. He didn't seem able to dismantle it. Sen Eva was staring as well, trying to figure out what had happened. Almost experimentally, she released a small bolt of red magic at the shield. Nothing happened, but when Serek tried to fire back at her, his magic couldn't get past it, either.

393

"Hmm," said Sen Eva. "That's interesting. Well, I suppose it will do for now, as long as you can't actively annoy me from in there." She turned away, dismissing Serek from her attention. Almost as an afterthought, she lifted a hand and sent small bolts of deadly energy at the Trelian soldiers, still fighting valiantly against Sen Eva's greater numbers.

They fell down dead without a sound.

Calen stared, shocked by what she had just done. He said a silent prayer for the fallen men. Sen Eva didn't even spare them a glance.

Serek turned to look at him, but Calen couldn't even begin to decipher his master's expression. He swallowed and pulled Maurel tighter against him, holding the shield firmly in place. It looked like he was on his own again, after all.

CHAPTER
TWENTY-FIVE

MEG WAS JUST FINISHING BREAKFAST WHEN she felt Jakl lurch suddenly through the link. She was so disoriented for a moment that she stumbled up from her chair, causing Nan Vera to leap to her feet in alarm, nearly dropping the baby.

"I'm okay!" Meg shouted at her. "Just—just give me a minute." She steadied herself with a hand on the table. *What?* she thought at Jakl. *What is it, what's wrong?*

In response, he sent her a terrifying image of one of the slaarh. She nearly screamed. It was just as horrible as her memories, and it was—oh, gods.

It was coming toward the castle.

She took off at a run, ignoring Nan Vera's startled cries and racing as fast as she could toward her parents' study.

She burst in, scaring them both. "Meg!" her father said. "What—?"

"Slaarh!" she said. "Coming here. Right now. Jakl can see it. I can't—I don't think I can hold him on the ground. I don't think I should. If it's coming to attack, he's the best defense we have."

Her parents stared at each other.

"There's no time to deliberate!" she said. "I'm trying to stay true to your wishes, but this — we can't just sit here and let it attack us!"

"You're sure?" her father asked.

"Yes!"

The king took a breath. "All right. Let him go."

She did.

She felt Jakl rush up at the sky as if gravity itself were his enemy, flinging himself to meet the invading creature before it got close enough to hurt them. To hurt her, especially.

Meg turned to run outside. She wanted to be there for her dragon, to see and help him, but Anders was suddenly there in the doorway.

"Something happened," he said. "Serek — he's trapped, something, I couldn't see it clearly, but it didn't work. They didn't —"

"Maurel?" the queen asked, getting to her feet. "What happened? Is she all right? Is she —?"

Anders shook his head. "I don't know. It wasn't even a complete vision. Just enough to see that Serek can't save her now."

"Meg," the queen said suddenly. "Meg can still save her."

"Merilyn!" the king said, at the same time Meg said, "What?"

"She is the only one who can get there quickly enough," the queen went on. "If we try to send anyone else — the mages, an army — it could be too late." She looked at her husband. "The dragon is already in the sky, Tormon. We've already broken our agreement."

The king was shaking his head. "No. Merilyn, listen to yourself. One of our daughters is already in danger, and you want to send Meg —"

"I can do it, Father."

"No, Meg!" he said, turning to her. "Absolutely not."

"I can. But Jakl can't take me there if he's here fighting the slaarh."

"No. I cannot allow it."

"Can't allow him to stop fighting here, or can't allow me to go?"

"Both! I don't —" He curled his hands into fists and pushed them against his forehead. "Meg, I can't let you put yourself in that kind of danger."

"Father," Meg said. "If Jakl dies fighting the slaarh, you know I'll be dead, too. So it's a choice of the danger here or the danger involved in letting me try to save Maurel.

If you could draw off the slaarh with soldiers, Jakl and I can get to Bellman's Pass in half an hour. Maybe less. Probably less. And I can get her back. I swear it."

"Meg, I can't —"

"Jakl will keep me safe, and if I can get to the others, he can help me get them home safely as well. There's no one else who can do that." There was no guarantee Jakl could really keep her anything close to safe, of course, but this was not the time for total honesty.

"What other choice do we have?" the queen asked her husband.

"Any other choice!" he said. "This is madness. Madness on top of madness. I never should have sent anything less than an army —"

"Sire," Anders said gently, "you did the right thing. My visions don't always make sense, but they are always right. Always. I know it doesn't look that way, but you cannot punish yourself now for that decision. Somehow, that was the best available course."

"And is sending another daughter into harm's way also the best available course?"

Anders looked troubled. "I don't know. But . . . it is true that the dragon can get there far more quickly than any man or horse. Time is not something we have in abundance."

The king suddenly looked at Anders with narrowed eyes. "How do we even know we should trust you?" he said. "Who *are* you? How do we know your visions aren't just tricks to make us act as you desire?"

Anders, taken aback, did not seem to know how to answer. The queen lay a hand on her husband's arm.

"Now is not the time to start accusing each other," she said. "We must deal with the problems before us."

"Perhaps — perhaps we could send a soldier with the dragon —" the king began.

"No," Meg said. "Jakl wouldn't carry a stranger off and leave me here. And I can't make him. It has to be me. And if — if there's any trouble, he might need me to be there, to help him."

Her father looked uncomfortable; she knew he didn't like to think too deeply about what her connection to the dragon really meant.

The queen turned away from King Tormon and took Meg's hands in her own. "Go, Meg. Please. Bring your sister home."

Meg nodded once. "Send those soldiers to take on the slaarh," she said. Then she ran from the room.

She knew she would have to wait for the soldiers to be ready before she let Jakl take her away, but she still felt a terrible urgency to get outside, to see with her own eyes

399

instead of only through the link. *Coming,* she thought at her dragon. *Keep fighting for now, but when I say, come down and get me.* She tried to send images along with her words, and she felt his understanding.

Pela nearly tackled her just as she was nearing the front door.

"Not now, Pela," Meg growled. Jakl had engaged the slaarh. She could feel them fighting, feel Jakl's anger tinged with fear. Most of all she felt his hatred of that abomination, his desire to destroy it as well as the human riding on its back.

There was a *human* riding on its *back*?

"This will just take a moment," Pela insisted. Meg realized the girl's arms were full of clothing. "I brought your riding clothes. New ones, actually. I had them made for you when I got a good look at those terrible rags you kept riding around in."

"Pela, there's no *time* —"

"Yes there is," she said calmly. "Time enough for this. It will be better if you change before you go. You don't want to tear up your legs."

She had a point. And Meg had to wait for the soldiers anyway.

They slipped into an empty room across the hall. Pela had her stripped down and dressed more quickly than Meg would have thought possible. At the last, she reached up and tied Meg's hair back with a pretty but strong-looking length of cord. "To keep it from your eyes while you're flying," she explained.

Meg met Pela's eyes and squeezed her hand in quick but heartfelt gratitude. Then she ran outside to see her dragon.

Jakl was magnificent, as she knew he would be, screaming and hurling flame and attacking with claws and gracefully dodging the return attacks from his ungainly opponent.

The soldiers appeared then, racing from the barracks with weapons at the ready, bowmen already launching bolts toward the monster, swordsmen waiting to see if any of the action got near enough to the ground for them to be useful.

All right, Meg thought at Jakl. *Come get me.*

He took a final swipe at the slaarh and dove for her, and the second he touched down she flung herself at his back. He was up as soon as he felt her slide into place atop him.

"Go," she whispered. "Go, go, go. Let's bring them home."

Jakl roared assent as he pushed himself forward, racing for the pass.

Lost in dragon-fueled imaginings of rescue and revenge, Meg gasped as screams — human ones — jerked her suddenly back to her immediate surroundings. Jakl reared, either in response to her shock or because he had seen for himself.

Below them, a pair of slaarh was attacking a farm near the road. She could hear people shouting between the terrible screams of the monsters themselves.

Jakl started for them without thought, and for a moment Meg felt as he did — the need to attack, to stop the creatures' destruction, to strike from above and burn them until they either died or fled. But then she pulled herself back, trying to focus.

No, she thought at her dragon. *We have to keep going. We cannot stop for this. We need to save Maurel.*

But then she thought of Tessel and faltered in her resolve. Where did her duty truly lie? Was she sacrificing those people in order to save her family? *No*, she thought. *This is different.* This was about saving Maurel, but also about stopping Sen Eva. About bringing her down before she could carry out her plans, which by all accounts would be a million times worse than anything the slaarh were doing now.

It was still hard to keep flying and leave those screaming people behind them.

Jakl pulled up reluctantly. Meg allowed herself one final look back, searing the scene and the sounds into her memory. She felt the fire boiling up again inside her heart.

Sen Eva would pay. She would pay for all of it.

CHAPTER TWENTY-SIX

CALEN STOOD THERE, HOLDING MAUREL, praying that he would be able to protect her from Sen Eva.

Sen Eva turned to him, her face cold and angry, but then something abruptly shifted. She got that faraway look again. And then she smiled.

The smile was more frightening than the anger had been.

"It's time. Finally." Her smile grew even wider.

Calen glanced at Wilem, who had watched all of this from where he'd sat down moments — only moments? — before. "Do you know what she's talking about?" Calen asked.

Wilem shook his head.

Sen Eva reached up and pulled on a delicate chain she was wearing around her neck. A polished blue crystal slid out from inside her dress. It took Calen only a moment to recognize it.

Oh. Oh, no. When she said it was time, she meant . . . time to finish what she'd been trying to do in the first place. What all of her efforts had been leading toward since the beginning.

Time to bring back Mage Krelig. That's what she meant. Time to open the portal and help him cross over.

Sen Eva had won.

And all the rest of them had lost.

He looked at Serek, who was still trapped like a bug in a jar. He was shaking his head, although whether in denial or plea Calen couldn't tell.

Sen Eva held the crystal in her left hand and held her right hand out before her, beginning to mutter the words of some incantation under her breath.

"Time for what?" Calen asked loudly, interrupting her concentration.

She stopped and frowned at him in irritation. "Be quiet."

"If you wanted me to be quiet, maybe you should have used a stronger sleeping spell," he said back. "Why didn't you just kill me, anyway? Aren't you worried I might stop you from doing whatever it is you're trying to do?"

Sen Eva stared at him for a moment, then burst out

laughing. "Oh, my," she said. "You do think highly of yourself, don't you? No, dear boy, I'm afraid you don't worry me in the least. And you should be thanking me instead of making a nuisance of yourself. You're about to see the beginning of a whole new world."

"I kind of like the old world," Calen said. "Why don't we just stick with this one?"

She rolled her eyes and made a gesture at one of her men. "Really, Apprentice. Annoying me is not your wisest course of action. And you're not going to distract me, so stop trying. Just be quiet now and watch. Maybe you'll learn something."

Calen opened his mouth to say something else — he didn't even know what, anything, just something to keep her from casting that spell — but before he could speak, the guard she'd gestured to slipped a rolled-up piece of cloth into Calen's mouth and tied it tightly behind his head. Another grabbed Calen's arms, yanked them behind him, and bound them tightly at the wrists. It startled him so much he dropped the shield he'd been maintaining. Luckily Sen Eva seemed to have lost interest in attacking him. He'd never even considered protecting against a nonmagical attack.

Wonderful, Calen thought. He tried to spit out the

gag, but he couldn't work it loose. Maurel looked up at him sadly; she couldn't help him, of course, since her own arms were bound as well.

Sen Eva glanced back at Calen for one more moment. "I suppose I did underestimate you once before," she said. "So just to be safe . . ."

She walked over to him, fingers spread wide on her outstretched hand. With no further warning, a web of orange energy flew from her fingertips. Belatedly, he braced for pain, for darkness, for death — no, wait, orange energy, not red. He tried to figure out what she had done. Nothing hurt; he could still move, he could still see and think and breathe . . .

She smiled at him. "Try casting," she said.

With a sinking feeling deep in his stomach, Calen did. He attempted a halfhearted sleep spell in her direction. Halfhearted because he already knew that it wouldn't work. That orange spell . . . she'd blocked him somehow, nullified his power. He was useless. Unable to cast the smallest thing.

Sen Eva's smile widened as nothing happened. Then she walked casually away from him, back to where she'd been standing before. Calen watched helplessly as she turned to face the cleared space between the tall rocks and raised her hand again, tracing an arc in the air before her. As he had seen happen once before, a portal shimmered into existence.

The shadowy figure Calen had also seen once before appeared within the portal boundaries.

"It is time," the figure said, echoing Sen Eva's words from a few moments ago. "The last piece has fallen into place."

"Yes, my master," Sen Eva said reverently. "Trelian has broken faith with Lourin, and even now the messenger-birds are flying to King Gerald with the news. His armies have been massing in preparation. The war is now inevitable. I set the wards just as you showed me, and I can sense the dragon in the air, sense the soldiers on the road. . . . I feel the change in the world, just as you said I would."

Her smile grew radiant. "Your time is now at hand, Master. And I am ready to help you across."

"Calen," Maurel whispered, "why is there a scary man hanging in the air like that?"

Calen shook his head, unable to answer. He didn't know what he'd be able to tell her anyway. *Oh, him? That's Mage Krelig, this crazy mage from hundreds of years ago who was exiled to another plane of existence where time*

works *differently and who wants to come back and take over the world. Sen Eva is about to help him do that. It is going to be very bad for all of us when she does.*

"Mother," Wilem said urgently, "you must know that he isn't going to give you what he promised. It's not possible. Father and Tymas are gone. He's just using you! It's not too late to stop this. Please."

Sen Eva didn't even glance at him. "Please be quiet, Wilem. You have no understanding of what is possible."

"At my command," Mage Krelig said now, "We will begin the spell. You must not stop once it has begun. Not until I have crossed over."

"I understand." She looked over her shoulder at the two closest men. "Watch them," she said, nodding at Calen and the others. One of them reached over with a heavy hand and pushed down on Calen's shoulder until he gave in and sat. Maurel promptly sat beside him.

Mage Krelig took a slow breath. "Begin."

Calen watched in horrified fascination as the edges of the portal began to glow white, then orange, then red, then violet, shifting along with the kind of energy that Sen Eva was casting. The portal itself grew larger, stretching vertically until it was just about the size of an actual door. He could see a faint echo of the spell on the other side, presumably being cast by Mage Krelig. The glowing intensified, and Calen could feel an unpleasant pulsing heat radiating from the portal. Sen Eva shifted uncomfortably but did not break her concentration. Calen longed to lunge at her, to knock her off-balance and interrupt the spell, but the men she'd set to watch them were annoyingly attentive. They'd stop him before he so much as tried to stand up. He kept thinking he should try anyway, just try to do something . . . but no. Better to wait for some other chance, some possible action that might actually work, rather than one that was sure to fail.

The magic energy intensified, and the edges of the portal actually seemed to be burning in multicolored flames. Calen realized that the other side of the portal was no longer shadowy and indistinct. He could see the other mage clearly now, standing in some dark space, all black rock surfaces and hard angles visible behind him. His face was unmarked, like Sen Eva's.

Something shifted — some piece of the world actually moved and *changed* and Calen could feel it, almost see it, as the flames around the edges of the portal grew into an inferno, nearly filling the interior space of the portal itself.

"Now!" the mage shouted from the other side, over the roar of the flames, and Sen Eva reached forward into that burning mess with her right hand. She screamed as the fire touched her but did not pull away.

All around them, all at once, the slaarh began screaming, too. Maurel buried her face against Calen's shoulder, and Wilem covered his ears with his hands. So did most of the men surrounding them. All Calen could do was lean his head down against Maurel's, trying to shut out the horrible sounds.

And then Sen Eva was stepping back, and as her arm drew back with her, they could see another hand, blackened and burned, gripping hers. And then the mage himself came through, stepping through the fire, then collapsing onto the ground at the base of the portal.

As one, the slaarh went silent. The portal winked neatly out of existence.

Oh, not good. Calen thought. *Not good, this is not good at all. Bright Lady, protect us. Great Harvester, please make this right.*

But it wasn't right. It was terribly, terribly wrong.

Calen looked at Serek, whose horror and dismay showed plainly on his usually well-controlled face.

Mage Krelig lay convulsing on the ground. Sen Eva

stared down at him, apparently uncertain whether to try to touch him. After a moment he rolled over onto his back, and Calen was shocked to see he was laughing.

"Master?" Sen Eva said hesitantly.

"Oh," Mage Krelig said, "it is good to be home."

CHAPTER TWENTY-SEVEN

FOR SEVERAL LONG MOMENTS, NO ONE said anything. Calen and everyone else stared at the man who'd just appeared. He was lying on the ground and looking happily up at the late-morning sky. He was old, Calen supposed, but not as old as you would expect someone to look after more than four hundred years. Everyone had said that time must move differently wherever the mage had been sent to, but Calen had never really understood how that worked. In any case, the man seemed older than Serek but not as old as Anders. His hair was gray and hung raggedly around his shoulders, and he had a scraggly gray beard as well. But his clothing seemed well made and not nearly as worn and dirty as it should be — as if he had perhaps kept it aside all these years, waiting for the day he would wear it upon his return.

Finally Mage Krelig himself broke the silence. He sat up with a grunt and looked around. Then he seemed to notice his burned hand for the first time.

"Huh," he said mildly. "Can't have that, now, can I?" He didn't move or even take a moment to focus, but at once a green and yellow glow surrounded his hand and forearm, almost solid in its intensity of color and brightness. Calen actually had to squint and then look away. It was like trying to watch the sun. Well, if the sun was partly green, anyway.

When Calen looked back, it was as though the hand had never been injured at all.

Mage Krelig glanced up at Sen Eva, who was clutching her own burned hand, and then the bright glow surrounded her hand as well. She gasped; the sensation of a healing that significant and fast must be intense, if not painful. Although the mage himself hadn't seemed to feel anything when he'd healed himself — or at least he hadn't shown it.

"Th-thank you," Sen Eva said, sounding shaken. She held out her hand and gazed at it in wonder. Then she seemed to come back to herself and offered her hand to Mage Krelig, to help him up. He waved it off, though, and stood up on his own.

"So, then, my dear," he said to her. "How have you prepared for me?"

"Everything you required has been accomplished,"

Sen Eva told him. "The men you see here are a mere fraction of the army I've assembled for you. The others are gathering in several different locations, as you instructed. We have more than a hundred slaarh, and I believe there are still a few more that might be brought over. The Magistratum rips itself apart from within, and the war is beginning. It will no doubt spark other conflicts as allies are drawn into the fight."

"Excellent," he said, nodding. Then he suddenly noticed Serek, still trapped behind his oddly solidified magic shield.

"Oho!" Mage Krelig shouted, grinning. "Is this one of my esteemed colleagues from the Magistratum?" He began to laugh again. "Oh, it is such a pleasure to meet you. We have many things to discuss, you and I and all your friends."

Krelig turned away as though dismissing Serek from his mind. Then he seemed to notice Calen, Maurel, and Wilem for the first time. "And what is this?"

"Playing pieces, Master," Sen Eva said. "The girl is a younger princess of Trelian —"

"Yes, yes, I'm sure they've served whatever purpose they were supposed to," the mage interrupted. "They are not needed any longer?"

Sen Eva's confident expression shifted slightly. She glanced at Wilem. "I'm — I'm not certain. It seems best to — to wait and see. Master."

"I don't like loose ends."

"I know. I promise I will take care of it."

He looked at her. "Is there something you are keeping from me? I am tired, Sen Eva. I do not have time for secret games. I must rest and regain my strength before I am called upon to use it. Destroy them and be done with it."

Maurel gasped in horror. Calen wished he could say something to comfort her, but even if he hadn't been gagged, there wasn't anything he could say. He tried again to access his power, but he was still blocked. A new thought froze his heart, suddenly. But no. It — it couldn't be permanent. It had been too quick, too easy for that. Just a lightly cast spell, barely any effort or energy at all. Surely he would be able to cast again in time. He had to believe that, because the alternative was too horrible.

Except — he'd forgotten. There wasn't going to be any time. They were all about to die.

I'm sorry, Meg, he thought sadly.

Suddenly Wilem shot past him, launching himself at the mage, who was still turned toward Sen Eva.

Sen Eva's eyes widened and the mage whirled, but not quickly enough. Wilem slammed into him and bore him back down to the ground.

"No!" Sen Eva cried. She pulled Wilem off the older man and thrust her son away from her. A burst of dark red magic energy from Mage Krelig's hands just missed him, shooting harmlessly up into the sky instead. They could all feel the power of it, though. Wilem stumbled and fell back to the ground, shaking his head angrily. Calen didn't know what Wilem had thought would happen, although he appreciated the effort. But Wilem was no match for a man of that much power. If this was what the mage was like when he was weak, Calen was almost glad he wouldn't be around to see him at full strength. The thought alone was terrifying.

The men around them had all backed away at the mage's display of magic. They weren't quite fleeing, but they clearly wanted to put as much distance as possible between themselves and what was happening here. Sen Eva had turned to face the mage and was reaching down once more to try to help him up. And putting herself, Calen realized, between Krelig and her son.

"I am sorry," she said desperately. "Please. He doesn't understand —"

The mage's eyes narrowed. "Your other son?"

Sen Eva licked her lips nervously. "Yes."

The mage was breathing heavily. He must really have been weakened from the crossover and then the healing and the attempt on Wilem. *Gods*, Calen thought. *How strong was he at full power?*

Slowly, Mage Krelig regained his feet. He stepped toward Sen Eva, and she backed away but did not move from his path. Calen felt ill. The mage was right in front of him now. "I cannot have dissenters in my ranks, Sen Eva. That boy has just earned his death." He looked at her and smiled then, a ghastly, evil expression. "Don't worry," he said. "You've lost a son before. I believe the second time is much easier."

Sen Eva's face drained of color. He pushed her roughly aside and then looked at Wilem, who was staring up at him defiantly. The mage was definitely slowing down; Calen could see the flicker of the spell gathering this time before it struck. Calen tried again, as hard as he could, to cast something, anything — a shield to divert the spell, a flame to set the man's beard on fire, a dancing teacup to distract him, anything, *anything*. Wilem was irritating and a problem and a liar, and Calen still didn't trust him, but he didn't deserve to die. Not like this.

But there was nothing Calen could to do to stop it.

Then Sen Eva threw herself back in front of her son. The spell hit her straight on, and she screamed horribly, seeming to claw at herself for the few seconds before the magic consumed her entirely. She crumpled within the fiery energy, the flames visible only to Calen but the effect on her body visible to them all.

Calen couldn't believe what he had just seen.

"No!" Wilem and Mage Krelig screamed together, each for his own reasons. Maurel just screamed, burying her face back in Calen's shoulder.

Mage Krelig tore his eyes from Sen Eva's blackened form and glared at Wilem with a new hatred burning in his eyes. He took a step toward him. Wilem didn't even notice. He was still staring at his mother's body.

Another flickering of deep red began to gather at Mage Krelig's fingertips. He was definitely weaker; each spell seemed to take a disproportionate amount of energy from him for reasons Calen did not understand and could not begin to sort out at the moment. But Krelig still wasn't weak enough. It wouldn't take a strong spell to kill them, after all. Just a thorough one, aimed with care. And Calen and Maurel, at least, couldn't even try to run.

Suddenly a welcome roar sounded in the sky above

419

them. Mage Krelig whipped his head around to stare. Jakl roared again, and Calen could almost see the dragon's desire to burn the man to a crisp right there.

Calen did not think he had ever been so glad to see anyone in his entire life. Dimly, in the back of his mind, he realized that this was what Sen Eva had meant when she said Trelian had broken with Lorin — Meg and Jakl leaving the castle grounds must have ignited the start of the war. But he couldn't care very much about that right now. Meg was here, with her dragon, and all was not lost after all.

"Meg!" Maurel screamed, trying to struggle to her feet but unable to quite manage it with her hands still bound behind her. Meg turned to locate her sister and stared in shock when she saw Calen. Jakl roared once more, shooting a stream of fire into the air before him. Now the black-clad men around them ran, scattering in all directions like beetles startled from under their rock.

Mage Krelig seemed transfixed, staring up at the girl and dragon who had appeared so unexpectedly out of nowhere. Wilem crawled quickly over and untied Calen's hands, then picked up Maurel and ran for some of the nearby rocks. Calen ripped the gag from his mouth and started to follow. Maurel was still screaming Meg's name, and this finally got the mage's attention. Calen looked back over his shoulder to see Mage Krelig staring furiously after them. Their eyes met suddenly, and Calen's legs nearly gave out beneath him at the insane power and rage he could see there.

And then the mage's features shifted in confusion and surprise. And pleasure? And suddenly the world stopped.

Calen blinked and stumbled to a halt. It had literally stopped. All around him. Meg and Jakl were suspended in the air midswoop. Maurel's face was frozen, her mouth stretched into a scream. Wilem was leaning forward, running for all he was worth, except he wasn't, because no one was moving.

No one but Calen and Mage Krelig.

"Interesting," Mage Krelig said, walking closer to Calen.

"What — what did you do?" Calen asked. A million tiny dots of every color imaginable seemed to hang suspended in the air around them.

"A little parlor trick," Mage Krelig said airily. "I can't hold it long, though, even at full strength, and can't repeat it for several months at least, so we've only got a moment." He looked at Calen appraisingly. "I know who you are. I've seen you."

Calen tried to speak around his terror. "You have?"

"Not your face." He said this as though a face were something like a shirt, that you could pull on and off at will. "Your power. Your . . . ability."

Calen stared at him. *What?*

"I have had many useful visions over the years. I have seen you more than once. And I have . . . *sensed* you; it was your magic at work in the room when I spoke with Sen Eva before she failed me the first time. You are . . . of interest." The mage looked around at the other people present, chuckling as his eyes passed over Serek again. Then he looked back at Calen and said, "And here I thought I would have to go and seek you out. You will need to come with me."

What?

"I — I can't do that."

"Of course you can. I've seen . . . that we might be of use to each other," he said. "You have an unusual talent, do you not?"

"I don't know what you're talking about."

"Of course, of course," Mage Krelig said. Then he winked. "But you know that you are capable of much more than what you have done so far, don't you, my boy? You know that there are things being hidden from you about the ways of magic, that there are things you are told never to do that some mages do quite often. You know that the rules that bind you are like a prison, and you have already begun looking for the key."

"No, I haven't," Calen said. "I don't even know what you mean. And the rules are — the rules are good. To keep people safe. And . . . and . . ."

Mage Krelig laughed again. "Keep people safe," he repeated. "Please. The Magistratum is trying to tear your claws off, keeping you a mouse-cat when you're meant to be a lion. You can't lie to me about this. I can tell. Your frustration radiates from you. You have tremendous power locked away inside. But clearly you've never been trained to really use it, or you wouldn't have been caught here as a prisoner of my — of *our* late friend."

"Sen Eva was not my friend," Calen snapped.

"No, no, of course not. Which is all the worse for you. She could have eaten you for lunch anytime she wanted. But do you know, she is not even that strong in the arts. Oh, she has — had — power, but it was the training, the knowledge that made her great. The same knowledge that I could give to you. I could give you that and more, my boy. Everything you ever wanted to learn. No secrets. No limits. No restraints."

Calen shook his head. He didn't quite trust himself to speak.

Because Mage Krelig was right about how badly Calen wanted to learn. He was right about how Serek kept holding him back. How the rules sometimes seemed like pointless obstacles. And hadn't he broken them on occasion? Hadn't he already decided for himself that some of the rules simply did not apply?

Only some, he reminded himself. *A very select number. And only with good reason. There's nothing to even think about here.*

But he was thinking about it all the same.

No. He tried to focus on what was real. On what he knew to be true. Mage Krelig was a monster. An evil, crazy monster. And what he was offering was to turn Calen into an evil, crazy monster, too. Like Sen Eva.

Never.

He should spit on Mage Krelig's offer. He should run, now, while the mage was busy holding this impossible spell, run away so that when time started again Calen would be out of reach and ready to be scooped up by Meg and Jakl, to be taken back home to begin planning the fight against the most terrible enemy any of them had ever encountered.

Except . . . he wouldn't be part of that fight. Serek wouldn't let him. Serek would keep him in the dark, unable to help, unable to do anything to protect his home and his fellow mages and his friends.

Mage Krelig was offering Calen everything that Serek refused to give.

They told you you would be involved with him, the little voice inside him said. *So go ahead. It's what they all expect you to do, anyway.*

That was crazy — Mage Krelig was the *enemy.* Calen could not, he could never . . . he could not believe he was feeling even the slightest bit of temptation.

But he was. He couldn't deny it. Some small, tiny part of him was tempted. To learn, to know everything he wanted to know. No limits. Nothing held back.

And then, beneath the temptation, another thought.

Maybe this was the opportunity he was meant to look out for. Maybe the cards had been telling him about this, this very moment, about this chance to grab the knowledge he yearned for. Not that he would ever really *join* Mage Krelig. Of course not. He was no traitor. He could never put himself against Meg. Or against Trelian. Or against Serek. Even when he couldn't stand his master, he didn't *hate* him. At least, not most of the time.

But if he could only *pretend* to join Mage Krelig, to go and learn and then come back — if he could pretend to join Mage Krelig in order to figure out how to defeat him . . .

This was it. This was the chance he was being given. It had to be.

And for a moment, he wavered on the brink of saying yes.

He looked at Meg and the others, frozen in time. Meg, who had come here to save them. Meg, who was his best friend, his only friend, the only one who truly believed in him.

The only one who needed him.

Who trusted him.

She would not want him to do this.

"No," Calen said. "Never."

Mage Krelig started to laugh again, a deep, rich, booming sound that filled the frozen silence around them. Then he stopped abruptly. "Ach," he said. "Losing my hold. You've got about five more seconds to decide." His lingering, easy smile vanished. He looked directly into Calen's eyes with deadly seriousness. "And if you dare to refuse me again, you ignorant, mewling whelp, I will rip apart every single one of your little friends into unrecognizable strands of bloody, screaming flesh. Accept, and I will let them live." He paused. "For the time being, anyway."

The world came abruptly back to life and motion. The first few seconds of sound were almost excruciating — Maurel was shouting; Meg was screaming in tandem with Jakl; Serek was beating against the inside of his shield prison, desperate to get free.

Mage Krelig looked at Calen for one more long moment. "Very well," he said. He turned toward the others, crimson streaks of magical energy gathering slowly about his hands. Hands that were raised in the direction of Wilem, of Maurel, of Jakl.

Of Meg.

"Yes," Calen heard himself say. "Okay, yes. I'll come with you. Just don't — don't hurt —"

Jakl swooped down close above them, but the mage ignored him, beaming at Calen. "Excellent!" he said, his good humor back in force. "Let's go someplace where we can talk."

Krelig gestured with one hand. There was an immediate answering scream from not very far away, the all-too-familiar-by-now sound of the slaarh.

Jakl turned to face the direction the sound had come from, but a shouted word from Meg brought him back around. He dove again toward the ground, and a burst of pure and perfect orange fire streamed from his open mouth into the empty air. Meg was shouting, and Calen

427

realized she was waiting for him to move away so she could attack Mage Krelig.

He didn't move.

The slaarh appeared above the trees then, screaming again as it came for its master. Jakl turned and landed heavily beside the rocks, clearly following Meg's instructions against his own desire to engage the other creature in combat. Wilem boosted Maurel onto Jakl's back, then climbed up beside her. Everyone turned to stare at Calen.

"Come on!" Wilem shouted. "Calen!"

The slaarh landed clumsily on the ground nearby and lay itself flat. Mage Krelig climbed up rather awkwardly; his casting was clearly catching up with him now. Calen didn't even want to imagine how much force of will and magic it would have taken to create the spell that had stopped time, let alone to hold it that way.

Calen looked at Meg. He met her eyes, fierce and lovely and confused. His best, truest, only friend. He wished he could explain what he was doing. That he was doing this for her, for them, for all of them. But there was no time, and no way.

He dropped his eyes and climbed up behind Mage Krelig. His stomach heaved at the feel of the creature's oozy skin beneath him, but he didn't turn back.

428

He heard Meg screaming his name, and Maurel too, and Serek was throwing himself against his shield. He wished he could tell all of them why he was going. And that he would find a way to use this, to turn things around. That he would come back.

He *would* come back.

He would go with Mage Krelig and learn his secrets. And then, when the time came, he would be prepared to fight him.

To destroy him forever.

He couldn't help looking back at Meg once more as the slaarh lumbered into the air.

Her face as she watched him ride off was like a knife in his heart.

CHAPTER
TWENTY-EIGHT

LATER, BACK AT THE CASTLE, THEY assembled in the same meeting room they had gathered in only a couple of days before. It was more crowded now. The king stood at the center table, bunched together with the Captain of the House Guard and the Master of Arms and the Commander of the King's Army, looking down at a large map of the continent. The queen sat in one of the elaborate chairs at one edge of the room with Maurel snuggled tightly in her lap. Wilem sat quietly under the watchful eyes of a guard. Anders and Serek and the mages from the Magistratum took up nearly half the room all by themselves. Even Pela was present, tucked in a chair in the corner and working busily at some piece of sewing in her lap and seeming to ignore everyone else completely.

But not everyone was there. Not quite.

"King Gerald's men are deployed along our western border," the king was saying, "and our scouts say their main forces are marching now."

"There has been no formal declaration of war from Lourin's allies," the commander said, "but we cannot expect anything else."

Meg tried to care about those things. She knew she had responsibilities here, people depending on her, a role to play in what happened from this point forward. She wanted to pay close attention and find a way to help. And she did care. She cared a lot. It was just hard to make her mind focus on any of those things for very long right now.

She looked over at Serek. His eyes were shadowed and dark as he spoke with his companions. She'd had to fetch Anders and two of the other mages to help release him from that invisible magical enclosure he had been trapped in.

Serek had asked Meg, more than once, whether Calen had said anything to her about what he'd been planning, what he had been doing at Bellman's Pass, if she could think of any reason why he might have chosen to go off with Mage Krelig in that way. But he hadn't, and she couldn't.

Calen hadn't said a word to her at all.

"Serek," the king said now, "what are your intentions? Can I count on your assistance here, or will your other duties draw you elsewhere?"

Serek exchanged an unreadable glance with Mage Anders. "I am . . . not yet certain, Sire. I am still hoping for an intervention from the council."

"Not bloody likely," one of the other mages muttered.

Serek ignored him and continued, "I remain your mage and advisor for the time being, at least. Although you know I cannot use magic to directly harm your enemies."

"Not Lourin. No, I know that," the king said. "But what about the others? If we find ourselves under attack by other enemies? I realize Mage Krelig may not be interested in us specifically, but he has already set his creatures against our people once." The soldiers had managed to bring down the slaarh that Meg and Jakl had left behind at the castle, but five more men now lay near death in the room at the end of the infirmary.

"His loss of Sen Eva will surely slow him down," Anders put in. "But we cannot expect that he will wait long to act. Especially since he appears now to have, ah, another . . ." He glanced at Meg, faltering.

"Don't you say it," Meg warned him, glaring. It wasn't true. It wasn't.

"Meg," her father said sadly, "you yourself told us what you saw. It seems clear that what the mages feared has come to pass. Calen has chosen —"

"No," Meg said. "Stop saying that."

"Princess," Serek began.

"No!" Meg screamed at him. The world went away for a moment, as it had done sometimes when she had been suffering from the nightmare rages, but this time she knew where the rage was coming from. Distantly, she noted that she could hear Jakl roaring outside the castle, hear him with her ears as well as feel him through the link. He was angry, too.

She realized suddenly that she was standing, that she had moved across the room, that her hands — her hands were fists, beating viciously against Serek's chest. She had slammed him up against the wall.

Everyone had frozen in shocked silence. Meg looked up at Serek's face. The sadness she saw there was worse than anger would have been.

"Princess," Pela said softly, suddenly at her side. "Princess, you must calm down." Gently, the younger girl reached up and took hold of Meg's hands, drawing them away from the mage.

"I'm sorry," Meg whispered. She backed away. "I just can't —" She looked at the ground, unwilling to meet anyone's eye. "There must be a reason. He wouldn't . . ."

She trailed off, because of course, he had.

Calen had willingly climbed up on the back of that

433

monster and ridden off with Mage Krelig. She wished she hadn't seen it with her own eyes, so she could pretend it wasn't true. She wanted to believe that he'd been under a spell, that he'd been confused, that he hadn't known what he was doing. But he had looked her right in the eye, and his gaze had been clear and aware and open and sad. He had known.

Serek's concerns, now validated. But she couldn't believe it. That wasn't Calen. It wasn't. He would never, never turn against them. He must have had some reason, some stupid, foolish notion that he could help save them by giving himself up.

He would never abandon her that way.

But he did.

She needed him, and he had left her. He had gone off with the enemy.

Nothing, not any other thing out of all the crazy things that had happened or could happen could ever have shocked her more. Not even Sen Eva's sacrificing herself to save Wilem. She had been astounded when Wilem had told her, and when Maurel and Serek had confirmed it. But even that was easier to accept than what Calen had done.

"Meg," her father said again. "Are you — are you with

434

us? I know how angry you are. But we need you here. You and — you and Jakl, both."

She looked up at him, surprised. "You're going to let us help? Directly?" She made herself ask the real question. "You're going to let my dragon openly fight for Trelian?"

The room had gone very quiet again. Everyone's eyes were on the king now.

He nodded, his expression an odd mix of reluctance and determination. "Even assuming we will have Kragnir on our side, a war against Lourin and its allies is not a fight our armies can win for us alone. And if this war is truly of use to Mage Krelig, if our fighting among ourselves is going to make his conquest easier, then we have a responsibility to end it as soon as possible. Your dragon, Meg — in him we have an advantage I cannot in good conscience ignore."

He looked at the queen, who met his eyes steadily, seeming to answer a silent question.

He turned back to Meg. "We have all seen how brave, resourceful, and dedicated you are." He held up a hand to stop her response. "You are also impulsive, and willful, and stubborn. If you are going to be of any use to us, you will need to learn to follow orders, to work with the others

435

who fight on our side, but . . . yes. If you are willing," he said, "I believe we will need you both to win this war."

"I am," she said at once. "We both are."

The meeting continued, her father's military advisors seeming very excited about the possibilities now open to them. The mages soon left for a meeting of their own, and Meg knew they were discussing not only what to do about Mage Krelig but also what might be the fate of the Magistratum if the mages could not come together in agreement.

Meg's mother caught her eye across the room. Maurel was sleeping, and the queen was stroking her hair. Queen Merilyn smiled just a little, and for the first time in a long while, Meg could see something other than fear and worry in her mother's expression.

I am going to make you proud, Meg thought.

Maybe she would never be the kind of princess-heir the people of Trelian could be comfortable with. But she would be the kind who could protect them, who could defend them from their enemies. She thought they would come to appreciate that.

She felt Jakl's excitement, his readiness to fly and fight at her command. *Not yet*, she thought at him fondly. *But soon. We are going to show them all what having a dragon on their side is truly about.*

She only wished that Calen could be here with them. Instead of ... instead ...

She tried to make herself think it: *Instead of on the side of our enemies.*

But she still didn't believe it.

He had left her. But not forever. Calen was her best friend. More than her best friend. More than family. And he always, always would be. No matter what. He had left her, but she was going to get him back.

And gods, was he going to be in trouble when she did.

RETURN TO THE BEGINNING
OF THE TRELIAN TRILOGY

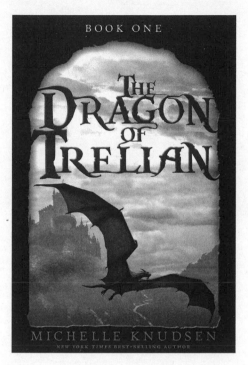

"This strong debut novel should find a
welcoming audience among Gail Carson Levine
and Shannon Hale fans." — *The Horn Book*

"A rich fantasy with everything you could want
in a book." — *Wands and Worlds*

Available in hardcover and paperback and as an e-book

www.candlewick.com

THE EXCITING CONCLUSION
TO THE TRELIAN TRILOGY

"An exemplary fantasy trilogy concludes with a blast. . . . Thrilling." — *Kirkus Reviews*

"This excellent fantasy trilogy . . . receives a worthy ending." — *Booklist*

Available in hardcover and paperback and as an e-book

www.candlewick.com